Dante

By

Eve Vaughn

Dedication

To my readers, thank you so much for supporting me, and keeping me going. I hope you'll enjoy reading this book as much as I've enjoyed writing it.

Prologue

1402

"Dante! Harder! Faster! Ride me!" Donna Perucci screamed as she clawed at his chest and thrust her hips to meet his every pulse and stroke.

Her melon-sized breasts jiggled furiously as he pounded into her. Though Dante's mission was to give her pleasure, it stayed in the back of his mind to be finished before her husband arrived home. A powerful man in Venice, Don Perucci would have his wife killed for committing adultery.

Dante's feelings for this woman writhing so passionately beneath him didn't spring from altruism, but for the loss of coin should anything happen to her. She'd become his most generous client over the past few months, and he depended on those funds to provide for his brothers. Most men in his position would worry about being strung up in the gallows, beaten, tortured, or possibly killed, but not him. There wasn't much harm a human could do to a vampire.

No, his concern rested firmly on the money.

Not so long ago, he'd been carefree, traveling and making a place for himself in the world. With no responsibilities, no one to provide for, and a warm bed with a willing body waiting for him in the many cities he'd visited, he'd lived the life of a nomad. He lived every day to its fullest and without responsibility — until one chilling moment in time irrevocably changed his life forever.

What should have been a joyous gathering with his parents and younger brothers had turned into a night that would stay etched in his memories until the end of time. It had been months since he'd seen his papa, mama, and brothers. He'd been filled with anticipation on this particular visit to Florence because Mama had recently given birth and he'd yet to meet the *bambino*, GianMarco.

The reunion had been all he'd hoped for. Like always, he'd be been welcomed home with open arms. Though his parents shared the kind of mad, wild love that seemed to consume them when they were near each other, they always included Dante and his brothers in their circle. It set high standards for Dante because he knew when he found his bloodmate, he'd settle for no less than what Maria and Giovanni had.

The night of his visit, Mama had cooked a feast in his honor. Nine- and eleven-year-old Niccolo and Romeo wouldn't leave his side, begging him to regale them with tales of his travels. GianMarco was every bit as precious as Dante imagined he would be. Later that night, his mama suggested the family take a stroll under the stars. Sensing his parents could use some time alone, Dante volunteered to stay behind with his brothers.

Mama and Papa never returned.

When a considerable amount of time passed and all his brothers slept peacefully, Dante went in search of his parents. His senses tingled and dread filled his heart.

They wouldn't leave their young sons for too long. As he continued his search, he was suddenly hit with the fresh scent of blood, and it smelled familiar.

Running as fast as his legs could carry him, he made it to the prone figures of his parents just as a cloaked figure flashed away into the night. Torn between chasing the mysterious attacker and checking on the seriousness of his parents' wounds, he chose the latter.

Weakened at the sight of the lifeless bodies, Dante collapsed to his father's side. Papa and Mama were dead. No human could have done this. A rogue. His mother's neck was torn to ribbons and her chest gaped open. Strands of bloodied blonde hair clung to her terror-frozen face. The same fate had befallen his father. There was a hole in his chest where his heart used to be. Papa's shirt had been torn completely off and written in blood across his stomach were the words *Il Diavolo*. The devil. A taunt. No ordinary rogue would have taken the time to send such a clear challenge.

But it made no sense. His parents didn't have any enemies that Dante knew of. They lived a relatively quiet life, blending in with the humans that surrounded them. A soul shattering pain ripped through his body. He wanted to scream and rage at the twisted fate that had befallen two of the most loving people he knew, but Dante didn't have the luxury of giving in to his grief. The thought of his younger brothers left unattended, set him on high alert. If this *Il Diavolo* had deliberately selected his parents for slaughter, it stood to reason he might turn his focus on the younger Grimaldis.

Before taking off, he gently closed his mother's eyes and kissed both parents goodbye. This would be the last time he would ever see them as their bodies would soon dissolve. "Whoever did this to you, I will make them pay."

With that vow, he raced home, where thankfully, he found the children safe. But they couldn't remain there in case the rogue returned. Days later with his brothers in tow, he'd found a small room to rent in Venice while he figured out how he'd provide for them. He needed a stable income and fast. He had very little money; most of it he'd earned doing odd jobs here and there.

The answer came in the form of a rich nobleman's wife. He'd caught her eye when he'd been out on the street, searching for work. When he was approached by her servant with an offer to be paid generously for services, Dante could hardly refuse. Upon meeting his would-be employer, it became quite clear what said services were. As much as he enjoyed sex, he balked at the idea of being some rich woman's glorified stud.

When she increased the offer, however, it made it difficult to refuse. Much to his shame, Dante agreed to whore himself in order to provide for his brothers. His rich *patrona* was so pleased with his bedroom skills she'd bragged about his prowess to her friends.

So here he was, giving the screaming woman the time of her life. It wasn't a completely distasteful experience, she was attractive and he liked to fuck but it was difficult to maintain his hard-on knowing this was merely a business transaction.

When her release came, it was a sweet, merciful relief.

"Oh, Dante!" Donna Perucci screamed her climax as a warm flow of cream coated his cock.

Dante stayed inside her until she stopped shaking, then eased himself out of her damp sheath. To his

Eve Vaughn

annoyance, she wrapped her plump thighs around his waist.

"No. Don't go. I need you again. My husband shouldn't be back for several hours. His new mistress should keep him occupied; that is, if Antonio is able to get it up, the impotent old goat." She released a satisfied trill of laughter.

Dante was well aware of Don Perucci's mistress, as he serviced her as well, but just because the don fooled around didn't mean he'd take kindly to another man fucking his wife. Besides, it was getting late and he needed to get home to his brothers. Leaning forward, he planted an open-mouthed kiss against Donna Perucci's white throat before meeting her dark, lust-filled gaze with his. "You are tired, Sophia." He whispered the words softly.

Her eyes widened, conveying her fear. He felt the heat of his glowing eyes but she'd soon forget she saw then. And just as he knew she would, Sofia relaxed. "Yes, I'm tired," she agreed.

"You intend to gift me with all the coin in your purse." Though his price had already been determined before their session, he told himself his brothers needed the money, just managing to push away his guilt at what was basically theft.

"Of course, everything I have is yours," Donna Perucci cooed.

A smile tugged the corners of his lips as he dropped one last kiss on her forehead. "Now, sleep, sweet Sophia."

"Hmm," she moaned, closing her eyes and giving in to the hypnotic rest Dante had demanded. Breathing a big sigh of relief, he untangled himself from her soft frame and donned his clothing before taking the coin she'd laid out for him, along with the remaining contents of her purse.

He counted his money and pocketed it. There was enough to keep his household comfortable for a month. Stealing one last glance at the sleeping figure in the oversized bed, he exited the room, flashing past the servants in a blur, not stopping until he stood in front of the little dwelling he shared with his brothers.

The faint sound of a baby crying in fury met his ultrasensitive hearing. GianMarco! A pensive, content child, the *bambino* rarely cried. Dante raced inside. "Romeo! Nico!" he called out. There was no sign of them. Fear shot through him. Those two knew better than to wander off by themselves, especially at night when they could easily fall prey to rogues.

He didn't know whether to go out and look for them or comfort the baby. His dilemma was solved on its own when the two children, one fair, the other dark, walked through the door with mischief in their eyes and their hands full of sweets. Their mirth was short-lived when they spotted their very angry older brother standing in the middle of the room, shaking with visible fury.

"Where the hell have you been?" Unable to control his temper, he stalked toward them and grabbed the boys by the fronts of their shirts. He lifted them off the ground and gave them each a shake.
"Where…have…you…been?" Dante pronounced each word with barely contained fury.

Romeo spoke, though his fear was evident.
"We…we only wanted to have a little fun. You never let us do anything. Mama and Papa —"

"Are dead! And I'm the one responsible for you two ungrateful children. What were you thinking to leave GianMarco on his own? He's just a *bambino*! And I suppose you stole those sweets you have?" Not waiting for an answer, Dante released Romeo and Nico none too gently. The boys hit the floor with loud thuds.

Dante regretted his actions the instant that happened. The stress of their situation had gotten to him, but it horrified him that he would take it out on his young brothers. They were practically babies themselves.

GianMarco's wails grew louder and more furious. A feeling of helplessness coursed through him as he collapsed to his knees, his face in his palms. He hadn't allowed himself to cry since he was a boy, not even when he'd found the mutilated bodies of his parents. But now, the sobs came freely. He cried for what had happened to his mama and papa, for his orphaned brothers who wouldn't grow up with their parents' love, and for what he'd become, a gigolo sleeping with wealthy women to make ends meet. And mostly, he cried out of fear. It was his responsibility to shape his siblings into the men they would eventually become. The thought was daunting and he was scared he was already failing at it.

In truth, he'd never had the chance to really get to know the children before his parents died because his visits never lasted long, but in the past several weeks of taking care of them, they had become his entire world. Tonight when he thought something had happened to them, it hit him how devastated he would have been.

As he gave in to his misery, two sets of thin arms wrapped around his shaking frame. "We're sorry, Dante. We won't sneak out again," Niccolo whispered against his ear.

Shamed at how easily his brothers were able to comfort him after his manhandling of them, Dante couldn't raise his head to look them in the eyes. "Please, one of you, bring Marco to me," he croaked, too full of emotion to get the words out properly.

Romeo scrambled to get the screaming infant and returned shortly. Dante took the baby and carefully rested him in the crook of his arm. He slit a vein in his wrist and put it against the baby's mouth. The bambino latched on and sucked furiously. Dante's heart contracted with love for this child and the two boys who stood beside him.

"I'm sorry for losing my temper with you. It was inexcusable. I need you to promise me to never wander off like that again. It's not safe for young ones like you to roam the streets at this time of night. If you two must go out, let me know and we can arrange something."

The boys nodded solemnly.

"We're sorry, Dante," Romeo said quietly, his blond head hanging in apparent shame.

"See that it doesn't happen again and no more stealing. Just because humans can't catch you, doesn't mean you can flaunt your powers. People fear what they don't understand, and I don't think I could handle it if anything ever happened to any of you. You three mean the world to me, and I will do whatever it takes to keep you safe."

"We know." Niccolo nodded. "We love you, too." They threw their arms around Dante.

The baby whined at being squeezed so tightly, but as if he sensed the magnitude of the moment, he quieted.

Eve Vaughn

"I will always be there for the three of you," Dante
promised. "Always."

Dante

Chapter One

They were dead.

He'd killed every single one of the bastards, yet the rage coursing through his body had yet to subside. In fact, his bloodlust demanded more casualties. Dante surveyed his blood-splattered surroundings, ready for another enemy to appear from the shadows.

Thump-thump. Thump-thump.

A still-beating heart caught his attention. Slowly, Dante stalked toward his prey, his eyes zeroing in on the rogue whose limbs he'd ripped off during battle. He lowered himself to his haunches and dug his talon-sharp nails into his enemy's chest. A pain-filled scream erupted from the rogue's throat.

"My fingers are only inches away from your heart. And you have one of two choices: You can either tell me where the children are and I'll end your life quickly, granting you the mercy you don't deserve or you could remain silent and I'll squeeze your black heart to a pulp. If you choose the second option, I assure you, your death will be slow and painful."

His red-eyed adversary stared at him with a hatful glare. "Fuck you, Grimaldi. Your precious family is as good as dead and soon you'll be as well." To punctuate his venomous words, he spit in Dante's face with a combination of blood and saliva.

With a hiss, Dante bared his incisors and ripped through his defiant enemy's chest and clutched his heart.

14

The vampire gasped, his eyes widening.

Dante tightened his hold on the pumping organ until it exploded in his palm. He kept his fist planted firmly in the gaping hole he'd created until he was satisfied the rogue was dead. Once he was on his feet again, he wiped away the rogue's spittle with the back of his hand.

Another mission complete, yet he was no closer to finding his nieces and nephews than he had been a week ago. Jagger, Nico's son, a vampire, warlock hybrid, could hold his own in most fights, but these weren't ordinary circumstances. The other three missing Grimaldi children were particularly vulnerable. Jaxson and Adrienne, Romeo's children, adopted into their family a short time ago were only six and three years of age. And human. They had to be frightened with what was happening with them. They had already suffered at the hands of cruel biological relatives before they'd been taken out of their home. It didn't seem fair that they would now have to contend with this as well.

It scared the hell out of Dante to think of the possible scenarios they could be facing, especially when most rogues viewed humans as food. And lastly, there was baby Gianna, Gia for short, Marco's infant daughter, not even a month old. She needed constant care and feedings. Would her captors give her the proper care she required or willfully neglect her?

A chill raced down Dante's spine as he imagined different scenarios. His thoughts strayed to Jagger. When his disappearance had been discovered, his blood had splattered the walls. What had they done to him and had the torture continued? He had to believe they were all still alive because to give up hope would cause his family to spiral into a dark place of no return. Marco had already lost one child. Fate couldn't be so malicious as to take a second one.

All the misfortunate and tragedy he and his brothers had suffered throughout the centuries rested at the feet of Adonis, a rogue hell bent on destroying the Grimaldis. Dante and his brothers had hunted relentlessly, but Adonis had remained elusive through the centuries. He was also their brother.

Recently, Dante had learned of yet another sibling: Giovanni, an elusive vampire, who seemed to pop up wherever they went in the last several months. It had been a shock to all of them to learn of not one more brother, but two. Seeing Adonis and Giovanni, so like them in features, there was no denying they shared a bloodline, but how? Papa had never spoken of the two other children he'd fathered.

Dante released a deep breath. Time was wasting and every precious second counted. He needed to move on to his next lead. The shrill ring of a mobile phone cut through the silence in the room. It wasn't his, as the one resting in his breast pocket was set on vibrate. It obviously belonged to one of the dead rogues. Answering it would hopefully lead to a clue.

He followed the sound of the ring tone and extracted the device from the pants pocket of one of the first rogues he'd killed.

"Yes?" Dante kept his voice low in hopes the caller wouldn't recognize he wasn't the intended recipient of the message.

"Snake?" the deep voice on the other end queried with uncertainty.

"Yes."

There was a slight pause. "The cargo is on the move. Our position has been compromised. It'll make it's final destination ahead of schedule. Niccolo Grimaldi busted up *El Corazon Negro* last night. The Romanovs were with him. I managed to escape, but other than myself, there were no survivors. Warn the others. Snake, are you there?"

"Yes."

"A bunch of us are meeting at Sidewinder's to await further instruction. I need to get out of here, but I'll call again when I'm able."

The phone clicked off and Dante stuffed it in his pocket. It would probably come in handy later if there were any other calls of importance. He had no doubt the "cargo" was the children. They were so close, he could feel it.

After coming up against one too many dead ends, Dante had received a tip from one of his agents regarding a group of vampires called the Serpent Gang, a band of rogues whose main goals were causing chaos and feeding on humans. Rumor had it that they were also mercenaries, performing tasks for the highest bidders, so it made sense Adonis was using them to hold his nieces and nephews.

Dante had sent his brothers to the gang's known hideouts. So far, he'd only heard back from Romeo, who still had no new information, and that phone call from the unknown rogue told Dante that Nico had no better luck. That only left Marco. He'd have to get out of here in case reinforcements came.

Back at the hotel, Dante paced back and forth, waiting for Marco's call. It worried him that he hadn't heard anything from his youngest brother thus far. GianMarco was more than capable of taking care of himself and had been on countless missions, but this was no ordinary assignment. A handful of agents had lost their lives to this particular rogue and his minions.

It seemed like ages ago when the entire family had assembled to celebrate the joyous occasion of Gianna's birth. But in truth, it had only been a few short weeks. Briefly, they'd put aside their worry over the threat of the mysterious brothers hanging over their heads to be thankful for the good things that had happened to them; like most of them finding their mates and the addition of the children to the family. The joy and good cheer they'd shared had been wiped out suddenly with the kidnappings. The timing had almost seemed deliberate, as if their enemy wanted them to know how easily he could snatch their happiness away.

He prayed they were okay.

His phone vibrated, interrupting his musings. "Dante here."

"It's me."

Relief flooded his chest at the sound of his brother's voice. Once it sank in Marco was all right, irritation took over. "Where the hell have you been? You should have checked in hours ago. Yesterday, in fact."

"Calm down, Dante. I had a narrow escape from a group of rogues. We lost two more agents, and I barely made it out of the skirmish alive."

"Anton and Dominic?" Dante closed his eyes in regret. In the past few days, the Underground had taken a hit in manpower. They'd lost five members in all. The situation was growing dire.

"Yes," Marco finally answered with a sigh. "They fought valiantly. Any news on your end?"

Dante told him about the phone call. "So now we have to figure out where Sidewinder's is. I can only infer from the call the kids are still alive. I believe the caller would have said otherwise if they weren't."

"They damn sure better be. If they so much as harm one hair on Gia's head, I swear…" A sob escaped from Marco, his voice filled with emotion. "I will not rest until every single one of them dies a slow, painful death."

"We'll find her, Marco. We'll find them all."

"It will kill Maggie if something happens to Gia."

It went without saying that it would be devastating for Marco as well. Now more than ever, Dante was determined to bring the children to safety. "We'll meet tomorrow in New York, at my penthouse. We're going to need all the reinforcements we can get. Paris and Aries, along with a handful of their pack members should be in attendance, as will Sasha's brothers."

"I'll see you then." Marco clicked off without waiting for Dante to respond.

Dante sank onto the nearest chair, letting his head fall into his cupped palms. He had to be strong for his family with these turbulent times ahead. But who would be strong for him?

Isis Vasquez paced her best friend's sitting room floor, nervous energy flowing through her body.

"Would you have a seat? You're making me dizzy with all that walking back and forth," Persephone Kyriakis snapped.

Isis sighed in resignation, raking her fingers through her hair. She was unable to keep still when she had so much on her mind. "I can't. As a matter of fact, I should be heading for Manhattan with your father."

Persephone raised one dark arched brow. "My, my, my. Someone is anxious and I know why."

Isis folded her arms across her chest. "I can't stand idly by when the lives of innocent children are at stake. I think it's awful how they were just taken the way they were."

"I agree and it's an admirable reason to want to help but let's not play dumb. The children aren't the only reason you want to volunteer."

Isis halted in mid pace. Folding her arms across her chest, she gave her friend a narrow-eyed stare. "Oh? You seem to be privy to information I'm not aware of."

A smile of pure mischief curled Persephone's glossed lips. "Isis, the only person you're kidding is yourself if you truly believe that, but if you need me to spell it out for you, it starts with a *D*, ends with an *E*. About six feet five inches tall, dreamy, dark blue eyes, and a killer body."

Heat crept up Isis's neck and stung her cheeks. "Okay, so I wouldn't mind seeing Dante again, but it isn't the main reason I'd like to go. I *need* to go."

"What *is* the main reason then? Ever since we overheard my father and Aries plan their trip, you've been jumpy."

Isis released a deep breath. She had feared her past would come back to haunt her one day, but she never figured it would come in this form. "They mentioned The Serpent Gang was embroiled in this mess, that they're likely the ones who are keeping the children hostage."

Persephone cocked her head to the side. "You're going to need to give me more detail than that."

"I was in a relationship with one of their members a long time ago."

"Are you serious? My father attempts to keep me unaware of his Underground dealings, but even I've heard of them. Why didn't you tell me this before?"

"Because your friendship means more to me than you could possibly know. But you're part of a powerful pack, and your father already has concerns about our connection because I have no pack allegiance. I didn't want to give him another reason to think less of me. I didn't want you to think less of me, either. I'm not proud of some of the things I used to do, and I haven't seen Black Adder for years. And I had hoped to put all that behind me."

Persephone's dark brows knitted together, while a frown caused her lips to droop. "Were you also a member?"

"I couldn't be a full member because I'm not a vampire, but because I was the leader's lover, they tolerated my presence." Isis lowered her lids unable to maintain the intense scrutiny of Persephone's gaze. "I can tell from your look that you don't approve."

"I didn't say that."

"You don't have to. Your expression says it all."

"What exactly is it saying?"

"That I'm a horrible person."

"I could never think that about you. I'm just trying to make sense of how you could keep the fact that you were once associated with one of the most dangerous groups of rogues in the immortal community a secret. They're responsible for a countless number of immortal and human deaths alike."

Isis bit the inside of cheek to keep herself from making excuses because there were none. She couldn't blame Persephone for judging her. The Serpent Gang fed off the weak, bringing chaos wherever they went. During her association with them, Isis had done things she now deeply regretted, but at the time, the need to belong had overridden her sense of right and wrong. "I know, Seph. It's one of the reasons I never mentioned it to you before this. I suppose if your father finds out, he'll see that our friendship is severed. Will you tell him?"

Persephone opened her mouth then closed it.

As the silence stretched, tension coiled within Isis's body until her nerves were ready to snap. "Say something." Persephone's friendship had been one of the things that had helped her out of a dark place in her life. Since the brutal slaughter of her pack by a group of Hunters and her rejection from her mother's former pack, Isis had been on her own. As a lone wolf, she'd done whatever she had to in order to survive, often things she was now ashamed of. Several of those things involved the Serpent Gang. Isis had been on a continuous downward spiral until she could no longer look at herself in a mirror. Once she'd finally turned her back on that life of mayhem and destruction, it had been a constant struggle not to fall back into her old ways. But one day she'd met Persephone, someone who didn't automatically label Isis as no good because she didn't have a pack. Lone wolves were usually shifters who had been shunned by their pack for behavior unbecoming of the pack. Most of these wolves later went on to become rogue, which earned them all bad reputations. Isis had been marked by that stigma by many, but not Persephone.

"Seph?" Isis prompted again.

Persephone swung her legs off her chaise lounge and stood in front of Isis to give her a tight hug. "I'm not going to stop being your friend. I just wish you would have been more open with me about your past before now." She pulled away and studied Isis with an indiscernible expression. "How did you get entangled with them in the first place?"

Isis sighed and gestured to the nearest chair. "It's a pretty lengthy story. Let's sit."

Persephone nodded returning to the chaise.

Isis plopped down on the edge of the chair and folded her hands in her lap. "You already know, I've always had an affinity for vampires, particularly the tall dark and dangerous ones. I guess it comes from being raised by a very conservative pack. My papa was a lot like yours, very protective but amplified. He had a very set ideal of how women in the pact should behave and at times, his rules were suffocating to the point where I wanted to rebel every chance I could get."

"I guess that's why I've been attracted to men who live on the edge, and no group embodies that as much as vampires. After my pack was decimated, I sought out my mother's old pack only to be told I'm a worthless mutt by my own grandfather. He told me if I showed up on their lands again, he'd send his pack out to erase me from

Earth, his exact words. He said I was an abomination who shouldn't have been born."

Persephone mouth formed a perfect oh as a gasp escaped. "You're kidding me, right? Pack relationships are very important. Your own grandfather said that to you?"

Isis bit the inside of her lip as a shudder wiggled up her spine. The memory of her grandfather's words still had the ability to make her heart go cold. He'd looked at her as if she'd been the lowest life form he'd ever come across. "Yes. He actually said that."

"Why? I don't understand. With your mother dead…"

"That didn't matter to my grandfather. In his eyes my blood was impure so I wasn't worthy to be part of his pack. You see, Pack Khan had several members with some type of psychic ability, like clairvoyance, telekinesis, mediumship and slew of other abilities. My mother could sometime gage events before they happened. It was these abilities my grandfather believed made Pack Khan superior to other packs. No one mated outside the pack. The problem lay with the small size of the pack. After a while inbreeding occurred, cousins and sometimes siblings mated." Isis barely stopped herself from shuttering as she had relayed that last bit.

Persephone's lips curved into a frown and her nose crinkled. "I vaguely remember hearing about a pack from Bangladesh that never mated out. I heard a lot of them succumbed to *Malum,* disease that wiped out so many of our kind, because of the weak gene pool."

Isis shrugged. "That could have been Pack Khan. They weren't the only ones who stuck to their own pack. But getting back to the story, my grandfather wanted my mother to mate with his brother, her uncle. My mother, of course, had no feelings for this man who was every bit the zealot my grandfather was."

Persephone curled her lips making her disgust evident. "So how did she manage to meet your father?"

"My father was visiting a neighboring pack and he and my mother happened to meet each other while they were both out on a run. From the way my mother described it, she realized she'd found the one she was meant to be with. They began to see each other secretly. My father, however being the traditionalist he was, wanted to ask for my grandfather's blessing when they decided to mate. Grandfather forbade them from seeing each other but my mother stood up to him. So she was given an ultimatum, do as she was told and marry her uncle or be banished from the pack. I'm sure you've already figured out the rest. My father took her back to his home in the Dominican Republic where they had me and we all lived until the pack was wiped out by hunters and rogue shifters."

"If my mother hadn't sacrificed herself so that I could make my escape, I'd be dead, too. I was only sixteen years old when it happened and I had never ventured off the island. I was terrified and didn't know how I'd survive. Pack Vasquez wasn't wealthy like my mother's old one had been so I had very few resources once my parents were gone. And if my father had money put away somewhere, I had no idea how to access it. I got the idea to seek out my grandfather because my mom told me about the grand compound in Bangladesh where her old pack resided. I thought for sure my grandfather would be happy to see me and that he'd forget his old grudge with my parents and take me into his fold."

Persephone crinkled her nose in a grimace. "Weren't you worried, he'd want to mate you to one of your cousins or something?"

Isis raised a brow.

"Sorry. Just curious."

"At the time, it didn't really cross my mind. Throwing myself on my grandfather's mercy seemed better than being on my own. For all I knew, the hunters would come back for me. I was terrified so I figure out a way to get to Bangladesh. I ended up selling the only valuables my parents owned and I begged on the streets, relying on other people's charity. At night, I would sleep in the woods in my second form for protection. After several weeks, I finally earned enough to purchase a boat ticket and some items I'd need for my journey. When I finally made it to the compound, my grandfather told me I'd wasted my time coming to him. He called me an abomination and it was because of me my mother had died. He said if she had obeyed him, she'd still be alive." Isis hastily swiped at the tear that had slid from the corner of her eye. Though it had been nearly two centuries, remembering that conversation still had the power to make her gut clench with anxiety. That feeling of worthlessness reared its head and gnawed at her soul.

"That was his loss, hon. You're much off better without those fanatics."

Isis shrugged. "Considering most of them have been wiped out and the survivors have gone into hiding, I suppose you're right. But I always wonder how different things could have been for me had Grandfather accepted me. Oh, well, that's neither here nor there. Anyway, as a lone wolf, I had to fight every day for my survival. I stole, fought, and did whatever I could to make it to the next day. After a while, I was just...tired. I looked to align myself with another pack for protection. Unfortunately, all the ones I encountered were unwilling to take me in. I'd been on my own for maybe a few years at that point and some even labeled me a rogue, *Malum* was prevalent around then and they didn't want to chance contacting it through me. I roamed South Asia for a while and moved on to Europe. I never stayed in one place for very long because of my fear of the hunters coming for me."

"It was around that time I had a chance meeting with a vampire by the name of Copperhead. I was smitten. He told me he admired my bravery and that I was beautiful. For someone who hadn't heard a kind word in years, I ate all his attention up. He was my first lover and I felt safe with him. I knew he did bad things but in my mind I justified it because he protected me. We were together for nearly a year before he introduced me to his crew. They weren't very welcoming toward me because I'm not a vampire, but after a while, I started to gain their trust."

"How? You didn't kill innocents, did you?"

"No. But my hands aren't completely clean. I delivered messages, and was the lookout for some of their jobs and I even got into a few tussles when they needed a little extra muscle. By then, I'd become pretty good at defending myself. After hanging out with them for a while, I caught the eye of Black Adder, the leader. And I know this sounds awful, but I was felt that if I was with the leader, it would secure my place in the crew. I didn't want to be alone again."

"So you dumped Copperhead, just like that? Wasn't he hurt?"

"It wasn't quite like that. Once Black Adder stated his interest in me, it was basically a done deal. Copperhead kind of just stepped aside and I allowed Black Adder to claim me for the reasons I already stated."

"Copperhead didn't, at least, put up a fight or even seem a little upset?"

"If he was angry over it, he didn't really show it. Besides, he replaced me within days."

"And how did that make you feel?"

Isis nibbled her bottom lip as she conjured up the memories from her past. "I was surprised, but to be honest, I wasn't in love with him and I don't believe he was in love with me, either. Don't get me wrong, I was grateful toward him for his companionship and his literally giving me a home. But I didn't kid myself into believing we had some grand love affair. I knew he saw other women behind my back and I turned a blind eye to it because I didn't want to be on my own again."

"Did you care for Black Adder beyond his position in the gang?"

Isis shifted on the chaise to make her position more comfortable. "Yes. Honestly, I'd always been intrigued by him but never dared say anything about it. He wasn't as classically handsome as Copperhead, but he had that certain something about him that would make any girl look twice. Besides being incredibly sexy, he excited me in way Copperhead never did. He had such a forceful personality, and said and did whatever he wanted. He was a bit of an anarchist and being that I had come from such a strict background, it gave me a secret thrill to be in his presence. So once we became lovers, he had some kind of hold on me I couldn't quite explain. Anything he would ask me to do, I'd do it like some devoted puppy. I was basically an unofficial member of their gang rather than just a hanger-on. I graduated from being a look out to more sinister tasks. I won't go into the gory details, but let's just say I did some things that weren't good."

Persephone frowned. "It's hard to reconcile what you're telling me. I know what the Serpent Gang is capable of, but I just don't see you involved in any of it."

Isis couldn't believe it herself. It made her shudder when she remembered some of the things she'd done. "I look back at that time with Black Adder and the Serpent Gang as just a bad dream. I've worked very hard to not be the woman I once was."

"Why did you finally distance yourself from them? Or did Black Adder end things with you? From the way you describe him, he doesn't seem like the type to let someone go unless it's his decision."

"And you'd be right about that, but I had to get away from them. They'd started dabbling in black magic. Somehow, they got mixed up with some vampire named *Il Demonio*, who promised them power beyond their wildest imaginings. He told them they'd practically be unstoppable."

Persephone tapped her chin appearing to be in deep contemplation before she finally replied. "*Il Demonio*? That name sounds familiar. I believe I overheard my father and Dante mention it. He might be the one who's behind the disappearance of the Grimaldi children."

Isis hopped to her feet. "That's it! That's how they're connected."

"Tell me what you know about the association with *Il Demonio* and the Serpent Gang."

"As I already explained, I broke things off with Black Adder shortly after his gang got involved with this particular vampire. I remember meeting him once and he made me extremely uneasy. By chance, I stumbled upon a strange ritual performed by a woman in a hooded cape but I couldn't make out her face. Actually, I didn't see much because someone noticed my spying. I wasn't supposed to be there, you see. Black Adder was careful to keep me away from all the mysterious dealings with this woman and *Il Demonio*. But, you know me. My curiosity was piqued and I had to find out what was going on because Black Adder had started acting strange."

"In what way?"

"Have you ever seen a human addicted to drugs?"

"Not up close and personal, but I've seen movie depictions of it. He was like that?"

Isis nodded. "I was concerned for him. After he got involved with *Il Demonio*, he changed. He started to shut me out and he was no longer interested in sex and he started having these wild unpredictable mood swings. But, he'd be perfectly fine after one of these mysterious meetings. The longer he went between each gathering, the more violent he became. His eyes would turn bloodshot red, and anyone unfortunate enough to cross his path was either killed or beaten to the point where they wished for death."

"So what happened when they caught you spying?"

"Two of the members grabbed me and the woman suddenly appeared in front of me, like magic."

"She must have been a witch."

"I guess so, but she didn't seem like she was. I didn't sense she was a true immortal, yet the power radiating from her was like nothing I'd ever felt. Black Adder stood by, not lifting a finger to help me as I tried to break free. In fact, I got the feeling he wanted harm to come to me. That's when things got weird. She touched my face and started to caress it. To say I was freaked out would have been the understatement of the century. She made strange comments about my looks and how I was perfect. For what, I'm not certain, but I didn't stick around to find out. I kicked her with all my might and she went flying across the room. I shifted and got the hell out of there. They chased me, of course, but I ran and didn't stop until I was sure they were no longer on my heels. I knew then I was alone again. But this time, I had actually managed to squirrel away some money I collected while I was with Black Adder. I had invested most of it and had managed to make myself enough to live modestly. I never did settle down in one place out of fear that I'd run into the Serpent Gang again. I've been roaming the world ever since. That was nearly fifteen years ago."

Persephone nodded. "That was around the time we met."

"Yes, I was just starting to get my life back together, and you came along at a time when I really needed a friend."

Persephone slid off the chaise, walked over to Isis, and gave her a hug. "Sweetheart, I'm not going to stop being friends with you because of your past, but I'm not the one you should be worried about."

"What do you mean?"

"If you meet up with Dante again, he might not be as forgiving about your past activities as me. You have to keep in mind, this rogue you mentioned has been tormenting the Grimaldi family for centuries."

Isis groaned inwardly. She had, of course, heard of Dante Grimaldi long before she'd met him. Most immortals had. He was a legend. However, she'd been disappointed so many times in her life, she didn't think anyone could possibly live up to the stories she'd heard about him. When they finally met however, not only did Dante meet her expectations, he exceeded him. He was every bit as handsome and charming as she'd been told he'd be.

What Isis hadn't been prepared for was the strong pull she felt toward him, it was stronger than anything she'd experienced before. Stronger than what she'd had with Copperhead, Black Adder or the random lovers she'd taken over the years. She wasn't sure what this meant but her pulse raced and her heart sped to a pace that would kill most humans when she was within a few feet of him. There were moments when she was certain he returned the attraction.

There had been one moment when she found herself in his arms but before anything could happen, they'd been interrupted. After that, he'd maintained his distance. Isis understood he was dealing with some unresolved issues and that the time to have even the briefest of affairs wasn't in the cards for them. But she couldn't help but think about what could happen between them once things had settled down. Isis felt her insides twist as she imagined the contempt he'd probably have for her if he discovered her past association.

"That's all I've thought about lately. This is why he can never know. But in the meantime, I can't sit back and do nothing when I can offer my assistance. I know things about the Serpent Gang that may be useful in finding the Grimaldi children."

"How do you propose to help without drawing suspicion? They'll probably want to know how you came across your information."

"I'll figure something out. For now, I need to catch up with your father before he leaves. I'm going to Manhattan one way or another." Isis would not be deterred. Though helping find the children was her priority, she couldn't help being excited at the thought of seeing Dante again.

33

Chapter Two

"I don't see why we can't kill the brats, especially the baby. All it does is cry. And one of those little fuckers bit me."

The sound of low-pitched voices roused Jagger Grimaldi from what felt like a deep sleep. His head pounded like a son of a bitch and his muscles contracted in pain. He lay face down and every single muscle in his body ached and he felt restrained. As his eyes adjusted to the darkness of the room, he noticed, two shadowy figures standing in the corner of his room. Their backs were to him. He closed his eyes and feigned sleep so he wouldn't draw attention to himself.

"The boy?" The owner of the second voice chuckled. "He kicked me when I brought food. He demanded I take him to his sister."

"You almost sound like you admire the child," the first one snarled. "He's a human, a lesser being. They're no better than animals."

"I agree but the kid has balls. I'd take that over some sniveling nonsense. One thing I haven't been able to figure out is why a powerful vampire family like the Grimaldis would raise the creatures as their own."

"Who the fuck cares? The Grimaldis aren't as powerful as everyone says they are. They're weak and their downfall is at hand. When they come for their offspring, they'll be defeated and forced to watch as we kill the children one at a time."

"What about this one over there? He's been unconscious since we captured him."

It took a concerted amount of effort to remain still as Jagger eavesdropped on the conversation. He hoped they stuck around long enough for him to discover their exact plans.

"He lost most of his blood in the scuffle. He's young, so it'll probably take him a while to heal. Plus, he's been put under a sleeping spell to make him easier to transport. There's no telling when that will wear off."

"Are you sure those charmed cuffs he's wearing will bind his powers? I heard he's related to the Romanov's. If he even has half their powers—"

"Quit worrying. You're starting to sound like a scared little bitch. Anything this guy can dish out, we can more than handle it. Besides, we've been assured the cuffs will work. Even if he does wake, he'll be as helpless as those human children and that baby."

For the first time since he came to, Jagger realized why he couldn't move his arms. They were bound behind his back. His muscled screamed for relief but none came. He wanted to open his eyes again to get a look at their faces but anymore movement would probably draw their unwanted attention.

"Well, he seems like he'll be out for a little while longer. Let's go check on the others. The baby probably needs to be fed again." The rogue's voice was full of disgust. "I wish we could just starve it but we have orders to keep them alive and healthy…for now. When I see Sidewinder again, maybe I'm going to tell him to find another fucking babysitter."

The second rogue chuckled. "You won't stand up to him and we both know it."

"Shut up, Viper. You and I both know this assignment is bullshit. I should be Black Adder's second-in-command."

The voices grew distant as they walked out the room and closed the door behind them. Once Jagger was sure they were gone and a good distance from the room, he rolled over to his back and sat up. The immediate blood rush made his head spin, sending him crashing to a supine position once again.

Jagger groaned as he allowed his body to recover from the shock of his sudden movement. The next time he attempted to sit up, he did it slowly, careful not to make any jarring movements. It was tricky with his arms behind his back. Jagger slowly swung his legs over the side of the cot and stood on trembling limbs before surveying his surroundings.

The room was bare except for the cot he'd been lying on and a bucket in the corner. The big door was solid wood with metal bars in the center like some medieval prison. He attempted to break the restraints, but they wouldn't budge. Regular handcuffs were no match for his strength. Jagger channeled his ability to manipulate metal but that too failed him.

He, then, remembered what one of the rogues had said; these cuffs were charmed. He plopped back on the cot with a frustrated sigh. Jagger had never felt so helpless in his life but he had to do something or the children were as good as dead.

Shaking his head to clear the fog surrounding it, he tried to recall how he'd come to be here. Slowly, the memories came flooding back. Camryn! Finally, she'd declared her love for him, a love he'd fought hard to earn. After a night of making love, they'd fallen asleep in each other's arms.

Later that night, he'd woken up full of energy ready to make love to his Camryn again, but her side of the bed was empty. Her scent had clung to the sheets and his cock was rock hard. He figured she might have gone to use the bathroom but when she still hadn't returned after several minutes, Jagger decided to seek her out. He donned his discarded clothing and was headed out the room when Camryn walked in but instead of acknowledging him, she brushed past him without a word and lay on the bed. Her eyes were open but something definitely wasn't right.

"Camryn?"

There was no answer.

He moved to her side and gently shook her. "What's the matter? Are you not feeling well?"

She was ice cold. If he didn't notice the slow rise and fall of her chest to indicate she was breathing, Jagger would have assumed the worst. Nonetheless, he began to panic because clearly, she was no okay.

"Her eyes may be open, but she's in very deep trance. She won't wake up for at least a few hours."

Jagger whirled around to locate the unfamiliar voice, yet he and Camryn were the only ones in the room. The timbre of the voice made it hard for him to determine the gender of its owner. "Where are you?" Who are you?" he demanded.

A chuckle, loud and menacing echoed against the walls. Jagger twitched with power as he readied himself to face the intruder.

"I'm the one who'll see you and your family in hell. You can make this easy for yourself and give up or we can do this the hard way. In either instance, make no mistake—you're coming with us. But if you give me too hard a time, I'll make the little ones suffer."

Jagger's blood chilled as cold as ice water at the reference to his young cousins. "Leave them alone!" he roared. "They're innocent."

Again, the owner of the raspy voice laughed. "It's too late, Nikolai Grimaldi. For them and you." Out of the darkness, three red-eyed rogues materialized from the wall, followed by a small, hooded figure. "I see you chose to do things the hard way." The voice belonged to the one in the cloak. Being in closer proximity, Jagger could now tell it was a woman. But who was she?

It didn't matter. They'd done something to Camryn and were threatening his family. Producing a large energy ball in his palm, he shot it toward the closest rogue. Instead of the expected result, the charge bounced off the vampire and slammed into Jagger's chest, sending him flying backward. He hit the wall with a thud.

The very fact that no one had yet to come to his rescue with a houseful of relatives told Jagger that the house had to be enchanted in some way. His family was still alive, otherwise he would have felt the loss of their connection.

Using every spell in his arsenal he could think of, he fought the three rogues off as best as he could but he was no match for the red-eyed creatures. These rogues were different from any he'd ever faced. They had somehow managed to turn all his attacks against him. Still, he refused to give up if for nothing else than to protect Camryn who lay helplessly in bed.

When the figure in the cloak whispered some indiscernible command, all three vampires jumped on him, biting and clawing and tearing into his flesh. The more he struggled, the more vicious they grew. Miraculously, they hadn't killed him. Instead, the woman stepped forward and pulled her hood back to reveal a young woman. There was something familiar about the intensity of her eyes and striking coloring, but he didn't have time to dwell on who she reminded him of because she raised her hands heavenward and lifted him off the ground with a telekinetic surge.

She then tossed him against the wall, over and over again. Jagger lost count of how many times before he blacked out. It brought him to the predicament he now found himself in. Obviously, he wouldn't be able to use his powers anytime soon and even if he could, he wasn't sure if he could best the rogues who probably guarded this place. But unless he figured a way out of this mess, he and the children were doomed.

"Absolutely not, Maggie. You're staying behind with Sasha and Christine," Marco stated firmly.

Maggie shot from her chair, nostrils flaring and eyes blazing. "If you haven't forgotten, Gianna is my daughter, too. And need I mention, Camryn has been in hysterics since she woke up to find all that blood. I made a promise to her that I'd help in bringing her little sister and Jagger home safely and I'm not going to back down from that vow. I need you to understand my position. I have a child who's missing, and as her mother, I refuse to sit back and do nothing."

Marco folded his arms across his chest. "Nico is fully capable of finding his son."

Maggie glared. "Do you have any idea how insulting that sounds? He has two parents, you know. You don't get to dictate that the womenfolk stay home just because we have vaginas. Our children were taken by some psychopath and I, for one, don't give a damn if you forbid me from going or not. I'm going!"

"And so am I," Christine chimed in, looking every bit as determined as Maggie.

Romeo shook his head. "Don't start, Christine. You'll be safer with the other women. Sasha's powers will protect you from harm."

A gleam of triumph entered Maggie's dark eyes. "Exactly. So why can't we go with you? I'm not human anymore. Neither is Christine, and as you just pointed out, Sasha is a powerful witch. I may not be an ancient like the rest of you, but when any of my children are in harm's way, I'll fight to the death."

"Which is what I'm trying to prevent. I can't lose you, too." Marco cupped his mate's face between his hands and gave her a quick kiss on the lips.

Maggie turned her head to the side and pushed him away. "And I can't lose Gianna."

"Maggie—"

Dante could take no more of this conversation. He pushed himself off the wall and moved to the center of the room. "Enough!" For the past hour, he'd been listening to this back and forth between his brothers and their mates when they should have been discussing strategy. "I suggest you six work this out among yourselves, but in the meantime, the children are out

40

there and there's no telling what's being done to them. Our time would be better severed if we stop wasting time arguing."

He paced the living room floor of his Manhattan penthouse. Secretly, he agreed with his brothers. Dante didn't doubt Maggie and Christine would prove to be fine allies. However, they were young vampires, each of them under a year old. Sasha, on the other hand, was probably the only one of his brothers' mates who could hold her own against these super rogues they were likely to face. But it was best Sasha stay with Maggie and Christine to keep them safe.

Sasha crossed the room to stand with her sisters-in-law. "He's probably right. There are forces working against us we haven't gotten a proper handle on. My brothers will be able to communicate with me and let us know exactly what's going on. We won't be completely out of the loop." She patted Maggie's hand reassuringly.

Steel Romanov nodded. "*Da*. We'll maintain contact Sasha. You have no need to worry."

Maggie opened her mouth as if she wanted to say more, but was forestalled when the doorbell rang.

Grateful for the brief intervention, Dante hurried to answer it. It was Paris and Aries. He was touched to know he could count on his friends in his family's time of need and they could use all the reinforcements they could get. "Paris, Aries, come in," he beckoned. Two more members of Pack Kyriakis followed, and to his surprise, so did Isis Vasquez.

Dante barely managed to tear his gaze away from the dark-haired beauty long enough to greet his friends properly. "Everyone is in the living room. My brothers are trying to calm their mates down."

Paris raised a brow. "Ah. Dissension in the Grimaldi clan?"

"Nothing we can't resolve. You have no idea how much it means to me to have you here, especially with your pack's current difficulties."

Paris offered him a tilted smile. "You've been there for my pack on numerous occasions. I wouldn't dream of missing out on this. Besides, Constantine is keeping an eye on pack affairs in my absence and he'll have his mate to keep him company. This is as good a time as any for him to practice for when he becomes Alpha."

Dante shook Paris's hand. "I'm still very grateful that you've come. And it's good to see you as well, Aries."

The younger shifter grinned, revealing his sharpened incisors. "You couldn't keep me away. I never miss out on the opportunity to bust some heads."

Paris rolled his eyes skyward. "My nephew sometimes speaks before he thinks, but please know, he understands the gravity of the situation." He eyed his nephew. "The objective is to find the children, Aries."

Aries nodded solemnly. "Of course, Uncle, finding the children is our priority but if we can take out as many rogues as possible in the process that would be a plus."

Dante smiled in approval. "I agree." Aries Kyriakis reminded him a lot of Romeo.

Paris gestured to the other three in his entourage. "You remember George and Theo?"

Dante nodded. "Yes, thank you for coming."

"And of course, Isis, Persephone's friend." Paris wasn't so gracious in his introduction of her; in fact,

Dante got the distinct impression his friend didn't approve of her presence.

"Yes, how could I forget?"

She glanced at him with that beautiful gaze that he found captivating. She bit her full bottom lip almost seeming uncertain. Since their last meeting, he'd thought about her often, wondering what would have happened had they met in different circumstances. At the time, he'd been battling the internal struggle of his feelings for his brother's mate. Being face to face with her now, however, reminded him of how much he'd enjoyed spending time with her. Unfortunately, his current situation was no better than the last, yet something inside of him was very pleased she was here.

Dante took her hand and placed a light kiss on the back of it. "I was sure our paths would cross again one day, but I didn't know how soon."

A faint tinge of red colored her golden brown cheeks. "I hope I can be of some assistance to you and your family."

"She insisted she come with us," Paris spoke abruptly, almost as if her presence was a nuisance to him.

The look of uncertainty entered her eyes again.

Dante winked in her direction to show her that he was happy to see her. "Well, I'm glad she did. Paris, why don't you and your pack join my family? I'll be with you in a moment."

The group of shifters headed toward the group already assembled but as Isis moved past Dante, he grabbed her by the wrist, halting her progress.

Her eyes widened in surprise. "Shouldn't we be joining the others?"

Dante shook his head. "In a minute. What are you doing here?"

Dark, winged brows flew together. "I wanted to help. You just said you were happy I was here. Didn't you mean it?"

He did. More than he cared to admit. In fact, that was the very reason why she shouldn't be here. At their last encounter, they'd nearly kissed and probably would have fucked had they not been interrupted. She was a distraction he didn't need.

For the past several centuries his world had revolved around his brothers, and now that they all had mates and families of their own, the identity he'd carefully built for himself had shattered. He was no longer their protector or the one they leaned on. Several weeks ago, when this revelation hit him coupled with his confusing feelings toward Maggie, he had decided to get away to clear his head.

Dante had sought refuge at his friend Paris Kyriakis's home, where he met Isis. She was quite possibly one of the most beautiful women he'd laid his eyes on. The first time they'd met, he found himself momentarily speechless. She'd seemed unreal to him.

With her long, thick wavy brown hair that cascaded past her shoulders and ended at the small of her back, and sinfully full lips, Isis Vasquez had the kind of beauty that made people stare. The first thing he'd noticed about her, however, was her large blue-gray eyes, which served as a breath-taking foil to the dark gold skin that hinted at her Latin and Bengali heritage. She was tall, at least six feet, with curves that would tempt a saint. But, it wasn't her looks that drew him to her. She exuded a confidence and intelligence he found extremely sexy.

Her presence would complicate things. She would be a distraction and that was something he couldn't afford on so important a mission. "Of course, I'm happy to see you, but I don't think you understand the gravity of the situation. All of us are going into this knowing that not everyone is coming out alive. It's dangerous and while I appreciate your offer of help, I can't in good conscience allow you to come with us, knowing something could happen to you."

Isis took a step backward, crossing her arms over her ample breasts. "And you doubt my ability to handle myself? I'm nearly two hundred years old, Dante, and the majority of that time, I've been without the protection of a pack. I didn't survive on my own by not being able to take care of myself. I can help. Besides, I have information that could be vital to your mission."

"Like what?"

Uncertainty flashed in her eyes but just as quickly as it appeared, it was gone. She raised her chin and connected her gaze with his. "I know about the Serpent Gang. Their hide outs and how they operate."

At the mention of the crew they'd recently scoured the world to find, he grew tense. The Underground had managed to take out a number of the lower ranks of the gangs, but the most dangerous ones of the lot still eluded them. Dante grasped Isis by the forearms. "*How* do you know of them?"

"If you'll let me go," she began calmly, "I'll tell you."

"Sorry." He raked his fingers through his hair. "Everyone has been on edge since the children were taken, including myself. If you know something, I need you tell me now."

She jerked her thumb toward the area where the rest of the group had assembled. "I think I should fill the others in at the same time so I don't have to repeat myself."

He had probably imagined it but Isis almost seemed evasive. Why she needed to be, he wasn't sure. Had she not come with Paris, whom Dante trusted with his life, he might have second guessed her motives. "Okay. Let's join the others." Placing his hand against the small of her back, he led her to where the rest of the group assembled.

Among the motley crew of immortals were his brothers, their mates, Steel, Cutter, and Blade Romanov, Wolf Wagner, Paris, and three others from Pack Kyriakis. These people would have his life in their hands, and they in his, over the course of the next several days.

"I think everyone has already been introduced and —"

"Ahem." Isis cleared her throat to remind him of his manners.

Dante couldn't keep the smile from tilting his lips. "I beg your pardon, Isis. Everyone, this is Isis Vasquez, a good friend to Pack Kyriakis. She's here to offer her assistance and incidentally has some information that might be of some use to us."

Romeo stood. "Any details you can give us will be appreciated. The children's lives depend on it. If I could just get them back—" He broke off, his voice clouded with emotion. The last time Dante had ever seen his brother Romeo come this close to crying was when he was a child. Seeing him break down like this broke Dante's heart.

A teary-eyed Christine wrapped her arms around Romeo's waist as she rested her head against his chest. "

They've been through so much already," she whispered. "But we have to hold on to hope that they'll be okay until they're rescued."

"We'll find them." Romeo dropped a kiss on top of her head, although uncertainty shadowed his expression.

Dante gently touched Isis's arm ignoring the slight spark as he made contact. "Go ahead and share what you know."

Isis wrung her hands in front of her and bit her bottom lip. "I understand you've recently learned the Serpent Gang is somehow involved in the children's disappearance. I...um, used to be friends with a member of that group and know a little about how they function and some of their hangouts."

Nico narrowed his gaze. "You're a shifter. From my understanding, they keep to their own."

"I said I was friends with a member, not one myself, and some years back, I didn't realize how ruthless the Serpent Gang actually was. I knew of them mostly through my friend."

"How did you get tangled up with this friend of yours in the first place?" Nico countered.

Isis released a deep breath. "It just happened, I suppose. Why does anyone become friends?"

"She's right. My best friend is a vampire and we became friends while I was still human. You could call that an odd pairing but this room is full of vampires, shifters and warlocks, and all friends." Christine chimed in. "I'm much more interested in hearing what she has to say about the Serpent Gang so we can find the children."

Dante nodded. He'd ask questions about her association later. "You're right, Christine. Please continue, Isis."

Isis granted him a grateful smile. "Thank you, Dante." She paused for a moment to look around the room before beginning again. "My friend was a high-ranking member of the gang, so I learned some pertinent info through him. I'm sure most of you are already aware of their reputation. They hate all weaker beings, mainly humans. At one time, they had even aligned themselves with another rogue organization to wipe out humans, but they abandoned that course when the Council stepped in to stop them. That was, of course, long before the Council became corrupt. Anyway, I severed ties with my friend when he and his crew got tangled up in something far too dangerous for my taste." She paused, and ran the tip of her tongue over her lips. Isis glanced in Dante's direction as though silently asking his permission to continue.

Dante nodded his encouragement.

"A vampire by the name of *Il Demonio* promised them great power which turned out to be some form of black magic. It made the members of the Serpent Gang incredibly strong and more powerful, but this magic was only temporary. When it started to wear off, they'd go through withdrawal. Their eyes would turn bloodshot red. It was a terrifying sight. Once I even came upon one of their ceremonies. It was being led by a woman in a hooded cloak. When I saw what was going on, I couldn't continue my association with them. They were doing the bidding of *Il Demonio* in order to get their next fix. It's probably what he's using to keep the Serpent Gang under his command. I've never actually seen him, but

I've heard the name whispered on quite a few occasions. I know of several of their hiding places. Some are here in the US, and there are a handful in Europe, a couple in South America, and one that I know of in West Africa."

"Would you be able to pinpoint these locations exactly? Specifically, where we could find a member by the name of Sidewinder?"

Isis nodded. "He's second in command. He has a place in L.A., but his home base is in Vegas. I would imagine he would most likely be at the latter if he's the one holding the hostages. He has a modest compound, but large enough to house a number of people."

"It's still possible they could be anywhere," Marco mused. "If you were to tell us of all the hideouts you can remember, I think we can go through each of them in teams."

"Good idea, Marco," Dante agreed. "Does anyone have any objections?"

The occupants of the room remained silent. "Good. Marco, I'd like you to take George and Steel with you. Romeo, you go with Wolf and Aries. Nico, Cutter, Blade, and Theo. And I'll go with Paris and Isis. Sasha, Maggie, and Christine will stay behind and serve as the line of communication between the teams." Dante knew each group would have their work cut out for them. If Isis's information proved correct, they should have the children back in no time, but if it wasn't, she had a lot of explaining to do.

Chapter Three

Adonis ended the call on his phone and slipped it into his pocket. He couldn't keep the grin from curving his lips. But then again, he didn't want to. Everything was falling into place. The Grimaldi clan was playing right into his hands. He expected them to catch up with him soon enough and that was when he'd have the revenge he'd sought for so many years. He'd make his *brothers* watch their loved ones die first and then he'd kill them, but not without torturing them first.

The help he'd enlisted was expendable. He could keep them in line with the spell Beatrice had cast on them. They believed he'd give them a power so great they'd be invincible—the fools. Once he achieved his objective, he might just kill them all for the hell of it. They were just the hired help. His true disciples lay in wait, ready to take out the Grimaldis upon his command.

"Good news?" Beatrice approached him from behind.

If he were jumpy, Adonis might have leapt at her sudden appearance, but he was so used to her moving silently, her comings and goings barely fazed him. "Yes. Apparently they've figured out who's holding their offspring, not that it will matter when I and my army finally strike."

"Good. Once they are out of the way, nothing will stop us from ruling the immortals of this world. No one will be able to stop m—us." She stroked her chin. "I noticed crow's feet in the mirror this morning. I'll need to make another sacrifice soon to restore my beauty."

Adonis groaned internally. He knew her well enough to realize when she was fishing for a compliment but he gave it to her nonetheless. "Beatrice, you're already beautiful. Perhaps, you should have killed GianMarco's stepdaughter when you had the chance. I'm sure she would have given you the essence you required."

Beatrice pursed her lips and glared in his direction. "I needed her alive to get into the house. Besides, the ritual would have taken more time than we had. I couldn't perform it and get those brats out of the house before my masking spell wore off." She walked to the wall on the other side of the room to look into the wall mirror, her favorite pastime.

She tilted her face from side to side, examining every angle. "If you would have allowed me to use your whore while she was still human, I wouldn't have had to make so many sacrifices to maintain my looks. Though I loathe admitting it, that arrogant bitch's face is nearly as perfect as mine. I'll just sacrifice the human child. She's young, but I have seen into her aura, and it promises great beauty, perhaps even more so than your slut."

"Beatrice," Adonis growled. "Nya is no whore. I'm the only one she's lain with since I made her."

Beatrice smirked at him through her reflection. "Such a passionate defense. Do you believe she cares for you, Adonis? Because from where I stand, I see nothing but contempt when she looks at you. No woman will ever love you as I have, or do." She finally abandoned the mirror to stand in front of him. She placed her small hands against his chest and stood on tiptoe to place a kiss against his jaw line.

"No." Adonis turned his head away from her questing lips. That familiar nauseous feeling bubbled within the pit of his stomach.

Beatrice narrowed her eyes to jade slits. "Why not? You never used to turn away from me. Let's do this for old time's sake?" She moved her hand down the center of his chest, not stopping until it clutched his cock.

Adonis pushed her away with more force than he intended, sending her sprawling backward to land on her ass. "I said no! We made a deal years ago, we wouldn't do this anymore."

She was back on her feet again, her features twisted with annoyance. "Have you forgotten I was the only one there for you when you had no one? Everyone turned their backs on you. Don Giordano couldn't get rid of you fast enough. The man who called himself your papa wanted nothing to do with you. Even your traitorous brother thwarts your every turn. *Bastardo!* And look at that *puttana* you bring to your bed. She's probably plotting against you as we speak, yet you keep her around and defend her as if she's worthy. I've have been the one in your corner from the beginning, yet it is I who you deny."

Adonis balled his hands into fists at his sides. "Don't pretend you didn't use me to get what you wanted. Were it not for me, those village idiots would have burned you at the stake for being a witch. *I've* been the one to lure those women to you, making it possible for you to fawn in the mirror every day and not see one single wrinkle. By rights you should be dead, so don't dare try to guilt me into bending to your will. It won't work."

Tears brimmed in her eyes and her lower lip quivered. "But, I'm the only one who truly loves you."

Adonis folded his arms across his chest unimpressed by her theatrics. "The only one you love is yourself. When I have my revenge on those bastards, we'll go our separate ways."

Beatrice's eyes widened. She rushed over to him and cupped his face between her palms. "No! You can never be finished with me." Pressing her lips against his in a long, hard, desperate kiss before pulling away, she shot him an angry glare. "*He* didn't want you. He left you for dead in order to live with his whore and those brats. When you begged him for help, he turned you away. And now you plan to do the same thing to me." She took a step back and smacked him across the face with the back of her hand. "You're weak! You are nothing! You are just like your father. Like *them*."

All the old rage and scorn roaring inside him boiled to the surface. Adonis yanked Beatrice against him and ground his lips over hers, giving her all the ire, pain, and darkness within him.

She clung to him, seeming to revel in the force of his temper. Beatrice tore her mouth away from his with a chuckle. "That's it. This is the man I know, the one who will make all of them pay."

"Yes," Adonis groaned. "I'll make them all pay."

"I've never flown on anything this grand." Isis took in the opulence of her surroundings, from the plush, cream leather seats, to all the amenities one could dream of. Paris and Dante seemed to take all these perks, which she was in awe of, in stride.

"The novelty will wear off after a while." Paris yawned from across the aisle, stretching his limbs and closing his eyes.

Dante chuckled. "Says the man born with a silver spoon in his mouth. Your grandfather Spyros made his first billion long before you were a twitch in your father's pants."

Paris smiled, opening his eyes to stare pointedly at his friend. "But you've been around a couple centuries longer than me and as I recall, you weren't exactly destitute when we met."

"That doesn't mean I haven't been. My wealth was built over time. In my younger years, I did what I had to in order to scrape by."

"And I applaud you for it, my friend. But there's no shame in enjoying the wealth you have now." Paris closed the shutter next to him, blocking out the sunlight. "I think I'll take advantage of this plane ride and get some rest." He closed his eyes then signaling the conversation was over.

Dante slipped out of his chair and took the seat next to Isis on the couch that faced the row of seats. A sensation of warmth shot through her body. Dante Grimaldi had this effect on her whenever he was in her general vicinity.

Being tall herself, she liked that he had her by at least five or six inches. Dante was all solid, rock-hard muscle, possessing a masculine beauty that would garner him, second, third and fourth looks. Isis couldn't pinpoint a feature she favored on him the most, from his cobalt-colored eyes, straight, patrician nose, and full, sensually curved lips, just right for kissing. Carnal images of him pressing those lips over every inch of her skin, infiltrated her mind and made her body heat elevate.

Sure his looks were extraordinary, but it wasn't simply his physical countenance that attracted her. He loved his family. From their previous conversations, it was clear to Isis he would do anything for them. He was the kind of man who loved hard and would do whatever it took to protect the ones he cared for. There was also a hint of danger about him that excited her.

He was the total package, and the more time she spent with him, the harder and deeper in love with him Isis fell.

She'd suspected her feelings for him when they'd met at Paris's house. But now, she was sure of them. Isis was almost certain he felt something for her to. There was a spark each time they touched, a particular look when their gazes met. Unfortunately, their current situation didn't allow time to explore these feelings, but she wouldn't ignore the opportunity if one arose.

"Isis?"

She jumped in her seat, startled back to reality. She'd been so lost in thought she hadn't realized Dante was speaking. "I'm sorry. What were you saying?"

He smiled wide enough to reveal perfect white teeth. "Can I go, too?"

She released a nervous titter. "What are you talking about?"

"Wherever you were just now. Do you want to talk about it?"

"Oh, I was just admiring my surroundings. It must be nice to travel this way." As explanations went, it was a pretty flimsy one, but she didn't think he was ready to discuss what she'd really been thinking.

"I find it hard to believe you haven't traveled this way before."

"It's the truth. I've flown before, of course, but my flights have always been commercial. The last time I was on a plane, I was stuck between a screaming toddler and a man who used my shoulder as a headrest while he snored in my ear. You know how sensitive a shifter's hearing is. I was in agony."

Dante laughed softly. "That's a pity. Hopefully, this trip will be more pleasant for you."

"It already is." She locked her gaze with his to let him know it wasn't just the plane ride that interested her.

Dante raised a brow but his smile didn't waver "When we met the last time, I didn't make the connections when you said your mother hailed from Pack Khan. I was once acquainted with the Alpha before he and his pack went into seclusion. I haven't heard from them in years but from what I saw, they were a pack of means."

"Yes. The Alpha is my grandfather but, since he didn't approve of the match between my parents, I wasn't welcome among them."

"My apologies. I didn't realize they'd shunned you as well."

Isis released a deep sigh of regret. "As far as they're concerned, my mother died when she chose my father over the wishes of her Alpha. From what I was told, my grandfather wanted her to mate with his brother. It was disappointing they wished to maintain their stance even though both my parents are gone, but I've had years to reconcile with the fact."

Dante placed his hand over hers and gave it a squeeze. Her skin tingled beneath his touch. "I admire how you've managed to not turn savage as most lone wolves do."

She bit her bottom lip. Isis might not be completely savage, but she'd certainly done things that could be classified as such. "It wasn't always easy." Realizing this conversation could quickly turn into a direction she didn't want to go, Isis quickly changed the subject. "Enough about me. What do you plan on doing once the children have been found?"

He hunched his shoulders in a brief shrug. "Our plans thus far simply involve getting them back. Of course, once we've ensured their safety and they're out of harm's way, I plan to personally get rid of every single member of the Serpent Gang. They may not be the masterminds behind this plan, but they made the mistake of getting involved. The very fact they hold my nieces and nephews hostage is reason enough for me to kill them. When I'm finished with them, I'll hunt down Adonis and gut him."

She frowned. The name sounded so familiar. "Adonis?"

"*Il Demonio*. Apparently, the vampire behind many of my family's misfortunes is none other than my own brother."

"I'm not sure I follow. Weren't all your brothers with us back at your penthouse?"

"I'm sorry. I forgot you probably aren't aware of all the details. We recently learned Adonis is our brother and there's another, Giovanni, but I'm not sure where he stands in this debacle. What's certain is they've both been nuisances over the years and we mean to finally put an end to it."

Isis noticed Dante hadn't moved his hand away from hers, so she returned the squeeze he'd given her earlier. That he was willing to share such intimate details of his life with her showed Isis he viewed her as someone he could confide in. She felt closer to him because of it. "How did you find this out?"

"For years, I've been chasing the vampire I believe murdered my parents and all I could come up with was the name *Il Diavolo*."

"I thought you said the name was *Il Demonio*."

"I did. Turns out, they were two different vampires. All these years, I believed we were after *Il Diavolo*, but he wasn't the one. Recently, they both revealed themselves to us. The one I'm positive is the monster we should have been tracking is Adonis. As much as I hate it, I only have to look at him to see my papa. The coloring is different, but he is a Grimaldi."

"And this other brother?" she probed gently.

"I felt the same connection with him as well. Even though they may be my brothers, I will destroy them both for their involvement in this."

"Was it a difficult decision to make?"

"Not really. We may share a bloodline, but Marco, Nico, and Romeo will always come first. They are the ones who matter to me."

If he was willing to kill a blood relation, she was sure he'd have no problem annihilating the Serpent Gang or everyone who was or had ever been associated with them. A chill ran down her spine. Dante didn't seem kindly disposed to anyone who'd had dealings with rogues and that meant her. What would he say if she were to tell him the truth now? Unable to deal with the guilt that slammed into her like a ton of bricks, she snatched her hand away from his. "Um, I need to go to the lavatory."

She hopped out of her seat and she rushed to the back, not stopping until she was safely in the bathroom. For a moment, just one brief point in time, she might have been able to tell him of her association with the rogue vampire gang in hopes he'd understand, but the adamant way in which he claimed vengeance told her otherwise. No matter what, she'd have to keep her secret and pray no one exposed her.

Isis turned on the faucet and splashed water against her face to calm down. As she patted her skin dry with one of the fluffy hand towels hanging on the wall, a knock on the door shattered her peace. She was taken by surprise to see Dante standing on the other side of the door, concern etched on his face.

"Are you all right?"

"Yes, of course. I guess I'm a little nervous about what's ahead of us."

That penetrating cobalt gaze of his roamed her face, seeming to see all the secrets she desperately tried to keep locked away. "I imagine we all are. This is your first mission with us, so I know how things can be a bit daunting at first."

Somehow she managed to smile, hating herself for lying to him. "I'm sure I'll be fine once we land."

"Probably." He cupped her chin and ran a thumb along the side of her face. "Not that I'd allow anything to happen to you."

"You almost sound like you mean it."

"I do. We've been skirting around the issue since you showed up at my penthouse, but there's something happening between us, isn't there?"

Isis caught her bottom lip between her teeth to hold back the emphatic yes she wanted to shout. Unable to trust herself to speak, she nodded.

"Do you have any idea what it's done to me to be so close to you without being able to touch you?"

"I have a pretty good idea."

He raised a dark brow. "You never said anything."

"Neither did you. I didn't want you to think I was stalking you. I mean, I felt a connection when we met right away, but I didn't want to assume you felt the same, although I'd hoped that you did."

"I did, but it didn't seem appropriate to bring it up. My head was in a weird place. Even now, I wonder about the timing of all this. My family is facing the biggest crisis we've ever dealt with and I can't stop thinking about you. I feel I don't have a right to experience these emotions when there's so much going on around me, but I don't think I can go another second without tasting you."

Before Isis could respond to his passionate entreaty, his lips were on hers, pressing forcefully, urging her lips to part with an insistent, questing tongue. Isis had wondered what their kiss would have been like had they not been interrupted, but her imagination couldn't have prepared her for the intensity of his mouth on hers. This kiss was more powerful, needier, and more fervent than she could have possibly dreamed of.

Shots of pure desire spread along every single nerve ending of her body, threatening to explode into a blazing inferno. Isis had never wanted anyone as much as she did this man. Twining her arms around his neck, she pressed her body against his and opened her mouth to grant him the access he sought, wanting to be as close to him as she possibly could.

Her pussy became wet and her body trembled as she thought of Dante fucking her until she couldn't take anymore.

He slid his hands down her back, stopping at the curve of her ass to cup and squeeze it. Dante molded his erection against her pelvis. He felt even larger than she'd imagined he'd be.

"You're already hot for me," Dante muttered against her mouth. "I can smell your cunt and the scent is driving me wild." With a groan, he shot his tongue between her parted lips and explored every inch the warm, wet cavern had to offer. Tentatively, she pushed her tongue forward to meet his, but then she pulled it back. Emboldened by his frantic caresses, Isis did it again, turning up the intensity of their kiss. Their tongues circled around each other in an erotic dance of lust.

Dante tasted so raw, masculine, and tangy, Isis couldn't get enough. Threading her fingers through his hair, she held his head to hers, giving as good as she got. He lifted Isis off her feet and placed her on the lavatory sink. The space was small, but they're bodies were pressed so tightly together, it didn't matter.

He undid the button on her jeans and pulled the zipper down before she could protest; not that she wanted to. Whatever this lusty vampire wanted, she would give it to him wholeheartedly. Grasping the sides of the sink for leverage, she raised her bottom as he yanked her pants down. She'd never been so glad to not be wearing panties in her life.

Isis's breath caught in her throat and a pool of moisture formed between the juncture of her thighs when he kneeled in front of her. "Dante," she panted. "What are you doing to me?"

Dante raised his head, his cobalt gaze catching hers. "I believe you already know, but if you need to hear the words, I'm going to eat your pussy and I'm not going to stop until you come. And then," he grinned to show his descended incisors, "I'm going to fuck you."

"Right here?"

"If you don't want me to, all you have to say is stop, but you're not going to, are you?"

"But Paris…"

"Is asleep."

"But he could wake up and —"

"You're making a lot of unnecessary excuses. We're adults and answerable to no one but ourselves." Dante pressed a kiss against the cleft of her pussy.

A shudder ran up her spine. There was no way she could deny him what they both wanted. "Oh, God," she cried out.

Dante smirked. "You mean, oh, Dante." He parted the sensitive folds of her labia and slid his tongue along the slick opening, sending shock waves of delight through her body. This was one of the very reasons she was attracted to vampires: the way they fed. Blood wasn't their only means of gaining sustenance. They also fed off orgasmic fluids and Isis didn't mind being Dante's meal.

Surrendering to the overwhelming sensations coursing through her body, Isis leaned against the mirror and spread her legs to offer him everything she had to give. Dante grazed her throbbing button with the pad of his thumb before latching onto it with his lips. He sucked on her clit forcefully, pulling at it, milking her pussy.

Unable to remain still under his passionate assault, Isis squirmed and wiggled against him. She bucked her cunt against his face, urging him to hold nothing back. Dante slid his middle finger into her slick sheath, and a groan tumbled from her lips. "Dante…oh. *Madre de Dios.* You're driving me insane." He was insatiable as he feasted on her as if he couldn't get enough.

Dante pushed his finger deeper into her channel and pulled it out to the fingertip. When he pushed yet another digit into her wet pussy, she wove her fingers through his dark locks. As Dante continued to suck on the sensitive nubbin, he fingered her, slowly at first, then steadily increased the pace, pushing Isis closer to her peak.

She'd lived for nearly two centuries and had had a handful of lovers, yet not one of them had driven her to such insane heights of passion. Every single inch of her body was alive and it was all because of Dante. Isis didn't think anyone else would do for her after this experience. She clamped her thighs over his head when he added one more finger, stretching her pussy to it so wonderfully. "Dante," she whimpered, so close to her peak she could hardly stand it.

He released her clit and eased his fingers from her cunt, but he wasn't finished with her yet. Far from it. He seemed as if he was only beginning. Dante licked her pussy with long, broad strokes, from the hood of her pulsing jewel to the crack of her ass. With a hungry growl, he positioned her legs up over his shoulders and circled her anus with his tongue.

She squirmed beneath his skilled tongue, thrashing her head from side to side. Any second she would burst.

Dante was ravenous, leaving no part of her erogenous zones unexplored. When her climax came, it was hard and swift, slamming through her body like a powerful jolt. "Dante!" she screamed, unable to hold back and uncaring if anyone heard them. Cream gushed from her pussy, and Dante lapped up every drop, relentless in his actions.

Even after he cleaned up all her juices with his tongue, he didn't stop, sending her spiraling to another peak. If she hadn't had the support of the sink beneath her, Isis believed she would have melted into a puddle on the floor like a blob of warm butter.

Just when she thought she'd pass out from pleasure overload, Dante finally lifted his head, his grin wide. "*Bella*, that was only the appetizer. I'm ready for the main course." His gaze never leaving her face, he undid his pants and pushed them down.

Isis allowed her gaze to travel down the length of his hard frame, stopping when she reached his jutting erection. He wasn't wearing underwear either and she could see why. There probably wasn't a pair big enough to contain that monster between his legs. *Dios*, he was huge. Dante Grimaldi was a legend in the immortal community, but he was probably an even bigger legend with the women who'd been fortunate enough to have been with him. His shaft was long, thick and she was ready to receive every inch of him.

"Do you like what you see?" He stroked his length for her benefit, making her mouth water in anticipation.

Her cheeks grew hot with embarrassment at being caught staring yet again. "You know I do. You're very…well endowed."

Dante laughed. "So I've been told. But right now, I'm not interested in the size of my dick. I'd much rather concentrate on getting inside your pussy."

Isis grinned. "Then why don't you stop talking about it and just do it?"

"Ah, a woman of action. I like that."

"Mmm, I think I have something you'll like a lot more." She ran her fingertips across her pussy.

His smile widened. "You've read my mind." Dante pulled her against him.

Isis wrapped her legs around his waist, eager to be one with him. Cradling her bottom with his forearm, he grasped his thick shaft with his free hand and guided the bulbous head into her wet sex.

"Please don't tease me," she begged, wanting every bit of him inside her.

Dante grasped her hips and drove deep into her pussy, not stopping until every single inch of his cock was in her. Even being aware of his size hadn't prepared her for the sensation of being deliciously filled by his hard, long, thick cock. "Dante, that feels so good." She gripped his shoulders, her nails digging into his flesh. "Please," she begged, not quite sure what she was pleading for. But whatever it was, if she didn't get it, she'd surely go mad.

He plowed in and out of her pussy, fucking her with slow, precise strokes. Catching her gaze with his, Dante bared his sharpened teeth before puncturing her skin where her neck and shoulder met. A spurt of adrenaline ripped through her body. Isis had been bitten before, but it had never felt quite like this.

Dante drank her blood, not missing a beat as he continued to plow into her. The untamed desire within her grew stronger. She tightened her legs around his waist and clawed at him, her nails breaking skin. Meeting him thrust for intense thrust, Isis ground against him, dangerously close to her third orgasm. Isis squeezed her muscles around his cock, sucking him inside her deeper still.

She doubted she could ever get enough of this sexy, addictive vampire. Her next climax tore through her like a powerful explosion. "Dante!" she screamed.

He tightened his grip around her as he grunted his release, shoving harder into her, spilling his seed into her cunt. He moved against her for a few more moments before lifting his head. "That was—" Dante broke off, panting.

Isis sighed in contentment. "Amazing. I know."

Dante pressed his forehead against hers. "Believe it or not, when I came in here, I didn't intend for this to happen. I only wanted to check on you, to see if everything was all right."

She gently touched the side of his face with her fingertips. "But now that it has?"

"I wouldn't change a thing. I knew you were special when I first saw you." Dante caressed her cheek.

Isis moved against his hand, reveling in his touch. She noticed he didn't admit to any deeper feelings, but that was okay because in her heart, she knew what they shared transcended mere sex. She'd have to be patient until he finally figured it out for himself.

"What are you thinking about, *bellissima*?"

Her heart leaped at his endearment. Unable to contain her joy, she hugged him.

Dante laughed. "What was that for? I'm sure you're well aware of how beautiful you are."

"It was for being you."

His cobalt gaze twinkled with mirth. "Thank you. Mmm, as much as I'd like to stay like this, it's probably best we freshened up. There's a full bathroom in the back of the plane where you can shower and you can have the room with the double bed. Our flight should be landing in a couple hours or so and it's a good idea if you get some rest in the interim."

"Or…we could shower together."

"I'd like nothing more than that, but if we did that, we end up doing a lot more than showering and resting and I must insist that you recoup before we prepare for our mission."

Isis wanted to do some insisting of her own but the firm note in his voice told her, Dante wouldn't be swayed. With reluctance, she unwound her legs from his waist, and his semi-erect penis slipped out of her with a wet pop. Dante lowered Isis until her feet touched the floor and kissed the top of her head. "The next time we do this, I'll make sure we have a nice soft bed at our disposal."

Isis pressed her lips against the pulse of his neck. "As you've already pointed out, there's one in the back."

He groaned. "I didn't realize how wanton you were."

"Only when it comes to you."

"Under any other circumstances, that's exactly where we'd be right now. But the next time I have you not only will it be in a larger bed, I'm going to require more than just a couple hours," he finished with a growl.

"After having sex in an airplane bathroom, a bed sounds awfully dull."

He lifted her hand and grazed her knuckles with his lips. "Oh, I can think of ways to make our next time together very interesting."

"Promise?"

"Of course, *bellissima*."

"I can't believe I'm finally a member of the mile-high club, although I suppose you're probably one several times over." She tapped his chest playfully.

"Actually, you've initiated me for this particular honor."

She found it hard to believe Dante didn't have offers left and right from women begging him to take them whenever and wherever. "You're teasing me."

"I'm completely serious. The opportunity never arose. Keep in mind, this form of travel is relatively new considering how long I've lived, but as first times go, I'm glad it was with you." Dante dropped a light kiss on her lips.

Her heart raced with emotion. Isis hoped more than anything else they'd experience a lot more firsts together.

Chapter Four

Liliana held her hand out in Nya's direction. "Take my hand and I'll get you inside."

Nya hated teleporting. It made her dizzy, but she'd have to do this in order to accomplish her task. Adonis had gone too far this time. She clasped on to the witch as instructed and squeezed her eyes shut. When she opened them again, she was inside a spacious penthouse apartment. Three women sat at the large dining room table, one of whom was one of the few people she considered a friend, Christine Grimaldi.

The women, who had been in the middle of what appeared to be a serious conversation, were immediately aware of their presence.

"Nya! What are you doing here?" Christine jumped out of her chair and ran toward her. Her movements were swifter and more fluid since she'd become a vampire. She threw her arms around Nya. "I was so worried about you. I haven't heard from you in weeks."

Most times, she was uncomfortable showing affection toward anyone, but she returned her friend's hug with a brief one of her own. "It couldn't be helped unfortunately. I'd like to introduce you to my associate. We've come to help. This is Liliana."

Christine gestured to the other two women who now stood on either side of her. "Nya, these are my sisters-in-law, Maggie and Sasha."

The petite brunette narrowed her brown gaze as she stared Nya and Liliana up and down. "Whose side are you on, exactly? Aren't you working for Adonis?" Sasha spoke with a thick Russian accent.

It dawned on Nya she'd seen this woman on the night Giovanni had intervened on Adonis's behalf. She should have known she'd meet some resistance, but her conscience wouldn't allow her to walk away without at least trying to convince them of her sincerity. "No... I mean, it's more complicated than that."

Sasha raised her brows in apparent disbelief. "Not really. You either are or you aren't. The only reason why I've haven't blasted the both of you is because you've somehow managed to get past the ward I put on this penthouse, which means you have no ill intent...for now. But don't think I trust either of you, not after you helped that bastard escape."

"Of course you have every right to be cautious under the circumstances, but as you've just pointed out, we mean you no ill will or else your ward would have kept us out."

The woman called Maggie, an attractive, pleasantly plump black woman, gave Nya a long, hard stare, seeming unimpressed with her explanation. "So why are you here?"

Christine intervened before she had a chance to reply, moving to stand between Nya and the other women. "Look, things are tense right now, but I trust Nya. If she really wanted to hurt us, she could. She's much older than all of us, and any witch who can get past Sasha's wards is probably no slouch herself. Let's at least hear what they have to say."

Nya had never been more grateful than this moment to have an ally like Christine. "Thank you, Christine. I have to be quick because there's not much time before he sends someone to find me."

"Who?" Sasha demanded.

"Adonis, but there's no need to worry. Liliana can get me out of here before that happens."

Sasha tapped her chin with her index finger. "Hmm."

Christine touched Sasha's arm. "Just give her a chance. For me.

The witch sighed. "Fine. I suppose you're right about them being able to get past my ward."

Liliana chuckled as if something amused her. "That's a powerful spell, baby witch."

Sasha narrowed her eyes and held up her palm to reveal a birthmark that resembled a flower.

Liliana gasped at the sight. "The mark of Hecate." Nya didn't know what it meant but the older witch seemed impressed by it.

Sasha nodded, lowering her hand. "My brothers assisted me with the ward. However, in time, I'll be able to handle such spells on my own. I'm still trying to get a handle on my complete power. Baby witch I may be, but I'm certainly strong enough to handle the likes of you and to protect my family."

"Then why aren't you out with the men looking for the children?" Nya couldn't help asking.

"I've been wondering the same thing myself. The men believe they're protecting us by keeping us away from the action, but I can't remain idle while my baby is missing. She's not even a month old." Maggie sniffed, quickly wiping a tear away.

Sasha put her arm around Maggie's shoulder. "We can't give up hope."

"I'm not, but I feel so helpless right now when I know I could be of more use by GianMarco's side."

"As you should be," Nya murmured. "Like I said, my time is running out. We have to formulate a plan to get to the children."

Anxiety entered Christine's eyes. "How much do you know?"

"I know a group called the Serpent Gang has the children. They're a dangerous band of cutthroat rogues. They've been in cahoots with Adonis for some years, doing his dirty work."

Sasha began to pace the floor. "Yes, we've already learned who's holding them, but we need to know where. If there's anything else you can share, please tell us."

Nya moistened her lips with the tip of her tongue. "From what I overheard, they're being held in Florence. That's where Black Adder's secret hideout is located. Only a few of his top ranking members even know about it. Is there a way to get in contact with the men to let them know?"

"They're all probably still en route, but I will try to establish a psychic link with my brothers and let them know. Are you sure of this, Nya?" Sasha asked softly, a hint of mistrust still underlying her voice.

"I overheard Adonis speaking on his phone with Black Adder."

Maggie folded her arms over her chest. "Why are you helping us anyway? You won't give us a straight answer on whether you're in league with Adonis or not. For all we know, you could be leading us into a trap."

"She's here to help. What does it matter? She's putting herself in danger by being here," Liliana retorted.

Nya patted the redhead on the arm. "It's okay, Liliana. I'll answer that question. I've never had a reason to care until now." She turned her gaze toward Christine. "You reminded me of my humanity, and for that, I owe you so much. For a very long time, I've merely existed in a state of apathy, not caring one way or the other what became of me. In many ways, I still don't, but I know if I don't stand up for what's right, I could become something far worse than what I already am. There's only so much one soul can take in a lifetime."

Christine wrapped her arm around Nya's waist. "I don't understand how you became entangled with Adonis in the first place but I know you're not evil."

The words *neither is he,* was on the tip of Nya's tongue, but she knew they wouldn't understand. There were times she had trouble making sense of it all herself, but she wouldn't get into semantics, not when the situation was already so tense.

"He made me a vampire. That bond is not an easy one to break. But getting back to why I'm here, you have to act quickly because I believe whatever he has planned won't bode well for the children."

Christine's sherry-colored eyes filled with unshed tears before her face contorted to an angry scowl. "Are you saying he plans to kill them? No! I'm not going to let that happen. I don't care what Romeo says; I'm going to get my babies back."

"Not without me you aren't." Maggie's eyes now glowed, a fierce bright gold.

Sasha stepped forward, determination etched on her face. "And of course me, but the rest of the team have has taken all the private conveyances to get to their destinations. We'll have to arrange for commercial airline tickets."

Nya shook her head. "No. That won't be a good idea. Adonis has men posted at all the airports within a hundred-mile radius. We have a jet at your disposal. Liliana will take you there. Giovanni will be waiting for you."

Maggie frowned. "He's *Il Diavolo*! Are you out of your mind? Do you expect us to go with someone who's been a source of pain for this family?"

Nya shook her head vehemently, wishing she had more time to explain the situation properly, but if she didn't get back to Adonis soon, he'd know for sure she was working against him. He already knew of her connection with Giovanni, though he'd laughed at the association as being no threat to him. *Giovanni is weak and would never lift a finger to harm me because his emotions will always get in the way.* If Adonis knew what she was up to, however, there was no telling what he'd do.

She didn't care if he killed her. Death was preferable to living with the blood of the Grimaldi children on her conscience, but if she could help her friend in any way, she would do it. "Giovanni's on our side," Nya finally answered.

Christine turned to Maggie and Sasha, her irritation evident. "I thought we already established that they're here to help. I don't know about the two of you, but I, for one am, not going to stand here and argue about the validity of Nya's claim when it gives me the opportunity to go get my kids instead of just sitting around talking about it. Whether you two come with me or not, I'm going with them."

"You'll be in good hands," Liliana assured them.

Maggie didn't appear so easily swayed. "Okay, let's say we believe Nya's reasons for helping us, but what are yours?"

Liliana smiled, although it didn't quite reach her eyes. "Let's just say, I have a score to settle with an old enemy. Once I take Nya where she needs to go, I'll be back to take you three to the airport. If it didn't take so much of my energy, I'd teleport you all, but the plane ride will provide me with the respite I'll need to recharge. Are you ready to go, Nya?"

Certain Liliana would take care of the Grimaldi women in her absence, Nya took Liliana's offered hand, but Christine grasped her arm. "Wait. You can't go yet."

"I have to." Nya closed her eyes against the concern in Christine's face. Her friend meant well, but she didn't know all that was involved and that was probably for the best.

"But Adonis is dangerous. He could kill you."

"Christine, my soul died a long time ago. What happens to my body is inconsequential." She brushed her lips against the young vampire's cheek. "Take care of yourself."

"Nya—"

Nya clutched Liliana's hand tighter, signaling her readiness. They were out of the penthouse before Christine could finish her statement. Nya hated long good-byes, and this one could possibly be their last. She only hoped her help hadn't come too late.

Dante glanced through the back window of Sidewinder's house. "There seems to be some kind of party going on. We're not going to be able to take all of them." Sneaking onto the grounds had been easy. There had been no one guarding the gates, and now he knew why. There was no need with all those rogues inside. Dante counted fifteen in this room alone.

There was no telling how many there were throughout the rest of the house.

"Really?" Paris murmured. "There don't seem to be that many. We've taken out more than this by ourselves before."

Dante didn't want to agree with Paris, but he was right. In most circumstances, he probably would have gone barreling into the house himself, but not with Isis around. She claimed she could take care of herself and Dante was sure she could, but he didn't want to risk her getting hurt. What had happened on the plane had changed everything and forced him to deal with feelings he still wasn't certain of. He might not have a complete handle on his emotions where she was concerned, but Dante did know if something happened to her, it would cause him a great deal of distress.

"Maybe there's a way to sneak into the house and check all the rooms without being noticed," Isis suggested, craning her neck to get a good look into the window.

"That may be a possibility, but I can tell that some of these vampires are pretty old. It won't be easy to slip by all of them," Dante mused.

Paris shook his head. "Or we can go in there and pluck off those sons of bitches one at a time. Why are we even standing here talking about it when we should be inside?"

"Because I'd like us all to get out of this alive," Dante countered.

"I have an idea," Isis volunteered. "I could go inside and distract them. You two can go in and search the rooms."

"No!" Dante spoke more loudly than he'd intended. Stealing a quick peek inside, he checked to see if anyone had heard him. The group inside seemed too engrossed with their discussion. "No," he whispered this time. "If you go in there, you'll be torn apart."

"I know these guys, remember? I can make up a story about hearing some news through the grapevine about the Grimaldi family, maybe feed them something to throw them off your scent."

Dante wasn't willing to budge on this matter. "It's too dangerous, Isis."

"I knew of the risks before I decided to come with you. If you want to play on the safe side, this is the best option."

"She's right, Dante. If Isis is able to distract them for even five minutes, it'll be long enough to tell if the children are inside."

Dante growled, baring his teeth. "Stay out of this, Paris."

Paris furrowed his brows. "Out of what? Because as far as I can tell, I'm already in it."

"You might be the Alpha of your pack but I'm in charge of this mission and I'm not going to allow anyone to take unnecessary risks."

"Anyone...or just Isis?"

"I'm not going to dignify that with a response." His friend was far too perceptive.

"It's reasonable plan, Dante. I understand you wanted to makes sure there are as few casualties as possible but the point is now moot. It looks like Isis has already made up her mind."

Dante frowned. "What are you talking about?"

Paris pointed over Dante's shoulder. Isis was already heading to the front door. Dante would have rushed to stop her before she could knock on the door, but Paris held him back. "Let her go. You're going to compromise us all."

"I can handle it, but what if she can't?"

"Then we'll back her up. If you weren't one hundred percent sure about her ability to aid us, why the hell did you allow her to come along? Don't tell me it was so you could have a convenient piece of ass on hand."

Dante grasped Paris by the collar. "Don't you ever fucking talk about her like that, again." His incisors descended in his anger.

Paris, on the other hand, remained unfazed by Dante's outburst. "Fine." He glared. "I won't besmirch the name of the fair Isis, but you need to get a hold of yourself."

Dante didn't particularly care for the shifter's tone, but he released Paris's collar. He suspected Paris didn't completely like the female shifter, but he'd have to get to the bottom of that later. For now, he had to make sure no harm came to Isis.

He stole another glance inside to see Isis surrounded by members of the Serpent Gang, yet they weren't attacking her. In fact, they almost seemed to welcome her. Dante hadn't been sure what their reaction to her would be, but this was unexpected. He frowned. She'd told him she had a friend in the Serpent Gang. Meaning one. Yet she seemed quite friendly with everyone in the room.

Paris broke into his thoughts. "Judging from the look on your face, my friend, you're thinking the same thing I am."

"You couldn't possibly know what I'm thinking unless you've read my mind without my consent, which I thought we agreed not to do to each other."

"I didn't need to. Your face says it all, but let's not argue. I suggest we figure a way to get into the house without drawing any unwanted attention."

"You're right. I believe I saw a window slightly ajar when we originally circled the house. It's on the second floor, however."

"That shouldn't be a problem. Let's go."

Once they made their way to the back of the house, Dante was relieved to see he hadn't imagined the open window. "The lights are off, so hopefully that means no one is in that room." He observed the windowsill was large enough for him to hold on to with one hand and jimmy the windowpane all the way up with the other.

Positioning himself beneath it, he bent his knees and leaped, catching on to the spot he'd targeted.

Quickly, he widened the entrance and slipped through. Paris followed seconds later. It took a moment for Dante's eyesight to adjust to the darkness. The room was completely bare. It could have been a bedroom or office had it been furnished.

"I think we should split up. I don't hear anything or anyone up here. I believe they're all downstairs."

Dante nodded in agreement. "I'll take the other side of the house and you stay on this side. We'll meet in the middle. Howl if you get into any trouble."

They were both careful as they slowly made their way out the door. Paris slipped into the next room and Dante made his way down the hallway on silent feet. Dante couldn't help but wonder what Isis was doing downstairs and why there was so much laughter. Unable to help himself, he walked to the stairway and cocked his head to the side to listen in on the conversation going on below.

"Black Adder would be interested in knowing what happened to you," one of the rogues declared.

"I've been around. I'm sure B.A. has other things to keep him occupied rather than worrying about what I'm up to," Isis replied with a trilling laugh.

"He was pretty pissed when you disappeared," the same rogue replied.

"Well, here I am. What have you boys been up to in my absence? Have you been staying out of trouble?" She almost sounded as if she was flirting. One thing was certain. Isis was much more familiar with this crew than she'd let on.

A hand fell on Dante's shoulder and he swiftly turned on his heel, ready to strike. It was Paris. "Did you check the other rooms already?"

"I, uh…"

"You were eavesdropping, weren't you? Perhaps, you're beginning to have doubts about her?"

"No." Dante walked away from the shifter before he said something he regretted. It didn't take him long to check the remaining rooms upstairs before he returned to Paris. "When we looked through the windows downstairs, we saw no sign of the children. The only other place they might be keeping anyone hostage would be in a basement. It might be too risky making it down there without being noticed. I'm going to project my thoughts to Isis."

"Good idea."

"*Isis.*" There was no reply, and he wondered if she was picking up on his mental signal to her. "*Isis,*" Dante tried again.

"*Dante? Where are you?*"

He released a small sigh of relief at the connection established with her. "*We're upstairs. Can you figure out if this place has a basement?*"

"*No. It doesn't. Did you find anything upstairs?*" Her answer came too swiftly, as if her knowledge of this place was that of a person who'd been here more than once. He made a mental note to ask her about it when they were away from this place.

I need you to leave now while their guard is still down.

Can't. You and Paris should get out the way you came in. I'll keep them distracted a bit longer and figure out what they know about the kidnapping. Sidewinder isn't here. Apparently he's away on business."

Dante would have bet every penny he had this so-called business had to do with the children, but then who were all these people in Sidewinder's house? *"What else have you learned?"*

"They're expecting an attack. They've recently learned the Underground knows about their involvement with the kidnapping. When we get out of here, we should probably warn the rest of the groups."

"Speaking of which, if you're not outside in ten minutes, I'm coming back in to get you."

"No! It would be too dangerous for you. I can handle this."

"Maybe, a little too well."

"What?"

"Nothing. You have ten minutes." Dante blocked his thoughts before he turned back to Paris.

The shifter raised a brow. "Well?"

"They're not here. Let's go outside. I told Isis we'd give her ten minutes before we go after her."

"Fine. Let's go."

Once they were outside again, Dante paced back and forth, worry making his heart beat erratically.

"Would you stop walking in circles? You're making me nervous," Paris drawled.

Dante glanced at his watch. Damn it. Only a couple of minutes had passed. How could he get through the next eight? "She's taking too long."

"If she runs into any trouble, we'll go in there."

Dante peeked through the window again. Isis was laughing with the rogues. What the hell? Something didn't sit well with him. Full of nervous energy, he turned to Paris and blurted out the question that had been plaguing his mind since they'd shown up at his penthouse the night before. "What is it you have against her?"

Paris lifted his shoulder in a shrug. "I'm careful of anyone who befriends my children. I respect my daughter's wishes of who she befriends, but if I have my concerns I keep a close watch on them. She and Persephone have become quite close, something that causes me great concern."

"And what are your concerns about Isis?"

"You know as well as I what lone wolves are capable of. Most of them are ruthless by necessity, but others are that way simply because they choose to be. Without the guidance of a pack, lone wolves can be quite dangerous. I've questioned Isis about her past, yet she gets evasive when I do. She seems fine on the surface, but I wonder what she's hiding exactly. I only say this because I care about you, but you should watch out for her. Is she a woman you can trust?"

"Of course. Why else would she be out here with us?"

"Why, indeed. How about taking another look at that cozy scene inside and tell me it doesn't make you wonder what she hasn't told us?"

Dante didn't want to agree with Paris, but his doubts were beginning to pile up. After all these years, he believed he may have finally found his bloodmate, but could he trust her?

Chapter Five

Jagger struggled to break his bonds even if every previous attempt had been futile. He believed he'd been conscious for quite a few hours and in that time, he'd learned the children were being kept in separate rooms. The little ones were probably scared out of their wits. He had to find a way out of here and save the kids and get them to safety. And then see his beautiful Camryn again. Where was she now? What must she be thinking?

He would give anything to hold her in his arms right now. For the hope of just one more kiss from her soft lips, he would find the strength to go on. Giving up hope was not an option. There had to be a way to get out of these cuffs. Finally, he decided if he couldn't get out of the handcuffs, he could at least get his hands in front of him.

Lying flat on his back, he managed to stretch his arms enough to get his rear through them. Jagger struggled for several more minutes before he was finally able to pull his legs through. To look at them, the cuffs seemed normal, though he knew otherwise. "*Reikius Imos Ish,*" he muttered.

An electric jolt shot through his body, stinging like crazy. Mere magic wouldn't get them off. He'd need to use his brain to get out of this predicament since it appeared the only way out of them was to break the spell or use the actual key. He wasn't sure which of the two guards he'd overheard had it. He did learn they went by the names of Cobra and Cottonmouth. There had to be some way to lure them to him.

Jagger looked around the large room for a means of escape. There were no windows and the door was solid oak. His gaze fell on a small nook next to the door and an idea popped into his head. He stalked to the door, banged on the wood with a hard thud, and then placed his ear against it.

When he heard nothing, he pummeled the door again. This time he heard light footsteps coming up some stairs. Quickly, he slid his body into the nook and waited. Jagger cringed slightly at the loud creaking sound the door made. He figured there had to be some kind of metal latch on the other side keeping the door locked. Jagger held his breath and willed his heart to stop beating so fast. He was sure whoever walked through the door would hear it.

He didn't have to wait long before a slender vampire with long, dark hair strolled in. Without hesitation, Jagger pounced on the rogue's back, throwing the chain that connected his cuffs around his neck and yanking hard. The rogue clawed and hissed, trying to fight off a determined Jagger.

Jagger's fury at being captured gave him the strength to crush his enemy's windpipe. He sank his descended incisors into the nape of his adversary's neck and tore out a large chunk. The rogue dug his talons into Jagger's arm, cutting into muscles and tendons. It hurt like a motherfucker, but Jagger hung on for dear life. If he couldn't kill this vampire, he would be the one to die.

The children depended on his survival. He let the rogue go long enough to grasp a fistful of his hair and yank with all his might. A hunk of scalp ripped off with all that hair, producing an agonizing scream from his red-eyed enemy.

Knowing he couldn't give his opponent a moment to retaliate, Jagger propelled him into the wall, not allowing the sound of crunching bone to slow him down. He, then, lengthened his fingers and morphed his hands into talon-like weapons. Even with the hindrance of the cuffs, his vampire abilities were functional, one of the perks of being a hybrid. With a swift lunge, he dug his hand through the rogue's back, plowed toward his heart and crushed it in his palms.

The rogue crumpled at his feet. Wasting no time, he searched the fallen vampire's clothing for a key, but to his frustration found nothing. Damn. He'd have to get out of here with these damned things still on, but first he had to find the children.

When he left the room, Jagger was taken aback by the large structure. He was at the end of a long, dark hallway. This place reminded him of the interior of a thirteenth-century castle.

Jagger made his way down the hallway and checked each room as he went. When the third door he tried opened, he saw a small figure lying on a cot with his back turned.

"Jaxson!" Jagger hurried over to the little boy, panic in his chest. He hoped the child was merely sleeping and nothing was seriously wrong with him. He gently shook the boy's shoulder. "Jaxson," he whispered.

With a wide yawn, Jaxson stretched his arms over his head and turned to face Jagger. The child rubbed his eyes. "Jagger!" He scrambled to his knees and flung his arms around Jagger. "I thought you were dead."

Even though Jagger couldn't return the hug as he wished, he was still relieved to find his young cousin alive and well. He pulled away with a frown. "Why would you think I was dead, little one?"

"I heard the mean men say they were going to kill you. Where's Adri? And where's my daddy?"

"I'm not sure where the girls are, but we'll find them. I promise. As for your father, I'm sure he'll be here soon. I know he will. Have they hurt you?"

Jaxson shook his head. "No, but they wouldn't give me anything to eat but bread and water. The bread had green spots on it." He scrunched his little face up in disgust.

"We'll get you out of here, but I have to find the others."

"Adri is scared of the dark." Jaxson poked out his bottom lip and looked like he was going to cry, but to his credit, he didn't.

Jagger's heart went out to the little boy. Seeing this small child's courage in the face of adversity firmed his resolve to get them all out of here in one piece. "I have to check the other rooms to locate your sister and cousin. Then I'll need to find a way out of this place. You wait here until I come back for you. Can you do that for me?"

"Can't I come with you? I can help. Daddy showed me how to throw a punch. I can hit someone real hard."

Jagger chuckled lightly despite the gravity of their situation. "I'm sure you can, little one, but you would be a bigger help if you stayed right here. I'll return when I can. Please do this for me, okay?"

Jaxson folded his arms across his chest and scowled. "I guess, but if you need me, I'll rescue you," he said solemnly.

"Thank you, Jaxson. I appreciate the offer," Jagger answered with equal seriousness. He gave his young cousin a brief smile of encouragement before slipping out of the room. There were seven more doors to check before he could find a way out. Carefully, he examined four more.

In the fifth room, he found a woman with flame-red hair that flowed past her waist. Her back was to him, and she was standing over what looked like a bassinet. She leaned over and picked up a swaddled bundle and cradled it to her chest. "She's a beautiful child."

Gianna!

"Put her down," Jagger growled. Wanting to rush at her but unwilling to endanger the baby, he remained where he stood.

"I'm sorry, Nikolai Grimaldi, but I can't do that."

His blood ran cold at the way she emphasized his last name as if it were poison on her lips.

"She's a lovely little thing, is she not? A female-born vampire. She'll be strong—if she grows up."

It took everything within Jagger not to rush the bitch and rip out her heart, but he had to think of his tiny cousin, so innocent to the evil surrounding her. "Put her down!" he roared.

"Or what?" She turned around to reveal herself to him. She was quite beautiful, but there was something off about her face he couldn't quite put his finger on. Bright green eyes taunted him, daring Jagger to do his worst. "Will you use your powers on me? I think not." She pushed back the blanket covering the baby's face and stroked a plump cheek.

Thankfully, the child was sleeping, blissfully unaware. If it weren't for the damn cuffs, he would have used a spell to blast a hole in her chest, while ensuring the baby's safety. Before the thought fully formed in his mind, the redhead raised her hand.

Bolts of lightning shot from her fingertips and sent him flying through the room. Jagger hit the wall with a heavy thud. Lightning sparked from her fingers yet again, sending another powerful electric current through his body. The sensation of being electrocuted grew more powerful by the second. He bit his bottom lip so he wouldn't scream out, even though the energy flowing within him was probably one of the most painful feelings he'd ever experienced.

Jagger refused to give the bitch the satisfaction.

She cackled with glee, obviously taking pleasure in his torment. As the jolts increased in intensity, a tear slid from the corner of his eye. Would he ever see his beautiful Camryn again? What about his mama and papa? The last thing that registered in the murkiness of his cluttered thoughts was the sound of a baby crying.

Since their journey to Vegas, Dante seemed standoffish. His treatment of her, wounded Isis's soul. She didn't understand how he could be hot one minute, making love to her with such vigor and passion, awakening her body to feelings she hadn't known, and then go cold the next, barely speaking to her.

When she'd finally left Sidewinder's house, Dante had given her an odd look. Isis hadn't paid too much attention to the disdain on Paris's face because she'd never had his complete approval. Other than to ask if the children were there, Dante had barely spoken more than two words to her.

She'd been waiting for an opportunity to get him alone, but it had been difficult because as soon as they had left Sidewinder's, they had headed for the jet to take them to their next destination, Vancouver. During the plane ride, Dante had told her to get some rest, but it was difficult to relax while he and Paris talked strategy in the seat in front of her, not because their conversation was distracting, but because it seemed she was deliberately being left out. By the time they'd landed, Isis was completely on edge.

Now she sat in the back of the car Dante had hired, close to tears. He pulled the car to a halt. "This is it. Another one of Sidewinder's hangouts. I'm parking here so we won't be detected. We'll have to walk a mile or so."

"Great." Paris opened the front passenger door. "I need to stretch my legs."

Dante was about to do the same, but Isis decided to make her move now or the opportunity would be lost. There was no telling when they'd next be afforded any privacy. Placing her hand on his shoulder, she stopped his progress. "Wait. Don't go."

He stiffened, his muscles tensing beneath her fingertips. "We need to go, Isis." His tone sounded distant, and she snatched her hand away as if she'd been slapped.

"Actually, I need to talk to you."

"What about, Isis? Paris is already outside and we need to join him."

"Could you give me five minutes? I doubt that would make a big difference to this mission. I promise I won't need any more of your time than that."

Dante released a deep breath and turned in his seat, directing his cobalt gaze in her direction. "Fine. What is it you'd like to discuss? I hope it's important, considering my nieces and nephews are still in danger."

She wasn't sure what she'd done to earn his scorn, but she didn't deserve to spoken to in such a condescending matter. "That didn't stop you from fucking me on the plane," she snapped, tired of his coldness. "I'm not going to allow you to treat me like someone you can just screw and then ignore on a whim."

Dante's eyes narrowed to dark blue slits and those sensual lips of his tightened to a thin white line. "Isis, I don't know what game you're playing but —"

"What are you talking about? Games? You're the one who's been treating me like a leper, and I think I'm entitled the courtesy of being told what I've done to offend you."

Dante opened his mouth to reply but a tap on the window forestalled him. "One moment," he bit out before opening the door. "Could you give us a few minutes, Paris?"

"Hurry up," the shifter growled. "I'm anxious to get this over with."

"Likewise, my friend. We'll only be a few minutes."

Paris nodded and walked away.

When Dante closed the door and turned to face Isis once again, it was with narrowed eyes. "Hurry up and get to the point, Isis."

"First off, don't talk to me like that."

His nostrils flared and a muscle twitched in his jaw as if his patience was wearing thin. "How am I talking to you?"

"Like I'm a piece of dirt on the bottom of your shoe. But if you're going to be rude, at the very least tell me what I did."

"I don't have time for this shit."

It infuriated her when he placed his hand on the door handle as if he would actually get out of the car without addressing her concerns, but Isis reached over the front seat and gripped his shoulder. The beast within her was threatening to erupt. "Were you lying to me on the plane when you said you wanted to be with me again or is that something you say to all the women to make them feel special? I didn't peg you for a user, Dante and I still don't. If I've angered you in some way, tell me what I did or at least be mature enough to tell me you're finished with me."

Dante clenched and unclenched his jaw, his lips going white as he pressed them together. He obviously wasn't used to women talking to him this way, but that was tough shit. Isis let no one back her into a corner, not even a man who she knew she was falling in love with. She hadn't survived the last several decades without knowing how to stand up for herself.

For several moments Isis didn't think Dante would answer her, but when he finally did, it wasn't what she wanted to hear. "Why are you so familiar with the Serpent Gang? You lied to me. You said you had *a* friend who was a member. You never said anything about being friends with the entire gang!"

A lump formed in her throat, her anger suddenly draining away. She should have known he'd catch on when she'd offered to go into the hangout with all those rogues in attendance. Dante was by far one of the most perceptive men she'd ever met. Silently cursing her stupidity, Isis cut her gaze from his for the first time since she'd initiated this conversation. She should confess her past and be done with it, but how could she make him understand? "It isn't what you think."

He swiveled in his seat to look at her full on, his brow raised. "Oh? You have no idea what I'm thinking. But go ahead and enlighten me. What exactly aren't you telling me because from where I was standing you looked pretty chummy with them. Maybe you were a member or still one and you've been leading us on a wild goose chase."

His accusation had the same impact as a punch in the stomach. "Is that what you really believe? That I'm capable of a plot that would involve harming children? Okay, so I didn't tell you I knew more about the Serpent Gang than I let on, but I disassociated myself from them years ago, so, no, I was never a member. They only allow membership to vampires."

"There's an exception to every rule."

"But not in this case."

"If you say so."

"I do because it's the truth. If you don't believe me, I don't know what I can say to change your mind. But if you truly believe I'm here to sabotage this mission then I'll stay behind. When you and Paris return, just drive me to the airport." She bit the inside of her lip to keep it from wobbling. Tears stung her eyes and she turned her back to him so he wouldn't see them. Isis expected Dante to get out of the car after her declaration, but didn't. Instead, the two of them sat in silence for an uncomfortable amount of time. Finally when Isis felt she was able to look at him without crying, she turned around to find him staring at her with his shrewd gaze.

Dante pinched the bridge of his nose and sighed. "Isis, you have to admit, it looked suspicious. My family is in danger, and your involvement with these rogues makes me wonder what you're not telling me. However, you're right. I should have questioned you before now instead of shutting you out. I, honestly, don't know where the two of us are headed, but I've been burned before, so pardon me if I'm a bit cautious this time around. I do know you make me feel things I haven't experienced with anyone else. But so help you, Isis, if I find out you've been lying to me, I'll kill you myself."

Isis could tell, Dante meant every word. Now was the time to come clean about everything, but the moment her lips formed the words, they got lodged in her throat. She couldn't do it, not when he was so close to realizing his feelings for her. Isis truly believed that once he could finally admit his love for her, he'd be more receptive to what she had to tell him.

"I *was* friendly with one of the members who introduced me to more of the gang and I hung out with them on a few occasions. I distanced myself from them because of the atrocities I witnessed. They were way too intense for me. If you believe nothing else, know that I'm here to help you and your family because I don't want anything to happen to the children and because I care very deeply about you." She took his hand in hers and hoped he could see her sincerity.

Dante brought her hand to his mouth and brushed it with his lips. "Forgive me, *bellissima*. I was being an ass. It's just...I'm worried about my family. Adonis has been fucking with us for so long, it's hard to let anyone new in. Do you accept my apology?"

Isis breathed a sigh of relief. Her heart leaped when she saw the tenderness lurking in his gaze. "Of course. And I understand where you're coming from. Just...tell me if you have a problem. Please don't shut me out."

"I promise. We'll be honest with each other from here on out."

She intended to tell him everything, just not yet. Isis hoped he didn't learn about her past from someone else before she was ready to tell him; otherwise things would be over before they could properly begin.

Chapter Six

"Sweetie, I know you're scared. I am, too, but you have to remain where you are so you'll be safe. Don't leave for anything, not to go to the store, or to take a walk. Don't even look out the window if you can help it. If you need anything, call one of the numbers GianMarco left for you and someone can take care of it. There are several agents guarding the house and there are wards to keep out our enemies." Maggie spoke as calmly as she could to calm down her near hysterical daughter.

"Wards? You mean a spell like that witch put on the house to keep out the people who took Jagger and Gianna?"

Maggie held the phone away from her ear at the sound of Camryn's high-pitched wail. "It's a different spell, a more powerful one. This one won't allow anyone in who has ill-intent. The first one—"

"Didn't work because I invited that bitch into the house." Camryn began to sob.

Maggie's heart broke. After Jagger and the children had gone missing, they'd all tried to piece together what had happened. It was then Camryn had told them about meeting a mysterious woman when she'd gone for a walk. And then later, she'd dreamt of the same woman asking for an invitation to come inside. Camryn had let her in, but it hadn't been a dream at all.

Maggie wished she could hold her daughter and assure her everything would be okay, but she couldn't. For one, she was on a plane, several thousand miles away, and second, Maggie wasn't completely sure herself. Her newborn baby was in the hands of a madman and there was no telling what he was doing to her at this very moment. Still, she needed to alleviate Camryn's worries. "Baby, you're going to need to stop blaming yourself. It wasn't your fault. Whoever this woman was, she obviously charmed you in some way."

"But because of me, Jagger, and Gianna are gone. And Jaxon and Adrienne too. Everyone must hate me but I can assure you, they can't hate me as much as I hate myself right now."

"Stop it. You're talking nonsense. No one hates you and no one blames you. I'm on a plane right now as we speak and I won't come back until Jagger and the children are safe. You have to trust me okay?"

Camryn sniffed. "I guess so."

"You have to be brave okay. I'm sure that's what Jagger would want."

"Mom…what if I don't see him again?"

"You will. Now, put your brother on the phone."

"Okay."

"I love you."

"I love you too."

There was a pause on the other end of the line before her son's rich baritone greeted her ear. "Mom?"

"Yes, it's me. How are you holding up?"

"Fine, although I'm not sure why we have to stay in this house the entire time. I'm missing work and my partner. Can't one of these guards just shadow my movements?"

She'd expected to be met with a little resistance from her older children on their forced isolation but when it came to protecting them, there was no negotiating. "Bryan is welcome to visit whenever he wants. He can stay there if he'd like, but no other visitors. But as for you and Camryn staying put, this isn't up for debate. Like I told her, if you need anything, have someone get it for you. You're not to leave the house. There are very dangerous people out there who want to harm our family. I already have one missing child. I'll be damned if anything happens to you and Camryn. So do me a favor and not argue with me about this."

Darren released a slow huff. "You're right, Mom. I'm sorry. Me missing a few days of work and sleeping at my own place can't compare to what you're going through right now. How are you holding up?"

"As well as can be expected. I just wanted to call and check up on you and your sister. I need you to watch out for her, keep her calm."

"I will. I just want you to take care of yourself. You say these people are dangerous and that worries me."

"I won't be alone but I appreciate your concern. I'll be back home before you know it with your baby sister."

"I love you, Mom."

"I love you, too. I'm going to end the call now because the service is breaking up a bit."

"Bye Mom."

"Bye, sweetie."

Maggie wiped away a tear that slid from the corner of her eye as she put her phone away. She was anxious to get to Florence and find her child. Why was the plane ride taking so long? She'd been to Europe a handful of times before, yet this trip seemed to take much longer.

Her poor baby, Gianna, needed her mommy and daddy. She hoped GianMarco was safe wherever he was. She hadn't heard from him since his team had departed from Dante's penthouse. He'd probably be furious to know she'd disobeyed his orders, but there was no way she was going to stay behind when their daughter's life was at stake.

Christine stirred in the seat next to her. "How are Darren and Camryn holding up?"

"Camryn is pretty much the same. She still blames herself for everyone being taken. Darren is feeling a bit inconvenienced because he's holed up in one place for an indeterminate amount of time. But what's a little inconvenience when it comes to safety? How about you? You holding up?"

Christine laughed without humor. "I'm a wreck but I'd be even more of one if I had stayed behind at the penthouse. Romeo's going to be pissed when he learns what we're up to," she mused, looking out the window. "God, why can't we get there faster? You'd think a private jet would get us there quicker than a commercial flight."

"I was just thinking the same thing. Is Sasha asleep? I haven't heard a peep out of her since we got on the plane."

Shrugging, Christine rested her head against her seat. "I think she said something about communicating with her brothers. Apparently, it takes a lot of concentration."

"I'm glad she's with us. Her powers will come in handy." Maggie paused for a moment before dropping her voice to a whisper. "What do you think of Liliana?"

Christine dipped her dark head closer to Maggie's. "She's all business. I don't get any bad vibes from her, but we'll still need to be careful until we're one hundred percent sure of her motives."

"That's a good idea. Are you nervous about meeting up with Giovanni?"

Christine nodded. "You know we won't hear the end of this when we see the men again, don't you?"

Maggie firmed her lips. "They did what they had to do and we're doing the same. Besides, we'll worry about them later. For now, I have my child to think of."

"But still, there's really nothing we can do about it until we land and according to Liliana, that won't be for another couple hours. We'll have to sit tight until then."

Maggie groaned, sinking deeper in the leather seat. "Easier said than done. You know, when GianMarco made me a vampire, I knew there would be dangers involved in being immortal, but not once did I believe I'd have to worry about my children. Camryn can't stop crying since Jagger was taken, and she blames herself for letting Liliana inside the house. One missing child is about all I can handle right now. I can't imagine how I would cope if all—I'm sorry."

Christine squeezed Maggie's hand in reassurance. "Don't worry about it. I know you meant no offense. Yes, it's pretty hard that both of my kids are missing but I lay the blame squarely on the ones who took them. They're my babies and it's killing me on the inside that I can't be there to comfort them right now when I know they're probably frightened out of their minds. What really gets me is when Romeo and I took them in, we swore to protect them and ensure no one could harm them again. I believed we were giving them a better life."

Maggie frowned. "What do you mean? You are giving them a better life. They have two loving parents and some much-needed stability. Who knows what would have happened had you and Romeo not adopted them? It's quite possible they could have ended up like me, growing up in different group homes, living off the system's charity, and being miserable for it."

"I appreciate you saying that, but Jaxson and Adrienne have been through so already. That monster who had custody of them abused them in ways that pisses me off just thinking about it. Jaxson suffered a few broken ribs and a fractured wrist from being kicked repeatedly when the state finally intervened. Adrienne was only twelve pounds at two years old because they nearly starved her to death. When I think of the hell they've already suffered only to go through this, I could just scream, cry, and tear shit up." Christine burst into body-shaking sobs.

Maggie, understanding exactly how her sister-in-law felt, threw her arms around her. "It's okay, sweetie. We can't give up hope." She held Christine until her tears subsided.

Finally Christine pulled away with a sniff, drying her wet cheeks. "Thank you. I think I needed a good cry."

"Sometimes, it helps."

"Are you ladies okay?" Liliana appeared beside Maggie's seat as if from nowhere. "I'm sorry for eavesdropping, but I couldn't help but overhear the two of you talking. The children are fine for now. Adonis wants them to be found alive. It's his plan to kill them in front of his brothers."

"Why?" Maggie demanded. "He's been tormenting our men for years, yet no one seems to know why. How could someone do this to his own brothers?"

Liliana grimaced. "Giovanni will be able to enlighten you as to the whys and hows, but in the meantime, I can tell you about myself. I know you're wondering who I am and what my role in all this is."

Christine leaned over. "The thought had crossed my mind."

"Mine, too." Maggie agreed.

A slight smile turned the corners of Liliana's lips. "My tale isn't a new one. It's one of revenge, something I plan on getting very soon.

"About three centuries ago, I was still quite young by immortal terms, not quite one hundred. I was apprenticing under my aunt, a powerful witch in our community. Our family was strong in the ways of nature and my aunt was teaching me to hone my skills. Around that time, people were wary of witches even though most of the ones accused of being witches weren't. My family rescued and gave refuge to those who were wrongfully branded for practicing witchcraft. One of those missions turned out to be our downfall. There was a young woman in the village, a widow who lived on her own, accused of murdering three women in our little community. But there was no evidence she'd laid a hand on them. They labeled her a witch, of course, and condemned her to be burned at the stake. When my aunt learned of this, she risked exposure to save this woman. We took her in and had planned to get her out of the area to somewhere safe. What we hadn't counted on was the claims being true." She paused, her brows knitting together as if reliving the memory was painful.

Maggie patted the witch's hand in comfort. She wasn't completely sure about the details, but she had a pretty good idea where this was headed. "But didn't you sense she was a witch?"

Liliana's lips tightened briefly and her green eyes flashed fire. "She wasn't, but we were unaware of her dealings in black magic or that she didn't live alone. With the help of her sinister partner, she stole my aunt's spell book and killed her. They came after me as well but I was saved by someone who has come to mean a great deal to me."

"Giovanni?" Maggie guessed.

Liliana nodded. "Yes. From then on, I've been helping him in his endeavors."

"Who was this woman?" Christine asked with a frown marring her brow.

"Her name is Beatrice. She came to our village after wedding a local farmer. He eventually died, but no one suspected foul play at the time because he was quite old. A lot of the single men in the village courted Beatrice after his death, but she turned them down, which was one of the reasons why my aunt believed in her innocence. She'd suspected Beatrice could have been set up by one of her spurned suitors, especially as it was a couple of them who leveled the accusations against her in the first place. What is that term people use?" Liliana tapped her finger against her chin. "Ah, yes. Sour grapes."

Maggie had to ask, although she suspected she already knew the answer from what she could determine from Liliana's tale. "Who was the sidekick you mention?"

"Adonis. He and Beatrice have a lot to answer for, but it's Giovanni's wish they come to no harm—yet."

Maggie was thoroughly confused. How could Giovanni truly be on their side if that was true? "Why would he want them alive when Beatrice and Adonis have perpetuated so much evil?"

Liliana sighed with exaggerated impatience. "It's not so simple. They're brothers. If you had siblings, would it be so easy to kill them off?"

Maggie was an only child as far as she knew, but if she did have a brother or sister, killing them would probably be a difficult decision to make. "I see your point. But, what about Beatrice? Couldn't he let you kill her, especially after what she'd done to your aunt?"

Liliana tossed a lock of her dark red hair over her shoulder as her expression became wistful. "Honestly, I wasn't strong enough to go against her at the time, but over the years my powers have grown, and now I'd make a formidable adversary for that bitch. However, when one has practiced black magic as long as she has, it possesses them. It takes on a form that sometimes even the most powerful witches and warlocks have trouble conquering. Giovanni didn't want me to risk my life challenging her, but he has another reason, a private one. I believe it's his story to tell, however. The rest you'll have to wait and hear from him."

Maggie hadn't known what to think of Liliana when they'd first met, but her heart went out to this beautiful witch who'd also suffered at the hands of their mutual enemy. Impulsively, she took Liliana's hand.

"Your loyalty is a credit to you. I hope you get the revenge you seek."

Liliana nodded with a smile. "Thank you, Maggie. I hope we can save the children before it's too late."

Maggie hoped so, too.

"What do you mean the women aren't there?" Dante demanded into the phone.

"They aren't at the penthouse," Marco barked into the receiver. "They left a goddamn note saying they're on their way to Florence — apparently to meet up with Giovanni."

"Like hell they did! All of them?"

"Yes."

"What did Romeo and Nico have to say about it?"

"What the hell do you think? They're pissed. No, they're enraged. I could fucking strangle Maggie right now!"

Dante could practically feel his brother's anger seeping through the phone. "Calm down, Marco. We're leaving Vancouver now. We should be back at the penthouse in a few hours. Can you hold tight until then?"

"How the hell do you expect me to wait for you when not only is my child in danger, but now my wife as well?"

"I understand how you feel, I'm none too happy that the women have disobeyed our orders but panicking won't change anything. Besides, you can't run off before I get back. There's strength in numbers. And we'll need all the backup we can get. The other teams have turned up nothing. In fact, except for the small band of the Serpent Gang we stumbled upon, there's been no sighting of other members. According to Isis, the ones we did see were low-level members."

"How does your friend know this? If you ask me, I'd be careful around her."

"Isis has been a big help. Look, we're in transit now so we'll talk about this later." Dante clicked off the phone without waiting for Marco to respond. First Paris had expressed his concerns about Isis and now, Marco. Dante wondered what his other brothers had to say on the matter. He wished he could shrug the comments away but he still had a few of his own suspicions, despite the brief explanation she'd given. He couldn't however, stop that nagging sensation in the back of his mind that there was more she had yet to reveal. But he wanted to believe her and because of that, he pushed those doubts away.

A long time ago, he thought he might have found his bloodmate, but it had been a ruse to break him, courtesy of Adonis. He prayed Isis was everything she appeared to be because he doubted his heart could stand another deception.

He glanced over to see her in the seat next to him. Hey eyes were closed and her breathing was slow and even. She was so beautiful while she slept. Unable to stop himself, he grazed her cheek with the back of his hand.

Isis released a soft sigh and her eyelids fluttered open. "Mmm." Blue-gray eyes that Dante could easily get lost in stared back at him.

Isis smiled at him, revealing white teeth. One front tooth was slightly crooked, but it made her smile all the more enchanting. The slight flaw in the midst of her perfection made her seem more real. "How long have I been asleep?"

"Not long. We should be in New York soon. Sorry to wake you."

"It's okay. I probably wouldn't have slept much longer anyway. I'm too full of nervous energy."

Dante smirked. "It didn't seem like it a few seconds ago."

She offered him a sheepish grin. "I guess I was a *little* tired, but I'm up now. What about you? You haven't gotten any shut-eye in the past forty-eight hours."

"I require little sleep. When you've lived as long as I have, there are many things one learns to live without."

"But I'm sure, you need to get some rest."

He shrugged. "Eventually. But I can go a little while longer without it."

"Were you able to make those calls?"

"Yes. I've heard back from my brothers. Thankfully, all their teams are still intact. Marco and his group are back at the penthouse. They ran into a dead end. There was no one in residence where they went. It was the same deal with all the teams."

Her finely winged brows flew together. "Do you mean no one was at any of the locations?"

Dante shook his head. "Not a one. I have a theory, however."

"And what's that?"

"They must all be where the children are or heading that way. My guess is, Adonis wants them heavily guarded."

"If that were the case, why would he call on the entire gang?"

"You, yourself, said the members in Vegas were mainly underlings. Maybe he has no need of them or he could be using them for another purpose."

Isis creased her forehead as if in deep concentration. "Actually, now that I think about it, they may not even be at the Vegas compound now. I remember one of them, a vampire named Asp, mention heading off soon. I assumed he was talking about himself, but he could have been referring to the group. Maybe if we had arrived a little later, they would've been gone too."

"You could be onto something. I'll send one of my agents to look into it. I'm glad you've come with us. We'd probably still be trying to locate the gang's hideouts."

Her brows shot up. "You've certainly changed your tune quickly."

"What do you mean?"

"You weren't sure you could trust me before."

Guilt assailed him because he still had his concerns, but he was willing to give her the benefit of the doubt. He'd overreacted and probably should have thought things through more thoroughly before lashing out at her. "This is a stressful period and sometimes, I act before I think. Forgive me?" Dante caught her by the chin and pressed his lips against hers. His cock jumped to attention, but unfortunately there wasn't much he could do about it. Dante promised their next time would be in a big comfortable bed. That way, he'd have room to explore her delectable body properly, tasting every inch of her golden skin.

"Mmm, when you kiss me like that, I think I can forgive you anything." She revealed her charming smile once again.

Dante caressed her cheek with his palm. "You probably should get some more sleep."

"I don't think I can."

"That's okay, because I get to look into your beautiful eyes."

A hint of red colored her cheeks. "Flattery will get you everywhere."

"Which parent did you inherent them from? They're an unusual shade."

"From my father, actually, although I've been told I'm the spitting image of my mother."

"She must have been quite lovely."

A haunted look entered Isis's eyes. "Yes. She was, but I could never see myself in her."

For the first time in their acquaintance, Isis was opening up about her past and it intrigued him. Dante wanted to know everything about her. "What were your parents like?"

"They were good people. I think you would have liked them. My father was Beta to his brother, my Uncle Luis. They were twins, actually. Papa wasn't much of a talker, but when he spoke, it was usually something profound. He rarely showed his emotions except to me, my mother, and his twin, but when he smiled it was always with his eyes. He was affectionate to those he cared about, but took his position in the pack seriously. He was very strict, however, and when I was younger I resented that because I felt stifled at times. But now, I realize he was that way to protect my mama and me."

There was a wistful note in her voice and Dante could feel the pain radiating from her.

He understood how Isis felt. Even after all these years, the death of his parents still tore at his heart. "And, your mother?"

A smile touched Isis's lips. "She was intense and so full of life. I think when she was with Pack Khan, they stifled her spirit. My father gave her the freedom to be who she was. I think that's part of the reason she fell in love with him. It's been a while since their deaths, but I still think about them all the time."

"There's no shame in your thoughts. I still feel the loss of my parents and it's been centuries. I often think or at least I hope they'd be proud of the man I've become."

Isis smiled, rubbing his arm. "I know they would. From what I understand, you took over the care of your brothers, becoming both father and mother to them. I've only met all your siblings briefly, but I can tell how much you all care for each other. Besides it's hard not to have heard about the famous Grimaldi brothers. You've done a lot for the immortal community. Were it not for the Underground, the rogue population would probably be out of control."

"Admittedly, I didn't begin the organization for altruistic reasons. It was more to root out my parents' killers, but over time, it grew to be much more. I'm happy to have accomplished what I have, but until I can avenge my parents' deaths, I doubt I'll ever be satisfied."

Her gaze cut away from his and a far-off look entered her light eyes. Dante sensed something was wrong, but figured she'd share what was on her mind when she was ready. "Dante?"

"Yes?"

"When you were younger, did you ever do something you weren't proud of?" Her voice sounded distant. It was almost as if she was trying to tell him something, but instead of analyzing her tone, he focused on her question.

Dante closed his eyes as the memories came flooding back. When he thought of the things he'd done for money to take care of his brothers, he shuddered. Those lean years, when he'd been the plaything to wealthy women and at times had resorted to petty theft, still haunted him, but he'd done what he had to and there was no point in dwelling on it. "Yes. I have. Unfortunately, there comes a time in everyone's life when they may have to make moral decisions that might go against their principles."

"Do you think it's possible for a rogue to be reformed?"

Where were these questions coming from? "I suppose it's possible, but I've never met one. Why do you ask?"

She raised her shoulder in a slow shrug. "Curious, I guess."

Dante raised a brow. "Is there something you wanted to tell me? You're not trying to confess to a nefarious past, are you?" he teased in hopes of making her smile. It didn't work. In fact, her face lost all color.

She shook her head, making tendrils of her dark hair fall all over her face. "No, nothing like that. But, w-what if I did say I killed a bunch of innocent people?"

Dante laughed softly. "Isis, I think you're more tired than you realize. Get some sleep."

Her mouth fell open, and then she closed it again. "Yes. Maybe, I am tired." She pressed the button to recline in her seat and closed her eyes.

Dante studied her profile for a moment, unable to shake the feeling she indeed had been trying to tell him something about her past. Was Isis a killer? No. It couldn't be. He was being paranoid again. Or at least he hoped so.

Chapter Seven

Adonis paced the length of the room as he grinned with self-satisfaction. His plan was coming together. If Nya did her part as his suspected she had, his brothers would fall neatly into the trap he'd set for them. Anticipation sizzled in his veins. Years of planning and waiting for the right moment to strike was finally upon them.

The door squeaked as it opened, but he didn't need to turn around to see who had entered the room. The scent of her fragrant skin was all the announcement he needed. His body quickened whenever she was near. After all these years, he still couldn't get enough of her and he doubted he ever would. "Where have you been, Nya?"

It had become a routine with them. Nya would sneak away from him, and Adonis would pretend he didn't know where she'd gone. There were times when she was able to give him the slip with the help of that witch and Giovanni. But most instances, he knew exactly where she was. Though her need to be away from him for long intervals grated on his nerves, he'd granted her that freedom because she always came back.

Adonis had even allowed her friendship with the human, Christine, but the moment that whore had become a Grimaldi, he'd forbidden Nya to contact her again. He was positive she'd just returned from warning *that woman* of his plans, but on this occasion, it was exactly what he wanted her to do.

"Out." Nya shrugged out of her leather jacket and flopped into a nearby chair to pull off her boots.

Adonis hated when she was vague with her replies. She talked less than any female he'd ever known and it should have been a refreshing trait, but he didn't like her keeping things from him. He liked it even less when she shielded her thoughts from him. He owned her. She was his. There shouldn't be secrets between them, yet he was forced into playing this game of cat and mouse with her. But that would change soon enough. As soon as he took care of his brothers and their families, Nya would fall in line. He'd make sure of it.

"Out where?"

Nya wiggled out of and kicked aside her too-tight jeans. "Here and there. Can we save the twenty questions for another time? I'm exhausted. I'd like to shower and then sleep."

His nostrils flared. Her flippant response incensed him. Adonis stalked toward her and grabbed her forearm. "Look at me when I'm talking to you!"

Nya raised her head to meet his gaze, her dark eyes glittering with barely suppressed fury. "If you're finished manhandling me, I'd like to finish getting undressed."

"I've put up with a lot, Nya, but no more. You will not leave here again unless I say. You won't speak to anyone other than me unless I say you can, and most especially, you'll stay away from Giovanni and that witch."

She placed her hands on his chest shoved him away. "You can't stop me."

"Oh, but I can. Where would you seek refuge? Giovanni? He can't help you. And neither can the Grimaldis. They'll hate you for what you've done."

Nya stiffened. Finally, he had her attention. "What are you talking about, Adonis?"

"I doubt your friend Christine would take kindly to the fact you've led her family to their demise. I know you went to New York to warn them. You see, my beautiful traitor, I was one step ahead of you this time."

A muscle twitched in her jaw. "Get to the point."

He chuckled, grazing her cheek with the back of his hand. She flinched away from his touch. "Even now you're full of fire and resentment, though I have the upper hand. I wonder if you'll still be so defiant when you learn of the part you played in the Grimaldis' downfall."

"I'm not in the mood to figure out your riddles. Tell me what you did."

He caught her chin between his forefinger and thumb. "It's not what I did, but what you did. When you pretended to sleep, I knew you were awake and eavesdropping on my conversation with one of my associates. I also noticed you skulking around the manor pretending not to hear me making plans pertaining to the Grimaldis. I let you hear what I wanted you to, because I knew you'd run to them. It was part of my plan. They'll come here and they will die. There's no way they'll be able to fight their way out of what I have planned for them." Adonis could barely contain the chuckle that erupted from his belly.

Nya's eyes widened as if he'd struck her. His usually cool, nonchalant femme looked to be on the verge of tears. "You're a monster. Whatever wrong you feel your brothers have done to you, those children are innocent."

"No one who carries the Grimaldi name is innocent. I'll make them pay for what *he* has done. It will give me great pleasure to obliterate his legacy."

She narrowed her eyes. "Is this all about your father again? Isn't it time for you to get over that shit?"

Anger barreled its way through his body and exploded. He grabbed Nya by the throat before she could react and lifted her off the floor, pressing her windpipe with his fingers.

Nya clawed and kicked in her attempt to break free, but his fury gave him strength. "You will not speak of matters you know nothing of. I've tolerated your disobedience long enough. You'll do as I say or you can die with the rest of them." He tossed her aside, sending her crashing against the wall.

She gasped for breath, but within seconds she was on her feet, eyes glowing and in battle stance. Her fury was palpable, but he didn't give a fuck. He was through with her siding with everyone but him.

Adonis turned his back to Nya, blocking out her anger mixed with anguish. He didn't want to care about her feelings, didn't want the love he felt for her to sway the course of his actions. She was one of the three people in his life who made him doubt himself and question his motives. But this time, she wasn't going to manipulate him with her cold indifference.

"You might as well kill me now, because I can't live like this anymore. You've already taken away my soul

117

and condemned me to this eternal damnation." Her words were shaky and more full of emotion than he'd heard from her in years. But those feelings were for other people. Not him. Never him.

Adonis whirled around to face her, his adrenaline pumping. "I saved you! You'd be dead were it not for me, you ungrateful bitch!"

"Maybe, I didn't want you to save me!" Her glare intensified. "Death would have been preferable to this existence. Dealing with you and that demonic witch. I want to hate you, but you're too pathetic for even that. I feel sorry for you. You're an evil twisted caricature of a ma—"

He slammed the back of his hand against her cheek before she could finish her statement. Nya's head snapped back, but she remained on her feet. A trail of blood oozed from the cut in her lip down her chin.

In all the years they'd been together, Adonis had never laid a hand on her in violence. His first instinct was to apologize but she needed to know her insolence would no longer be tolerated. He had killed people for less.

Nya turned her back to him but not before he witnessed the pain swimming within the depths of her dark eyes.

His heart sank. "Nya, I—"

She shook her head. "Don't, Adonis. I don't want to hear whatever you have to say. You're so hell-bent on your course of revenge that you're willing to destroy my last link to the life I once had."

"For God's sake, you were a fucking slave! Viewed as less than human by the ones who called themselves your owners. You were subjected to rape, beatings and humiliation on a daily basis, yet you stand there and imply you were better off than with the eternal life I've gifted you with?"

She raised her shoulder to a nonchalant shrug. "I've only traded one hell for another." She turned to face him. "Do you honestly believe this life is preferable to the one I'd endured before? You have my every move followed. You tell me where to go, what to eat, how to think. Isn't that just another form of slavery?"

"You have far more freedom than you've ever known. I've given you riches, you've lived in luxury and walked among kings. But, you still hold it all in distain."

"A gilded cage is still a cage."

"Are you in a cage when you're crying out my name when I fuck you? You may fool yourself into believing you don't want to be with me by running to Giovanni and that Grimaldi slut. But, you always return to me. You and I know they can't provide you with what your body craves most, and that galls you, doesn't it, my dear? You say you hate me, but I'm the only one who makes your body weak with desire, your pussy wet, and feeds your hunger. Admit it."

Nya glared. "I'll do no such thing. I despise you."

Adonis snickered. "So you've said, but your body tells me otherwise. Nya, I've tolerated a lot where you're concerned, probably because I care for you more than I should, but not anymore. Your disobedience ends now."

She balled her hands into fists at her sides and lowered her lids. If he didn't know better, Adonis would have suspected she was going to hit him, but instead with a trembling voice she pleaded, "Please spare the children and if you can, Christine. Your fight is with the Grimaldi men, not them."

Knowing how proud Nya was, Adonis realized how much it must have hurt to humble herself before him. But he wouldn't let her pleading sway his course. "My fight is with the Grimaldis period. You won't dictate to me how to handle my affairs."

She flared her nostrils and shot him with a look that could have killed him dead, if it was possible. Nya bent over and picked up her jeans and boots and headed toward the door.

Adonis teleported to the hallway. When she opened the door, he was waiting for her on the other side. "Going somewhere?"

"Out, now move."

"You must have thought I was joking. You're not going anywhere. Do you think I'd let you leave to warn my brother? What kind of fool do you take me for?"

Her full lips curled into a sneer. "You can't keep me here!"

"But, my dear, I can." Adonis whispered a chant under his breath, sending Nya's limbs into temporary paralysis. Her eyes widened as she fell forward into his waiting arms.

"What have you done to me?" she demanded as he carried her to the bed. Dropping her in the center with deliberate ease, Adonis ignored her question. Instead, he searched through a chest at the foot of the bed to produce some shackles. Placing them aside, he sat beside her on the bed. "Don't do this to me!" Her eyes blazed with fury.

Adonis hunched his shoulders. "You only have yourself to blame. I've been generous with you, yet you constantly go behind my back." He took his time undressing her, admiring her dark, lean body, curved in all the right places. His cock jumped to attention, and he willed himself not to take her right then and there. There'd be plenty of time for that later.

When he had her completely naked, he cuffed each of her wrists to one of the bedposts. The cuffs had about a foot of give, making it possible for her to bend her elbows once he enabled her to move on her own again.

Nya's eyes glowed a deep onyx shade and she bared her incisors at him, but Adonis continued with the task of securing her properly. He cuffed both ankles, anchoring them at the foot of the bed, arranging her spread-eagle. Only when he was finished, did he stand back and admire his handiwork.

His gaze raked up and down her bare flesh. "You have a beautiful body, my dear. Though I'm sure, you're probably tired of me telling you that."

"Go to hell!"

Adonis chuckled. "I've been there and back already, Nya." He snapped his fingers, releasing her from the spell. "You can move now."

Nya struggled against her bonds with gritted teeth. "What's the matter with me?" she muttered more to herself than to him.

"Fight all you like, my beauty, but you'll never get out of them. Let's just say those cuffs are special. Not even your magnificent strength can break them."

Comprehension dawned on her face, and a look of pure malice crossed over her face. "I hate you!"

Seeing Nya lose her cool fascinated him. She so rarely allowed her emotions to show. It told Adonis he had the upper hand and he loved it. "You're beginning to sound like a broken record, but I don't think you hate me at all and it burns you up inside, doesn't it?"

She turned her head away from him, setting her jaw.

He raised his voice. "Doesn't it?"

"No," she bit out.

Adonis chuckled as he ran a fingertip over one blackberry-tipped breast.

Her body quivered in reaction.

"See? I barely touch you and you start to shiver with desire. Your mouth might say one thing, however, your body says another. But make no mistake, just because I want you, doesn't mean you can dictate to me. The Grimaldis will die, and if you try to stop me again, you'll regret it."

"Then go ahead and kill me," she challenged. "Because as soon as I get out of these restraints, I'm going to align myself with the Grimaldis and take you down."

He caught her face in his hands, forcing her to meet his gaze. "Who says I'm letting you out of them anytime soon? I actually prefer you like this, all naked and helpless. Ready to be fucked." He threw back his head and released a throaty laugh before covering her body with his. "You're already hot for me, despite your words; you can't get enough of me, can you?" He covered her mouth with his.

Nya clamped her lips firmly together. If she thought to deny him what he wanted, she had another think coming. She belonged to him and he would have her. She looked so beautiful spread wide open for him. Ready for his cock. The scent of her arousal belied her protests. Perhaps, he should have chained her to his bed sooner, although he did enjoy the way she clawed at his back and clamped her powerful thighs around his waist in the throes of sex.

No matter how he took her, she excited him. Beatrice said Nya was his weakness, but Adonis didn't give a damn. And there was not a single thing either woman could do about it.

Adonis ran his tongue along the crease of her lips, gently teasing them apart. Her resistance waned as she moaned and her nipples pebbled. Clasping her head between his palms, he pressed his lips more firmly against hers, the need to possess her driving him.

With a sigh, her lips parted, granting him the access he sought. Thrusting his tongue inside her mouth to explore the sweet recesses inside gave him an indescribable thrill. The taste of her was like wild nectar. No matter how many times he had her, touching Nya was always a brand-new experience. It wasn't long before Nya's tongue shot forward to meet his. She pulled it back before boldly circling his.

Adonis wanted to laugh. He knew she would give in to him eventually, just as she always did. No matter how much she claimed to despise him, her body didn't. It craved his, wanted his. Needed his. They were made for each other, and whether she cared to admit it was inconsequential to him. She belonged to him and he fully intended to brand her until she could think of no one else but him.

He broke their kiss to nibble on her full bottom lip, his teeth digging in deep enough to break skin. She gasped as the sweet, coppery taste of her blood filled his mouth. Damn, he ached for her. It had been weeks since he'd taken her, and Adonis didn't want to rush because after tonight, he'd be far too busy to spare this time with Nya. Not that he planned on denying himself. No, he'd take her when and where he felt like, but this would be the last time in a while he'd be able to revel in his mastery over his beautiful lover.

He took his time tasting and licking the fleshy texture of her lips. His body burned for hers. His dick was rock hard and though he wanted this to last, Adonis didn't know how much longer he'd be able to hold out. Already the heady aroma of her cunt intoxicated him, and he desperately wanted to bury himself deep inside of her slick folds.

Nya squeezed her eyes shut. Adonis refused to let her pretend she was anywhere other than in his bed. He grasped her face. "Look at me! I want you to know who the victor is tonight. There will no pretense." When she didn't comply immediately, his grip tightened on her face. "Open them!"

She popped her eyes open then. They were full of her normal defiance, but this time it was mixed with the unmistakable look of unadulterated lust. "Why do you have to torment me like this?"

A smile tugged the corners of his lips. "Because I can. Because you're mine. Because we're bloodmates."

She cut her gaze away from his. "Don't say that."

"Why not? Deny it if you must, but it's true. Your mixed-up moral sensibilities tell you not to feel anything for me, yet your heart, body, and soul recognizes what you won't admit. We belong together."

"No! You brought me over. That's the only reason why I remain with you."

Adonis released a hearty chuckle. "You can keep telling yourself that, Nya but it won't make it any less true. Now, let me love you properly." He brushed his lips against her collarbone and placed kisses across her chest."

Nya narrowed her eyes. "I could never love you."

He raised a brow. "I see. So what would you do if I were to leave you in this high state of arousal? It wouldn't matter, because you have no feelings for me. Am I correct?"

Her nostrils flared and her breathing grew shallow, but Nya remained silent.

"I think we'll put your statement to the test."

Adonis rolled off of her and nearly made it off the bed when she growled. "Don't you dare leave me like this! Finish what you started."

It wasn't an admission, but he knew it had taken a lot out of her. She was too damn proud for her own good. He'd enjoy taking her down a notch. "Oh? I thought you wanted nothing to do with me?"

"I didn't say that. I said I didn't love you," she said through clenched teeth.

Adonis sighed with a shake of his head. "You beautiful liar, you. No matter. I can prove just how much you do indeed love me."

He stood and undressed before rejoining her on the bed. Adonis trailed his finger down the center of her body between her small but well-formed breasts to her flat stomach. He halted when he reached the nest of tight curls between her quivering thighs. "Shall I stop?"

In answer, she bucked her hips against his hand, silently demanding his attention. Unable to resist, he slid his middle finger past her slick labia and into her sopping wet channel. *Dio*, she was so hot, she nearly scorched his flesh. Nya squirmed against his hand as he fingered her, slowly at first before adding a second finger and ramming into her harder and deeper.

"Oh!" she cried out, moving her hips as best as she could. Adonis was nearly tempted to remove her restraints and let her go wild as he knew she would, but he couldn't chance it. Not tonight anyway.

It satisfied him to see how turned on she was for him, but finger fucking her wasn't enough. He had to be inside her right now! Adonis slowly eased his fingers out of her cunt and brought them to his lips, making sure he didn't spill a single drop of her delicious cream. "Mmm."

Unable to wait another second, he positioned himself between her spread legs and guided his cock against her entrance. "Look at me, Nya," he commanded softly.

This time she obeyed without argument. Her body shook. "Hurry."

Needing no further encouragement, he thrust into her tight pussy, reveling in her wet heat. The snugness of her cunt felt like coming home. It gripped him in a sensual vise so strong Adonis didn't know how long he'd be able to hold out. Bracing his arms on either side of her body, he moved into her until he was balls deep.

They gasped simultaneously. It felt so right. So fucking good. "Nya." He shut his eyes briefly to savor this moment. Right now, nothing else mattered. Not Beatrice. Not Giovanni. Not the Grimaldis or his quest for revenge. They were the only two people in the world as far as he was concerned.

"Adonis," she whispered so faintly he almost missed it.

"That's right, Nya, tell me how much you want me. That you need me. That you can't get enough of me." With each word he spoke, Adonis pounded into her, harder and faster. "Tell me!"

"I want you. Need you. Can't get enough of you!" Nya lifted her pelvis to meet each of his thrusts. Her cunt gripped him tighter still. "Oh, God, Adonis. I shouldn't feel this way but—"

"You feel this way because we belong together. It's time you finally accepted it." As he continued to surge in and out of her, he rested his weight on his forearms. He let his incisors descend and sank them in the juncture of her neck and shoulder. The blood rush, coupled with the extraordinary feeling of being inside her, was so intense he reached his peak. Spasming against her, Adonis shot his seed deep inside her pussy.

Nya screamed his name as she shuddered and squirmed uncontrollably, signaling her own orgasm.

Adonis remained inside of her, wishing this moment would never end. But it would. Nya would go back to pretending she didn't care about him and he would proceed with his plan to destroy the Grimaldis.

Nya's body ached from exertion. Adonis had taken her three more times, exploring every inch of her body, and her most tender regions were sore. His mouth and hands had been everywhere, and to her utter shame, she had loved it.

But much worse, she finally admitted to something she'd been fighting for the last several decades. She did care for him, more than she wanted to. Whether or not they were bloodmates she didn't know, but no one set her body on fire quite the way he did. She felt conflicted caring for someone who was capable of such evil.

Nya wanted to believe somewhere deep down there was good in him. She'd seen glimpses of it over the years, but it was a side of him he kept carefully hidden. Nya had told herself she stayed only because of the hold he had over her and the threat that he'd take out her last link to her past, but now she wasn't so sure.

But none of that mattered anymore because in his quest for revenge, he'd crossed the line. Since becoming a vampire, she'd done her best to shut off her feelings not just for Adonis, but for everyone and everything around her. Too wrapped up in her own private pain, she'd encased her heart in a cold, hard shell, letting only a few people in, but not all the way. Now he threatened to hurt one of the few people she called friend, and her conscience would not allow her to remain passive any longer.

If she could find a way to break free from her restraints, there was only one thing left for her to do.

Kill Adonis.

Chapter Eight

Romeo slammed his fist through the wall, creating a gaping hole. "I'm going to strangle Christine for this."

Isis flinched at the palpable ire radiating from his every pore. She'd never been happier to be her. She certainly didn't want to be in the shoes of the Grimaldi women at the moment. When she, Dante, and Paris had gotten back to the penthouse, they'd found three very furious vampires.

Niccolo paced the floor, practically wearing a trail in the plush wine-colored carpet. GianMarco muttered curses under his breath, and Romeo proceeded to cause major damage to the walls.

"Watch it, Romeo. I don't think my poor walls can withstand any more of your assaults." Dante's half-hearted scold sounded tired. He'd been on the phone since he'd arrived, trying to get the whereabouts of the women.

Romeo turned on his brother with bared teeth. "What the hell do you expect me to do? Christine is a young vampire. She has to feed. Not to mention she's not strong enough to battle the rogues we've faced."

Isis felt the need to offer comfort. "Maybe you're underestimating her. A mother can be very fierce when protecting her young."

Cobalt eyes narrowed to slits of blue fury. "And who the hell are you to say what I should feel?"

"Romeo!" This time Dante's tone was more forceful, but Isis was used to defending herself.

She took no offense at Romeo's outburst. Had their roles been reversed, she didn't know how she'd handle the situation. She'd probably be as frantic as he, if not more so. "I know because if my mother hadn't fought so valiantly to protect me from Hunters, I'd be dead. My mother gave her life so I could live. She, too, was young, but she took out four Hunters single-handedly. At least, Christine will have the assistance of Maggie and Sasha, who, if I understand correctly, is a powerful witch. My mother didn't have that luxury."

Romeo clenched his fists at his sides as his body trembled. He seemed to fight some internal battle before a heavy sigh whooshed past his lips. "I'm sorry. I shouldn't have spoken to you like that."

Isis offered him a smile to show him no harm was done. "It's okay. You have every right to be concerned about the safety of your family. I think we're all pretty tense over this situation."

Romeo nodded and then hung his head. "I can't lose them."

Dante strode across the room and caught his brother in an embrace. "As long as there is breath in my body, I'll protect this family. We'll find them, Ro, and when we do, we'll make every single person involved in this scheme pay."

The touching scene before Isis pulled at her heartstrings and made her a little jealous. She missed being part of a family, having that support system from a group who'd have your back no matter what. Isis felt an affinity with the Grimaldi clan because even in these times of turmoil, the love they shared for one another was apparent.

"Where do we go from here?" Niccolo finally broke the silence. He hadn't said much since they'd all gathered, but his expression remained bleak.

Dante released his younger brother with a sigh. "Well, I've—" He was interrupted by the loud, shrill ring of his mobile phone. Pulling the device out of his pocket, he pressed a button and put it to his ear. "Dante here." He gave nothing away as he listened to what the caller on the other end of the line had to say. "Yes. Thank you. Would you tell them to stay where they are until we get there?" Another brief silence followed. His eyebrows shot up suddenly. "They're with whom?"

"What is it?" GianMarco demanded.

Dante waved his brother off. "Yes. Just make sure they remain there until we arrive. We'll deal with them then." Dante clicked off without waiting for a reply.

"Well?" practically everyone in the room chorused.

"They've landed in Italy and are en route to Florence, and they're traveling with the witch, Liliana, to see Giovanni," Dante informed them. "That was Steel. He's made contact with Sasha. He and the twins are on their way back here. They were having trouble reaching her for some reason. He mentioned something about outside interference."

Isis frowned. "Was some kind of spell involved?"

"Probably. It's the only reasonable explanation I can think of why Sasha's brothers couldn't get in touch with her through their powers. They had to combine their abilities in order to accomplish that feat."

Niccolo looked at his older brother expectantly. "And what of my son? Have they learned of his whereabouts?"

Dante shook his head. "I'm afraid not. They'll be joining us shortly, so we'll be able to ask them if they know anything else when they get here. In the meantime, I need to call some of my agents who are already in the area. They can at least keep a lookout for the women should they see them."

Unable to keep still any longer, Isis stood. She wandered to the balcony's sliding glass door and stared outside. She was as anxious to save the children as Dante was. She knew firsthand what it was like to lose a loved one.

It tugged at her heartstrings to see how Grimaldi brothers interacted with one another. Maybe it was selfish of her to want to be a part of their inner circle but she was tired of being on her own. She wanted to be a part of a unit that took care of and loved each other. She wanted someone to hold her at night, maybe even have a few pups of her very own. And Isis wanted that with Dante. In her heart, she knew he was the one meant just for her.

The only obstacle standing in her path, however, was her past. The secret she guarded was tearing her up inside. It was true she'd come here to help Dante and his family. But, there was another reason she hadn't admitted even to herself.

Isis sought redemption for her past transgressions, freedom from a pair of big brown eyes that haunted her dreams.

Wrapping her arms around herself to stave off the shiver that suddenly coursed through her, Isis tried to fight the memories she'd tried desperately to suppress over the years. Even before the Serpent Gang had aligned themselves with Adonis, Isis had misgivings about spending so much time with them. Her feelings had never been more apparent than the night she'd gone along with a few of the gang members who'd wanted to "raise hell," for lack of anything better to do.

That hell had been visited upon an unsuspecting young family of humans. The group attacked their victims maliciously, taking out every single one of them. As disturbing as that was, Isis had been most bothered by the little girl they'd found hiding in a corner, her huge, frightened brown eyes filled with horror.

In her shifted form, Isis had advanced on the child, yet didn't have the heart to actually kill her. How could she, when she, too, had once been in a similar predicament? *"Run,"* she'd telepathically commanded the child, but the girl was too frightened to move.

Unfortunately, in the end, sparing the child hadn't mattered. One of the members, a vampire called Cobra, had finished the little girl off mercilessly. It was the last time Isis had ever gone out with them to hunt. Soon after, she began to distance herself from them. Their alliance to Adonis and the witch had been the final straw.

"A penny for them." Dante's soft voice broke through her thoughts.

With a slight shrug, she kept her gaze averted. "Nothing really." How easily that lie had tumbled from her lips. Yet another sin to add to her other misdeeds.

"Oh? That was a pretty ferocious frown you were sporting just now."

She stiffened. There wasn't much she could get past him. "I guess I'm worried about the children. The Serpent Gang doesn't care if they kill little ones."

Dante placed his hands on her shoulders. "I'm worried about them as well, but we can't give in to those worries. Otherwise, we'll lose hope. The good news is the women have been located and will wait for our arrival before they make a move. We probably should have included them from the start, in a lesser capacity of course. But they have just as much of a vested interest as their mates."

Isis nodded in agreement. "I think they're very brave, if not a bit foolish."

Dante snorted. "Foolish isn't the word for it. Insane comes to mind, but I suppose I can't fault them for what they've done. If the roles were reversed, I probably would have done the exact same thing. Even though the women have put themselves in harm's way, I'm proud of them. My brothers are lucky to have such worthy partners, willing to fight by their sides."

"My meeting with them was brief but from what I can tell, they're amazing women. But I guess, one would have to be extraordinary to win the heart of one of the famous Grimaldi brothers."

Dante chuckled softly. "You make us sound like deities."

Isis stole a look over her shoulder. She noticed a few sets of eyes trained on them with more than a little curiosity. "Can we go out to the balcony for a minute? I need air."

"Sure."

Once outside, she finally turned to face him. Her breath caught in her throat. He was so handsome. Was it only a short while ago when they'd shared that passionate interlude on the plane? His cock had been buried so deep inside her cunt, it had felt like they were one entity. "I know this might sound strange, but to me you guys are."

His brows flew together in bemusement. "We're what?"

"Deities. You said I spoke of you and your brothers as though—"

"Ah. But, we're not."

"You're legends in the immortal community."

His lips twisted into an ironic smile. "The legend has probably become bigger than all of us. Sometimes our reputation has benefited us, but most other times, it's a burden. You have no idea how many enemies come after us simply to say they tangled with the Grimaldis and lived to tell the tale. Honestly, even after we get through this ordeal— if we get through this ordeal, we'll never completely be in peace."

"I didn't realize."

"Our lives are complicated, but you take the good with the bad. I'm pleased my brothers have at least found mates to ease their paths through eternity."

"They're very fortunate." Isis took a deep breath before continuing. "I need to clarify my statement. I don't want you to think I'm some sycophant. I've always admired you and your brothers because of the work you've done to take out rogues. My entire pack was wiped out by Hunters and I know your Underground has been instrumental in ridding the immortal community from that threat. You might not think what you do is a big deal, but your work means a lot to people like me. It helps to know my parents didn't die in vain."

"Thank you. That actually means a lot. Like I explained before, I got into this line of business for my own selfish reasons but if what I've done helped to keep other immortals and other innocents safe, then it's worth it." He smiled making her want to melt.

"I'm sure I'm not the only one who admires your work."

A comfortable silence fell between them as they stared at the stars. Isis was finally the one to break the quiet. "I notice how family oriented you are. Do you see yourself eventually settling down...with a mate?"

"Of course."

"And what kind of woman are you looking for, Dante?"

He took a step closer and lowered his head until his lips were mere inches from hers. "I never knew the answer to that question until recently. But I'm beginning to have a pretty good idea." Dante cupped her face between his palms and brushed her lips with his. "And you, *bellissima*? What kind of man are you looking for?"

Isis hadn't realized she was holding her breath until a *whoosh* of air pushed its way out of her lungs. She moistened her suddenly dry lips. "I think you already know."

He cocked one dark brow. "How would I, if you've never said anything?"

"There really hasn't been much time. As a matter of fact, I feel guilty having this discussion with you right now when so much is going on."

Dante caressed the sides of her face with his thumbs. "Crazy, isn't it? Even through all this madness, I can't stop thinking about what's happening between us. There's a connection, isn't there? I felt it upon our first meeting, but the time wasn't right. Now, probably isn't either but I don't think I can go another day without letting you know."

"What?" she whispered when he didn't finish.

"I once believed myself to be in love a couple times, but in both cases, my feelings were misguided. It's shaken my confidence in that emotion, but I want to explore these feelings I have for you…that is, if you are in agreement."

"Yes!" She didn't have to even think about it. Tilting her head to receive his kiss, she wrapped her arms around his neck.

The kiss, however, never came because the balcony's glass door slid open.

"If I'm not interrupting anything, Steel, Cutter, and Blade have returned." Paris spoke in a way that made it clear he wasn't amused at catching Isis and Dante in each other's arms.

Dante's mouth twisted into a half smile of regret. "We'll pick up our conversation later."

Isis dropped her arms to her sides with a nod as she tried to conceal her disappointment.

When she would have followed Dante inside, Paris stepped onto the balcony and closed the door. Without waiting for Isis to answer, he stepped in her path. "I'd like a word with you."

Isis frowned. Paris didn't deign to have many conversations with her unless it pertained to Persephone. "Shouldn't we be in there with the others?"

Gray eyes narrowed momentarily. "They can wait. What I have to say to you won't take long."

Isis stilled, readying herself for what was to come. Paris didn't look as if he wanted to exchange pleasantries. "Okay, say what you have to say." She had tried to inject casualness in her voice, but her heart raced a mile a minute.

"I'm sure you're aware I've never quite approved of your friendship with my daughter."

A ghost of a smile briefly flitted across her lips. "Yes. I know. You've never said anything directly, but I sensed it. But do you think it's really appropriate to bring this subject up now?"

"Maybe not your association with Persephone, but I do think something should be said about the one with you and Dante."

Her lips tightened briefly. Though she had the utmost respect for the Alpha of Pack Kyriakis, he had no right to sit in judgment of her relationship with Dante. "I don't really see how that's any of your business."

"I'm making it my business, Isis."

Isis's brows flew together in her agitation. "You may be the Alpha of Pack Kyriakis but you are not the ruler of me. What gives you the right to think you can interfere?"

"I don't know. Why don't you tell me, Isis, or should I say, Coral?"

The gasp escaped her mouth before she could stop it. He knew! But how? She'd been so careful to keep her past a secret. The only person who knew was Persephone, and Isis was positive her friend wouldn't have said anything. There was no use in pretending she didn't know what he was talking about, so she leaned her head back to meet his glittering gray gaze. "That was my past and that's where it belongs. But out of curiosity, how did you find out?"

He smirked. "I'm glad you're not going to insult my intelligence by denying it. That explanation of your old association with the Serpent Gang didn't quite sit well with me, so I decided to make some inquiries of my own while you and Dante were in the airplane lavatory…getting to know each other better. I made a few calls. I had to wait for my answers, but I also found it strange how easily you were able to converse with one of the most deadly group of rogues without getting into a scuffle. So it didn't surprise me when I received the information I was looking for. My source seems to remember a shifter who used to hang out with the gang, and she wasn't merely an onlooker. Care to explain?"

"I wasn't a member."

"You had a code name. They don't give code names to nonmembers."

"Not usually, but they made an exception for the leader's lover. I was in a relationship with Black Adder, it's true, but I disassociated myself from them a long time ago. Please believe me." If Paris went back inside and told Dante everything she could forget about developing anything with him."

Paris crossed his arms over his broad chest and gave her a stern look of disbelief. "Oh? Why should I believe you? After all, you've been oh so honest up to this point."

Isis closed her eyes briefly and took a deep breath. "You're right, but the truth is, I didn't know how my news would be received."

"For someone who is no longer in contact with them, you sure seemed friendly with them in Vegas. It would make one think you were still a part of the group."

"Actually, I didn't leave them on good terms. And I had to do a lot of fast talking when I walked into that house. It was touch and go for a little while."

Paris raised a cynical brow. "Yet you walked out of the house unscathed."

"I think they let me go because they didn't think I posed a threat. Look, I can't say all the choices I've made have been good ones, especially my dealings with the Serpent Gang, but it's my past."

"One which could jeopardize this mission, and all this just so you can get laid," he accused through clenched teeth.

Something inside her snapped. "Look, I respect your Alpha status, but it gives you no right to say things like that to me. Whether you believe me or not is up to you, but I'm telling the truth. I haven't been in contact with them for years. Yes, part of the reason I volunteered to help is because I have feelings for Dante, but I also want to do the right thing. When I overheard you talking to Aries about the Serpent Gang, I thought my knowledge of how they operate and where they're located would come in handy. If you can't see that, then it's your problem, not mine."

Paris's eyes narrowed to gray slits of fire. "Brave words for one in such a precarious situation. Okay, let's say I accept you're telling the truth. What do you think

Dante will say when he learns the truth—and he will eventually. He's too thorough not to. The only reason he hasn't yet is because he's besotted with you. I'd hate to find out you're manipulating him through his developing feelings for you."

Her mouth gaped opened then closed. "I resent the implication."

"Oh, I'm not implying anything, Isis. I'm flat-out saying it. Dante means a lot to me and my family. He's been hurt before and I don't want to see it happen again."

"I would never—"

Paris held up his hand. "I'm sure you don't think it would hurt him, but considering what he and his brothers have already been through—are going through—do you think he'd take your being a rogue lightly?"

"I'm not a rogue."

"But you were and that's all that will matter to him."

A chill went down her spine. He was probably right. It was one of the reasons she hadn't confessed her nefarious past to Dante yet. She didn't want to lose him now when they were getting so close. "Will you tell him?" Her breath caught in her throat at the thought.

"I doubt I'll need to because he'll find out for himself soon enough. If I were you, I'd come clean. He may not take it any better than he would if he finds out on his own, but he might go easier on you if you do. I won't say anything to him for now, out of respect for your friendship with my daughter, but if you make one single misstep or if I find you've been playing both sides, all bets are off."

Isis wished the ground would open up and swallow her whole. She'd been delusional to think she could keep her secret to herself. Shutting her eyes against Paris's hard scrutiny, she sighed. "Whether you believe me or not, I won't betray Dante. Like I said, I'm not proud of everything I've done in my past, but I won't do anything to jeopardize this mission."

Paris's nostrils flared briefly. "See that you don't." He turned to go inside, leaving her alone. She was frightened that she might just lose out on love before it even began.

Chapter Nine

Dante couldn't quite put his finger on it but there was a change in Isis shortly after their conversation on the balcony. She'd always come across as a confident woman, never afraid to look anyone in the eye. But in an instant she'd become something else. He wouldn't have exactly called her timid but whenever he spoke to her she seemed nervous about something and refused to meet his gaze. He was almost certain it had something to do with the conversation she'd had with Paris. Whenever he'd ask Isis or Paris, neither would tell him and it frustrated him. Only a short time ago, he and Isis had made a pact to be more open with one another so he didn't understand what gave.

Isis didn't take the seat next to his on the plane. Instead, she stretched out on the couch and closed her eyes. To look at her now, one would think she was asleep, but he could tell she wasn't by the way she'd tense whenever he shifted in his seat. Her full lips drooped into a frown and her hands trembled just enough for him to take notice. Once they arrived at their destination, there would be little time to talk. Needing answers, Dante closed his eyes and attempted to link his mind to hers.

She didn't answer immediately and for a moment, he didn't think she would.

"I know you're awake."

"Yes, Dante?" The voice in his mind sounded tired, the slight tremor giving her away her wariness.

"Are you okay?"

"I'm fine. It's been a long couple of days."

"It has been for us all but it's more than that and we both know it. Tell me what's wrong."

"Nothing is the matter."

"If it were the case, then you wouldn't seem so jittery every time I attempt to have a conversation with you. And we both know whatever it is that's bothering has everything to do with what you and Paris talked about back at the penthouse."

No reply was forthcoming and Dante opened his eyes to look at her from across the aisle. Isis, who was now in a sitting position, looked straight ahead, her stoic expression unreadable. He didn't like the wall she'd erected between the two of them and planned on tearing it down before this plane ride was over. *"You can't keep ignoring me. I could always ask Paris what you spoke of."*

She turned her gaze in his direction, her face still a blank slate. *"I know you've already asked him and if he'd said anything, you wouldn't be asking me now."*

Dante slid out of his seat and walked over to join her. She stiffened when he sat close enough to her for their hips to touch. *"You're correct. He won't tell me either, but I was hoping you would be forthright with me in light of our previous conversation. Weren't you upset with me for not telling you why I'd been upset? Well, now it's my turn. I thought we agreed to be more open with one another."*

"We did, but there are some things better left alone."

He found her answer a bit unsettling. *"I never took you to be a hypocrite, Isis. You can't have it both ways, Isis.*

Either we're both honest with each other or we have nothing left to say to one another.

She released a mental sigh. *"Dante, the thing is, I do want to tell you."*

"Then what's stopping you."

"It's complicated. You were right about the conversation I had with Paris being the cause of my being distant but it has nothing to do with how I feel about you."

"Then make me understand why you can't tell me about it."

She took his hand in hers and met his gaze for the first time in hours. *"It has something to do with my past. Paris is very thorough when it comes to his offspring and me being friends with Persephone, he of course did a little digging into my background. He wasn't too thrilled with what he found but."*

He raised a brow. Now Dante was more curious than ever. *"What did he find Isis?"*

"I...can't tell you just yet. But I promise I will tell you, I just need to gather my thoughts.

He yanked his hand out of her grasp. *Time for what? Why can't you just come right out and tell me?"*

Isis folded her hands in her lap and hung her head. *"Because, I don't want you to think less of me. As I've already told you, being a lone wolf, I had to do whatever I needed to do in order to survive. I didn't always make the best choices but I've done my best to atone for what I've done. And, I'm going to tell you about it. But can we talk about it after we rescue the children?"*

Whatever Paris had turned up had left Isis frazzled but he could feel her sincerity. Though he wanted to push the issue, one look at her tense face and Dante relented. *"Could you at least answer one question for me?"*

"I'll try my best."

Dante bit his lip to hold back the frustrated retort on the tip of his tongue. *"Does your former connection to the Serpent Gang have anything to do with what Paris found out?"*

She shut her eyes briefly and ran the tip of her tongue across her lips. *"I'd rather not say. Not yet anyway."*

"Are you fucking kidding me?" he roared, forgetting to mind speak in his anger.

Isis flinched. Several pairs of eyes turned in their direction. Dante hated losing his cool, but most especially he despised this game Isis seemed to be playing. Ignoring the curious onlookers, he focused his attention on Isis, who once again averted her gaze from him. *"Well does it?"*

"You're getting angry with me and you don't even know the full story yet. What will you do when you learn what you want to know?" She turned in her seat to face him again, her eyes wide and pleading, silently imploring him to hear her out. *"What I can tell you is that I promise on my life that I will not jeopardize this mission in anyway. I will fight at your side just as fiercely as anyone else on the team. I only ask that you give me a bit more time. I'm only asking for a little time because you mean a lot to me whether you're ready to hear it or not. And I don't want what I have to tell you to be a distraction from the mission or...us."*

Dante wasn't sure what to say. He was usually very good at reading people and from where he sat, Isis seemed quite earnest in her declaration. Besides, if Paris thought she would be a detriment to the mission he would have told him. *"Okay. I'll give you time, but whatever it is I learn, it better be from you. I don't want to hear it from anyone else."*

"Of course. Thank you, Dante." Her eyes glistened with unshed tears.

His head told him to ask more questions, probe deeper, but his heart wouldn't let him. Unable to go another second without touching her, Dante cupped her face in his palms and planted his lips at the corner of Isis's mouth. He brushed a stray teardrop from her cheek with his thumb. *"Don't cry. I know you're here to help, and I appreciate it. Without you, we wouldn't have figured out where the hideouts were so quickly. You're doing a good thing by risking your own safety for this cause."*

She curved her lips into a smile. *"That means a lot to me to hear you say that."*

"Just know, my patience will extend but so far."

Isis nodded. *"I understand."*

Dante momentarily tightened his grip on her face. *"I'm serious, Isis."*

She gulped. *"I know. I'll keep my promise."*

"Good. I don't care for broken promises or the people who break them."

Maggie clutched Sasha's arm. "Are they really upset with us?"

Sasha grimaced. "According to my brothers, they're definitely not happy and I believe that's putting it mildly. But you and Christine only have GianMarco and Romeo to contend with. Not only will Niccolo give me a piece of his mind, but my brothers will give me an earful as well, especially since I used a spell to keep them from contacting us until it was too late for them to bring us back. They weren't pleased about that."

"Well, I, for one, am glad you did it. There's not much they can do about it now, can they? We're doing ourselves no favors worrying about it now, I suppose. They should be here by tomorrow morning at the latest," Christine chimed in from the other side of the room. Her arms were wrapped around her body as she glanced out the bedroom window. She'd been quiet most of the journey. They had arrived in Florence only a few hours ago.

Liliana had brought them to this villa which was located on the outskirts of the city. Giovanni was supposed to have greeted them, but had some pressing matter to attend to and had left a message stating he'd return shortly. Maggie wondered for the hundredth time if she'd done the right thing by coming here, but she only had to think of her daughters and all doubts faded away. She could tell Christine had those same doubts, judging from the forlorn expression on her face.

Maggie joined Christine at the window, placing a hand on her sister-in-law's shoulder. "Don't worry, honey, Romeo will probably be a little angry at you for leaving against his wishes, but he'll get over it."

Christine put her hand on top of Maggie's. "Believe it or not, my concern isn't with what Romeo will think. I already know he'll be pissed. I'm wondering how the children are holding up and what's happening to them. Jaxson tries to be brave and I'm scared he might do something that would—"

"If you continue to think that way, you'll only end up driving yourself crazy. I'm holding on to hope that they're fine. They're just waiting for us to come get them and we will."

Christine nodded. "You're right of course. I wish I could be as sure as you."

Maggie let out a mirthless laugh. "I'm not. I'm just as scared as you are but I think I'd be somewhere in a corner crying if I allowed myself to give in to despair. Will you be all right, Christine?"

"I don't think it's possible for me to be all right until my family is intact again. It's a little different for you and Sasha. Not to take anything away from the agony I'm sure the two of you are dealing with, but I feel that no one can understand what I'm going through. You both have adult children and I'm pretty new to this motherhood thing. The two of you—" She broke off, shaking her head vehemently.

"What?" Maggie prompted, trying to understand.

Christine lowered her head, her eyes squeezed shut. "If I said what was on my mind, you'd probably think it was really shitty of me."

Sasha moved to Christine's other side and took her hand. "We won't think that. If you can't share your feelings with your family, who can you share them with?"

Christine flexed the muscle in her jaw before speaking "It's just…if something were to happen to Jagger and Gianna, heaven forbid, there could be more children for you down the road. Maggie, you have three birth children. My kids… if —They're it for me." She broke off stuffing her knuckles in her mouth.

Maggie rested her hand on Christine's shoulder. She didn't know the pain of infertility her sister-in-law had suffered through, but she could sympathize. Christine was now a vampire, immune from all the human deficiencies and ailments that had shadowed her life before Romeo made her immortal. However, she still wouldn't be able to give birth because her ovaries had been removed due to health issues some years ago. Maggie had since learned vampire blood could heal a number of things, but it couldn't fix what wasn't there before her change.

"I don't think that was a terrible thing to say at all. You're right, Sasha and I could never understand that particular pain, but I empathize with you and ask that you have faith that we will find them. Alive."

Sasha patted Christine on the shoulder. "I agree."

Christine's lips twitched to a brief smile. "Thank you for being so understanding. This is all so surreal to me. It seems like only yesterday I was on my own with no hope for a future or family. And then, Romeo came into my life and changed it all. He helped me realize my dream of becoming a mother. I may not have given birth to Jaxson and Adrienne, but they are just as much mine as if I had. In fact, I feel that my bond with them is stronger because of it. I believed once we became a family, I could give them the life they deserved, the one they'd been deprived of. Jaxson still has nightmares about what those monsters used to do to them. And Adrienne, she's a bright child, but she doesn't speak much and has a distrust of people that isn't natural in such a young child. And now this. I swore to protect them and I failed." Fresh tears streamed down Christine's cheeks.

A reply was on the tip of Maggie's tongue when the bedroom door opened.

"Am I interrupting anything?" Liliana stood in the doorway.

Maggie, Christine, and Sasha moved away from each other. "We're just having a moment," Maggie answered. "How much longer do we have to wait before we see Giovanni?"

Liliana stepped into the bedroom. "He should be here shortly."

Maggie was tired of waiting and refused to bite her tongue while they played the waiting game. "Where is he anyway? I thought he would be here when we arrived. What business did he need to take care of?"

The redhead stepped further into the room, her expression neutral. "I'm unfortunately not able to disclose that information. It's of a private nature."

Maggie narrowed her eyes, placing her hands on her hips. She liked Liliana, could tell the witch was an ally, but it didn't mean Maggie would accept this runaround. Even when they'd been on the plane, Liliana had evaded more questions than she'd answered. "I think we're entitled to know something, considering how we've traveled halfway around the world based on your information and faith."

Liliana didn't seem the least bit intimidated. One auburn brow shot up in surprise.

Sasha placed her hand on Maggie's arm, giving it a gentle squeeze as a warning to stand down. "Liliana, understand our position. We're very anxious to get our children back. Give us some hope, some reason to stay and wait for someone who we'd all thought to be our enemy. That's all we ask. Every instinct in my body tells me to go out on our own to find our loved ones, but still we stay. The least you can do, is tell us what we want to know."

The stubborn purse of Liliana's lips gave every indication she wasn't willing to relent on the matter, but Maggie returned the witch's stare, determined not to back down. Sasha was right. Why should they wait?

Finally, the redhead relaxed her rigid stance. "It's really not my story to tell, but before you arrived, he received word from one of our contacts regarding a favor he was doing for a friend. It's all I can say right now, but I assure you, if it wasn't important, he'd be here. I've been assured he'll join us soon."

Liliana's vague explanation did nothing to soothe Maggie's concerns; if anything, it served to further irritate her. What was more important than finding the children? She was on the verge of asking exactly that when she sensed another presence in the room.

Maggie turned to see a tall, dark-haired vampire. Her mouth fell open and her eyes widened.

He stepped farther into the room, a smile of amusement tilting lips that were too familiar for comfort. "Ah, so we meet again, Maggie."

Maggie blinked as she tried to figure out whether she'd stepped into a dream or not. She moved her mouth in an attempt to form words, but nothing came out.

"Who is this?" Christine asked with an undertone of wariness in her voice.

Liliana smiled, her attention focused on the newcomer. "Ah, Giovanni, the women have been anxiously awaiting your arrival. Perhaps now, you can put their concerns to rest."

His piercing green eyes scanned the face of each occupant. "It's a pleasure to finally meet my brothers' mates."

Maggie's body shook with tension as she fought to regain her speech. Like a volcano, it finally returned in an eruption. "You!" she managed to get past her lips before the room went black. Her last conscious memory was of a familiar pair of strong, corded arms wrapping themselves around her before she hit the floor.

Chapter Ten

Isis stared out the car window, not particularly looking at anything. She hadn't traveled so extensively in her entire life, yet seeing new sights didn't give her the pleasure or sense of awe it should have. At the very least, she should have been thinking of the important mission ahead of her but her mind wasn't on that, either.

There hadn't been much time to speak with Dante after she'd made the promise to tell him everything later because no sooner had she resolved to tell him the truth about her past than GianMarco had wanted a private word with him. Then Steel, and after him, Niccolo needed Dante. If she were to tell him then as she'd planned to, it would have been a distraction he didn't need. The irony of it was had changed her mind. She was going to tell him because she didn't want the secret hanging over her head. She wanted to be completely honest with him to see if they could work past it. Now, that opportunity was lost.

Her stomach was twisted in knots. Part of her was a little relieved at the brief respite because it bought her more time. It shouldn't have been so hard to confess, but the risk of him turning her away scared the hell out of her.

Isis sank her teeth into her bottom lip until she tasted the coppery sweetness of blood. When she remembered some of the atrocities she'd perpetrated, shame filled every pore in her being. She couldn't take back the things she'd done, but they were behind her. Hopefully, Dante would realize it as well.

"We're here, Isis."

Isis had been so deep in thought she didn't register the gentle shake on her shoulder. Startled, she jumped in her seat before noticing the vehicle had stopped.

Dante smiled at her, a silent look of inquiry lurking within the depths of his cobalt gaze.

"Oh, I didn't realize."

"Obviously. Let's go." Pushing the car door open, he slid out in one fluid motion with an ease most men his size would have envied.

Isis took a deep breath. With reluctance, she followed him outside, already missing his proximity. The others were already headed to the entrance of the house. Waiting in front was a witch with long dark red hair. She assumed it to be Liliana, based on the description she'd been given.

Dante approached the witch first. "I presume Giovanni is present?"

The redhead inclined her head slightly. "Yes, as are the others. Please come in. We've been expecting you all." She moved aside just enough to allow them entrance. Isis noticed the way Liliana's gaze followed Dante's retreating back and the small smile that touched her lips. Her appreciation of Dante was quite obvious, and the way Dante had greeted her told Isis they had met before. Something fierce and possessive reared inside of Isis.

Clenching her fists at her sides in an attempt to rein in her temper, she drew closer, but as she approached Liliana, Isis had the distinct impression she'd seen the witch somewhere and by the close scrutiny she received, it was clear the feeling was mutual.

Cautiously, she made her way past Liliana when long, thin fingers wrapped themselves around her arm, halting her progress. The others had already gone ahead of her. Isis stared pointedly at the hand holding her steady.

"What are *you* doing here?" Liliana's lips barely moved as the whispered words were delivered through clenched teeth.

Isis pulled her arm out of the other woman's grip. "I'm here to help."

"I see. Just like you helped the Serpent Gang before?" The redhead twisted her lips into a sneer. "Don't look so surprised. I know who you are. You remember me, don't you?"

Isis wanted to be sick. She could feel all color draining from her face as it hit her where she'd seen Liliana before. It had been around the time Isis had begun having doubts about her association with Black Adder and his crew. Ironically, the incident which came to mind was the last time she'd stepped foot in Italy. For some reason, Black Adder had been interested in attacking a group of gypsies, except something had gone wrong.

Isis hadn't wanted to go along in the first place, but like always, her lover had questioned her loyalty to him, which usually won him most arguments. Though she'd gone with the group, she didn't participate when the gang descended on the unsuspecting band of nomads. In fact, she'd distanced herself from them, unable to stomach the carnage.

It was the same scene, different set of victims all over again. But this time there was a twist. A bright light erupted within the camp and the woman standing before her shooting her a hostile look had appeared. Using her powers, Liliana had conjured up a powerful storm, providing the perfect distraction for the group of gypsies to escape.

Black Adder had barked orders to go after the witch, but she'd made it rain even harder and sent thunderbolts of lightning crashing down on the gang. Isis barely avoided being hit by one herself. As she ran for cover, Isis had come face-to-face with Liliana. Though her heart had not been in the fight that night or for a long time before then, Isis was prepared to defend herself. But instead of attacking her as Isis suspected, Liliana had said ominously, "Beware of the company, you keep." And then she'd disappeared.

It had been the strangest encounter she'd ever experienced.

Isis finally managed to get the words past her parched throat. "That's a closed chapter in my life. I've put it behind me." No matter what she'd done in her past, Isis wouldn't be intimidated by this woman because of it.

"Perhaps it is, or maybe, it isn't. The only reason I spared your life that day was because you didn't participate in the massacre your friends committed, but you did nothing to stop them, which doesn't absolve you in my eyes. So I ask again, what are you doing here?"

Isis had the foresight to realize that getting indignant would do her no good. Taking a deep breath to hold back an angry retort, she met Liliana's steady gaze. "Like I said before, I'm simply here because I want to help. You, obviously, know of my past association and because of it, I believe I can be of some assistance to the family. I have plenty of knowledge about the inner workings of the Serpent Gang."

One auburn eyebrow rose. "Are the Grimaldis aware of this?"

"Of course."

"Hastily spoken words usually aren't true."

"But these are. I promise, I'm not here to cause trouble. I'm not that person you saw years ago."

Liliana stroked her chin with her thumb. "If they're aware of your past, then if I mention it to the others, there'll be no surprises?"

Isis was caught in a lie and her only option was to brazen it out. "Of course." If Liliana did back up her threat, maybe it wouldn't be such a bad thing anyway. At least then, she wouldn't be carrying around this huge burden of guilt.

"You're an awful liar."

Their gazes locked in what seemed to be a battle of wills. If Isis backed down now, Liliana would only see it as a weakness and she couldn't afford that. "Will you let me pass? I can't stop you from telling the others about me if that's what you've made up your mind to do, but you're not going to stop me from walking inside and joining the rest of the group. I made a vow to help and I have no intention of breaking it."

"So, you'd be willing to challenge me? I'm much older than you, shifter."

Isis shifted her hands until her claws grew to sharp points and held them up to show she wouldn't be bullied. "And I'm much stronger than I look. Would you like to put it to the test, witch?"

Liliana pursed her lips into a thin line of annoyance.

"Isis, why are you still standing out here?" Dante appeared behind Liliana.

Isis put her hands behind her back, hoping he hadn't seen anything. Pasting a smile on her face, she answered, "Liliana and I were just having a chat. It seems we've met before—a very long time ago." Though her reply was directed toward Dante, her gaze never left the witch's face.

With obvious reluctance, Liliana took a step back. "Yes, a conversation we'll continue later." The casual tone didn't hide the underlying venom beneath the redhead's words.

"I'm looking forward to it," Isis returned, her insides shaking. She'd have to tell Dante before Liliana did. She'd do it the first chance they were alone.

Dante shot her a questioning look, but Isis turned away, unable to meet his gaze. "Is everything all right? You seem a bit jittery."

Isis shook her head. "I think all this traveling is starting to catch up with me."

Dante searched her face, his dark blue stare not missing a single detail. "You probably need to rest. You didn't sleep much on the plane or in the car."

"No. I'll be fine."

"Are you sure?"

"Yes."

Liliana shot Isis another narrowed glance. Her stiff stance told Isis she still had reservations and would be watching her. That was now two people who knew her secret. It felt like the walls were closing in on her.

Finally, Liliana refocused her attention on Dante, and bestowed a smile on him. "Giovanni will be with us, shortly. He was here briefly to greet the women before being called away again on a personal matter. I spoke with him moments before you arrived and he'll be here within minutes."

The grim expression didn't leave Dante's face. "Good. I'm anxious to hear what he has to say. Maybe, I'll finally get the answers I've been chasing for years."

"Yes," the witch agreed. "All will be revealed to you soon enough."

Isis flinched when that dark gaze fell on her again. Somehow, she had a feeling Liliana wasn't referring to Dante's questions. Isis prayed Dante would understand when he learned the truth.

Jagger's eyelids felt as though they were being anchored by fifty-pound weights. He let out a soft groan and, after a brief struggle, managed to open them slowly. It took him a few moments to remember where he was and why he was there. This weakness was even worse than the first time he'd come to.

Damn it, if it weren't for the cuffs, he could have used his powers to best that witch, who he realized wasn't a witch at all. She was very much human. Making him draw the only possible conclusion; she practiced black magic. Even as her burst of energy had seared through his flesh, it had felt strange — evil. The sheer force and ease with which she'd been able to wield such power told Jagger she'd been practicing it for a very long time.

It must have been she who had bound him and charmed these cuffs. That explained the heaviness in his body, as if his strength was being zapped from him a little bit at a time. There was a spell to undo the works of black magic, but his lessons under his mother and uncles had yet to extend to that point.

Muttering a curse under his breath, Jagger managed to wobble into an upright position. The room was darker than he remembered. Scanning his surroundings, he noted this wasn't the same room at all. Blinking to adjust his eyes to the darkness lurking within every nook and cranny, he noted his current jail was much smaller than the last one. There was no furniture, not even a cot to lie on. It was bare bones, not much larger than a walk-in closet. Had they put him here because they believed this place could hold him?

If he died trying, he'd find a way out.

At least his cuffs were still in front of him, making it easier to maneuver. One thing he had figured out about the blasted things: They were impervious to his strength and spells, but that didn't mean he couldn't slip out of them. His hands were too big at the moment to push through the cuffs, but there was one other way he could free himself of them. No matter how excruciating that option was, he had to try or else he and the children were as good as dead.

Jagger had only to think of Camryn, the love of his life, to decide that any pain he would suffer was worth it, if it provided him the opportunity to escape. Desperation had brought him low, but the love in his heart for his woman and family would get him through this ordeal.

After struggling to his feet, Jagger tested the sturdiness of the wall. The unevenness of the hard stone assured him it was exactly what he needed. Taking a deep breath, he curled his fingers into tight fists before slamming one of them into the wall with all his might.

The splintering of bone greeted his ears before he actually felt a wave of white-hot pain shoot from his fingertips to his shoulder, tearing into his body like a dull blade. Tears sprang to his eyes as he caught his bottom lip between his teeth to hold back the howl lingering in the back of his throat. The last thing Jagger wanted was to bring someone to the room, at least not until he was free.

Before he could psych himself out, he punched the wall a second time, further pulverizing his already shattered hand. Bright spots of light danced before his eyes, he was close to passing out and throwing up. But, he wouldn't. Couldn't. He needed to stay focused in order to escape and find the children. There was no telling what that bitch had done with the baby.

Jaxson had seemed fine for the time being, but where was Adrienne? Sweat beaded along his forehead and temples as Jagger fought to remain conscious. He took deep breaths as he leaned against the wall and tried not to focus on the agonizing ache not only in his hand but in his entire body.

"Come on, you can do this," he muttered to himself. He'd already completed the toughest part of his task. There was only one more thing left to do. Gripping the cuff shackling his now broken hand, he yanked and pulled, skimming it over the nearly boneless appendage until he was able to slip it off. A grunt escaped his lips before he could stop it, but at least one hand was free.

Now he'd have to play the waiting game and heal before he repeated the process with his other hand. Nothing would stop him from getting out of here.

Chapter Eleven

Dante felt Giovanni's presence in the room before he actually saw him. It felt surreal to know he would finally have the answers he'd sought for years. The tension in the room was palpable.

The witch, Liliana who had entered the room ahead of Giovanni, spoke first, breaking the tense silence in the room. "Giovanni, as you can see, everyone has been anxiously awaiting your arrival."

Dante's breath caught in his throat. It was like seeing a ghost. Except for his deep green eyes, this vampire was the spitting image of his papa.

A small squeeze of his hand briefly drew Dante's attention to Isis, who stood by his side. She smiled as her eyes silently conveyed her support. Her presence was somehow reassuring, and now more than ever, he needed it. Dante redirected his attention to the vampire who stood in the center of the room.

Giovanni took his time to gaze upon each occupant as though committing their faces to memory. He walked over to GianMarco and Maggie.

Marco eyed the older vampire warily, protectively pulling his mate closer.

Giovanni smiled, undeterred. "GianMarco, it's pleasure to finally meet you face to face. And this is Maggie?

Marco nodded his blond head stiffly, his arms tightening around Maggie's shoulders.

"You remember me, don't you, Maggie?"

Her mouth opened, but no words came out.

GianMarco's eyes turned from their usual amber shade to a dangerously glittering hue of silver. "What are you talking about? When have you two met?" His body shook visibly with suppressed anger.

Giovanni, however, seemed unfazed in the face of Marco's hostility. "Relax, GianMarco. All will be explained soon enough." Turning away from Marco and Maggie, he focused his gaze on Nico and Sasha. The centuries-old vampire practically glided across the room until he stood in front of the couple. "Niccolo, I'm very pleased to meet you. You as well, Sasha, bearer of the mark of Hecate."

Sasha furrowed her brows, not bothering to hide her surprise. "How did you know?"

"I have my sources. I, also, know you're just coming into your powers. I'm sure once you have a proper handle on them, you'll be more of a force to be reckoned with than you already are."

Without waiting for a response, Giovanni focused his attention on Romeo and Christine. "Romeo, welcome to my home, I'm happy to see you. Christine, I'm very pleased to see you've recovered from your health scare."

Romeo's expression remained stony, while Christine whispered a shaky, "Thank you."

There was something about the way Giovanni introduced himself to each brother, almost as if he'd finally found something he'd been looking for that he'd lost. There was almost a look of longing as he glanced at each man, almost as if he were seeking something only they could provide. Dante, however, wouldn't be swayed no matter how hospitable Giovanni pretended to be. There were too many years of unexplained agony inflicted on his family for Dante to immediately absolve the one man who knew why.

Dante narrowed his gaze. "We didn't come here to exchange pleasantries. What we want are answers and a reason why we shouldn't kill you." He stalked over to the older vampire until they were toe to toe. Balling his fists at his sides, he fought to reign in his temper.

Giovanni nodded in what appeared to be contrition. "Dante, I'm not your enemy. Please," — he gestured to a chair between Isis and Paris— "have a seat and I'll tell you all you want to know."

Wanting to protest, yell, fight, and whatever else to ease the warring emotions inside him, Dante continued to glare at Giovanni. Even if this wasn't the vampire that had been behind all the misfortune that had befallen the Grimaldis over the years, Giovanni was still responsible for allowing Adonis to escape and because of it, the children were taken.

"I think everyone is on edge as it is," Paris spoke. "I can only imagine what it would feel like if my pups were in danger, but it's probably best if we listen to what Giovanni has to say and then we can make an informed decision on what our next move should be."

Paris was right. With a resigned sigh, Dante slid into the empty chair. "We want to know all of it."

Giovanni inclined his head slightly. "I understand. We'll save the formal introductions for another time. I'd first like to thank everyone for being here on such short notice. I wish I would have been able to meet you all in more agreeable circumstances." He paused briefly, agitation lined his face. He placed his hands behind his back and began to pace the length of the floor. With each stride, Giovanni seemed more bothered, until finally he halted, turned to his audience as he released a deep breath. "Adonis has been dealing in black magic for centuries now, which gives him an extra advantage in addition to his age."

Dante arched his eyebrow. Generally, black magic was something only bound Warlocks or Hunters dabbled in. There were a few humans who played around with it, but since the wicked arts were not easy to master, many mortals ended up dead from trying.

"How did he get involved in it? I mean, why would a vampire need to?" It was the very same question Dante had wondered.

Giovanni's lips twisted into a grimace as if the answer pained him. "I see you haven't guessed. Like myself and our father, Adonis was born human, unlike you, Dante, Niccolo, Romeo and GianMarco."

This news was surprising to him. Just from looking at Giovanni, he knew they were related through their father, but he never knew his papa had not been born an immortal. It wasn't a subject that had ever been broached. "Papa never said." He spoke more to himself than to anyone in the room.

"I think you should tell them everything from the beginning, Giovanni." Liliana moved across the room to stand beside him. She placed a hand on his chest. "They need to hear it all."

Giovanni nodded. "Yes. I know this. It's just... I'm having a difficult time figuring out where to begin."

"The beginning would be nice," Marco growled.

"Of course, but I'll need to sit down. My story is quite long and it isn't pretty." He pulled up a chair from one of the far corners of the room and moved it to the center to give everyone a good view of him while he spoke.

Giovanni sat down raking his fingers through his hair. The muscles twitched in his face and he seemed to struggle to find his next words.

Dante flexed and unflexed his fingers with impatience. He wanted to tell the older vampire to get on with it, but something stopped him. A fleeting emotion he didn't quite recognize briefly flitted through the depths of Giovanni's serious gaze.

After several moments of silence, Giovanni finally spoke. "My tale begins with a girl. She was by far the most beautiful woman in her village and because of it, she was much sought after. Men from neighboring towns would visit the tiny *villaggio* to catch a glimpse of her just to see if the stories of her loveliness were true. She —"

"I'm sure you have a point to this, but you need to hurry up and get to it." Romeo's nostrils flared, his narrowed cobalt gaze conveying every bit of impatience Dante felt.

Giovanni held up his palm. "To understand the present, one must first learn from the past. Bear with me, brother."

A scowl twisted Romeo features into an angry mask. "Don't fucking call me that. We're not —"

"Romeo!" Dante shook his head. "Let him finish."

Giovanni gave Dante a slight smile. "Thank you. As I was saying, this girl's beauty had become renowned, but all the attention went to her head. After a while, she'd come to expect the admiration and adulation as her due. She'd received a number of marriage proposals, but was unwilling to accept the fate of being a mere farmer's wife. Word traveled to the don of the land about this particular beauty and she was summoned to his castle. This was exactly the type of suitor the girl was looking for. Though the don was getting on in years and the girl wasn't quite sixteen, it placated his ego to have such a prize as his next mistress."

Maggie gasped. "She was just a baby. He took advantage of her."

Giovanni shook his head. "It was a different time. Most women back then were already married with a couple children by the age of fourteen. If anything, the girl was approaching spinsterhood. Anyway, she saw the don's offer of protection as her opportunity to enter the lifestyle she dreamed of, though once she became his mistress she wasn't content to simply remain his bed warmer."

"Why didn't he offer for her hand?" Christine asked.

"Because the don was already married to a woman from a very powerful family. But this didn't matter to the girl, who by the way was quite cunning. She managed to convince the don to install her in the *palazzo*, instead of one of the don's many other elaborate properties. This was an insult to the *patrona*, but the don was so enchanted by his young lover there wasn't much he wouldn't offer her. Besides, it was no secret the don was unhappy his wife had not provided him an heir, although there was plenty of evidence to support the fact he was the sterile one." Giovanni twisted his lips in derision.

"After the girl moved into the palazzo, the *patrona* fell ill. Some said unnaturally so. Within weeks, she was dead. Many of the villagers whispered of seeing the girl visiting the hut of an old woman known for mixing tonics and potions. Others say, the *patrona* died because she lacked the will to live upon suffering the humiliation of having her husband's mistress under the same roof. It's pretty safe to say, however, that the girl had left nothing to chance where getting what she wanted was concerned." Giovanni stood up again and resumed his fretful pacing.

Dante wanted him to get to the end of this tale just as much as anyone in the room probably did, but as the story unfolded, he had to admit it was a riveting one. Biting his bottom lip, he held back the many questions swirling around in his mind. Patience wasn't one of his strong points and sitting through this was definitely a test.

After what seemed like an especially long pause, Giovanni continued. "The don, concerned with producing an heir, took a new wife."

"But you said the don loved her," Christine pointed out.

The storyteller shrugged. "I said he was enthralled by her. There's a difference. Besides, love had nothing to do with it. In those times and even today, powerful people treat marriage as a business arrangement. It's true the don adored his beautiful young mistress, but she was still just a commoner, not fit to bear his heir. This, of course, didn't sit well with the girl, who felt her charms should have been enough."

"But they weren't?" Christine asked.

A slight smile touched Giovanni's lips as he shook his head. "No. As I said, within weeks the don was married, again. Discontent with her lot, but not ready to give up on her quest to be the next *patrona*, the girl decided to capitalize on the don's infertility. Knowing how much he wanted a son, she was determined to get him one. On a side note, she'd been unfaithful to the don even from the very beginning, but she'd always managed to avoid an accident." He air quoted the last three words. "Her target was a young stable boy by the name of Giovanni, fifteen to her eighteen years at the time, and like any other hot-blooded male, he was in her thrall."

Dante couldn't hold the gasp that tumbled from his lips. Unable to contain his energy, he bounded to his feet. "My father?" He sought out the faces of his brothers. Judging from their expressions, they were thinking along the same lines as he.

Giovanni nodded. "*Our* father." His narrowed gaze said it all. He would no longer be denied their connection. "Our father was infatuated with her, but he wasn't as malleable as her other conquests were. He had honor, and his loyalty to the don prevented him from giving in right away when she blatantly threw herself at him. This intrigued the girl because no one had ever resisted her before. It took a while, but she finally wore down his resistance. Not long after, she was with child. Being naive and enamored with his lover, Papa tried to convince her to run away with him so they could be married and raise their child together. She, of course, laughed in his face and told him his usefulness had expired."

Dante snorted. "A little premature, considering she couldn't know if she was pregnant with a son."

"This is true, but she was so used to getting her way in most cases she didn't for a minute doubt her child was anything but. As it turned out, she did, in fact, give birth to a son, which she promptly declared as the don's. Eager to latch onto anything which disproved his sterility, he accepted her lie and was so grateful he made her his third wife."

"But what about his second one? Wasn't he still married? Divorce was nearly impossible back then," Dante mused.

Giovanni nodded his agreement. "There was no need. The second *patrona* fell ill not long after the girl conceived. She suffered from the same mysterious illness as the don's first wife."

"Wasn't the don suspicious? He might have been forgiven for thinking his first wife died of natural causes, but when the second one succumbed to the same sickness, didn't he suspect something?" Niccolo wondered out loud.

"One would think so, but he had his heir. The girl had finally achieved her goal. Once she had the power she desired, she returned her attention to Papa. He presented a challenge to her. He wanted nothing more to do with her after being used. The new *patrona* was not used to being told no and refused to take that as his final word. She set out to seduce him, but he remained firm in his resolve to keep things platonic. Only when she used a love potion, she'd gotten from the medicine woman she sometimes frequented, was she able to resume the affair. I was the result. Of course, I'm sure you've already figured out Adonis was the first child I spoke of. She named me after our father to secretly taunt the don, and in her twisted mind she believed it would keep our father close."

"If our father wanted nothing more to do with your mother, then why did he stay?" Dante demanded. If there was one thing anyone couldn't dispute about his father, it was his integrity. It was understandable Giovanni may have been under the influence of a love potion, but why did he stick around long enough for Giovanni's mother to use such a concoction on him?

The older vampire sighed. "He wanted to be near his son, and my mother wasn't above using a little emotional blackmail. By the time I'd come along, he had double the incentive to remain in his position. He couldn't claim us as his own or it could mean our deaths and his. Besides, he was a poor servant. Adonis and I had the opportunity to grow up in a style that he couldn't provide. Once the love potion wore off, he stayed clear of her as he vowed he would. In the meantime, the don poured all his affection and love onto Adonis, molding him to be the kind of man worthy of the Sarducci name. For all his lack of foresight where his young wife was concerned, he was a hard man and every bit the proud aristocrat. He was determined to make sure Adonis knew how to use his station in life."

"And you?" Dante asked softly, wondering if the don was a contributing factor to Adonis's evil.

A humorless laugh escaped Giovanni's lips. "Me? He simply ignored me unless it was convenient for him or he wanted to reprimand me for some transgression he believed I committed. Looking back, I think deep down he knew we weren't his sons. We looked nothing like him, you see, but at least Adonis had our mother's coloring. Other than my green eyes, I didn't look anything like either one of them. So, I stayed out of his way. In the meantime, my mother found a way to manipulate our father by using me. She'd bring me to him when the don wasn't around, and when Papa didn't fall in line with her wishes, she'd keep me away from him. As I grew older, I became close to this man who I believed was merely a servant. I think I always knew he was my real sire because I felt nothing for the don. I would sneak off to see Papa when Mama was distracted or with one of her many other lovers. My bond with him strengthened in those instances."

So many questions flowed through Dante's mind. What about Adonis? And how did *his* mother come into play?

Giovanni held up his hand. "All will be answered in time, brother."

Dante should have been annoyed at how Giovanni had read his mind, but he only had his self to blame for letting his guard down in his eagerness to hear the rest of the story. Somehow, he managed to contain his curiosity.

"Despite the don's attempt to mold Adonis into what he deemed a proper aristocrat, Adonis was sensitive, kind, and quite giving."

Snorts of disbelief sounded throughout the room.

Giovanni scowled, showing annoyance for the first time since he entered the room. "Adonis was not always the way he is now. He shielded me from the don's wrath on numerous occasions and he was loved by all. Even my mother held some affection for him, or at least as much as one such as she could have."

"So what happened?" Dante demanded.

"Again, I must ask you to hold your questions until I'm finished. I promise, all your questions will be answered in due time, but this piece is very important. Now where did I leave off? Ah, yes. My mother. It came to pass when the old don grew ill. His sisters and their families came to visit, believing they would be burying their relative. Before anyone asks, yes, Mother was up to her old tricks again. Adonis was thirteen at the time and I eleven, so she believed with the don gone, she could bend the heir, Adonis, to her will, thus making her power absolute. She'd underestimated the don's family, however. They'd long suspected Adonis and I weren't the don's sons, and that being the case, his oldest nephew was the next in line to inherit his title and lands." Giovanni paused. "To shorten this already long story, the don's family and my mother didn't get along, and even though she knew they were watching her like a hawk, she couldn't stay away from our father."

"She was in love with him," Dante mused, rubbing his chin.

Giovanni smiled, shaking his head. "Hardly. The only person my mother truly loved was herself. No, the term I'd use is obsession. He was the one man who wasn't so easily swayed by her charms. Through it all, the *patrona* wasn't completely unaware of the precarious situation she found herself in with the don's family, so she used her charms to seduce Fabricio, the don's true heir. And like countless men before him, he fell under her spell. Unfortunately for her, he was so enthralled he'd seek her out whenever she wasn't in sight, which is how it finally happened. Fabricio followed my mother to our father's quarters and was doubly shocked. Not only because he'd fancied himself in love with her, but he'd not laid eyes on the stable master thus far. It was quite obvious to him Adonis and I were the servant's children, and seeing my mother forcing her attentions on this servant was all the proof of her duplicity he needed.

"Realizing her predicament, my mother tried to convince Fabricio not to say anything, but she hadn't counted on his ambition. He took the information and used it against her. When confronted with the news, the don could no longer ignore what had been right before his eyes all along. Papa was dragged from the stables and beaten to within an inch of his life before being sentenced to death."

"My mother was denounced and Adonis and I were labeled bastards. To say the don was furious for having been made a fool of so publicly was an understatement. He ordered her to be dragged through the village naked and declared an adulteress. The villagers threw stones and shouted curses at her. We walked beside her as she was shamed for the world to see. Adonis and I tried to shield her as best we could, but one of the rocks caught me in the temple and I nearly passed out and Adonis had taken such a pelting he was barely conscious. It's quite possible the three of us would have died were it not for a powerful storm. Like magic, the sky went black and it rained like nothing anyone had ever seen before. The villagers scattered and the soldiers who'd held us captive ran away. However, we had nowhere to go. Shamed and humiliated, we were now outcasts. We were shunned by everyone except Old Sophia, the healer my mother had gone to for her remedies over the years. She—"

"The one who'd been supplying your mother with the poison?" Romeo interrupted.

Giovanni nodded. "Yes. Old Sophia had plans of her own, you see. She intended to steal my mother's beauty for her own, but that was all to come later. In the meantime, our father was scheduled to hang and would have if not for the aid of a young female vampire who took pity on him. Her name was Maria. "

"*My* mother," Dante whispered more to himself than for anyone else's benefit. "How did she get involved in all this?"

"Shortly before my mother's affair with Papa was discovered, he befriended a young woman who he'd become besotted with. At the time, he didn't realize she was a vampire. Upon learning his fate, Maria helped him to escape with the aid of a charm she received from a witch she knew. She had been responsible for the storm that day."

"Why would she want to help your mother?" Dante asked.

"It wasn't for my mother, but for Adonis and me. She couldn't allow the sons of the man she'd fallen in love with to die. Once she saved Papa, she had no choice but to bring him over; otherwise he would have died from the injuries inflicted on him."

"I see." Dante nodded in understanding of his parents' twisted past. From what he understood, his mother had been a young vampire when her family had been killed by rogues. She'd barely escaped with her life. Even after many years had passed, Mama didn't like speaking of the loss of her family. "Go on," he prompted Giovanni.

"Papa and Maria sought Adonis and me out in time to save Mama from Old Sophia. It turns out the 'old woman' was far older than anyone suspected, though her

177

true appearance was that of a younger woman. She used the old lady guise to lure in her victims into a false sense of security. We learned after the fact that she practiced black magic and intended to use it to steal my mother's essence. It's what kept her alive. Papa and Maria managed to kill the old woman, but barely. Sophia was quite powerful, having used the wicked arts for so long. Papa was furious at the danger our mother had put Adonis and me in, and he told her he'd take us with him. I was willing to go, but Adonis was not. He believed his loyalty lay with our mother. Besides, he was a little resentful to know he wasn't the son of a powerful don but that of a servant. My mother was still obsessed with Papa and thought she could use us to hold onto him, but she hadn't counted on Maria. When he rejected her, I think the little sanity she was holding onto began to slip away. I'm sure it was a difficult decision for him, but he let us remain with her, though he was never far away. I would sneak off to meet up with him."

Dante frowned. "I'm finding it difficult to reconcile how Papa could have left his sons in the clutches of a madwoman."

"If I needed him, I knew how to get in contact with him, so technically, he never left us. I think at the time he believed Mother might actually care a little for us and perhaps, we would keep her out of trouble. Mother, in the meantime, thought he would love her again if she was young forever. She'd stumbled upon Sophia's books and scrolls on the black arts and began to practice some spells of her own. But she was most interested in the one that would keep her forever beautiful. The spell required human sacrifice, however. She began luring young women to her cottage where she would kill them, stealing their souls and beauty, much like Sophia had done before her. Once Papa caught wind of it, he renounced her and demanded Adonis and I come with him. By then, I was fifteen and Adonis seventeen, old enough to make our own decisions. I wanted to go with him, but once again, Adonis refused. His hatred for our father had only grown over the years, mainly because Adonis blamed our papa for what Mother had become.

"I think Papa would have killed my mother for what she'd done had Adonis not protected her. He backed off, but Papa knew if she remained alive more innocent women would die, so he gave her an ultimatum: leave the area or he would kill her. She screamed at him and called him *Il Diavolo* and said he was heartless. Slightly insane she might have been, but she was no fool. She and Adonis packed up and disappeared. It broke Papa's heart to see Adonis leave, knowing it wasn't likely the rift would ever be repaired between them. I went with Papa and Maria and for the first time in my life, I was truly happy. Anyone could see how much in love those two were. They both cared about me and I grew very affectionate toward Maria. I'd finally discovered a mother's love. Eventually, Papa brought me over because I'd fallen quite ill from pneumonia. It was often fatal back then. From that point on, we lived a relatively peaceful existence, and our family grew with your arrival, little brother." Giovanni smiled as he directed his gaze toward Dante.

Something tweaked within Dante's heart. For the first time, he truly felt bonded to this other vampire, his brother. "You were there when I was born?"

"Yes. I held you in my arms when you were just a *bambino*."

"Why didn't you stay? I don't remember you!" Dante was suddenly angry for not having known about Giovanni. Why hadn't he been told?

"Ah, but I remember you and to answer your question, with your birth I was reminded of the brother I'd left behind. With Papa's blessing, I left his home to seek Adonis out and perhaps reason with him. Despite everything, we had always been close. What I didn't expect when I found Adonis and my mother was them terrorizing a young witch. They'd murdered her aunt and intended to do the same to her."

Dante's gaze fell on Liliana. He didn't need to be told it was she who Giovanni had referred to.

"I'd been away from them for a long time and a lot had changed. Mother had been practicing black magic for years and Adonis was beginning to dabble in it as well. What was worse, Mother's hatred for Papa had grown. He was the one who got away, and somehow she convinced herself he was the cause of all her problems. She, in turn, had made Adonis hate Papa, too. I, sometimes, wonder if I had stayed with my mother and Adonis if I could have changed the course of certain events. But by the time I did return. it was too late. They'd both gone more than a little mad. Despite all the havoc they'd wreaked, I couldn't kill them. Especially Adonis. I finally understood what Papa had felt all those years ago. I tried to convince Adonis to come away with me, but my mother's hold on him was too strong. I thought I finally had a breakthrough when he told me he might consider coming with me if I made him a vampire." Giovanni closed his eyes briefly and bowed his head as if that particular memory was an especially painful one.

"Forgive me, but I did. I thought I was saving him, but I only made things worse. It was all part of her plan. She'd told Adonis to tell me that. He never had any intention of coming away with me. I so desperately wanted the old Adonis back, I had been willing to commit any sin. In my mind, he was still the loving, sensitive boy I remembered. I'd even seen glimpses of the brother I once knew, but my mother's hold was too strong. Even after I learned of what she'd done, I still worked on him, and for a little while I thought he just might break away from her, but I underestimated my mother. I should have known she'd use anything in her power to manipulate him." His face twisted into a grimace of pure disgust.

"What?" Dante asked with bated breath.

"The night we were to leave, I waited for him but Adonis didn't show at the designated meeting spot, so I looked for him. I don't think I'll ever forget what I saw." The blood drained from his face only to be replaced by a greenish hue.

Dante could literally feel his older brother's anguish. Whatever it was he'd seen, must have been so devastating it was difficult to speak about. But Dante had to know. *Needed* to understand. "Tell us. What did you see?"

Giovanni clenched his hands into tight fists and closed his eyes as though struggling to get the words out. "She was screaming at him and telling him he was nothing. That he wouldn't make it without her. That he was a hateful demon spawn. She continued to rain insults on his head until he broke down. This was my brother. My *older brother*, the one who'd protected me from the don's wrath, who made me feel loved in the face of our mother's indifference, who'd been my best friend. I couldn't take another second of the abuse she was dealing out and I was about to storm into the room and defend him but something stopped me. I don't know why, but I stood by the door and continued to watch them. They were so involved in their spat, neither one of them noticed me or even sensed my presence. My mother then told him she was the only one who would love and understand him and then she..."

He paused to take another deep breath. "She started to kiss him. On the mouth, in a way no mother should kiss her son. And to my utter revulsion, Adonis returned her embrace. They fell to the floor in each other's arms. Something told me this wasn't the first time. That bitch must have been doing that to him for years, probably since he was a boy. Looking back, the signs were there, but I didn't understand. That night I left and never went back. I stayed away for years, too disgusted to face them, but while I kept my distance those two must have plotted and schemed until the night they killed Papa and Maria. I'd learned of what they'd planned through some connections of mine and how they'd scrawled '*Il Diavolo*' in blood near their bodies. I knew, then, they wouldn't rest until you were all dead. So began my dual life. I took on the persona of *Il Diavolo*. Despite their evil deeds, I protected them. Not for her, but for Adonis. I was always one step ahead of you, throwing your organization off the scent. I even employed moles to infiltrate the Underground. Remember Trent Black?"

Dante clenched his fists in outrage. "It was you! You killed him!" He stood up, anger shaking his body.

"He was going to tell you the truth, Dante. I couldn't allow that to happen."

"So you were working with Adonis all along!" Romeo accused.

Giovanni shook his head in denial. "No. I kept you from getting to Adonis. There's a difference."

"I don't see much of a difference if you're protecting him," Dante pointed out.

Giovanni raised his chin in defiance, apparently not ashamed of his actions. "While I was throwing you off his scent for centuries, I afforded you, Romeo, Niccolo, and GianMarco the same protection. I employed agents to penetrate his group as well." He turned to face Maggie. "Maggie, do you remember our meeting? It was at the train station. It was I who taught you that chant that saved you on the night of Adonis' attack. You would be dead otherwise."

She slowly nodded in response. "Yes. I remember now. You helped me."

"I've been there for all of you just as much as I have for him. I've been following the Underground making sure to provide backup even when you weren't aware of it. I've had people watching you, making sure no harm came your way as best as I could. Sometimes, there were problems because Adonis has built quite an impressive army but now, I've come to the point I've most dreaded for years. Because I knew there'd come a time when I'd have to choose a side." His sounded so forlorn Dante almost offered Giovanni comfort but managed to remain where he was standing.

Dante raised a brow. "And you choose ours?"

Giovanni inclined his head to indicate his affirmative answer.

"Why?" Dante asked.

"Because I finally realized I've been protecting the man he once was, not what he's become. I cannot abide this last scheme. He and my mother have gone too far. As much as it pains me, Adonis has to die."

Chapter Twelve

"I feel terribly for Giovanni. Imagine living like that for hundreds of years, torn between a memory and a promise." Now that she and Dante were alone again, she couldn't stop thinking about the heart-breaking story Giovanni had woven. Shortly after his revelation and more questions from the group, Giovanni suggested they retire to get some much-needed rest. He'd said they all needed to be at full strength when they finally confronted Adonis and the army of rogues he'd have guarding the children. Giovanni had pointed out that Adonis' plan required all of the brothers to be present before he actually enacted his plan which was to kill the children in their presence. He believed resting and then talking strategy would be the best course of action.

His proposal was met with dissension from the group, who at that point was too keyed up to sit around and play the waiting game, but Dante had surprisingly agreed with Giovanni. The villa was large enough to accommodate everyone with their own rooms if some of them were willing to double up. Isis was more than a little pleased when Dante had offered to share a room with her but he had done little more than pace back and forth across the room with barely suppressed energy. She watched from the edge of the bed with her hands folded in her lap.

Finally, he paused long enough to acknowledge her. "I'm sorry for being so distracted but understandably what my brother had to say was a lot to take in."

"You say that with such ease now."

"Say what?"

"Brother. Before when you mentioned a familial connection with him, it was spoken with a little disdain, but just now, you said it so naturally."

Dante gave her a half grin. "You're right. I didn't realize it until you just mentioned it. I admit, my guard was up before this meeting and even now a part of me still wants to remain cautious purely out of habit. But, I was struck by his sincerity. I felt his pain and it was real. I believe he was telling the truth. It's odd how strongly connected I felt to him. It's also incredible how he was there when I was born. I just don't understand why my parents never told me about him. "

Isis' first instinct was to walk over to Dante and wrap her arms around him for comfort but he began to pace again. "Maybe, they wanted to protect you and thought the best way to do it was to keep Giovanni and Adonis a secret."

"You're probably right."

"I can't imagine what Giovanni must have suffered through as a child, growing up in such an environment. I was fortunate to have a loving family, albeit briefly so to know the depravity of his mother." She shuddered. "Beatrice…and Adonis. That's horrible. What kind of mother would do that to her own son? It's sickening."

Suddenly, Dante stopped in his tracks and turned to face Isis. "For so many years, I've been chasing a dream."

"I'm not sure I follow you."

Dante took a seat on the bed within an arm's length of Isis. "Everything was so clear before today. I saw this situation in black-and-white. There was a mad rogue who for some reason was hell-bent on destroying my family. His reasons didn't matter; what did was that I wouldn't rest until he was dead."

"I feel a but coming," Isis prompted when he took a long pause.

"Everything I've been conditioned to believe has basically been obliterated. I don't know which way is up, what's right or left. *Dio*! I can't wrap my mind around the fact that this has all been about a woman scorned." Dante raked his fingers through his ink black locks, frustration radiating from every muscle in his body.

"It sounds to me like Giovanni's mother probably got everything she'd wanted in life because of her looks, but being denied something—or should I say someone— was more than she could handle. Most people learn to handle disappointment, but having stuff handed to you or never being told "no" can't be a good thing. The only conclusion I can come to, is there was perhaps some mental illness there to begin with. Besides, practicing black magic for as long as she has may have contributed to her psychosis."

Dante cocked his head to the side with a look of deep concentration on his face. He stroked his chin. "You're probably right, but it galls me that my parents were murdered because some selfish bitch couldn't get her way. I always believed there had to be some elaborate reason why someone wanted us all dead. Why they'd brutally slaughtered my parents and killed GianMarco's family. It's not like my past is squeaky-clean, so I believed my parents might have done something someone couldn't forgive, but this is unacceptable! Papa and Mama are gone because of the whim of a psychotic narcissist," he raged.

Isis scooted closer to him and rested her head on his shoulder. There wasn't a thing she could say to make matters better, but at least she could show Dante she was there for him.

Silence fell between them, but she could feel the tension flowing through his body. Now that they were alone, she should finally tell him about her past association with the Serpent Gang. It was on the tip of her tongue to do just that when, Dante turned to face her. He wrapped his arms around her and buried his face against her neck and pressed a kiss against her sensitive skin. "Thank you."

"For what?" she asked breathlessly. Only Dante had the power to make her forget everything around her except him.

"For being you."

Her pulse raced and her heart beat a tattoo against her chest. Isis snaked her arms around his waist and snuggled closer. The bond between the two of them could no longer be denied. Raising her head for the kiss she knew would come, Isis parted her lips.

"Beautiful," he whispered before pressing his mouth against hers in an urgent, hungry kiss. Dante grasped the sides of her face as his tongue plowed forward and he devoured her like a starving man given his first real meal in months.

Beneath the onslaught of his insistent lips, Isis gave back as good as she got, pushing her body against his until the hard wall of his chest crushed her breasts. She met his tongue with hers. His taste was amazing, so wonderfully male and wild.

Her senses reeled and her body shook with need for him. Their interlude on the plane had only whetted her appetite. She wanted more, craved it, and she wouldn't be satisfied unless this encounter ended with his cock in her pussy. Isis squirmed in his arms, trying to ease the searing heat between her thighs. A wild, animalistic need to be possessed by him came over her and slowly drove her insane. The raging fire deep within her core spread through her entire being. Her passion unleashed, Isis pushed Dante down, pinning his shoulders to the bed.

Cobalt eyes widened in surprise before she released a low growl from the back of her throat and covered his mouth with hers. This time, Isis controlled the kiss. She couldn't remember the last time she'd been so hungry for anyone. She'd never been so hungry for anyone. But it only made sense. Dante belonged to her. He was her man and she his woman. Every time they touched only confirmed they were meant for each other.

Isis lengthened her canine teeth as her arousal grew. Isis nipped his bottom lip until she tasted the coppery sweetness of his blood which only served to fuel her savage need for him.

Dante bucked from beneath her as if he was making an effort to break free of her hold, but Isis tightened her grip. She was strong, but was aware that her strength was no match for his. Dante could push her off and have her beneath him in the blink of an eye. And she appreciated his willingness to let her take charge. Besides, his mock struggle turned her on.

"You're so fucking sexy," he murmured beneath her mouth.

Isis chuckled. "That's my line." She leaned forward and ran her tongue along the shell of his ear, tracing its outline and savoring the taste of his skin.

Dante raised his hips, pressing his erection against her pelvis. A shiver raced up her spine as she remembered how hard and thick his cock was and how it had felt pulsing inside her pussy. It wouldn't be long before his stiff dick was inside her again, powerful, throbbing and taking her to a mind-shattering release. Just the thought of it sent her blood roaring through her veins, heating her from head to toe.

Unable to hold back, she gripped his shirt and ripped it apart, baring his chest to her hungry gaze. Isis smiled as she gazed upon his taut, body. Dante Grimaldi was perfection personified, from his chiseled pectoral muscles to the ripped valleys and hollows of his washboard stomach. As she ran her fingers over his chest, her stare locked with his.

"What? Why did you stop?"

She slid the tip over her tongue across her bottom lip. "I want you so much." Did that deep, guttural whisper belong to her? So full of longing and need? There was no place in the world she would rather be than right here with him in this moment.

His cobalt gaze briefly glowed. "Then take me, *bellissima*."

No further encouragement was necessary. Isis lowered her head and circled his nipple with the tip of her tongue before catching the flat disc between her teeth. His sharp intake of breath followed by a low moan prodded Isis to continue nibbling and sucking the now hardened tip.

"Isis! What are you doing to me?"

She raised her head long enough to give him a wink. "Taking you. Isn't that what you wanted?" Isis caressed his taut body, stopping only when she reached the fastening of his pants. She fumbled with his zipper, frantic to see him completely naked.

Dante tried to assist her, but Isis smacked his hand away, wanting to undress him on her own. "No. Let me."

A grin tilted his full lips. "Did I mention how much I admire a take charge woman?"

"No. Tell me now."

"Isis, I love what you're doing to me."

She wished he would tell her how much he loved *her*. Isis was hopeful he'd eventually realize his feelings for her. For now, she'd settle for his body. Eager to see every single inch of him, she removed his shoes and yanked his pants down his hard, muscled thighs. She pouted. "Underwear?"

He chuckled. "I like to change it up every now and then."

"Well, these definitely have to go." Lengthening her nails, Isis ripped his black silk boxers to shreds. "Mmm." She ran her gaze over his long, blood-engorged cock. He was every bit as thick and big as she remembered.

Dante reached for her, but she pushed him back down, exerting more than a little force. The beast within would not be satisfied until she had her wicked way with him. Placing her palms against his chest, Isis dragged her nails down his body.

Dante gritted his teeth with a sharp intake of breath. "You're going to be the death of me, woman."

"But what a way to go." She couldn't get enough of the sight of his beautifully proportioned form. It was as if he'd been molded by the hands of a master from a special piece of clay that could only bring forth perfection. She had to taste him!

Moving down his body, Isis pressed a trail of kisses against his abdomen until she reached the nest of dark hair between his thighs. His musky, masculine scent greeted her nostrils, making her want him with a rawness that took her by surprise.

"Stop teasing me," he growled, grasping the sides of her head and guiding her to his rigid shaft. Dante raised his hips, bringing his cock closer to her lips.

"Ready for it, baby?"

"You have no idea."

She raised a brow in challenge. "Oh, I think I do," she whispered, and wrapped her fingers around his cock as she slowly took him into her mouth.

Isis found it empowering to have this Dante at sexual her mercy. Tightening her lips around Dante, she swallowed him inch by delicious, hard inch. He felt so good. Tasted so good. When she bobbed her head up and down his length, he twitched and writhed beneath her oral seduction.

"Isis, your mouth is magic. This…feels…so…good." His words came out in breathy pants. He threaded his fingers through her hair, strengthening his hold as he bucked his hips and sent his cock deeper into her mouth until she had ingested all of him.

Isis gripped him harder and sucked faster. With her free hand, she cupped and fondled his balls, exploring their texture. She wanted to send him beyond the edge of reason. Dante couldn't keep still; he yanked on her hair and continued to squirm wildly. She found his response to her caresses thrilling. To know she was the cause of so much pleasure was intoxicating. Her cunt was so wet and hot she didn't know how much longer she could continue before impaling herself on his rock-hard dick.

A loud groan rumbled from his throat. "I need you now!"

Defiantly, she continued sucking his cock with the perverse desire to send him closer to his peak.

"Isis!" Dante stiffened and began to shake before he shot his seed into her mouth.

Greedy for every ounce of him, Isis sucked fervently, catching every drop of his essence. Taking her time, she ran her tongue up and down his rod like an ice pop.

"Enough!" Dante slipped his hands beneath her armpits and pulled her roughly against him until their mouths melded together. Their tongues dueled, pushing back and forth, battling for supremacy in a fight as old as time. Without breaking the tight seal of their lips, Isis and Dante tore at her clothing until she, too, was naked and ready.

The contact of bare skin against skin served to further heat her already hot flesh. The friction created as they rubbed together made Isis delirious with lust. The overwhelming need to join with him became too much for her to handle. Finally breaking the kiss, breathing ragged, she straddled his lean hips.

Locking her gaze with his passion-filled one, Isis held his cock within the circle of her eager grasp.

"Stop fucking teasing me, woman." Dante bared his descended incisors. His dark blue eyes were now a shimmery, glowing silver. Grabbing her hips, he lifted Isis high enough for her to part the damp folds of her labia and guide his cock into her channel.

With slow ease that belied the tumultuous desire raging within her veins, she gripped his dick with her cunt, squeezing and sucking him deeper. A gasp escaped her lips and Dante groaned simultaneously. Isis didn't need to be told how he felt because she knew. His body shook and his eyes were shut tight. His breath came out in shallow huffs.

She stilled, allowing herself to savor the sensation of being so decadently stretched by his thickness. Digging her nails into his sides, Isis began to gyrate on his cock, searching for her rhythm. "You feel so…mmm," she moaned. There were no words to adequately describe the feelings coursing through her. Being one with this vampire who made her heart sing was an emotional roller coaster ride of lust, love, joy, hunger, and absolute pleasure. While earth-shattering, their time on the plane couldn't come close to this experience. He was so deep inside of her Isis wasn't sure where she ended and Dante began.

Isis suspected every time she was with Dante would be better than the last, each encounter taking her to a different place, making her feel invincible and as if nothing mattered save the two of them. Nothing compared to this and Isis wasn't sure anything ever would.

"Dante, I love—" Isis caught herself and squeezed her eyes shut. No. Even though her heart was bursting with emotion, something told her not to share too much too soon. Besides, she couldn't burden him with her feelings when he was already dealing with so many familial issues. Right now, all she planned to do was give him this temporary relief and total pleasure. But later, once the children were safe with their parents and their enemies defeated, then she was going to give Dante Grimaldi all the love he could handle and more. "I love being with you like his," she amended, hoping he didn't notice her slipup.

"Me too," he whispered back, an easy smile curving his sensual lips.

As she moved her hips up and down and began to bounce on his cock, Isis leaned forward to press kisses against his torso.

Dante ground against her, tightening his already firm grip on her hips. He lengthened his fingers against her heated flesh and dug into her skin. "I've never wanted anyone as much as I want you, Isis. You're so damn hot…so fucking tight," he grunted. Eyes closed, he rolled his head from side to side, arousal giving his skin a pinkish tint as the blood rushed through his body.

She scraped her extended canines against his chest, evoking a sharp cry from his lips. All her senses were stimulated. The scent of their bodies locked together hit her nostrils, and his touch seared her skin. The sight of him so turned on by her, made Isis want him even more. They moved together in time to the rhythm of their erratically beating hearts, a choreographed dance of sex and passion so powerful she could have wept.

Dante released her hips and wrapped his arms around her waist. Then, with a quick, fluid motion, he shifted to a sitting position, driving deeper into her hot cunt.

Isis planted her knees on the sides of his hips and gripped his shoulders, increasing the pace. Her ass slapped his thighs and juices dripped from her pussy.

With a groan, Dante nuzzled her breasts. Shooting her a hungry look, he opened his mouth to reveal gleaming fangs before sinking them into the top of her breast.

Isis inhaled sharply. The link created between them as he drank her blood sent her to the edge.

Her climax was explosive, sending shock waves of heat raking through her body. She scored her nails down his back. "Dante!"

He shook and thrust harder and faster with frenzied motions until he stiffened and shot his seed up her channel.

Isis gripped his cock with her pussy walls, milking every drop of his essence. Temporarily sated, she sagged against him. "That. Was. Incredible."

Dante carefully unhinged his teeth from her skin and licked a dot of blood from the corner of his mouth. "Yes, it was. You were a wild woman." He smiled, seeming quite pleased with himself.

Her heart did somersaults. She loved this man with all her heart and she hoped for the day when he was ready to return it.

Isis had never felt this content in her life as he held her. She could stay like this forever, enjoying the silence. Enjoying him.

Dante placed a kiss on the top of her head. "I'd love to stay like this, but we should get some rest. We have a long day ahead of us tomorrow."

Isis didn't want this moment to end, but like all good things, she knew it had to. It briefly crossed her mind to mention her past while he was this relaxed, but decided against it. She didn't want her news to be a distraction and there would be another opportunity.

She hoped.

Chapter Thirteen

"This is the place." Giovanni threw the words over his shoulder as he led the way up the dark, winding path to what looked like a large brownstone that had been converted from an industrial building. Odd in appearance, it stood alone, as if everything around it had been demolished, leaving this lone, gothic monstrosity. A row of trees surrounded the house, blocking out the moonlight.

The dark cloak of night still concealed the team, producing shadows, which proved to be allies. Dante quick-stepped toward Giovanni until they were standing shoulder to shoulder. *His brother.* No matter how many times he thought of it, he was still surprised at how easily he had accepted Giovanni into his heart after all the years of cat and mouse and the surrounding mystery. Dante understood Giovanni's conflict; he was torn between two factions, wanting to do the right thing but sometimes dwelling on the dark side to accomplish his goal. Dante knew this path well because he'd walked down it on countless occasions for several years.

While he'd never consider his younger brothers burdens, the responsibility of ensuring their safety had sometimes been a test to his moral compass. The years of agony and restlessness Giovanni must have endured touched what Dante had always considered an impenetrable part of his soul. He and this vampire he'd once believed to be his enemy were kindred spirits.

His thoughts drifted toward Adonis. Was there a chance he could be redeemed or was it too late? Whether it was or not, he wasn't sure if they could turn back from the course they'd already set. "Are you sure this is where the children are being held?" He spoke in a whisper to Giovanni who now stood statue-still, looking straight ahead with his head cocked to the side. "My source tells me this is the place, but something's not right. It's too quiet. Do you hear that?"

Dante crinkled his forehead in concentration. "No. I hear nothing."

"Exactly. Not a thing. There should be night sounds, owls, crickets, and the like. The wind's not even rustling the leaves. It feels like we've stepped into some kind of void."

"I was thinking the same thing. There's some kind of magic working around us," Steel Romanov added. His blond brows were knitted together and it was clear he was also trying to figure out what was going on.

"My brother is right," Sasha agreed. "I'm not sure what kind of magic it is, however, it doesn't feel natural. I believe black magic is involved but it doesn't seem that powerful. I don't get a sense that it's being wielded by someone who's practiced it for hundreds of years." She held her hands up as if she was trying to grasp something from the air. She then lowered them, shaking her head "I can't get a read on this."

"Sasha, do you think it's those rogue vampires we've encountered? The red-eyed ones?" Cutter asked, thumbing his chin. "Black magic has given them strength beyond what they're supposed to be capable of, but the power they exude isn't quite enough to create this kind of magic even if it is weak, except..."

"If there were a lot of them, it would," Blade finished for his twin.

Dante frowned, not liking where this conversation was headed. He wasn't naive enough to think Adonis wouldn't be prepared for them, but just how many of those bastards lay in wait for them? Not that he was scared, but as always, he worried about the safety of his group and particularly his family. Pretty much all the members in their team could handle themselves in battle, but what about Maggie and Christine?

Against his and his brothers' better judgment, they'd allowed those two to talk them into coming along. In the back of his mind, he knew the women wouldn't have stayed put regardless of whether they were granted permission or not; their children's lives were on the line, after all. But would that decision end up costing them more than they bargained for? Dante shuddered to think of the agony his brothers would suffer if anything happened to their mates, but he knew Romeo and Marco would guard the women with their lives.

"Whether there's a hundred of them or a thousand, if this is where the children are being held, we have to go in there. We may be outnumbered, but we have an advantage. There are three powerful warlocks and two witches among us who could counter any black magic spells they might try to cast on us. Not to mention the shifters are on our side. Paris and his pack have always proved to be valuable allies in battle. The rest of us are also battle ready." Straightening his shoulders, Dante naturally fell into his role as leader and began to bark orders. "Steel, I'm going to need you and your brothers to see if they're using any wards on this building. Sasha and Liliana, the two of you need to cast a spell on this structure so that no one gets out unless they go through us. Paris and Aries, I'll need you two to split your pack up and take the other entrances inside. We're going to need to hit them from all sides. Wolf, go with them. I'll need three volunteers to go with Isis to scout the area for the children."

Maggie raised her hand. "I'll go with her!"

"No, you'll stay close to me as we discussed." GianMarco gave his mate a narrowed stare.

"Don't even think about it," Romeo growled, shooting Christine a stern glare when she looked as if she, too, would speak up.

Dante nodded. "It's for the best that you stay close to Marco and Romeo, ladies."

Christine pursed her lips. "But —"

Dante held up his hand to halt whatever it was she'd intended to say. He, then, turned to face the others. "Stefano, Julian, and Huck, how about it?" he asked three of the Underground agents who'd joined up with them after they'd left Giovanni's.

Once the duties were meted out, each subgroup broke apart. Before Isis went off with her team, she walked over to Dante. His heart raced and pulse quickened from her nearness. If they weren't about to go on one of the most important missions in their lives, he probably would have taken her in his arms and shown her just how much their encounter of a few hours ago had meant to him. It worried him slightly at how easily he wished to be alone with her instead of focusing on this mission which was sure to be dangerous. The woman had truly bewitched him. Shaking his head to clear it of his carnal thoughts, he nodded in acknowledgement, not wanting to reveal what was really on his mind. "Yes, Isis?"

Concern lined her face as she grasped his hands. Her blue-gray gaze searched his face for several moments before she spoke. "Be careful." Giving his hands a squeeze before releasing them, she turned on her heel and walked off with her group without giving him a chance to reply. Dante wanted to call her back but couldn't. Too many lives were at risk.

Giovanni whispered to him, "Something isn't right. My source said this was where the kids would be held. I know this is one of Adonis's main hideouts, but there's something off about this place. I'm starting to have a very bad feeling."

Dante frowned. This wasn't exactly the best time to tell him this. The atmosphere around here was strange enough as it was without Giovanni's premonitions. "Why?"

"I can't really say, but it's a feeling I have."

Dante shrugged. "Well, there's really no time to ponder it now. We're here, and you said your source told you this is where the children are being held."

Giovanni sighed. "I know, but I had men who were supposed to follow up with me, and I haven't heard from them. They usually get back to me promptly. I probably should have told you this earlier, but I didn't want to concern you." He paused to rake his fingers through his dark hair. "You're right. It doesn't matter at this point anyway. We go in when we get the signal from Sasha and Liliana."

Giovanni seemed nervous about something, and in the short time Dante had known him, he hadn't found edginess to be one of his older brother's natural characteristics. Maybe something was wrong. Dante took a moment to check the rest of their entourage, ensuring everyone was there and accounted for.

"Dante, how well do you know Isis?" Giovanni's words filtered into Dante's mind.

Dante stiffened, surprised at his brother's question. *"Well enough. It's a hell of a time for you to ask me something like that. Why the sudden interest in Isis?"* Was it mere curiosity or something deeper? A burning anger ripped through him the likes of which he'd never experienced where any woman was concerned. He thought he'd been jealous before, but that had been nothing compared to how he felt right now.

"Calm down. I'm not asking for the reason you're thinking, but I am concerned. It's clear you two have feelings for each other, but Liliana has told me something I think you should know."

Dante frowned. What did Liliana know about Isis, and if it was something so dire, why was Giovanni telling him about this now? *"What?"*

"Maybe she bears watching is all."

Dante narrowed his eyes. *"You can't fucking say shit like that and expect me not to want to know what the hell you're talking about. What is it I should know about her?"* He'd almost said the words out loud, but managed to maintain the telepathic link with the older vampire.

What Giovanni would have said next remained unknown because Liliana chose that moment to reappear. "It's done. Once we enter the house, none of our enemies will be able to escape."

Giovanni nodded. "Then we go."

Dante gestured the rest of the group forward and made his way to the front entrance, a large oak double door with two iron handles. A lion's head with a metal ring in its mouth served as a knocker. There was no point in trying to sneak in. Whoever waited on the other side probably knew someone would come for the children. He caressed the door and gave it a push, testing its strength to discern how much force would be needed to break through. Once determined, he sent a mental signal to Paris and the others waiting at the other entrances that they'd enter on three.

Dante turned to the group. "Keep your head and look out for each other. We don't know what we'll be up against, but whatever it is, we have to be ready for it. Once I bust through this door, we go. Remember the plan and we can all get out of here alive." Taking a deep breath, he whispered a silent prayer for the safety of his family and comrades.

Balling his hands into tight fists, he pounded the door with enough force to knock it down. The sound of splitting wood and squeaking hinges created enough noise to wake the dead, and Dante tensed in anticipation, expecting their enemies to descend on them any second now.

When nothing happened, he wondered why, but it didn't stop him from crossing the threshold. It was darker inside the house than it had been outside. All the curtains were drawn or the windows were blackened; he couldn't tell which. Dank, stale air assaulted his nostrils, and the dampness of the air seeped into his clothes and chilled him to the bone. The place seemed abandoned, as if no one had stepped foot inside for years, yet he couldn't shake the sensation of being watched by malevolent eyes.

A dark evil lurked within the house, but he couldn't see anything, even with his extra-sensitive vision. Why didn't they come out? His nerves were on edge and every muscle in his body was tense in anticipation.

"What now? It doesn't look like anyone is here," Nico murmured from his left.

A rumbling unexpectedly shook the house, nearly knocking Dante off balance. "I think you have the answer to your question, Nico. Shit!" An unseen forced shoved him in the chest, sending Dante stumbling backward. This time he did fall, but returned to his feet in a flash.

Several pairs of glowing red eyes appeared from out of thin air, and invisible hands wrapped themselves around his throat. What the fuck? Only those menacing eyes remained visible, but the attack against him was no less dangerous. Someone or something attempted to squeeze the wind from his esophagus. Dante strained to steal a glance at his team members only to see they, too, were in similar predicaments.

They all seemed to be fighting off their own assailants. The warlocks and witches began to chant simultaneously, likely in an attempt to counter their undetectable foes. The house was suddenly bathed in light, but despite the illuminating sheen it produced, their attackers remained invisible.

Dante caught Steel's eye. "Do...something," he managed to gasp, gripping the unseen hands wrapped around his neck. Shifting his fingers, he lengthened them to talons and dug into his invisible adversary's flesh. A primal cry reached his ears. He, now, knew they could be hurt—whatever they were. But why the hell couldn't he see these motherfuckers? And he wondered about their incredible strength. They seemed more powerful than the rogues he'd encountered previously.

A howl tore through the air, the sound of a shifter going through its metamorphosis, but it wasn't the deep, throaty bay of a male. It was more feminine. Isis! He had to get to her and make sure she was okay. Bringing his knee up, Dante connected with what he hoped was the invisible villain's midsection. He must have hit his mark because his opponent's grip loosened on his throat, giving Dante the opportunity to grasp at the rogue's forearms and toss him off. Though this momentarily freed him, Dante was caught by what felt like a fist smashing into the side of his face. Realizing he couldn't rely on his sight to fight this battle, he used his ears to guide him.

Sidestepping another oncoming blow, Dante threw his fist out and connected with a solid object. A body. Quickly taking advantage of nailing his target, he grabbed the figure and head-butted it before slamming his knee into its middle.

Dante pummeled his unseen enemy, unleashing every ounce of his might and all his frustrations of the past several months. As he continued to throw punches, an arm hooked around his neck, yanking him away from his target. The force of a fist slammed into his stomach.

Whatever spell the rogues were using to make themselves invisible must have been hard to reverse, because the warlocks and witches continued to chant. The black magic surrounding them was probably more powerful than anything they'd dealt with before.

Taking blow after blow, he struggled to break the tight hold he found himself in. A loud scream rent the air, followed by the acrid scent of death. His heart plummeted within his chest, and he prayed the smell didn't belong to one of his allies or worse, his family. Managing to turn his head, he saw Julian fall to the ground, his eyes lifeless. Niccolo held on to something, while Romeo tried to pull an invisible enemy off Christine.

Giovanni appeared by his side, whispering something under his breath in a tongue Dante couldn't discern. Whatever had been said must have done the trick because the rogues holding him captive became visible. Barely. They were still translucent, but at least he could, now, make out their outlines—just in time to see one of the creatures come toward him with fangs bared, its intention seemingly to rip out Dante's throat.

With no time to dwell on what his brother had done to make their enemies detectable, Dante ducked and caught his enemy with a fist to the chest. Giovanni grabbed the rogue behind Dante and kicked it in the midsection. Another howl filtered through the room, reminding Dante to find Isis to ensure her safety.

He ripped through the side of his attacker's face with his sharp claws, and pulled off a large chunk before gouging out its eyeballs with his thumbs. Dante stuck his fingers through the now empty eye sockets and pulled his enemy's face apart, to expose the skull beneath. The rogue screamed in agony, madly clawing at the air now that it had been rendered blind.

Bloodlust gripped Dante, giving him the strength to tear through the evil vampire's chest until he reached its heart. Pulling his fist back, Dante smashed it through the now gaping hole, connecting with the pulsing organ to deliver a deathblow. Before the body hit the ground, two more semi-invisible fiends were on him.

Managing to twist out of their viselike grips, he grabbed them by the backs of their heads and smashed them together, cracking skulls and stunning them in the process. Using their temporary incapacitation to his advantage, he repeated the move, then tore through the chest of the one on his right and yanked out its heart before stuffing it down the other's throat. His team might have been outnumbered but the rogues had ignited a fury within him that stirred his menacing need to make these motherfuckers pay. He intended to make every death as painful as possible.

One rogue clawed his face, shredding flesh. Dante gritted his teeth against the pain, making a mental note to make this one suffer more. He circled his hands around his antagonist's throat and squeezed with all his might. Its eyeballs bulged and looked as if they would pop out of their sockets. Releasing his grip, Dante smacked the sides of the rogue's head like he had cymbals. Blood oozed out of its ears, but it wasn't enough to suit Dante's bloodthirsty mood. Opening his mouth with descended incisors, he clamped onto the exposed throat, ripped out a large chunk, and spit it back in the rogue's face.

From the corner of his eye, he caught a glimpse of Nico being knocked backward and Dante came to his senses, realizing there was no more time for dallying. He had to take care of business and help out where he was needed. With a fist through the chest, he found the creature's heart and gave it a tight squeeze until it exploded. Without hesitating, he rushed to assist Nico with the three red-eyed vampires attacking him.

Dante pulled one of them off his brother, enabling Nico to hop to his feet and deliver a staggering hit to the rogue closest to him. Luckily, Dante's enemy this time around wasn't as strong as the last three, and unlike the others, was clearly visible. Why was this one so different? Not that it mattered; he'd be dead like the rest.

After he dispatched his tenth rogue, he lost count, but they seemed to keep coming. Thankfully, from what he could see as he quickly scanned the room, no one else in his group had fallen, although there had been several close calls. Romeo's head was nearly taken off, but with the assistance of his friend, Wolf, he turned the tables on his foe, much to Dante's relief.

Surprisingly, the women were holding their own. Dante saw Maggie kicking the shit out of one of the rogues, while Christine straddled another one on the ground and banged its head against the floor. There was definitely something to be said about a mother protecting her young. Romeo and GianMarco stayed near their mates, providing them the backup they needed.

It seemed, however, that the more enemies they fought off, the more came at them. There seemed to be close to a hundred of them. He had to get to Isis! Fighting his way through two more opponents, Dante made his way to the other side of the house. He found her in full shifted form, a graceful wolf with a dark brown coat. She was smaller than the male shifters but no less dangerous. Isis reared back on her paws, snarling at an advancing adversary. Baring a mouthful of sharp teeth, she sprang forward, knocking the rogue onto the ground before clamping her jaw down on its shoulder.

Like the ferocious beast she'd become, she bit into his arm and tore it to ribbons. Though her opponent managed to toss her off, she was on him again in an instant, ripping into his chest until she found the heart. However, before the thing died, it cried out, "You fucking traitor, bitch!"

What the hell was that supposed to mean? He didn't have time to dwell on the question before two more creatures came after him. Ducking, he missed a blow flying his way before dealing out one of his own. Taking one of his adversaries by the arm, he spun him around and slammed him into another one. Their skulls cracked when their heads collided.

With a low growl, Isis jumped at the closest red-eyed vampire and sank her teeth into its face. Savagely tearing off flesh, the rogue became unrecognizable as she continued to claw away at him until only tattered shreds of tendon and broken bone remained. She was vicious in her attack, not stopping until the creature beneath her paws lay dead. Not bothering to pause for a rest, she pounced on another rogue. Blood coated her fur and pieces of flesh stuck between her teeth. Dante had never been more thankful in his life to have someone on his side. He knew then she would be able to handle herself, though he didn't want to stray far.

She may have been fierce in battle, but his protective instinct wouldn't allow him to leave her side even as she vanquished yet another one of the monsters.

During battle, Dante noticed a peculiar phenomenon. Some of their enemies possessed that see-through quality, while others he could see just fine. As one of the shimmery rogues threw him against the wall, it finally dawned on him where he'd seem some of these vampires before. The Serpent Gang. He couldn't identify the semi-visible ones, but the others were definitely members of the gang they'd been trailing for weeks. It seemed as if every single member was here and they were even more powerful than they had a right to be.

"Dante, watch out!" Sasha called before a fist crashed into his jaw. Woozy, he fell back. Stars danced before his eyes and blood filled his mouth. His own. The balled fist came forward again, but the snarling creature was lifted off its feet by an unseen force. Dante saw Sasha raising her hands in the air, controlling their enemy's movement as Isis leaped through the air, catching it with a vicious swipe of her paw.

Sasha let the rogue fall to the ground with a thud as Isis went to work. One of the red-eyed fiends grabbed Isis by the tail and swung her around like a rag doll, banging her against the floor. She howled in agony, struggling to break free of its grip.

"Isis, hold on!" Dante would have been at her side were it not for a pair of arms wrapping around his midsection and squeezing him in a massive bear hug. Dante slammed his head back, connecting with his foe's face to break free. A long metal rod came flying through the air toward his head, and by the sheerest of luck, he twisted out of the creature's hold just in time. The foreign object pierced his enemy's skull, knocking the rogue to the ground. Someone else would have to deal with the writhing vampire, because Dante needed to get to Isis.

He backhanded the rogue with all his might, making it angry enough to focus its attention on him, and most importantly, let Isis go. He pummeled the thing, backing it into a corner, but even then he didn't stop. If anyone messed with his woman, they were fucking with him. Dante was so caught up in punishing the bastard for daring to lay hands on Isis, he didn't have time to think about the magnitude of what he'd just admitted to himself. Isis was well and truly his woman. Maybe he'd known it from the moment he'd laid eyes on her, but there had been far too much going on.

There was too much happening now, but seeing her in danger had awakened the feelings that had been dormant. The discovery of new love gave him the second wind he needed to fight through several more of the creatures. If Adonis's plan had been to exhaust them, it was certainly working. He'd never battled such a large group of adversaries at once, but after what seemed like an eternity, it seemed that their foes' numbers had finally diminished.

"Isis, come with me," he called to her. They had to search for the children. She raced to his side and looked up at him with eyes that were now dark green ringed with gold. Her tongue hung out as she panted for air, obviously as worn out from the fight as he was. "Are you all right?" He brushed his fingers against the back of her head.

Her ears perked up. *"After this is over I think I'll sleep for days, but other than that, I'm fine."*

"You were taking some lumps over there."

"So were you. Shit!" Without warning, she jumped past him and knocked another one of their opponents to the ground. He must have been coming after Dante, but she'd saved him, making short order of dispatching the fiend.

Dante looked around him to ensure he wouldn't be surprised by another attack. Surveying his surroundings, he was thankful to see his brothers alive and holding their own. Giovanni had a rogue by the throat, holding him in the air with one hand while punching him in the face with the other. Romeo held the arm of one foe, while Wolf grasped the other and they yanked them off. Sasha and Maggie tag-teamed another rogue, while Nico and Marco prevailed in their own fights.

He tore through the house, relieved to see most of his comrades were also still alive, despite their having been outnumbered. Both sides were nearly even now, and he knew they wouldn't have been able to accomplish what should have been an impossible feat without the skill set of each team member working together. The diminished group of rogues gave Dante and Isis the opportunity to properly search the house.

They cautiously made their way through each room, only to be greeted by at least one or two of those red-eyed motherfuckers. As a team, he and Isis killed everything that dared to cross their paths. As their search continued, Dante grew agitated. There was no sign of the children and he was beginning to believe this was one elaborate set up. And what was worse, something else was bugging the shit out of him, but he couldn't remember what it was.

When they came to yet another room, a tall, muscular, ebony-skinned vampire with waist-length, dreadlocked hair and glowing red eyes stood in the middle of it as if he'd been waiting for them. But unlike the other rogues who'd immediately attacked them, he laughed. "Isis. It took you long enough to get here," he greeted with a wide, malicious grin.

Dante recognized Black Adder, the leader of the Serpent Gang, from pictures and a few near encounters. But why would he be waiting for Isis?

Isis snarled at the red-eyed beast, rearing back on her hind legs as if she was about to spring, but Dante forestalled her. He wanted a piece of this rogue himself. He flashed across the room to the Serpent Gang leader with hands clenched into fists. Before Dante could reach him, Black Adder dissipated and reappeared on the other side of the room.

Baring menacing fangs, the rogue tossed his head back and laughed. Dante rushed at him again, but with the same result. This dance of cat and mouse continued for several more moves. Even when Isis tried to catch up with Black Adder, he would already be out of the way. This black magic shit was pissing Dante off, and when he finally got his hands on that bastard, it wouldn't be pretty.

Black Adder reappeared above them with his back clinging to the ceiling as if he were a spider, forcing Dante and Isis to crane their necks to see him. The rogue laughed again. "Isis, there's no need to continue the pretense. Tell your boyfriend whose side you're really on. Everything was arranged after your little trip to Vegas, remember?"

Dante stiffened. Had she been playing him all along?

"Don't listen to him, Dante. I don't know what he's talking about," she projected to his mind.

"Isis, there's no need to hide your thoughts from me. We're connected, remember? Forever and always. When you promised to be mine, the link between us was created, never to be broken. I'll forgive you for what you did on that plane, and" — his grin widened — "a few hours ago." Black Adder focused his red gaze on Dante. "Was it good, Grimaldi? She's always been a wild piece of ass. I can't fault you for sampling some of that sweet shifter pussy, but you had to know you could never possibly handle someone with her insatiable appetites."

The thought that had plagued him earlier returned full force. That comment from the rogue who'd accused her of being a traitor suddenly made sense.

Dante's heart plummeted within his chest. It was his worst nightmares coming true. This was a setup and Isis was a part of the entire conspiracy. Paris had tried to warn him, as had Giovanni. But he'd stubbornly trusted her, believed she could never do him harm, that she had feelings for him. His beliefs had proven false. It was happening all over again for him— another Flora situation—but this was far worse.

Several emotions warred within him all at once: rage, pain, sadness, disbelief, confusion, and most of all, betrayal. She'd betrayed him. Isis was a liar, who'd led him to believe…

The rage won out. Springing in the air, he reached for the ceiling, managing to catch an off guard Black Adder in a viselike grip. Stunned by the swiftness of his capture, the other vampire attempted to break free from Dante without success.

"No! Dante, don't! Listen to me!" Isis's voice filtered into his mind, but he was beyond listening, especially when it came to anything she had to say to him. Her attempt to save her boyfriend further enraged him. He slashed his talons against Black Adder's face.

His adversary slapped his hands over Dante's ears. Hard. His ears rang, but he kept his fingers locked around the rogue's throat. A fist slammed into his stomach and the air whooshed from his lungs, making him loosen his grip. Black Adder followed that move with a punch to the chest, sending Dante flying across the room. By the time he'd lunged to his feet, the Serpent Gang leader was gone.

Breathing raggedly, he focused his attention on Isis, who stood in the center of the room. She'd shifted back to her human form. Blood covered her naked frame from head to toe. Dante wasn't sure whether to take her in his arms or choke the hell out of her.

Her eyes were wide, silently imploring him, but for what he wasn't sure. One thing he did know: He wasn't in the mood to listen to any more lies. He'd trusted her. What they'd shared had all been a ploy to lead them to their demise. Not only had she managed to dupe him, but Pack Kyriakis as well. Paris was generally an astute judge of character, but apparently not as good as Dante thought.

He clenched his hands into fists at his sides, willing himself not to kill her right there on the spot. Though he didn't like battling women, he would take the bitch out if she made one wrong move.

She held her hand out to him, but he gazed at it with all the contempt that welled inside him.

"Dante, I don't know why he said the things he did, but they weren't true. I swear. I'd never betray you."

His nostrils flared, and he barely resisted the urge to call her a liar. Too angry to even speak, he continued to stare directly into her deceitful eyes. How many times had he looked into them thinking she was the most genuine and open person he'd ever met? When he'd gazed into those eyes, he believed himself invincible, that he could conquer anything and anyone. She had been the reason he saw light again when the dark had threatened to consume him. Yet, it had all been a lie. All of it!

216

Eve Vaughn

This had been a setup from the start, and if Isis was in on it, perhaps Giovanni's source was too. After all, there was no sign of the children and "the source" had told him they'd be here. With all the rogues they'd battled, Dante suspected Adonis hadn't counted on them surviving, or maybe he'd wanted them to, but barely. Knowing Adonis's sadistic streak, he probably intended to keep the children alive long enough for them to witness the children's murder. Everything was finally coming together. Would Adonis be making an appearance soon? Or, perhaps, Beatrice.

Isis wrapped her arms over her bare breasts. The movement drew Dante's attention to her again. His tongue cleaved to the roof of his mouth and the words wouldn't come.

"Please say something." Her eyes glistened with the suspicious sheen of tears. Knowing what a good actress she was, Dante didn't buy it for a minute.

Remembering his rule not to hit a woman unless he needed to defend himself, he turned on his heel and made his way out of the room, leaving her standing alone in the room. He hesitated for the briefest of seconds, hoping deep down that she could offer some kind of explanation, something to show him he'd misconstrued the situation, but her silence spoke volumes.

He flashed out of the room and raced back toward the stairs. His team still fought on valiantly, but the numbers were now on their side. His group now double and, in some cases, triple-teamed the remaining rogues.

Grief hit him when he saw two more of his agents along with two shifters among the casualties. Paris would mourn their loss when all was said and done.

Seeing Giovanni take on a rogue in a one-on-one situation, he hurried over to offer assistance. Grabbing the creature from behind, he held on tightly while Giovanni smashed his fist through its chest, pulled out the heart, and threw it on the ground before crushing it beneath his heel.

His chest heaving as he attempted to catch his breath, Giovanni inclined his head. "Thank you, Dante."

"Anytime."

A troubled expression marred the older vampire's forehead. "This was a trap."

"No shit." Dante snorted, trying to push Isis's betrayal from his mind. She was dead to him. As far as he was concerned, she only existed somewhere in a distant dream—an unpleasant one. From here on out, he intended to focus on the task at hand; finding the true location of the children. "And we should probably get the hell out of here before another gang of rogues appear. Most of us may have survived this wave, but I don't know if we'd be able to handle another onslaught. Not only that, we're dealing with black magic the likes of which I've never seen. And, what the hell did you chant to make those things appear the way you did?"

A slight smile quirked Giovanni's lips for a brief moment. "Sometimes one must fight fire with fire. Like I said, I've had to do many things over the years out of necessity, and one of those was learning the black arts."

"What happened to your source? I thought it was a reliable one."

"She is. I would trust her with my life, which leads me to believe something has happened to her."

It suddenly dawned on Dante who Giovanni's source was. "Nya? You trusted information given by her? She's Adonis's whore."

"I'll let that comment slide, Dante, but only this once. And, yes, I'd trust her with my life."

Dante swept his arms out. "Then what was all this about? Why aren't the children here like she said they'd be and why were all these creatures stronger than normal rogues?"

Giovanni released a sigh. "This conversation is probably best left for when we get out of here."

Dante nodded. The sooner they left this place, the better. And the sooner he got away from Isis, the better his heart would be.

Chapter Fourteen

Numb. The cold fingers of pain and despair wrapped themselves around her heart so tightly she could barely breathe. Falling to her knees, she allowed her blood-matted hair to hang over her face like a curtain of shame. For as long as she lived, Isis would never forget the expression in Dante's eyes. If she could have, she would have wiped away the anguish that had briefly flitted across his face but had quickly been followed by anger. No, rage. He'd quickly masked the emotions, but she'd seen them nonetheless. And, it hurt like a deep cut to her soul.

The most difficult part had not been his look, however. It was how he hadn't even asked her if any of it was true. He had looked right through her as if she wasn't in the room. Dante hadn't bothered to demand an answer. It made her doubt that he actually had feelings for her after being so certain. Isis couldn't bring herself to be angry with him for not fighting for her. She'd brought it all on herself for not telling him about her association with the Serpent Gang when she had the chance. Now, it was too late.

She hadn't laid eyes on Black Adder in years, however, he wasn't surprised to see her. In fact, from the way it appeared, he had expected her. Isis didn't understand why he had lied about meeting her recently.

He'd always been possessive of her, but when she'd run off after witnessing that ritual he'd been involved in, he had never sought her out. She'd taken that as a sign that he'd moved on. Apparently, that wasn't the case.

Hastily wiping away a tear, Isis wobbled to her feet. She needed to get to the extra clothing she'd hid not too far from this building. In her haste to shift, she'd ripped her outfit to rags. For the first time since Dante had left her alone in the room something struck her. The silence. There was absolutely no sound to be heard. The noise of battle was gone. She must have been in here longer than she realized.

Despite seeing no one around her, Isis couldn't shake the feeling that she wasn't alone. The hairs on the back of her neck rose, and she had the distinct impression of being watched. Whirling around, she surveyed every nook and cranny of the room, but saw nothing. She shifted her hands to claws, preparing to defend herself as she remembered how the invisible foes had come out of nowhere.

When a chuckle assaulted her ears, Isis straightened to her full height, alert now that her suspicions were confirmed.

"You're just as beautiful as I remember, Isis." The deep, velvety voice that used to make her quiver with lust now filled her with disgust.

Bile rose in her throat but she forced it back down. She bared her extended canines and glared in the direction of the voice. "Show yourself. That's the least you can do, considering the stunt you pulled." For all she knew, Black Adder intended to kill her. But, she wouldn't let him take her down without a fight.

Dante

In a mist of smoke, Black Adder materialized. "As you wish, beautiful." His coal black gaze skimmed over her in a slow perusal. His smile was malevolent. "Mmm, even when you look a mess, you're still gorgeous."

"Fuck you! Why did you tell Dante I was in on this?"

He raised one broad shoulder in a shrug. "Why not?"

Fury seared throughout her body, propelling her feet forward. She caught him with a vicious swipe of her fist. The move obviously caught him by surprise, because he crashed into the wall. Black Adder was instantly on his feet again, his eyes red and fangs bared. "Cunt!" He rushed at her, but she dodged the fist thrown in her direction.

Claws out and ready to take him on, she planted her feet on the floor, but instead of attacking again as she anticipated, the red glow left his eyes and he smiled. "Come on and fight," Isis taunted. "This is what you wanted, isn't it?"

Black Adder moved his head from side to side, cracking his neck. "Among other things, but I thought you deserved to suffer a little before I kill you."

She sneered. "You always were a sadistic bastard."

"And, you were always a power whore. I see you're up to your old tricks—latching on to the alpha in the group. What's the matter? Did you try your wiles on the Kyriakis Alpha and he turned you down? Did he see past your tight little pussy and ass? I guess one fuck was enough for him."

"Shut up," she hissed between gritted teeth. "You couldn't be further from the truth. I have no more

222

interest in him than he has in me. And whatever you may think, it wasn't completely about the power. When I was with you, it was because my feelings were genuine."

He raised one sinister brow. "Oh? So you didn't cast my friend aside for me or did I imagine it? You know what you are? You're a leech, Isis — too weak to stand on your own. And Grimaldi finally recognized it. I'm surprised you managed to snag him. Beautiful though you may be, I always thought he was a bit more astute than to fall for someone like you."

The more he spoke, the angrier she became. She clenched her fists, digging her nails into her palms until they bled. The first punch she had landed had been a lucky shot. The next one wouldn't be so easily accomplished. Isis forced herself to make no sudden moves, deciding the way to handle the situation was to allow him come to her and then counterattack. To even have a chance at getting out of here alive, she'd have to keep a cool head no matter what he said to provoke her. Black Adder was the type to play mind games with his prey before he went in for the kill.

She raised her chin in defiance. "What's the matter? Jealous I found someone much better than you? In and out of bed?"

He snarled, clenching his fists at his sides. "You always were a bitch. That's why I liked you so much, but you've become soft over the years. All that gushy love stuff never would have occurred to you years ago, but you've been dying to tell Grimaldi how you feel. You disappoint me, Isis."

She stiffened. He seemed to know way more about what was going on with her than he should have. "What would you know about what I've told Dante?"

His smiled to reveal his fangs. "I think it would surprise you how much I know. For instance, I know you've been struggling with this so called secret of yours these past few days. You believe yourself to be in love with Grimaldi and you think he might feel the same for you. But you're too scared if he knew about your past, he'd drop you. Oops. Too late for that, I suppose." His laugher was cruel and gut-wrenching.

A chill ran down her spin. It was one thing if he was having her followed but somehow he'd managed to get inside her head and violate her by stealing her thoughts. His taunts had hit home in more ways than she would ever let him know. The man was a sadistic devil whom she wished she'd never gotten involved with. "How do you know these things?"

"Did you think I'd let you walk away from me without any repercussions, bitch? I told you, we're connected. I can read your every thought and have known all your moves since you thought you'd seen the last of me. By the way, why do you think you and your friends weren't killed when you went to Sidewinder's Vegas compound? You thought you were being so brave by going in there with a group of my gang, but it was on my orders they didn't touch you...or Grimaldi and Kyriakis as they rummaged through the house."

Isis gasped in horror. Dante was right. She had led them to danger, albeit unwittingly. "How?"

Black Adder rolled his eyes. "You still don't get it, do you? My alliance with Adonis has given me power beyond what the likes of one such as you could understand. It's also given me the ability to link to your thoughts without your knowledge. I've been waiting for the proper opportunity to pay you back, bitch. No one fucking walks away from me until I say they can."

"How long have you been watching me?"

He sighed impatiently. "Not much has changed, I see. You still don't listen. I haven't followed you. I've had no need to. I said I've linked myself to your thoughts and when I choose to, I can tell what you're thinking and what you're feeling. I've been doing it off and on for a couple years, but things have gotten pretty interesting within the last few months. Mmm, mmm, mmm, but those were some interesting nights you've spent lately."

Casting aside her resolve to wait for his attack, Isis charged at him again, but this time he was ready for her. He sidestepped her grasping hands and caught a handful of her hair. Black Adder smacked her across the face and then backhanded her, making Isis's head reel. When she tried to hit him, he caught her fist in his and squeezed until her bones shattered, but even if it did hurt like a son of a bitch, she wouldn't give him the satisfaction of hearing her scream. A wave of fire shot to her shoulder, and spread through her entire body. The pain was incredible, but she continued in her attempt to break free.

The harder she fought, the stronger his grip became. If she got opportunity, Isis could shift to get the added strength she needed and to speed along the healing process.

While he still held her crushed hand in his grip, he grabbed her by the throat and squeezed, cutting off her air supply. He was so strong Isis could barely move, and she grew woozy.

"Now listen, you whore. Did you fucking think you could leave me, try to ruin our plans, and expect to get away with it? This was the night the Grimaldis were supposed to meet defeat and you helped them!"

"What are you talking about?" she got out telepathically.

"You and your fucking boyfriend ruined everything, bitch!" He released her throat long enough to backhand her again.

Blood gushed from her nose and now split lip. A red haze covered her eyes as dizziness took over and she fought to remain conscious. There was no way she'd let this fight end like this. "You're crazy."

"At one point, I was crazy for you. So crazy, I thought maybe I'd give you another chance, which is why I maintained a link with you."

Isis hoped the look she conveyed held every single ounce of contempt she felt for him. Injecting every bit of venom she could muster into her voice, she said, "That's called stalking, you psycho. If I disappeared from your life and made no effort to contact you, it should have been a sign I wanted nothing further to do with you."

Black Adder slapped her hard again, and Isis's head snapped back. His eyes now glowed the eerie blood-red she'd come to associate with rogues touched by black magic. "Isn't it ironic that just when I was about to seek you out again, you start snooping around my hangouts? So, I kept this mind link with you. And lo and behold, here you are."

Isis moistened her blood-caked lips. He was way too powerful for her to take out herself. Her only chance of survival at this point was to keep Black Adder talking and catch him off guard. There seemed to be one thing that hadn't changed about him, and that was his love of bragging about every single thing he felt he'd accomplished. "You couldn't have known all my thoughts, B.A."

The rogue snorted. "No. The power granted me wasn't strong enough to keep the link permanent, so I used it sparingly. It was enough. I knew your thoughts would lead you here; all you had to do was take the bait we'd set for you."

"What bait? What are you talking about?"

"Apparently, I'm not the only one who's had to deal with a traitorous bitch. He knew his lover would warn the Grimaldis, and he used that to his advantage. I learned through you that Giovanni had fallen for the intel. You played right into our hands."

It was on the tip of her tongue to point out that his plan hadn't worked out quite as well as he'd thought since the Grimaldis had survived this melee, but she wisely kept that tidbit to herself. She needed to save all her energy for healing and escaping.

Black Adder chuckled. "Didn't I tell you there's no point in masking your thoughts from me? I can read them, if I so choose." He grasped her chin tightly and brought his face within an inch of hers. His hot breath bathed her skin. "If we wanted the Grimaldis dead, don't you think they would have been? Think about it, Isis. There were way more of us than there were of them. Legendary fighters they may be, but they're not invincible."

"They certainly could have handled your sorry gang, but who were the others?" When she saw the semi-visible rogues, Isis didn't recognize any of them as members of the Serpent Gang. She didn't think anything of it at first, but considering how difficult the initiation was to get into the gang she doubted its membership had grown that much since she'd distanced herself from them. But, the ones they could see clearly had been members. Isis didn't understand the difference.

Black Adder rubbed his thumb over her cheek in a circular motion. Her skin crawled, but she fought the urge to push him away. The more information she had, the better. "They were Adonis's men, sent to assist us. Your warlocks and witches shouldn't have been able to break the visibility spell, not even a little. Seems like someone in your group may have been practicing a little black magic of their own to counter the spell. Probably Giovanni, the interfering bastard," he muttered that last line more to himself than to her.

His grip loosened as he talked more. Her hand started to itch as the bones slowly knitted together. Good. She needed to keep him going just a little longer. He tossed his head back, and the small, neat dreads that had framed his face fell behind his shoulders once again. A far-off look entered his gaze and he seemed to go into a trance. Isis debated whether she should disturb his thoughts or wait for him to continue speaking.

The decision was taken from her when he focused his hard stare on her once again. "There's going to be some retribution for him for what he's done."

She knitted her brows together. "Who?"

"Giovanni. Adonis didn't want him harmed, but I owe him something for this."

Isis was more bewildered now than she had been before this conversation. None of this was making sense. "I-I...your gang members were completely visible while the others weren't. Why was that?"

He laughed. "Oh? You noticed, did you? They were all supposed to remain unseen, but like I said, the spell was countered, sort of. My men were expendable. The spell cast on them wasn't as strong as the one performed on Adonis's men. They were only there to beef up the numbers."

Her mouth fell open. "You sold out your own men? You let them get slaughtered?" It wasn't that Isis gave a damn about any of the fallen members of the Serpent Gang, but considering how Black Adder used to preach about brotherhood among his group, it shocked her that he would sacrifice them so easily.

"You see what I've done as a betrayal, but I saw it as an opportunity. They promised me ultimate power. Haven't you already witnessed what I'm capable of?"

"So what? You can teleport. Whoop-dee-fucking-do."

With a growl, he raised her above his head and tossed her against the wall as if she weighed little more than a handful of feathers. The back of her head hit the wall so hard it left a crack. Before she could recover, he was on her, holding her up by the forearms and shaking her until her teeth rattled. "Shut the fuck up, bitch! I'll have the last laugh. Your precious boyfriend and his brothers may have won this round, but they won't survive the next time. Once I'm granted the power promised me, I could take them all out on my own, and Adonis will finally have his revenge. But for now, I'll have mine." He raised his fist to punch her, but this time their bodies were perfectly aligned, allowing her to knee him in the groin.

Black Adder hollered in surprise, releasing his tight grip on her. Using his reaction to her advantage, she went into midshift, not having time for a full transformation. It still gave her the extra strength she needed to slash her claws down the side of his face. Her hand, though almost healed, was still in pain, but she used it to shove him across the room. Instead of falling to the ground, he dissipated and reappeared behind her. In a swift move, he grasped the sides of her head and twisted so hard, the bones snapped. Her body went numb as she fell to the floor in a heap.

In its weakened state, her body shifted back to her human form. An injury like this would take a lot longer to heal from and this temporary paralysis would be her downfall. She squeezed her eyes shut. Death was near and she'd never see Dante again. Never get the chance to tell him how much she loved him. There were many things she regretted in life, but that would be her biggest. Tears stung her eyes, but she quickly blinked them back. She wouldn't let this bastard see her cry.

Advancing on her with panther like strides, Black Adder reached down and grasped her by the arm until her feet dangled above the floor. "Good-bye, Isis." Arching his taloned hand, he brought it down to deliver the death blow, but the room exploded with a big ball of light before his hand connected.

"Don't. She's worth more alive at the moment."

Isis almost wept with relief when she heard the sound of a raspy female voice. She'd heard that voice before but in her fight to remain conscious, Isis couldn't figure out where. She couldn't turn her head to see who it belonged to.

Black Adder glared at Isis before looking past her. "She's no use to us."

"We'll kill her, but not just yet. Wait until Grimaldi comes to us and then we'll take care of her right before his eyes," the woman replied.

"He's not interested in this bitch anymore. I've taken care of that."

"I wouldn't be too sure about that. For some inexplicable reason, the Grimaldis have a soft spot for damsels in distress, and I doubt Dante Grimaldi is any different. Let's keep her alive long enough for them to come to us."

"But our army has been decimated," Black Adder argued.

"Do you doubt the power I possess?" The female's voice was sinister and cold.

Black Adder shook his head, sending his dreads flying around his head. "No. But—

"It would behoove you not to question me. Your life can easily be forfeit along with the rest of your men. I'm not pleased that our plans didn't play out the way I'd anticipated, but there are plenty more tricks up our sleeves. If we wait it out, they'll come to us."

Black Adder tilted his head to the side, his expression one of bemusement. "How would they find us?"

"That's for Adonis and me to deal with. Do as you're told." A cloud of smoke surrounded them, and Isis sensed she and Black Adder were on their own again.

A deep growl rumbled from Black Adder's throat before he dropped Isis on the ground and kicked her in the ribs hard enough to make the bones splinter. Thankful she was beyond the point of feeling pain, she closed her eyes tightly as he stomped on her leg, shattering it. "Fucking cunt. Don't think because of this temporary reprieve I won't eventually kill you."

A black haze blanketed her, and though she fought it as best she could, she closed her eyes, wishing they wouldn't open again.

Jagger snapped his shoulder back into its socket, his head still pounding as if he'd been hit with a sledgehammer. How long had it been since he'd jumped out of the tower window of this medieval-style castle? With the slight slant of the castle's wall, he thought he might be able to slide down, but with two shattered hands, he hadn't been able to hold on long enough to make it all the way down and had fallen at least fifty feet. He'd crashed into the dried-up moat. Though he had the agility to land on his feet if he maintained concentration, the battle wounds from his escape attempt were too painful to ignore. Jagger cursed under his breath as he gritted his teeth against the immense ache. He needed to channel all his energy into getting out of this place without alerting the guards inside.

Jagger uncurled his body and attempted to stand. He crumpled to his knees again as shards of raw agony ricocheted through his body like white-hot pins of torture. If he were an ancient like his father or possessed the apt magical skill of his mother and uncles, the healing process wouldn't take nearly as long. Bright lights danced before his eyes, and he felt himself spiraling into a pit of despair. Closing his eyes, he rested his forehead against the cold, dry earth beneath him. A vision of big brown eyes infiltrated his mind.

Camryn.

His bloodmate. She was the reason he still lived. Jagger was sure, were it not for thoughts of her to keep him going, he wouldn't have made it this far. Jagger believed some of the soreness throbbing within his heart was partly the pain she, too, must be feeling at their separation. "I will come back to you, Camryn," he whispered. But first he'd have to get far enough away from the castle so that the black magic surrounding it would lose some of the pull it had on his power. To Jagger's dismay, once he'd managed to free himself from those charmed cuffs, he realized the entire structure had been blessed with a black touch, and his powers were still ineffective.

Using strength he didn't know he had, Jagger swayed to his feet and hobbled toward the edge of the moat. The next challenge was actually getting out of the sunken-in land, and it took him several breathless minutes to succeed. He limped away from the castle as fast as his damaged legs could carry him. Only when he was surrounded by the cloak of the wooded area a few thousand feet away from his former prison did he rest. His one regret was leaving the children behind. Ideally, he would have liked to take them with him, but once he'd made it out of his cell a second time, he realized he'd have a better chance of rescuing them if he could locate his mother or uncles so they could pinpoint the children's location. At least that way, they'd bring reinforcements to save his little cousins. Besides, none of them would have survived that fall. He was thankful to have found the window that afforded him his escape.

There was no doubt in Jagger's mind that the redheaded witch intended to kill them. He just had to rely on the hope that his family would get to them before she decided to make her move.

Using the support of the nearest tree, he focused his attention on a chant to communicate with his parents. *"Mama. Papa. Can you hear me?"* He projected his thoughts out as he silently prayed to be heard. When no response came, he tried his uncle. *"Uncle Steel. If you can hear me, please respond."* When that didn't work, he called out to his uncles Cutter and Blade. Nothing. Even though he received no reply from anyone he'd called to, Jagger could feel them. They were close!

He ventured on, hoping that getting far enough away from the castle would do the trick to establish communication. Jagger hobbled along for what seemed like a couple miles before he tried to contact his family again. When he tried again, there was still no response from his parents or his uncles.

Fuck! He was screwed. Not only did he not know where the hell he was, but his magic didn't seem to be working properly. How much farther would he have to go before he could reach anyone? Just as despair began to set in, a voice penetrated his mind.

"Jagger."

The call was so faint that he couldn't get a proper handle on who it was from. At first he believed he'd simply imagined it, but when he heard it again, his hope soared.

"Jagger."

"Papa. Is that you?"

"Yes, mio figlio. *Tell me this isn't some cruel joke and it's really you."*

Jagger leaned against a tree for support, overwhelmed by his relief to finally have contact with someone. *"It's me, Papa. I've managed to get out of the castle*

I was being held in, but unfortunately, I couldn't take the children with me. I'm sorry. I tried."

"Don't be so hard on yourself. I'm just happy that you were able to get away. We'll rescue the children. Are they all right?"

"I'm not sure. But, I think so. I saw Jaxson and the baby. They were still alive and well from what I could tell, but I didn't see Adrienne. I can only assume she's being kept in a separate room. That witch knocked me out before I could find her, and when I came to again, I knew my best bet would be to get out on my own and get help."

"You did the right thing, Jagger. It's best you got away so that we can get a lock on your location. We were unable to feel you before now."

"There's some kind of dark magic that's unlike anything I've ever experienced. It's surrounding the castle and probably why you couldn't communicate with me. There's a woman there who can do things that no mere mortal should be able to do. Not even those who practice the black arts."

There was a pause before his papa answered again. *"I'll have to tap into your mother's or uncles' knowledge about it. My understanding of it is quite limited, but if we're dealing with what I think we are, we may be in for more trouble than we imagined."*

Jagger frowned. *"I'm not sure I follow, Papa."*

"I'll explain as soon as you're back here with us. In the meantime, get as far away from that castle as possible. She can probably sense your whereabouts, and you need to put some distance between yourself and this woman before she realizes you've escaped. Jagger, do you know where you are?"

"Judging from the architecture of the castle, I'd say somewhere in Italy, maybe the northern part. I've just gotten out of the forest and haven't run into anyone to verify my

supposition." He began to walk as he maintained communication with his father, but suddenly stopped as a tingling sensation took over. *"Strangely, I feel you too. I mean, more so than before. Are you near?"*

"We're outside of Florence, at your Uncle Giovanni's villa."

"My who?"

"We'll fill you in when you're here with us. Your mother and uncles are at this moment working to pinpoint your exact location so we can come get you."

There was one thing Jagger needed to know before he forged on. *"Papa, how is Camryn holding up?"*

"She's safe. She has been sent to a secret location with her brother where they are being guarded by several agents. They would protect her with their lives."

Jagger sighed with relief. Now, all he needed to do was survive this ordeal so that he could see his bloodmate again. *"Good."* A sharp pain tore through his chest as he shifted his weight on the balls of his feet. He inhaled sharply.

"Are you all right, Jagger?"

"Nothing's wrong that I won't eventually heal from."

"We'll find you. As long as we keep this link between us, we'll be there in no time."

Jagger gritted his teeth and continued on, moving through the pain. Finally, there was hope where there had previously been none. He just might survive this ordeal after all.

Beatrice cackled with delight. "Fool," she whispered under her breath as she watched the warlock, vampire hybrid totter off in the cloud of mist she'd created and held in her palms like a crystal ball. He was foolish if he believed he was able to escape without her knowing it.

She had learned from observing Nikolai Grimaldi, he had that damned Grimaldi bullheadedness. It would be his downfall just like the rest of his family. She was still highly peeved those *bastardos* had somehow managed to kill off the army she and Adonis had built, but no matter. Those grunts had been expendable. She had planned on killing them once they'd run out of usefulness anyway, just as she would finish off Black Adder…eventually.

She wondered if she had been too ambitious but quickly cast those doubts away. The plan had been for the Grimaldis to be ambushed by all hundred rogues. Only Adonis's men had been in the know of the real mission while the Serpent Gang had just been there for manpower, which is why she hadn't injected half as much power into the spell protecting them as she had the others. Everyone except the Grimaldis themselves was fair game, but she'd wanted the Grimaldis alive when the battle was over. Well, alive enough to be taken and bound in her castle as they watched their precious offspring die.

Her plan had been so perfect, but she hadn't counted on the incompetence of her men. They had failed her! How could a hundred men be defeated by such a small group? It was just another black mark against the Grimaldi men. She would enjoy watching them die, just as she had their father. They were all just like him, even that traitorous son of hers who was even worse for siding with them after he knew what their father had done to her.

She was born to rule and hold power, and it would have been hers had it not been for that self-righteous Giovanni. The *original* Giovanni. She was sure he was the reason their affair had been discovered. He had set her up and rejected her. Rejected *her*, the most beautiful woman in all of Italy, perhaps even the world. She had yet to see anyone in her long lifetime fairer than she.

Never forgetting that humiliation and shame she'd suffered because of him, she made him pay. But Beatrice wasn't content to stop there. She'd made it her life's work to wipe out his entire legacy, except her precious Adonis. As long as she could keep him under her thumb, they would rule the immortal communities together. Though she wasn't technically immortal, with the help of his vampire blood and her secret weapon, she would maintain her beauty and live forever. She would, of course, have to get rid of that *puttana* Adonis believed he was in love with. She'd allowed his indulgence long enough. With that nuisance out of the way, order would be restored and everything would be as they were meant to be.

But first she would allow the Grimaldi boy to lead his family here to their demise. She wouldn't fail where the others had.

Chapter Fifteen

Dante watched Nico pace back and forth across the room, his strides impatient. His hands were clenched at his sides, and the muscles in his jaw twitched like a fluttering heartbeat. "This is so frustrating! I know my son is close. I felt him and I know Sasha did, too. What's taking them so long? Why haven't they brought him back, yet?" He halted midstep to face the others in the room. "Do you think they may be in danger? We should try to locate them." Anxiety turned his usually amber-colored gaze silver.

As much as Dante could sympathize with his brother, he could barely focus on what was going on around him. His nephew had managed to escape but all he could think about was Isis. He didn't understand how she could make love to him as if it had actually meant something to her and then, turn around and betray him. He'd been fooled once before, but Dante had truly believed in his gut that Isis had been different. He didn't feel deception coming from her. It was true she had been secretive but he in no way could have imagined this was what she'd been hiding. It was like the Flora incident all over again, but this time the hurt cut much deeper. It was real, the kind of pain he would not easily recover from. He'd been so sure about Isis, so positive that she could be — was the one, but while he'd been rejoicing in the discovery of his new feelings she had been scheming to destroy him.

Paris and Giovanni had tried to warn him, but he'd been too blinded by her protestations of innocence to listen. As he imagined Isis with Black Adder plotting and laughing behind his back, it made his blood boil. That rogue had touched her, sucked on her generous breasts, and had probably ate her pussy until she begged for completion. It almost sickened him to think they were doing that at this very moment while his heart had been ripped asunder. Bitch.

If it had been Adonis's plan to bring Dante to his knees by sending the beautiful Isis his way then he'd nearly succeeded, but never again would he allow a woman to touch his heart the way Isis had. He cursed his stupidity for not seeing through her ruse. He felt doubly foolish for now listening to his initial instincts where she was concerned.

"Dante. Are you listening?" Nico demanded, cutting into his brooding thoughts.

He shook his head in order to focus his full attention on his brother. "I'm sorry, Nico. What were you saying?"

Nico tightened his lips briefly. "I said we should go to them. I've been trying to establish a link with Sasha for a while, now, and I haven't been unable to. They said they would be in touch by now."

Romeo stood up from the couch and stretched. "I'm inclined to agree. If Sasha and the Romanovs had found Jagger, wouldn't they have gotten in touch with us by now?"

Dante nodded. "You're probably right, but I don't think we need to send the entire group out just yet. The women need their rest. They fought valiantly, but they're not used to these types of missions and need to recharge. Besides, we'll need some people to stay behind just in case of a surprise attack. The three of us can go. The others can stay behind." Dante turned to the rest of the occupants in the room. "Is everyone all right with the plan?"

"That's fine with me," Marco answered from a loveseat in the far corner of the room. His arm was around Maggie, whose eyes were closed. She snored softly unaware of the conversation happening around her.

Giovanni entered the room wearing a ferocious frown. He was followed closely by Liliana. When they'd all returned to the villa, he and the witch had immediately excused themselves to another room and hadn't been seen since. "Where are you three going?"

Upon looking at the lines of stress on his older brother's face, Dante could tell something was wrong. "Is everything okay?"

Giovanni shook his head. "No. Nya is missing. We've been unable to establish contact with her. Usually, Liliana is good at creating a telepathic links from any distance."

Dante raised a brow. "Nya? Why would you be worried about her?"

"Because something may have happened to her." Giovanni's tone brokered no further argument.

Dante, however, couldn't understand why his brother seemed to care so much for Adonis's lover. "Or, maybe she doesn't want to be found. It's possible she's working both sides. You assured me she could be trusted, but I still have reservations. Liliana's inability to get in contact with her isn't helping your defense of her. For all we know, she could have set a trap for us by supplying you with the wrong information." From what he'd remembered of the long-legged vampire, she didn't seem to care whose side she was on. "How can you be so sure she had nothing to do with the plot against us?"

"I've known her for a long time and things are a bit too complicated to go into details at the moment, but I know she's not involved in this. She only gave us that information because she believed it would help us." Despite the certainty in Giovanni's voice, Dante remained unconvinced. If his brother wanted to be a fool, that was his problem, but no longer would *he* fall for the lies of a woman with a pretty face. Was Giovanni fucking Nya? If that was the case, her pussy must be amazing.

Without warning, the older vampire turned toward him in a blur, his eyes blazing green fire. His lips were compressed into a thin white line. *"If you want to keep your thoughts to yourself, I'd suggest you do a better job at masking them next time."*

Dante raised a brow, refusing to be intimidated. No one had asked Giovanni to read his mind. *"Well, are you? Fucking her, I mean? Seems like she doesn't care where she's getting it from, if you ask me. Is the pussy so good that you'll allow yourself to be led by the bal—"*

Before Dante could finish his thought, Giovanni grasped him by the collar and lifted him off his feet. *"Don't even think it."*

"Take your hands off of me before I make you." Staring down into that now menacing glare, Dante realized his brother was no more willing to back down than he was.

Marco, Romeo, and Nico were by them in a flash. "What the hell is going on here?" Marco demanded.

Before, Dante knew his younger brothers would have sided with him in any argument with Giovanni, but something had happened. They had accepted him as family and the three of them seemed to have some internal debate on whose side to take.

Giovanni slowly lowered Dante to his feet. "Nothing," he answered curtly. "Dante and I need to have a word in private, but before we do, I'd like to know where you three planned to go before I came in the room?"

Nico shifted his gaze between Dante and Giovanni before answering. "We're going to search for Sasha and her brothers. They've been gone long enough."

Giovanni relaxed his stance, not bothering to look in Dante's direction. "That won't be necessary. They are near. All of them."

Nico's brows flew together. "How do you know? None of us have felt them. Don't you think I would feel my mate and son?"

Giovanni dipped his head in agreement. "Of course you would, if there weren't dark forces still surrounding Jagger."

"What do you mean? He's managed to escape. I don't understand any of this." The anxiety was evident in Nico's voice.

Anger still welled within the deepest pits of Dante's soul. He wanted to smash something, yell, or just plain kill someone, but seeing the worry in his brothers' faces, he remained as calm as he could be. He wouldn't let some scheming bitch break up his family. Taking a deep breath, he focused on the current conversation.

"Knowing what I do about what my mother is capable of, it puzzled me that Jagger was able to escape, no matter how clever or strong he is. She wouldn't have allowed it. There's some kind of ward working around him so she is able to track his movements. That he was even able to contact you earlier was probably because she wanted him to," Giovanni explained.

"Does that mean she and Adonis are headed this way?"

"No. I think she may want Jagger to lead you back to where he'd been kept. That's more than likely where the children really are."

Dante narrowed his eyes. Something didn't quite fit. His brother had been a bit evasive on the topic of his mother. It was apparent he was holding something back and Dante wanted answers, now. "Spill it. You haven't told us everything, have you?"

"I wanted to make absolutely certain before I said anything, but I think my mother may have a demon attached to her, hence the incredible power she now possesses. And if that's the case, it will be difficult to kill her."

Marco threw his hands up in frustration. "What? Demons? After all we've already had to contend with?"

Giovanni shook his head. "Demon in the singular."

Dante crossed his arms over his chest. "Explain."

"When someone has practiced the black arts as long as she has, they eventually attract a demon, who will slowly take over their body a bit at a time until it eventually consumes them. The demon feeds on negativity, and my mother has plenty of it."

Nico frowned. "My understanding of demonic possession is that eventually the demon will need a new host once its current one has no more usefulness."

A humorless smile briefly twisted Giovanni's lips. "You're basically right, but as I've already stated, my mother is full of negative energy. A demon will have plenty to feed on for decades to come. Besides, as long as she continues to murder innocent people to maintain her youth, the demon will be satisfied. She is the perfect hostess."

Dante had learned a lot more about black magic in the past weeks than he had in his lifetime, but he did have some working knowledge of demons. Humans, no matter how much they knew or how long they practiced the dark craft, should not have possessed the power to create those invisible red-eyed rogues.

And then there was the way Black Adder had disappeared into mist. There were many powers a vampire eventually acquired with age, but an ability such as that was rare even among the ancient ones. Now, he understood the source of Beatrice's powers completely. Though true immortals were impervious to demon possession, she wasn't one.

He'd only seen one other possession in his lifetime, but the demon had to be extracted from the host in order to kill either one. "It won't be an easy task defeating her."

Giovanni nodded. "You're right, but it can be done, especially when we have a witch who bears the mark of Hecate."

Nico's brows furrowed together. "Absolutely not! I will not allow Sasha to be used as a sacrificial lamb!"

Before anyone could respond, they were interrupted by the sound of newcomers entering the villa. Steel and Cutter entered the room first, followed by a tattered, bloodied Jagger being held up by his mother on one side and Blade on the other.

"*Mio figlio!*" A sheen of moisture glistened within the depths of Nico's amber eyes as he rushed over to his son.

"Papa." Jagger's voice was small and weary as he went into his father's embrace.

Nico held Jagger tightly as if he couldn't bear to let him go, stroking the back of his head. "My son."

Sasha wrapped her arms around her two men, tears streaming down her face. "My baby."

Dante's heart contracted at the warm scene before him. One would have to be heartless to remain unaffected by such a display. Silence engulfed the room as everyone watched the mother, father, and son reunion. Dante would probably welcome his nephew back once his parents had their turn but for now, he felt he was intruding on a private moment, so he turned away.

Giovanni caught Dante by the arm. "*Outside, now. What I have to say is not meant for the others to hear.*"

He didn't like Giovanni's commandeering tone. Dante stared pointedly at the hand gripping him. However, for the sake of not causing a scene, he allowed himself to be led out to the terrace at the back of the villa.

"You needed to get out of there before you ruined Nico and Sasha's moment."

Dante's brows flew together and he pounded his chest. "Me? He's my brother. Credit me with a little more tact."

Giovanni crossed his arms over his chest. "He's my brother, too, or have you forgotten?"

"I believe I have more right to claim it, don't you think?" The second the words left his lips, Dante realized how fucked-up that sounded. Giovanni's face remained expressionless, but Dante sensed an acute ache emanating from the older vampire. "I'm so —"

Giovanni held his hand up. "Don't. Your apology isn't necessary. It's a stressful time for us all."

Dante released a deep sigh. He had to get it together. Just because he'd been tricked by a heartless bitch didn't mean he should lash out at his loved ones because he was hurting. No matter his current state of mind, he had to keep his composure. Getting angry about his situation wouldn't change things. "But, you have it, nonetheless. I don't know what's come over me." He raked his fingers through his hair in frustration.

It was so much easier dealing with issues when they weren't his. He told himself to stop thinking about her, to not let her invade his every thought and affect his actions.

"Just so we're clear, Nya is as much Adonis's victim as the children are."

"You don't need to explain yourself to me. Obviously, you're privy to things about her the rest of us are not. However, you have to pardon me, if I'm a little skeptical about a source who spends most of her time with the enemy."

"Not everything is black-and-white, as you know. If it were my place to tell you the history she has with Adonis, I would, but it's not. Maybe one day you'll know, or not, but don't judge her by the standards of someone you feel has disappointed you."

Dante narrowed his eyes. "I don't know what you're talking about."

"Cut the bullshit. You and I both know something is wrong and that something is Isis. Whether you want to talk about it is your business, but you need to get over it and quick. When this is all over, you can brood all you'd like." Giovanni sighed. This is probably my fault anyway."

Dante shrugged with a nonchalance he didn't quite feel. "How is this, your fault? You tried to warn me about her. Paris did, too. I should have listened. Next time, I won't allow my dick to do my thinking for me."

Giovanni shook his head, a troubled expression furrowing his brow. "No. I shouldn't have said anything to you. At the time, I thought I was doing the right thing, but now I'm not so sure."

"Look, I know you mean well but I don't want to talk about her right now. And if you don't mind, I really need to be alone right now to clear my head."

Giovanni's steady, all-seeing gaze roamed Dante's face, conveying a wealth of meaning. "As you wish, but there is something I need to make clear to you about my relationship with Nya before I leave you to your own devices."

Dante wasn't in the mood for a lecture, nor did he want to hear about the sordid details of his brother's sex life. Could it be his brother had also gotten so wound up in a bunch of pretty lies he couldn't see the truth? As far as he was concerned, if Nya was with Adonis, then he'd kill her, too, if necessary. "No explanation needed. In fact, I don't want to hear one."

Giovanni's green eyes turned such a deep shade of jade they nearly looked black. "But, you will listen to me. Considering what she's already done for me, done for your family, you, at least, owe me the courtesy of a hearing."

Dante smirked. "Exactly what has she done other than play both sides?"

"It's been difficult to always keep track of Adonis's movements. In the last century, it has been Nya who has kept me informed of his plans."

This didn't quite add up for Dante. "I don't follow. Why would Adonis allow her to spy for you and continue to take her back? If I've learned anything about him, it's that he wouldn't be the kind to suffer such a betrayal lightly."

"Exactly, yet she continues to put her life on the line over and over again."

Dante snorted. "This still makes absolutely no sense."

"It's complicated, and like I said before, it's not really my story to tell, but you do know the strength of a bond created when one of our kind brings a human over?"

Dante nodded slowly. Only in the case of bloodmates did a vampire usually bring a mortal over although there were some exceptions. That link between creator and new vampire was stronger than most. Some would argue it was more powerful than that of mother and child. In essence, when a vampire brought someone over, it was like giving birth, if only in the metaphorical sense. The blood exchange required was a pure sharing of essences; the new vampire had a piece of its creator's soul, making it hard for him or her to break away without it actually being a painful process. Unless there was already a bond to begin with as was the case with Giovanni and Adonis and that of father and son. It wasn't often a new vampire chose to leave the one who made them.

In his experience, there were only three reasons vampires turned humans: For love, as was the case with his brothers Marco and Romeo; to save a life, as was the case of his older brothers and father; and to enslave. Dante wondered if it was the latter.

"It's a bit of the first and the last option."

A low growl escaped Dante's throat. "Don't do that. You are not allowed into my thoughts without my permission."

"Then you should be more careful to shield them around me. As long as you've lived, it's a lesson you should be well aware of." Giovanni released a lengthy breath. "I apologize. You're right. I shouldn't do that to you. I'm so used to doing it to others that I sometimes don't know when to stop. I've only recently gained the ability to touch people's minds even though they are locked. It's come in handy for what I've been up against. I promise I won't tap into your thoughts again unless you grant me access."

The obvious sincerity in Giovanni's tone mingled with another emotion, which sounded a lot like despair. Could it be that he was in love with the mysterious Nya? That had to be it; otherwise, Dante didn't know why his brother cared so much. "No, I'm the one who owes you the apology. I'm acting like an ass. My problems do not justify my behavior."

"That's one of the issues. If you continue to bottle your emotions up, they'll fester until one day they explode."

"But we're not talking about me, remember. You were telling me about Nya."

Giovanni closed his eyes briefly and opened them again slowly. "Of course. Like I was saying before, the dynamic between Adonis, Nya, and I is complicated for reasons I can't get into. Everything isn't so cut-and-dried, but Nya is my friend, nothing more. Before she met Christine, I feared for her. I actually still do."

"How?"

As if he was struggling to determine the right words to say, several seconds of silence passed before Giovanni responded. "She's been spiraling for some time now."

"That normally happens if…"

"It wasn't a vampire's choice to be turned. That she's managed not to fall into that dark descent after all this time is a testament to her will and strength. Recently, she's found another reason to hold on, but it would all be for nothing if something isn't done about Adonis."

"So she really doesn't want to be with him? He's using the bond they have to hold her to him."

"I wish it were that simple. They've been together for several decades; feelings do eventually get involved."

"Are they bloodmates?"

"Again, it's not for me to say. But, I'd like to ask you to not judge her. There are things at work here even I don't fully understand. Nya carries a heavy burden and I owe her a lot. She's saved my life on more than one occasion."

"I know you said you're not at liberty to discuss what's going on with them, but can you at least tell me why Adonis allows her to spy for you? Why wouldn't your mother have said anything?"

"If it were up to my mother, she would be dead by now, but Nya's death wouldn't serve any purpose to her, except in vanquishing a rival. My mother needs human sacrifice in order to maintain her unnatural immortality. As for Adonis, his feelings for Nya run deeper than even he would let on. But to be perfectly honest, I don't think even they quite know what to call each other."

"I see," Dante murmured, not really seeing at all. If anything, he was more confused than before, but it seemed Giovanni was stubbornly convinced of Nya's innocence. He just couldn't see how Adonis would keep her around if she wasn't truly on his side. Dante supposed she would remain an enigma he'd never figure out.

"I don't think you do, brother, but it's okay. All I ask is you respect my wishes where she's concerned."

Dante nodded. "Since I owe you for all you've done for us, I will as best as I can. However, if she does anything to jeopardize the family, I will take her down with no questions asked."

A muscle twitched in Giovanni's jaw as he clenched his teeth together. Finally, he nodded. "I only have one more thing to add before you join the others out front."

"What?"

"I' just wanted to apologize again for doing you a disservice in sharing my misgivings about Isis. It wasn't my place."

Dante clenched his hands at his sides as tension slid through his entire being. Not trusting himself to speak, he remained silent, turning his back to his brother.

"Not that it's any excuse, but I was made aware of something before we'd gone out that first time and it concerned me. Normally, I would have taken the time to mull it over and give it the proper degree of thought it deserved, but believed I was protecting you." Giovanni took a deep breath. "This is coming out all wrong. What I'm trying to say is maybe she's not as guilty as I initially believed her to be."

Dante didn't want to hear anyone's defense of Isis, especially Giovanni's since he obviously couldn't see past the wiles of Nya. "Do you think what you've told me really matters after what I saw? What I heard? She's a goddamn traitor, and if she would have had her way, every single one of us would be dead. My skin crawls when I think of how I let her touch me, when she'd been plotting our demise all along. She and her real lover are probably plotting their next move. All this time I sensed something wasn't quite right, but I was so enthralled by her. She played me for a fool. She betrayed my trust as well as our family's, so there's absolutely nothing you can say to make things right. And, I'd rather you not try again. I meant what I said before. I don't want to fucking talk about her again. Do. I. Make. Myself. Clear?" He met Giovanni's unreadable stare, refusing to back down.

Anger emanated from Dante's every pore and the need to lash out grew with each passing second. Giovanni looked to be on the verge of speaking but was halted when Marco joined them on the terrace.

"Is everything all right out here?" Marco's gaze swept over Dante's face and then shifted to Giovanni's.

No! Dante wanted to yell. Everything was fucked! The children were still in the clutches of some evil psychopath. They were possibly facing a force none of them was prepared for, but despite all this he couldn't stop thinking about Isis and how she'd made him feel when he believed she was genuine. He had been so close to admitting to her the depths of his feelings that he'd begun to imagine a future with her. Cloaking his thoughts, he managed not to let the words slip out of his mouth. He took steady, deep breaths to get the erratic beating of his heart under control.

Giovanni finally answered for the both of them. "Yes. Dante and I were getting some air. It seems he's as anxious as I am to find the other children. How is Jagger, by the way?"

Marco frowned not seeming to believe the explanation he'd been given. He gave Dante and then Giovanni another once-over before answering. "A little worse for wear, but his mother and uncles are healing him so he'll be as good as new very shortly. We'll need him to lead us to our destination, but, of course, Nico and Sasha are reluctant to put him in the line of danger once again. Plus, Nico and Sasha are arguing about the role she'll play in taking down the demon, if, in fact, one has attached itself to Beatrice."

Giovanni's lips tilted in a humorless half smile. "There's no doubt in my mind one has. Having Sasha's powers at our disposal is an asset we can't afford to squander. I'm sure once Nico understands the magnitude of what we're up against, he'll relent."

Marco laughed without humor. "You obviously don't realize how stubborn Nico can be, but I see your point. I see his as well because if Maggie had to be the catalyst in order to defeat Beatrice, I too would hesitate. It's been hard enough to not go insane with worry about Gianna."

Dante cursed under his breath, realizing yet again he'd been so wrapped up in his own selfish issues he had failed to offer the comfort he knew his brothers needed. Walking over to Marco, he wrapped his arm around the younger vampire and placed his head against his. "I promise you on my life, we'll get the children back alive."

Giovanni moved to Marco's other side. "And, I second that promise."

"Is this a private party or can anyone join?" Romeo asked, stepping onto the terrace. His usual devil-may-care expression had been replaced with one fraught with tension and sadness.

Dante reached out and took Romeo's hand in his and pulled him close. "How are you holding up, Romeo?"

Romeo's lips twisted briefly in a cross between a grimace and a smile. "How am I supposed to feel? I'm torn between happiness, guilt, and helplessness. I'm happy Nico has been reunited with his son and Jagger is back with us and in one piece. But then, there's this guilt that's eating me up inside at the jealousy I feel. It hurts that I envy my brother having his son back to the point where I can't stay in the room with them for more than a few minutes because I want my children back. And, I feel helpless not knowing the well-being of Jaxson and Adrienne, wondering if they're hurt or scared about what's being done to them. And, that I'm not there to protect them." He squeezed his eyes shut and lowered his head.

If Dante wasn't mistaken, he'd seen tears glistening in Romeo's cobalt gaze. It was the closest he'd ever seen Romeo come to crying, and it tore at Dante's soul. It wounded him to see his brother like this, especially when he didn't know what words to offer to make it better.

"If it makes you feel any better, Romeo," Marco began. "I felt the same way. Gia is so small and unable to defend herself. She needs us to survive. I made a vow to my wife that no harm would ever come to her and our family, but look at what has happened. I've let her down."

Dante felt every bit of the ache radiating from his brothers tenfold. He happened to glance up to see a pained expression cross Giovanni's face as well. He felt it, too. Before he could offer words of comfort, Nico joined them.

"I was beginning to wonder where you'd all disappeared to."

Dante pasted a smile to his face, not wanting Nico to see his anguish. It wasn't his fault Jagger had made it back and the others hadn't. "Here, we are. I thought you, Sasha, and Jagger might prefer a little privacy."

Nico inclined his head. "I appreciate it. They're healing him now. His body was mending on its own, but it would have taken a while to get him back to normal because he's so young. They're also purging him of all the dark magic surrounding him. I'm thankful to have him back alive. I thought I'd go insane with worry. I'm sorry about..."

Marco patted Nico on the shoulder. "It's okay. We're happy for you and I know you care and we appreciate it."

"We'll get your children back. They may not be my children, but they are yours and because they are a part of you, I love them too."

This time a genuine smile curved Romeo's lips. "Thank you, Nico. That means a lot, and I hope you don't think Marco and I begrudge you your happiness in the reunion."

"I know you don't." Nico sighed. "So I guess the question that remains is where do we go from here?"

"It's time for the confrontation that's been eluding us for centuries," Dante answered. And this time, he knew after the showdown between him and Adonis, only one of them would be left standing. He had never been more sure of anything else in his life.

Chapter Sixteen

The pounding in her head was the first thing Isis noticed when she came to. She attempted to open her eyes, which felt as if they were being held closed by two-ton weights. She gagged as the rancid smell of rotting flesh and stale blood assailed her nostrils and traveled to her esophagus. She frowned. She didn't know what was happening but she had to get away from the stench.

Slowly, she managed to open her eyes only to find herself in a dark room. That scent. That putrid odor was strong and she had a feeling it contributed to the throbbing in her head. She must have suffered a bad head wound if she still felt the side effect. Her skull had probably been cracked. Hopefully, the ache would fade away soon.

Comprehension finally dawned as she remembered her last conscious thoughts. Dante! The look of pure hatred he'd sent her way hurt far worse than any of the blows Black Adder had delivered.

Anger singed her blood as she recalled the trick he'd played on her. If she got her hands on that asshole, she'd squeeze the life out of him. Even back then when they'd been lovers, she'd known how menacing he was. Back then, it had excited her. Now, his attitude nauseated her. It was embarrassing to know she'd aligned herself with him and the first group that had accepted her after her grandfather had rejected her.

Her thoughts drifted back to Dante as she shut her eyes against the dull ache within her heart. He was her mate, the one she wanted in her life always, and he had to know it, too. But she understood why he was angry with her. She couldn't even blame Black Adder because had she told Dante about her past association with the Serpent Gang, he might have actually listened to what she had to say in the face of Black Adder's lies.

Her former lover had been so convincing that even she would have believed the worst of her. It was no wonder why Dante had been so ready to discard her. Because of that, she could never hate Dante Grimaldi. She loved him, and Isis believed their love was worth fighting for. If she managed to get out of the mess she was in, she vowed she'd do whatever it took to make him believe her and realize they belonged together.

For now, Isis had to throw all her energy into escaping. When Black Adder was ready to finish her off, someone had saved her. At the time, Isis couldn't figure out where she'd heard that voice before, but now she was sure it belonged to the cloaked figure she'd had seen during that mysterious ceremony she'd stumbled on. It had to be Beatrice. It all made sense now.

Isis had seen the fear Beatrice had inspired within Black Adder so it was clear that Beatrice wielded a power beyond anything she had ever witnessed. Otherwise, the usually arrogant leader of the Serpent Gang would not have shown such deference, especially to a woman.

Isis stored that information away in the back of her mind for later use as she switched her focus to escaping. Slowly, her eyes began to adjust to the darkness, and she looked around. She was in a room bare of furniture except for the large cot she'd regained consciousness on. Surveying her surroundings, she noticed heaps of something she couldn't quite make out on the floor. Isis suspected it was the source of the stench.

Swinging her legs over the cot, she stood and realized she was still naked. It was just as well. It would be easy to shift without the encumbrance. Grabbing the blanket off the cot she'd been lying on, she wrapped it around her body toga style and made her way to the closest pile on the floor. She'd only taken a couple steps before halting. It was a corpse. A rotting, stinking corpse and judging by the smell of it, the body must have been there for a few days. Upon closer inspection, her stomach lurched at the gory sight before her. What used to be human no longer had a face. Maggots and flies crawled in and out of the gaping holes where a face should have been. It had been a woman and a young one, if she went by the smoothness of the bruised, naked skin.

Unable to take the sight before her, Isis turned away and inspected yet another cadaver, which was in the same condition as the first. She didn't need to examine the other two to know she'd find something similar. She didn't understand why there would be dead human corpses lying around. The stink was now firmly embedded in her nostrils, and if she didn't get out of this room soon, she'd throw up. There was nothing more offensive to a shifter than rotting meat. That was probably why she had been tossed her in here: to make her suffer.

Upon further inspection of the airless room, she noticed a big wooden door almost cloaked amid the stone walls. She sighed with relief at seeing her means of escape, but that relief was short-lived. Grasping the door handle, she yanked, but to no avail. Hoping the first time was a fluke, Isis tried again with the same result.

Dammit! She hadn't used her full strength, but it shouldn't have been that hard to open a damn door. With her next attempt, she did use all her might, only to find the damn thing wouldn't budge an inch.

She took a few deep breaths to calm herself down. Silently counting to ten, Isis took a step back before giving the door a powerful kick. All it caused was a dull throb in her foot. Something was definitely wrong here. She tossed the blanket she'd wrapped around herself aside and went to her hands and knees, channeling her fur form. A howl tore from her throat as her insides shifted and fur sprang from her pores. Her muzzle elongated, teeth sharpened, bones snapped, and muscles contracted until she had fully shifted.

Once she was completely in wolf form, she hurled herself against the door, using every ounce of strength in her being. The door still didn't move. Her suspicions were confirmed; there was some kind of enchantment surrounding it otherwise, she would have busted the door down easily. She should have known her captors would leave nothing to chance, especially after all she'd learned about black magic. What she didn't understand was why Beatrice would want to keep her hostage. She could be of no possible value to the Grimaldis. Dante certainly wanted nothing to do with her.

She shook her head to rid herself of the memory of his disdain and growled at the obstruction blocking her escape. Frustration ate away at her like acid. She had no idea of how to get out of this mess she found herself in.

Isis lay on her belly, muzzle to the floor as she contemplated her next move.

A sinister laughter bounced off the walls and Isis bounded to her feet once again, her ears perking up.

"There's no use trying to escape. You're well and truly caught."

Black Adder.

She turned toward his voice and focused on the ball of smoke that appeared behind her. In the darkness of the room, she could only make out the silhouette of his muscular figure and the gleam of his white teeth. Advancing on him would do her no good. She'd learned that particular lesson the hard way. Isis could at least get the answers she needed. *"Where am I?"*

"You're exactly where you're supposed to be, although if I had my way, you'd be a distant memory. Beatrice seems to think you may be of some use."

"I don't see how, because I'd rather die than to help you."

Black Adder laughed, a deep, throaty sound of pure, evil glee. She hated it. "Oh, but that's exactly how you'll help us. You'll die right in front of lover boy."

Her heart caught in her throat. She would rather he just hit her than taunt her this way. The reminder of the lost special bond between her and Dante was nearly more than she could take, not that she'd let Black Adder see he'd gotten to her. *"News flash, asshole, Dante and I are finished, thanks to you."*

"Hmm, I should think so, too, but Beatrice doesn't agree. Maybe he still cares for you. Or not. In the meantime, how about I reacquaint myself with your delectable body one last time before you go?"

She took a step back. *"You wish. You might as well kill me now if you think for a minute I'd willingly fuck you again."*

"I never said I needed your cooperation." Before she could respond, he teleported to her side and gripped her by the neck. His nails dug into her flesh, but this time the fight between them wouldn't be so one-sided. She owed him big time.

Isis turned her head and locked her teeth over his forearm, biting down hard enough to rip off a chunk of his flesh and hang on. Black Adder screamed in anguish as he tried to shake her off, but she was determined not to let go without creating serious damage. He punched her in the head to free himself. Isis tightened her grip in return, ignoring the pain as adrenaline pumped through her veins.

His blood filled her mouth and Isis was thoroughly satisfied to know he was in pain. With his free hand, Black Adder gripped her throat, cutting off her air supply, finally forcing her to let go. She swiped him across the face with her paw, her claws gouging his skin. He released her, but she wasn't going to lose her advantage by hesitating. Springing forward, this time she went for his throat. Teeth sinking into his arteries, she bore down as hard as she could.

Isis wanted him to pay for all his past transgressions and for the lies he'd told Dante. With a shout of pain, he punched her in the midsection hard enough to make her gasp for breath, thus freeing himself from the death grip she'd had on him.

He was ready for her next attack. One hand gripped the now gaping hole in his neck, and he shot currents of electricity from his free one. The jolt slammed into her so hard Isis flew backward and hit the wall. She hadn't been prepared for that blow and wasn't given a chance to recover before his hands were locked around her throat.

Barking and snarling, she fought to break free, clawing at him. But he held her out of reach. "You always were a stupid fucking bitch. Did you think you could best me?" His eyes glowed bright red in the darkness.

There was only one hope for her. She concentrated on shifting back to her two-legged form, although the grip around her neck made it difficult for her to breathe. She made it midway through her transformation before Black Adder punched her in the stomach, stopping the change. Fur still covered her body, but she was mostly human in shape.

Black Adder snarled, "You can't hope to best me, Isis." His grip cracked a bone in her neck. Gritting her teeth against the pain, she brought her knee up to meet his groin. The surprise of her assault made him loosen his grip, giving her enough leeway to twist free. Extending her leg again, she kicked him in the balls harder than before. He fell to his knees.

Balling her hands into fists, she dealt him a right hook followed by a left uppercut. When she lunged toward him, she met the floor. He'd dissipated into a puff of smoke only to reappear behind her. Black Adder gripped her by the hair and yanked hard enough to break her already cracked bone.

Isis howled. He could break every single bone in her body but she refused to let it end this way. He'd bested her once before, but she wouldn't let him do it again, no matter how powerful he was. She could barely move her head as the pain flared in every single nerve ending of her body but her determination gave her the strength to stand her ground. That, and her desire to live.

If she lived another day, it would give her the opportunity to see Dante again and convince him of her feelings for him. Without that chance, she had nothing to fight for.

Instead of going in for an attack as she had before, she waited for him to come to her. With fangs bared and talons curled, he flew at her. She moved out of the way before he reached her. Black Adder ran toward her again, but Isis grabbed one of the corpses and tossed it at him. The momentary distraction gave her the opportunity to mount an attack of her own. Isis kicked him in the face as hard as she could, knocking him to the ground, she then used the heel of her foot to stomp his head into the floor.

Isis didn't expect to be struck again by another bolt of energy. This time it was more powerful than the first jolt, sending her flying across the room. The back of her head smashed into the wall, and she slid down its length, unable to ignore the pain. That jolt hadn't come from Black Adder. She would have lifted her head again, but her neck was too unstable to support it.

"Silly fool," that voice she had come to dread, hissed. "Did you think it would be so easy for you to escape? No one gets in or out of this fortress without my say-so." Isis had been so caught up in her fight with Black Adder, she hadn't noticed the presence of a third person in the room.

"And you were instructed to leave the shifter alive."

"I wasn't going to kill her," Black Adder countered in a sulky tone.

"I was watching. I'm always watching. I've had enough of your incompetence. You are no longer of use to me."

Isis somehow managed to roll to her side just in time to see the room illuminate with light and a charge of electricity shoot at the large vampire. He screamed, "You promised me power!" Falling to his knees, Black Adder began to shake as he tried to counter Beatrice's shock waves with some of his own. But his magic was nothing compared to the redhead's.

Then, to Isis's horror, a large beast appeared almost as if from thin air. Its presence filled the entire room. Unlike anything she'd ever seen before, this large brown monster with its slimy skin looked like something out of a B-grade horror movie. He advanced on Black Adder and commenced ripping the vampire to shreds. The creature snarled and grunted as he devoured and fed. When the thing was finished, all that was left of Black Adder was a bloodied pile of bones.

The monster disappeared as quickly as it had appeared. Isis opened her mouth to scream when Beatrice's menacing gaze fell on her. "And now, for you."

Before Isis could contemplate fighting back, another powerful jolt tore through her body. This time she welcomed the oblivion that followed.

Adonis stalked back and forth across the room, ignoring his lover who remained chained to the bed. Tonight was the night. His revenge would finally be complete. The time had come to make them pay for the years he'd suffered, for snatching away his birthright, and for thwarting everything he'd envisioned for himself. There was a time when he could have let them all be. His grudge had been with the man who'd sired him. But, the brats wouldn't leave well enough alone.

Every stronghold he'd created had been thwarted by Dante's so-called Underground. His younger brothers' interference in his plans opened old wounds and made him realize he couldn't rest until he wiped them all out. As long as they lived, they served as a reminder of what could have been his and what he'd lost. Once he was done with them, he could start all over again and rebuild his legacy within the immortal community, taking whatever he wanted, whenever he wanted. And no one would stop him.

There was no point in having so much power at his disposal without using it to rule. He wouldn't squander his powers like Giovanni. Adonis paused for a moment as he thought of his brother. Out of a sense of loyalty to their shared lineage, Adonis had been careful to leave him unharmed. But Giovanni had not chosen his side and they both knew what the price would be. Death. In a way, it almost saddened him to know things would end this way but there was no turning back now that his mind was made up.

"It's not too late to change your mind, Adonis." Nya spoke for the first time since he'd entered the room.

She'd basically ignored his presence since he'd locked her up. To hear her speak in defense for the other side, the side he'd fought so hard against for all these years, was yet another betrayal. Instead of the anger he expected to feel, however, sadness welled within him. Beatrice was right; he was on his own.

Walking to the bed, Adonis touched the cuffs binding her wrists and whispered a chant under his breath. He allowed his gaze to sweep over her naked frame. Despite her treachery, Nya still had the power to make his body tighten and his cock stiffen to near pain, but he wouldn't take her. She, too, had chosen. It had only been his stubbornness that had made him hold on to her when he clearly should have set her free long ago. "You're free to go." Adonis turned away from her, not wanting to see the look of triumph he was sure would be dwelling within her dark eyes.

No sound of her breaking free of the bonds was forthcoming. Instead, he was met with silence. He had expected her to jump at the opportunity. "I said, 'you can go'. The chains are no longer enchanted, not that my setting you free will help your friends now. They're on their way, you know. Beatrice has foreseen it."

Still there was no response. Why didn't she answer? Why was Nya giving him hope that she didn't actually want to leave him when he knew there was none? He had dreamed of her being by his side when he eventually brought the immortal world to its knees.

Adonis turned to see her in the same position he'd left her in. Nya's gaze was fixed on a point somewhere across the room, though he got the sense she wasn't really looking at anything. If he didn't know better, he would say her usual stoic features were shadowed by an emotion she'd never allowed him to see before. Sorrow.

The anger that he believed had deserted him returned full blast. Who the hell was she anyway, to make him feel this way? Fuck her! "Get out of here, you conniving bitch. Go to Giovanni and his newfound family. You are no longer welcome here. We are enemies." Stalking back to the bed, he grasped the chains anchoring her wrists and gave them a powerful tug, ripping them out of the wall. She could have easily broken them herself, but he was growing impatient with her passive-aggressive behavior. "Now go! Get the hell out of here and die with the rest of them."

Her arms fell to her sides, but her gaze remained set at the same point beyond him.

Grabbing her by the forearms, he hauled Nya against him and shook her, and all the while his body responded from the mere feel of her skin beneath his fingertips, her scent, and her beauty. Instead of fighting back as she normally would have, she took it, further driving his rage. He tore off the chains anchoring her leg and lifted her fully off the bed. He spun her around and slammed her against the wall, then pressed his body against hers. "Do something!"

Finally, her big dark eyes locked with his. "You're setting me free, but we both know as long as one of us lives, the bond between us will remain unbroken. And when you die, the part you gave to me will die as well. I'll live the rest of my existence as an empty shell, craving something I can never have."

Adonis narrowed his eyes and spanned her throat with his hand, his thumb grazing the pulse in her neck. Her breathing was shallow as if she found it painful to do so. Torn between squeezing the breath from her lungs and pressing his lips against her luscious ones, it already felt like a piece of him was dead. "And the fault lies with you, my lovely. Had we truly bonded, that wouldn't be. Besides, I don't intend on dying tonight, but you will, if you go to him. I will spare you otherwise."

She cut her gaze away from his momentarily and her lips tightened. "Despite what you think, there was never anything between me and him—except friendship."

"Of course, there wasn't. I would have smelled him on you. Besides, I'm not talking about the use of that delectable body of yours. You've shared things with him you kept from me, and I resent the hell out of it. That you would go to him when you know how it drives me insane makes you just as heartless as you claim I am."

"He and Liliana were friends to me when I needed them, as was Christine. You, on the other hand, are so filled with rage and vengeance you've let it consume you. You've allowed it to shape who you are. You've let Beatrice manipulate—"

"Shut up! You know nothing about it. About her. She's the only one who's remained loyal to me. She has never betrayed me."

"The only person Beatrice cares about is herself. Do you think if you were to deviate from her plans she wouldn't kill you, too? She's twisted. Pure evil, and there's nothing about her that can be redeemed. But you…"

He tightened his fingers around her neck, pressing against her windpipe until she gasped to breathe. "I don't need to be redeemed. Dante, Romeo, Niccolo, and GianMarco Grimaldi will die tonight along with the rest of their family; every single one of them and all of those who get in my way, including Giovanni. When they're all dead, I'll go after every single member of Dante's Underground and take them out for crossing me. That way everyone will know I mean business. I intend to rebuild my army and no one will stand in my way."

"And that's it? That's how it will be forever and ever?"

"Of course. You have the opportunity to be there with me."

She shook her head. "You're truly insane if you think Beatrice doesn't have plans of her own."

"I'm sure she does, but they have nothing to do with me."

"You're wrong. And you offer me a choice that really isn't a choice. I can't be part of this any longer, and if it means my death, then so be it. Kill me now because not only will I go to Giovanni when I'm out of this hell on earth, I will help him take you out."

Even though her words cut him sharper than any dagger he'd ever encountered, he wouldn't let her know it. He sneered at her. "Don't think you mean enough to me to waste my time." And with that he slammed her into the wall again. Her head hit it with a loud thud.

She winced, but didn't release a whimper. "I'm sorry." The whisper was so soft Adonis believed he might have imagined it.

Releasing her, he turned his back on her. He'd been so close to caving in to his desire for her, but he wouldn't show weakness when this moment called for strength. "And what exactly are you sorry for, Nya?"

"I'm sorry for what you've become. What you've let her make you into. It's still not too late to stop this. Giovanni would—"

"Not another word, Nya." He clenched his fists at his sides and shook with tension. She obviously thought this was a game if she believed she could she change the course of his plans with a few pretty words. This final showdown was inevitable. He walked to the door and halted. With his hand on the knob, he glanced over his shoulder to see Nya slumped to the floor, her arms wrapped around her legs.

He'd never seen her like that before and something within him wanted to reach out and offer comfort, but to do so would be to give in to something he could not abide. Adonis would not be weak for anyone, not for Giovanni or Nya. Not even for Beatrice.

"If our paths cross tonight, Nya, I will kill you without hesitation."

She closed her eyes against his words and released a heavy sigh. "And, I, too, will do what I must to stop you from this course of destruction."

Adonis gritted his teeth, hardening his heart against the sight of her. "Now we know where we each stand, there's nothing left to say." Not giving her a chance to answer, he swept out of the room and was surprised to see Beatrice standing on the other side of the door.

One red brow was raised and she wore a mockery of a smile. "See? I told you it wouldn't end well with her. You should have let me kill her when I had the chance. I can still do it, if you'd like."

Nya should have meant less than nothing to him, but despite what she'd done, he couldn't bring himself to give the okay. "If she dies, it will be by my hand."

"As long as you realize, she has to go. Forget about the slut for now. Our enemies are approaching. They are very near. Our minions may be few, but there are still enough of them to take care of the others. The Grimaldis belong to us."

Adonis nodded. When he would have walked past her, she grabbed his arm. "This is what we've been working for. Finally, they will fall and the legacy of Giovanni will be wiped out."

Beatrice's features were so twisted in that moment she lost some of her usual beauty. A hint of the demon that possessed her shadowed her face. She used to be his everything, but now she was just a twisted, bitter woman who was holding him back from his real purpose. Once this was over, he'd be glad to see the end of her. He'd go his way and she'd go hers with little regret on his end.

"Yes, it'll soon be over," he finally answered.

She widened her smile to reveal sharp, pearly white teeth as she reached out to him, but he managed to sidestep her embrace. The old sickness welled in his stomach at the thought of her unnatural touch. Brushing past her, he didn't answer as she called to him.

Chapter Seventeen

The war had finally reached its culmination. Every battle fought had led up to this. Dante would finally face *Il Demonio* head on. Adrenalin raced through Dante's veins. His heart pounded so quickly it probably would have killed a lesser being. He'd waited for this moment for years and now, it was here. He was anxious to face Adonis but scared for the safety of his family and allies. No matter the outcome, there would be a lot of bloodshed and many would fall. But, he was ready.

Standing with him a short distance from the castle was team which consisted of the same group from before. They were joined by several more members of The Underground which Dante was thankful for. They would need all the reinforcements they could get. He'd have to put his trust in them and they in him. If they were all to make it out alive, they'd need to watch each other's backs more closely than they ever had before. The witches and warlocks twitched with the magic flowing through their bodies, and the shifters were already in fur form.

Stealing a glance at his brothers, Dante could tell they were as tense as he felt. He turned to his nephew. "Are you sure this is the place, Jagger?" he asked needlessly, simply wanting to hear a voice in the silence of the night. Dante already knew this was where his nephew had been held hostage. He could feel the great evil surrounding this castle, an evil so strong it threatened to choke him.

Jagger nodded wordlessly.

"Is there anything that has to be done, magic-wise? I'm sure there are powerful wards surrounding this building." Dante directed his question toward Sasha and her brothers. Nico had needed some convincing, but he'd finally relented in his decision to use Sasha to their advantage, if it needed to come to that.

Sasha frowned at the structure before them and shook her head. "There's not much we can do until we're inside. As you can see, the gate is open for us to go in. Giovanni will probably know some dark spells to counter whatever Adonis and Beatrice cast. My brothers will be able to assist Giovanni with that. I will, of course, take care of the demon, although I can't do it alone."

"You'll have my assistance and Giovanni will be doing what he can as well," Liliana added.

Jagger moved to his mother's side and wrapped his arms around her. "And you will have me as well, Mama. I may not be as powerful as you, but I can lend my magic to strengthen yours."

Sasha rested her head against her son's chest. "Thank you. Your help will be much needed."

"We'll all have to work together, if we're going to get out of this alive," Dante reiterated. "If you are one-on-one with your adversary, but see a teammate is being triple-teamed or more, it's easier for two of you to join up and defeat your enemies together. This is something we already know, but this lesson was never more necessary than tonight. Some of us may not make it out of this alive, but I'll make damn sure I get as many of you as possible out of this battle alive."

Marco, Romeo, and Nico grasped their mates, pulling them close as if they were all sharing their last embraces. The intimacy of the moment made Dante's thoughts stray to Isis. He couldn't understand why he couldn't get her out of his mind after what she'd done. She was probably inside now, lying in wait with her lover to kill him and his family.

He balled his fists at his side, pressing them together so tightly His fingers went numb. Dante refused to let her distract him, and he wouldn't go easy on her if she got in his way.

Giovanni exhaled deeply. "It's time."

The group huddled together, everyone exchanging meaningful glances before forging ahead. For the first time in centuries, he felt an emotion he believed himself no longer capable of where fighting was concerned; fear. But, he would use this emotion to his advantage to keep himself and his team alive.

The moment the entire group stepped over the threshold of the castle, the gates slammed behind them, barring any avenue of escape. "Stay close," Dante commanded.

A powerful chill seeped through his clothing and penetrated his skin, making him shake. His stomach turned as the offensive stink of something old and rotten assailed his nostrils. It was the scent of death and something else he couldn't quite determine. An invisible energy brushed against him, sending an involuntary shudder down his spine. There was a powerful evil here. In his years of searching for Adonis, he'd encountered glimpses of it, but never had it gripped him as strongly as it did now, anchoring him to where he stood.

Taking a deep breath, Dante forced himself to walk farther into the castle. He felt as if he was stepping back into the fifteenth century. There was nothing modern about this castle, from the setup of the great hall to the wooden furniture, which was splintered and swollen from age and misuse. It didn't sit well with him that they had yet to encounter Adonis, Beatrice or any of their minions. Dante might not have been able to see them, but he felt the presence of many surrounding him and he didn't like it one bit.

No sooner had the thought crossed his mind than a force pummeled him in the chest and sent him flying through the air. He crashed into the wall with an "Umph!" The back of his head took the brunt of the blow, and his senses reeled. Using every ounce of agility he possessed, Dante managed to land on his feet, but just barely.

To his dismay, the members of his team each seemed to receive their own attacks. A loud, throaty chuckled echoed through the hall.

Anger coursed through his body, and the blood pounded in his head. His bloodlust had been awakened and someone was going to feel his wrath. Dante let his incisors descend to the sharp points that would tear his enemies to pieces. Shifting his hands, his nails lengthened to razor-sharp claws. The heat from his eyes spread throughout his entire body. Whoever had been behind that assault may have caught him off guard, but it wouldn't happen again. "Show yourself!" Dante whirled around the room, eyeing every corner for any foes. His breathing came out in short huffs and never had he been more ready to battle as he was now.

Nothing happened.

"What the fuck," he muttered under his breath.

"They're toying with us," Giovanni answered. "Don't let down your guard."

"Not a chance." Dante surveyed his surroundings, ticked that his enemies remained invisible.

Giovanni closed his eyes tightly and began to meditate. When he finally opened them again, his normally green eyes were a glowing red. "They want you to lose control. If that happens, you're more likely to make mistakes."

"Shit!" Romeo shouted and began to advance on the older vampire. "He's one of them!"

Giovanni backed away from a stalking Romeo. "Calm down, Romeo."

Rage-filled cobalt eyes glowed before Romeo threw a fist.

Giovanni stepped aside, barely missing the punch. "Stand down. I'm not one of them."

Dante put himself between his brothers to defuse the situation. "Wait a minute. I think he's telling the truth." As damning as those eerie red eyes were, for reasons he couldn't explain, he believed Giovanni. Considering the trouble they had had with red-eyed rogues before, there was no reason Dante should have believed him, but instinct told Dante to give Giovanni an opportunity to explain. "You've got exactly sixty seconds to tell us why you resemble one of those tainted rogues."

Giovanni closed his eyes again and when he reopened them, they were their usual green hue. "I've already told you, I've had to dabble in black magic in order to stay two steps ahead of you and Adonis, and sometimes, there are consequences for the things we do."

Dante tapped his foot impatiently. "I'm not sure I follow."

"One can't mess with the black arts unless they're willing to deal with the consequences. It becomes addictive. It's a craving that can't be satisfied until the next infusion of power. Why do you think there are so many followers willing to do Adonis's and Beatrice's bidding? They hunger after that next injection of power until it drives them insane."

Marco narrowed his eyes and looked Giovanni up and down. "And you want this power, too?"

"Not so much want it, but need it in order to keep my sanity. I knew this was one of the effects before I began using it, but my options were limited."

"I suspected this was the case," Sasha mused.

Nico turned to his mate. "You knew this and never mentioned it."

She shook her head. "You have to keep in mind I'm only coming into my powers. Remember, my father kept me bound for decades, and I still have a lot to learn. I know of black magic, but my familiarity with it isn't as extensive as Giovanni's."

Dante raised a brow. He could excuse Sasha her ignorance given who her father had been, but he wondered about her brothers. He turned to her brothers. "Blade? Cutter? Steel? Perhaps, this was something you could have told us about?"

Steel shoved his hands through his hair with a sigh. "I wish it were that simple. There are several layers of it that even we don't know of. And, if one practices for as long as Giovanni, Adonis, and their mother have, different levels are achieved that even we can't imagine. I now, at least, understand why those rogues seemed stronger. Injected with a more powerful brand of black magic, they would hunger for it more. Fight harder. My only concern now, comrade, is will Giovanni make it through the fight without his need consuming him?"

Judging by how red Giovanni's eyes had turned, Dante wasn't sure he could answer that question and he didn't have time to. An explosion went off that rocked the foundation beneath him. He'd been warned not to let his guard down and that's exactly what had happened, but it wouldn't again.

"Come out," he shouted.

"If you insist." A woman with long, dark red hair that tapered to her waist appeared out of thin air. Garbed in a green silk gown that clung to a petite but well-curved frame, she appeared taller than she probably was. There was something regal about her carriage. And her eyes were the same shade of green as Giovanni's. Beatrice. From the unblemished porcelain skin to the straight patrician nose and the thickly lashed eyes, she was stunning, but hers was a cold beauty that could freeze a man in his tracks. It was a touch-me-not kind of loveliness that hinted at the danger lurking beneath the surface.

She smiled at them as if this were a social visit. "Welcome to my home, Grimaldi family and friends. I'm so embarrassed you've come before I had a chance to tidy my home up. There were once many servants here, but you know how the saying goes: Good help is hard to find, is it not?"

The woman was truly insane, or maybe they were the crazy ones. Why else would they be standing here instead of going after this psychotic bitch?

She snapped her fingers, and the castle was abruptly illuminated with candles and lanterns. But not only that, the entire inside transformed. All the broken-down furniture was suddenly restored and a thick, expensive-looking carpet cushioned the floor beneath their feet. A large dining table appeared with place settings as if a big meal was about to be served. "Now, this is more like it. You remember this place, don't you, Giovanni? This was yours and your brother's birthright before that *man* came along and destroyed everything." Her smile slipped momentarily.

Dante shot his older brother a glance. What the hell did she mean by that? Was there something else Giovanni was hiding from them?

The muscles in Giovanni's jaw twitched as he clenched his teeth together. "This was never our birthright and you know it. He wasn't our father and I'm glad I wasn't sired by a selfish megalomaniac who was gullible enough to fall for your charms."

Beatrice's placid expression gave nothing away except for a brief flaring of her nostrils. "You always were a disappointment to me. I should have taken that potion to terminate my pregnancy when I knew I carried you."

Giovanni didn't so much as flinch but Dante could feel his brother's pain. No matter how evil she was, it had to be damaging to hear such a thing from one's own mother. "It's a mistake you may yet regret, because I intend to kill you."

She smiled. "Somehow, I doubt that. You're not half the vampire Adonis is, and you made him, didn't you? You're so weak and worthless, Giovanni. That is why I named you after *him*. He was weak, too."

"What the fuck are we standing around here for? Let's waste the bitch." Romeo seemed ready to pounce, but Giovanni threw his hands out, holding him back.

"No. Not yet."

Romeo, however, wasn't ready to listen to reason. "I can take her!" He sidestepped Giovanni, ran forward and halted abruptly.

In her arms, Beatrice cradled a sleeping child. A tiny little girl.

"Adrienne!" Christine cried out. She began started forward, but Maggie and Sasha managed to hold her back.

"Let her go!" Romeo roared. His hands trembled at his sides. Romeo was not one to hold back, but for the sake of his daughter, he somehow managed to restrain himself.

Beatrice cradled Adrienne against her, stroking the child's hair. "Such a precious little darling. She will be a beauty, this one. As well as this *bambina*." Adrienne vanished from her arms only to be replaced by an even smaller child. A newborn.

"No!" Marco yelled.

"Oh, this bitch is dead." Maggie released Christine and stepped forward, but Dante grabbed her arm.

"She wants you to go to her and that's not a good idea." As much as Dante wanted to rush Beatrice, it couldn't be done while she was holding one of the children.

That evil green gaze turned in Dante's direction and he nearly stumbled back at the sheer malice within it. "Dante, leader of the Underground. You might not have been as moved by the children as your siblings, but I don't want you to feel left out. I think she might be of some interest to you."

Before he could question her, the bundle in her arms was replaced by the unconscious figure of a very naked Isis. Beatrice held the limp figure effortlessly against her body as if Isis were a doll, even though the shifter was taller and heavier.

This made no sense. For what purpose was Isis being held, when they were working on the same side. Was this some kind of trap?"

"Your ladylove has lost her usefulness to our dear departed Black Adder, but has she to you?"

Her words were like a bucket of ice water to his face, drenching the last vestige of hope he may have had. So Isis had been working for the other side all along, but it looked like Beatrice had no problem killing off those who worked with her. As much as Dante wanted to remain unmoved, he couldn't.

Despite her duplicity he couldn't help remembering how she'd tasted, how she'd felt in his arms, and the sound of her laughter and the way her eyes twinkled when she was happy. As much as she deserved to die for her betrayal, he couldn't let it happen. Not like this, anyway. If for some reason after this was all over their paths crossed, it would probably be to her detriment, but right now, his protective instinct had shifted in to overdrive.

Shit. He had to be out of his mind for even thinking of sparing her, but he would — as long as Isis didn't try anything.

Dante didn't have a chance to reply before Isis, like the children, disappeared and Beatrice stood alone once again, but no one dared to approach her. She had the upper hand and she knew it. The bitch.

Her green gaze roamed the face of each occupant in the room. "I see we're all here and the festivities can soon begin." She moved toward the head of the table with such fluid movements, it almost seemed as if she were floating. Her feet barely touched the ground. She took a seat with a smile.

Dante stole a glance at his brothers. They were apparently as confused as he felt. Something was about to happen. Something big. "Where's Adonis?"

Beatrice waved her hand dismissively. "He'll be here soon enough, but I thought I'd introduce you to my guests since you brought along a team of your own. It's only fair for me to even the score, is it not?"

At each seat appeared red-eyed rogues who seemed bigger and hungrier than any of the ones they'd faced before.

"Did someone ask for me?"

Heads turned toward the newcomer's voice.

Adonis entered the room with the same nonchalant smile his mother wore. He scanned the room, his avid gaze missing nothing. "I see everyone is finally here. So, which one of you wants to die first?"

Chapter Eighteen

No longer could he hold back nor would he be held back. All his pent-up frustration would explode if he didn't get his hands on Adonis. Flashing toward the redheaded vampire, Dante was grabbed by two of the rogues who'd sprung from the table. They tried to stop him as he advanced, but he was too full of fury and adrenaline to be held back.

He slammed an elbow into his closest adversary's face, and managed to duck an oncoming blow to the head. One of his enemies, however, hit him from behind, shoving his fist directly into his kidney. Dante yelled his rage, not allowing himself to feel pain. Twisting out of the firm grips holding him, he grabbed each rogue by the arm and made them crash into each other.

Their heads smashing together created a loud thud, but it only seemed to make them angrier. Fortunately, the collision made them loosen their grips, enabling Dante to free himself. He had to survive these attacks if he was to have it out with Adonis.

Out of the corner of his eye, he noticed Beatrice at the head of the table, surveying everything happening in the great hall with a smile her face almost as if she was watching an amusing television show. If he could make his way to her, he'd gladly kill her as well.

Dante ducked another oncoming blow and dealt out one of his own, catching one of the creatures in the stomach. He followed the assault with a kick in its nuts, using every ounce of his strength. His foe fell to its knees and coughed up blood. Dante brought his knee up and connected with the downed rogue's face with a loud crunch. He didn't have a chance to relish his advantage before another one of the red-eyed beasts grabbed him from behind, catching Dante's hair and giving it such a hard tug his neck nearly snapped. Dante pulled away, but only by losing a big chunk of his hair. Furious, he turned on his adversary, caught it by the sides of the face, and head-butted him.

Once the creature was temporarily stunned, he sank his fangs into its carotid artery, and blood splashed against his face. Dante tore off a chunk of the rogue's flesh, making it scream. Seeing another approaching enemy in the reflection of his opponent's eyes, he swung his captive into the oncoming foe who'd tried to sneak up on him, sending both of them flying. Not giving either creature a chance to recover, Dante was on them, ripping through clothes and tearing into flesh.

Though they fought back, he'd weakened them enough to give him the advantage. Taking one rogue by the face with both hands, he twisted its head until its neck shattered. He continued to twist and turn it to a grotesque angle. He then tore into its chest cavity and yanked out the thing's heart before flinging it toward the head of the dining table.

He heard the sound of cold laugher coming from Beatrice. She remained seated like a queen on her thrown clapping every so often. The woman was demented.

Dante lifted the second rogue off its feet and threw it toward the demoness to show his contempt.

With a wave of her hand, she redirected the oncoming body in Dante's direction, making it necessary for him to duck. With a growl, he raced toward her, only to be snatched back again by another pair of hands followed by a kick to the rear. He stumbled forward and landed facedown. Before he could recover, a heavy body straddled him and grasped his head on either side with large palms. Claws dug into the sides of his head and the rogue holding him down banged his head into the cold, hard floor.

Though slightly disoriented, he struggled to break free of the tight grip, wiggling and writhing, but the thing keeping him captive was strong. "You're going to die, Grimaldi," the beast taunted with a raspy voice before he sank sharp fangs into Dante's back.

Dante howled in pain, but he refused to quit fighting. Reaching back, he grabbed his opponent's wrists and furrowed his claws into the rogue's skin, ripping those hands away from his head. With the firm hold he now had on the thing, he managed to roll over and throw it off, but in the process, the rogue tore out a piece of his flesh with its teeth. When he regained his footing, Dante ducked as the red-eyed creature charged toward him. Dante tackled it and in the process sent them both flying to the floor, this time with him on top.

He was tired of fucking with this thing. What he really wanted was a go at the redheaded ball of evil still sitting at the table and laughing with wicked delight. The rogue screeched as Dante used his thumbs to squash its eyeballs like grapes. Pink goo mixed with blood spurted down the monster's face, but Dante was far from finished with it. He slammed his fists into the rogue's mouth, shattering all its teeth. Using his advantage, Dante ripped through his enemy's chest and wrapped his fingers around its pulsing heart. He clenched it between his fingers, squeezing it like a stress toy. "No. You're very wrong. You're the one who's going to die." And he compressed the heart until it exploded in his grasp.

It suddenly dawned on him that these rogues had a weakness. The flesh. One of the reasons, it was so difficult to kill ancient vampires was as they grew older, their bodies became more impervious to physical attack. Some of the blows he'd taken tonight would have killed the average mortal and seriously wounded a much younger vampire. Though these rogues had some magical qualities about them and the strength of an ancient, their flesh gave away their age. It now made sense why it had been so easy to damage them once he got his hands on them. These creatures weren't ancient and they could be killed the old-fashioned way: by ripping their goddamn hearts out.

His group might have been outnumbered and would probably fight for hours to come, but he was in this battle for the long haul. Two more of the red-eyed creatures approached, and Dante sprang to his feet. He was ready to take them both on.

Isis's body ached all over. She groaned as she moved her head to the side. She felt as though she'd been put through a shredder put back together and then put back through again. She was sore in spots she didn't realize she had. Even the bottoms her feet stung. Her hair even hurt and she wasn't sure how that was possible.

Each breath she took set her lungs on fire. She contemplated not moving again. Ever.

Small hands touched her shoulder. "Miss Lady. Wake up."

She winced. "Lemme 'lone," she moaned. If she could turn over, she would. Her mind was murky and she couldn't think past the cloud of pain shrouding her.

"Miss Lady. Wake up!" This time the hands shook her, seeming to jar every bone in her body.

She swatted at the nuisance, only finding air. Was the sound of a child's voice simply her imagination, or was she in some sort of hell where the demons sent to torment her for the rest of eternity were actually in child form?

"Miss Lady, please wake up. Don't die."

Dammit. The kid wasn't going away. Her eyelids felt as if they had been glued shut. With some effort, she opened one to find herself back in a dark room illuminated by one candle. She hadn't imagined her little tormentor after all. It was indeed a child, a little boy.

Understanding finally dawned, slapping her fully awake. She opened her eyes and sat up abruptly, ignoring the pain. Though she'd never seen so much as a picture of him, this boy had to be Jaxson Grimaldi, Romeo and Christine's son. He glanced at her with solemn, light brown eyes.

Isis brought her knees to her chest. It all came back to her now. She had been taken hostage by Beatrice and was then attacked by Black Adder and some other creature she couldn't begin to describe. She couldn't, however, remember how she'd gotten here.

"Jaxson?" she whispered, afraid she was imagining this entire episode.

The child nodded. "Are you okay, Miss Lady? I thought the witch killed you," he said sotto voce.

She moistened her dry lips with the tip of her tongue. "Why are you whispering, Jaxson?"

He looked over his shoulder before answering. "I think she can hear us."

Isis balled her fists in anger. That monstrosity of a woman needed to pay for putting such an obvious fright into this child. "Don't worry. You're with me. I'll protect you."

Doubt creased his forehead. "My daddy will find us and protect you."

Despite the gravity of the situation, Isis couldn't help but see the humor in his statement and she chuckled softly. "Gee, thanks for the vote of confidence, kid. Where are your sister and cousin?"

"They're over there." He pointed to a small cot in the corner of the room. Jaxson placed his fingers over his lips. "Adri just woke up, but the baby is sleeping. Gianna was crying, but I held her until she went to sleep again. That's all she does really, sleep."

Isis wobbled to her feet and realized for the first time since she'd come to that she was still naked. Though Jaxson's attention was focused on the two figures on the cot, she crossed her arms over her breasts. This was awkward. Nudity was natural among immortals, especially shifters, but this child was neither. She shifted just enough for fur to cover her bare skin.

Jaxson gasped as his eyes widened. "Are you a werewolf?"

290

She saw no point in correcting him. "Umm, something like that."

"Are you going to eat me?"

Isis couldn't hide her smile. "I'm on a strict no children diet."

"Oh. Will you turn into a wolf?"

"If I need to, yes. Let me get a look at the girls okay?"

She hobbled toward the cot, each step a painful reminder of her encounter with Beatrice and that...well, whatever the hell that thing was. Just as Jaxson had said, his sister was wide awake, lying on her side with her thumb in her mouth. Her dark eyes looked so empty, almost as if she was in a catatonic state. The poor little darling. "Is she all right?"

Jaxson shook his head, his lips drooping in a ferocious frown. "I don't know. She's been sleeping a lot, too. I think the witch did something to her. Adri doesn't talk much, but she won't even talk to me."

Isis's heart went out to the child. She would have hugged him but she wasn't sure how he'd receive comfort from a stranger.

Her gaze cut to the baby, carefully swaddled in a wool blanket. She seemed to be okay at least for now. Isis had no doubt Beatrice would be back to kill them all. She wasn't the type of woman to keep hostages for long. Somehow, she'd have to get them out of here before that happened.

She kneeled to meet Jaxson's gaze. "I'm going to need your help, okay?"

Jaxson cocked his head to the side, his gaze roaming her face as if he was trying to decide whether he could trust her, before he finally nodded. "Okay."

"I'll need you to stay in this room and watch the girls. You're going to have to be a big boy and protect them with your life."

He flexed his little biceps. "I can do that, but if you need me to help you fight the witch, or those bad men, I'm your guy. My dad showed me how to beat people up." He hit his fist against his palm. "But don't tell my mom; she gets mad about stuff like that.

Isis smiled at his preciousness. "I appreciate the offer, Jaxson. I'll keep you in mind if I need some backup, and I promise your secret is safe with me. In the meantime, don't go anywhere and do as you're told, okay?"

He nodded. "I won't let anything happen to them."

"I know you won't." He wasn't hers but she was proud of him just the same. She was certain Romeo and Christine would be as well if they could see him now. This child seemed to be without fear even though she could smell the emotion on him, yet he was still willing to face their enemies head on. Jaxson may not have been born a Grimaldi, but he definitely had their characteristics. Like his father and uncle.

Isis winced as thoughts of Dante crept into her mind. She swiftly pushed them away. She'd deal with them later. Standing to her full height, she surveyed the room for possible escape routes. There was a window that looked to be boarded up, but she couldn't determine just how high they were off the ground. She walked over to it and gave the boards a hard shove under the protest of aching muscles. The boards collapsed under her strength, giving Isis the opportunity to gauge how far a leap to the ground it would be.

Damn. It was too high. She could survive the fall, but the children wouldn't. The only other option would be the big oak door. If it was anything like the one she'd been imprisoned behind before, it was probably enchanted. To her surprise, however, she didn't have to test it before it flung open.

"Stay behind me and don't move, Jaxson. If you see an opening, take the girls and run, okay?" Isis said over her shoulder to the little boy, hoping he wouldn't try to play hero.

She was on the verge of shifting when the newcomer entered the room.

Instead of Beatrice or one of the red-eyed henchmen she expected, a tall, dark-skinned femme strode through the door. Isis had never seen her before but she glanced at the other woman warily. This could easily be someone sent to do Beatrice's bidding.

Whoever the vampire was, if she was looking for a fight, Isis was more than ready to give it to her. The feral instinct of a she-wolf protecting her cubs took over. They may not have been her children, but they were in her temporary charge and she was ready to protect them with all she had. The heat in her eyes spread through her body and her insides began to contort as she readied herself for a full shift.

Dark eyes narrowed as they fell on Isis. "Who are you?"

That was an odd question for someone under Beatrice's or Adonis's charge to ask. Fur popped from her pores, lining her body. "I should be asking you that question. If you've come here to kill us, I won't make it easy for you."

The femme raised one dark brow and kept her steady gaze on Isis as she walked farther into the room.

"Stay back, bitch."

The vampire didn't bat an eye. "Funny, but isn't that what you are?" She turned her gaze toward the child standing behind Isis. "Jaxson, are you okay?"

He poked his head out from behind Isis. "Yes, I'm okay, but I want to go home."

The femme stepped past Isis and hunched down to the child's level. "We'll get you out of here, okay?"

Isis frowned. "You know this woman, Jaxson?"

Jaxson nodded. "It's Miss Nya. She's my friend," he answered, fixing his narrowed gaze on the vampire. "Where have you been? You said you'd come back and visit. You made my mom sad."

Nya stroked the side of Jaxson's face. "It made me sad to be away." For a brief moment, a flicker of emotion flitted across her face. Regret, maybe? Isis couldn't tell because as quickly as the emotion appeared, it disappeared. She stood up again and walked over to the cot. After she studied the girls for several moments, she turned to Isis. "They've been charmed."

"What do you mean?" Isis didn't like that she was losing control over the situation. "How do you know this?"

"It doesn't seem like the spell will have any lasting effects on them, but it was probably something done to keep them quiet or at least in a sleeplike state most of the time."

Isis noticed the femme didn't answer her question but she wasn't given an opportunity to press the issue, because Nya turned on her heel and headed to the door.

Isis caught up with her, catching the vampire by the shoulder. "Where are you going?"

Nya shrugged off the hand and pointed to the door. "Don't you hear it?"

Isis turned her head toward the now open door, her ears perking up. There was some kind of commotion going on in the distance, and though she couldn't quite make out what it was exactly, she didn't need to because she already knew. The battle was happening. Right now! "I have to go help."

"Then, maybe you should fully shift before you head down to join them." Dark, unreadable eyes looked Isis up and down as if Nya found her wanting.

"Why should I trust you? And why did you come in here, if it was your intention to leave them. I thought you said you wanted to help."

"My goal was to locate the children and ensure their safety. Now that I have, there's something else I need to do."

"And what's that?"

"Regain my soul," Nya answered cryptically. "If you're ready, let's go."

Isis looked over her shoulder to make sure Jaxson would stay put. "Don't go anywhere, okay?"

Once she got his assurance, she followed Nya out and pulled the door closed behind her. Isis went to her hands and knees and morphed to her fur form. The previous aches weren't as glaring as her healing accelerated once she'd shifted. She was ready.

Dante

Chapter Nineteen

Dante drop-kicked his adversary in the chest before flying toward it with his claws extended. He took advantage of the momentum he'd picked up. He ripped into the rogue's neck and twisted, tearing of hunks of flesh before biting into the side of its face. He chomped on his screaming victim's face until there was nothing but bone and ligaments.

The rogue fell to the floor in a dead faint. Dante raised his foot and stomped through the creature's chest to squash its heart beneath his heel. With each kill, his bloodlust increased along with his strength. Never before had he felt such rage and passion during a fight. Years of frustration radiated through his very core and dispatching rogues was a way of relieving it.

Like their prior fight with the translucent minions, these vampires seemed to come out of nowhere. There was no apparent end to their numbers, but as he fought on, he noticed instead of being triple and double-teamed, he was now facing one at a time. Dante took a moment to survey the room briefly to see how his team and family fared. Nico pummeled one of the red-eyed creatures and was obviously winning. Marco back-handed one of the rogues so hard it went sailing through the air. Romeo had one in a headlock, making it eat fist. Maggie held a creature from behind, her fangs sunk deeply in its neck while Christine rained punches on its body.

Dante didn't have a chance to breathe a sigh of relief before one of Beatrice's minions appeared from nowhere and grabbed Jagger from behind. Flashing across the room to offer his nephew assistance, he was stopped when a big ball of dark fur flew in front of him. He saw a shifted wolf pounce on a rogue that had obviously been about to advance on him.

He recognized that wolf. Dante didn't know where she had come from or why she decided to help them after what she had done. If she thought to switch her loyalties now when his side was gaining momentum, she was too damn late. "What the fuck are you doing here?" he demanded through gritted teeth, hating the part of himself that was actually glad to see her.

She raised her head momentarily, her maw dripping with blood, before turning back to her antagonist. *"What I've been doing from the beginning — helping you, whether you believe it or not."*

"Just stay the hell out of my way." Dante remembered the reason why he'd headed this way in the first place. Jagger. She'd made him lose his concentration, yet another strike against her. He refocused his attention in Jagger's direction in time to see Steel come to his aid in the form of sending an iron poker from the fireplace through the rogue's skull. Jagger took over from there, using his own powers to telekinetically pull the poker out and shove it back into the rogue's body. Over and over again.

The numbers were about even now, and there was nothing he wanted to do more than to get his hands on Adonis and Beatrice. He could feel Beatrice's cold green eyes on him. Slowly, he turned to face her. No longer was that easy smile curving her red lips. Instead, she looked more than a little annoyed, her forehead puckered and her nostrils slightly flared.

She, apparently, didn't reckon on them surviving another rumble of this magnitude, but she hadn't counted on the Grimaldi fortitude and determination. Nor did she count on how badly they all wanted to take her and Adonis down. His cut his gaze toward Giovanni, who had just moved out of the path of one of Adonis's attacks. Dante was torn. He didn't know whether to advance on the witch while none of her helpers were around or assist Giovanni, who looked to be in need of his assistance. The decision was taken out of his hands, however, when she pushed her chair back and stood.

She wasn't very tall, probably a few inches above five feet, but the imposing shadow she cast gave the illusion of her being larger than life. Dante knew better than to underestimate her. The trick would be to get his hands on her while dodging the magic.

Beatrice folded her arms across her chest. "Should I be impressed by your display?"

"You ought to be, since you're about to get a taste of it for yourself."

Her mouth twisted as did the rest of her features, wiping away the artificial beauty of her face. "Somehow, I doubt that. You're no match for me."

Dante walked toward her with easy strides, careful not to make any sudden moves. She would probably easily avoid such a maneuver anyway.

"I would stay there if I were you. Unless, you don't care about the fate of those poor, dear children."

He halted. She'd used the one thing he couldn't fight against. If only the children weren't a part of the equation, he'd tear her limb from limb, but he still didn't know where she was keeping them. Fuck! He glared at her. "No matter what I do, you intend to kill them anyway, don't you?"

She chuckled, flipping a lock of red hair over her shoulder. "We haven't known each other that long, but you seem to read me so well. You look like him, you know."

"Who?"

"Your father. You are the walking image of him, right down to the eye color. I always thought Gio favored him the most, but I see I was wrong. That's why I think I'll make your death the most painful. You'll die like him, too. Do you know he begged as he lay dying? Oh, not to spare his pathetic life because even he wasn't stupid enough to think I would. He cried for his precious Maria and for her *bambinos*. It was music to my ears, especially as I splattered his little bitch's blood right before his eyes. Tears ran down his face, like he was a child. It was pathetic. Are you a crier, Dante?"

The more she spoke the greater his fury grew. That she could casually talk about the murder of his parents, as if it had been an amusing event instead of the great trauma he'd remembered it to be, made him see red. No longer thinking clearly, he charged toward her, but she teleported to another spot. "You're as pathetic as he was. You can't hope to beat me. I know more than any mere mortal ever has before."

"Yet, you are one," Dante reminded her.

She shook her head with a smile. "I'm better than one. I'm even better than an immortal. I'm a goddess.

And, you will find out for yourself soon enough. Shall I let you in on a little secret, Grimaldi?"

Dante forced himself to stay calm as he contemplated how to catch her while her guard was down. "What?"

"I killed your father because he was a weak fool. A *pitiable*, weak fool."

"No, you killed him because he didn't want you. So who's the pitiful one? He wasn't impressed by your so called beauty. How does it feel to be cast aside, Beatrice?" he taunted, noticing the unattractive sneer that snarled her lips. He could tell he was getting to her and he hoped it was enough of a distraction to attack. "My father never talked about you. Not even so much as thought of you. You probably believed you were significant in his life, but you were barely an afterthought to him, once he was rid of you. You hated that he saw past your exterior to see the withered dark soul of a bitter woman. You're angry because he chose my mother, a woman whom you couldn't hold a candle to. And you know it, don't you? So don't pretend there was any other reason for what you've done. You're a maniac who couldn't get what she wanted, pure and simple."

"Shut up!" she screamed at the top of her lungs. The entire castle shook with a boom, but Dante could tell Beatrice was shaken. This time, she wasn't able to disappear before his fist connected with her jaw.

She crumpled to the floor, holding the side of her face. Her eyes turned the same bright red as her followers'. "You'll pay for this with the blood of the children."

When he would have rushed at her again, she vanished in a mist of smoke.

His heart sank because instinct told him she was
going after the children. He had to find them even if it
meant tearing this castle apart stone by stone.

"Promise me you'll stay right here and don't move.
And if possible, be very quiet. If someone tells you to
open the door, don't do it, okay? I know this place is dark
and scary, but it's much scarier in the castle where the
witch is." Nya didn't want to frighten the little boy more
than she needed to, but she had to impress upon him just
how precarious his situation was.

Just as Nya and the shifter headed downstairs to
help the Grimaldis, Nya realized she couldn't leave the
children where they were. Even if they were away from
Beatrice, she could easily appear in the room. Suddenly
remembering the little hut in the woods where she
sometimes went to clear her head, Nya decided she
would take the children there.

In one of his more generous moods, Adonis had
charmed the house, making it impervious to other spells
so that she could have her privacy. She had no doubt in
her mind, however, he could come and go as he pleased,
or seek the children out, but at least Beatrice wouldn't be
able to. And, Nya had a feeling Adonis would be too
caught up in battle to think about the children. It had
been Beatrice's idea to abduct them in the first place,
after all.

Nya had told the shifter to go ahead while she
checked on the children one last time. Taking the baby in
one arm and Adrienne in the other, she bade Jaxson to
follow her as she secretly prayed that Beatrice wouldn't
come looking for the children anytime soon. She led

them down the servants' stairs to a hidden underground tunnel she often used to get out of the castle.

Jaxson stumbled a couple of times as he tried to keep up with her, and she ended up carrying all three children at once. Swiftly, she negotiated her way around trees and bushes until she came upon the old shack. Dark and dank though it was, it was the only place she could think of where they'd be safe, at least temporarily.

She squeezed Jaxson's shoulders, careful not to shake him since he now held the baby. Adrienne sat at his feet with her thumb in mouth, her eyes slightly glazed. "Do you understand all I'm saying to you?"

The child finally nodded.

"Good."

She managed to scrounge up a few candles she'd stowed away during her last visit and lit them so they would have some light. "Remember what I said. The girls' safety is in your hands." It was a lot of responsibility for a six-year-old to have, but the alternative was far worse. They could either stay in the castle and wait for Beatrice to return to them or they remain here out of her reach.

"I won't let you down, Miss Nya." He cradled the baby closer.

"Thank you, Jaxson. I know you won't and I'm very proud of you."

She left the children behind without a backward glance because it nearly broke her heart to see them standing in the middle of the room looking so innocent and so lost.

Dante tore through the castle looking for her. "Come out, Beatrice. Your fight isn't with the children, it's with me. Come out!" he yelled again, his heart beating frantically. Fear and worry guided his steps. It frightened him to acknowledge the consequences of not finding them before Beatrice. They were just babies. He'd promised his brothers nothing would happen to the children, but now he wondered if he could keep his oath.

"Beatrice! Don't hurt the children. Take my life instead!"

"That can be arranged." Beatrice appeared in a haze of smoke in front of him and shot out a bolt of power so strong it felt as if he was being ripped asunder.

"Where are they, you bastard?" Her face had turned a bright red and had contorted into what looked like a grotesque mask. She no longer resembled anything close to beautiful.

That shot of magic seeped into his bone marrow, sending pain through every single cell in his body. Winded, he wobbled back to his feet. "What are you talking about?"

She struck him with another bolt. Dante had once accidentally stepped on an active power line and had been electrocuted to the point where he could barely move. He almost wished for that feeling again. The force of her magic sliced through him like a million sharp needles.

"What have you done with the children? Where are they?"

The children were gone? If they had managed to escape, it was probably because someone had helped them. He was grateful to know they were out of Beatrice's reach for now, and he could worry about their whereabouts when this was over. If he managed to get out of this alive. At the moment, excruciating pain like he'd never experienced seared through him like a thunderclap, and his mind grew fuzzy.

He had to fight through this for his family. He charged forward, unmindful of the pain. It would have to be his ally for now, making him aware he was still alive. He forced his way through the wave of power she shot toward him and tackled her to the ground. She screamed her frustration, but before he could wrap his fingers around her neck, she was gone, again.

Shit. The bitch was more slippery than an eel. As he hopped to his feet, Dante was propelled into the wall face-first.

"Give up, Grimaldi; you have no hope to defeat me." Beatrice's breathing was heavy and she didn't sound nearly as confident as she had earlier. He could only hope that she was losing steam. Even with all her years of practicing the dark crafts, she'd probably never fought any real battles, never mind battling against anyone as old as he.

Whirling around, he flashed over to her, moving fast enough to grab her by the arm and spin her into the wall, returning the favor. She crumpled to the ground.

This time when she screamed the sound was definitely something not human. It was low, guttural, and unearthly, almost as if her voice had come out of a synthesizer.

What the fuck? Dante took a step back and remembered what Giovanni had said about the demon. It was coming. And from the sound he'd heard, it would be here soon. Regardless, he wouldn't back down from it no matter what. As Dante was on the verge of kicking her in the midsection, Beatrice shot her hand out and a bolt of lightning hit him, even stronger than the first two hits.

A wet, sticky substance seeped down the front of his chest as he fell backward and landed on his ass. Blood! Dante placed his hands on the floor, using his arms to hold him up. It was difficult to move. More than it had ever been. He could feel his strength ebbing away and he wasn't sure how many more of those bolts he could take.

Beatrice made it to her feet first, her face bleeding and left arm hanging lower than the right. He must have dislocated her shoulder when he'd thrown her into the wall. Her eyes were no longer the bright glowing red, but a deep, dark crimson, and all her teeth had grown large and pointy. They were so big, they overlapped each other and she couldn't close her mouth.

Some kind of transformation had happened and he didn't understand what it was. "You will die now."

She raised her hands and hit him again, harder than ever. Dante fought to maintain consciousness, but the ache in his body was so unbearable he could barely breathe. His heart skipped several beats and he sensed it was on the verge of stopping as he fell to his knees to meet the cold earthen floor beneath him. He closed his eyes to catch the tears that threatened to spill. The tears weren't for his pain, or the imminent sensation of death coming, but the taste of failure, of letting his brothers down. Before everything went completely black, he heard a howl in the distance. Isis. She would meet the same fate as him if Beatrice exerted the same amount of power as she had with him. His heart was well and truly shattered because a revelation suddenly hit him. He loved her, had felt so all along. And just as he acknowledged that fact to himself, he fell into the arms of sweet oblivion.

"There's no point in running, brother. Remember when we were children and we'd race? You could never catch up to me." Adonis sent another beam of light in Giovanni's direction, which he barely managed to dodge.

Giovanni's plan to wear Adonis down seemed to be working. Adonis was using his power more than he had probably ever needed to. His eyes had gone from blue to red several times before staying red. Unfortunately, some of the sparks his brother sent out had connected. "We're no longer children, Adonis." He ducked and flew across the room, catching his brother in his chest. Each time he managed to land a punch or kick, it felt as if he were hurting himself.

Giovanni had never wanted things to come to this, hadn't wanted to pick sides, but Adonis was no longer the brother he once knew. His mind was gone and had been replaced by that of a crazed, power-hungry rogue. He was doing the right thing by going against Adonis, but it still didn't make his decision any easier.

Claws outstretched, Adonis charged forward and grasped Giovanni by the shoulders, applying enough pressure to make it hurt. Badly.

Giovanni made the mistake of grunting in protest. Adonis laughed. "Don't you see? You're no match for me. You never were."

Giovanni grabbed Adonis's shoulders, demonstrating his strength. "You shouldn't underestimate me. One would think you would have learned that lesson a while ago. If it weren't for me, you would have realized all your plans by now."

"And for that, I should make your death slow and painful, but because we share a bloodline, I will spare you that fate. Give up and I promise to kill you quickly."

Sadness filled Giovanni's heart as his gaze roamed Adonis's face, desperately searching for something within him that was redeemable. Those sneering lips and blood-colored eyes were a mockery of the jovial youth he once was.

Giovanni brought his knee up and rammed it into Adonis's midsection. "Never!"

Adonis snarled and let go long enough to slam his fist into Giovanni's chest. He stumbled backward but managed to right himself so he wouldn't fall to the floor. They were evenly matched where strength was concerned and this would be a battle of endurance, if ever there was one.

Adonis threw himself at Giovanni and they both crashed to the ground. As his rogue brother threw punches, Giovanni blocked, but suddenly Adonis gripped the side of his head and sent a heat bomb coursing through his body.

Giovanni convulsed and writhed in agony. Twitching uncontrollably, his muscles began to shut down one at a time. He'd seen Adonis use this attack on another vampire before. It seemed that he'd been the one to underestimate. Adonis still had plenty of magic left within him.

"Your death will be the only one I regret today." Adonis raised his fist and Giovanni prepared himself for the deathblow, but a brilliant light filled the entire hall and flew at Adonis in a fiery yellow ball. Its impact was powerful enough to knock Adonis off Giovanni.

A soft hand touched his brow. Giovanni sighed in relief. He was so sure he'd seen the end. "Lili, thank you." His muscles still contracted adding to his other aches.

"I'll heal you." She kneeled at his side and placed her hands over his chest. "My strength is yours."

It took a moment for her words to set in. But by the time they did, it was too late. She sent something akin to an electromagnetic pulse through his body and it was like a soothing balm to his ache. Once again, he could move and within seconds, he felt as good as new. Better than new. Liliana had transferred some of her power to him.

Giovanni rose slowly. "Why did you do that? By giving up a piece of you, you've made yourself vulnerable."

"I've kept enough for myself, but you need my powers more than I do right now. You'll never have a normal life while your mother and brother are still around to terrorize others."

He was truly touched by her selflessness. She'd always been a good ally and there was no way he could possibly repay her for all she'd done for him. "You're a good friend to me, Lilli. I don't know what I would do without you."

Neither one of them had noticed that Adonis had gotten back to his feet until Liliana was plucked into the air by an invisible force that sent her sailing across the room to hit the wall with a sickening crunch.

"Lili!" Giovanni raced across the room but was halted in his tracks when a blunt object hit the back of his head. Stumbling, he stuck out his arms to brace himself against the fall. He was up on his feet in an instant with descended fangs. The regret Giovanni had been battling earlier vanished in the face of Adonis's cold smirk. There would be no holding back from this point on.

Chapter Twenty

Isis pounced at the witch, catching her on the arm. Beatrice attempted to shake her off, but Isis held on, sinking her teeth deeper into her adversary's skin until she heard the crunch of bone. She'd hang on for dear life if it meant saving Dante. Her love for him gave her the courage to forge on with this fight against a creature she wasn't certain she could beat.

Dante's family seemed to be holding their own against the rogue threat downstairs in the great hall. In fact, the numbers of their enemies had dwindled to the point where both sides were now evenly matched. Just as she had gone on her search for Dante, she saw Giovanni and Adonis squaring off. She was sure the others would aid him, if the need arose. But her main focus had been on finding her lover as quickly as possible.

Instinct told her he was in trouble. There was no reason why she was so certain of it, she just was. Seeing him chase after Beatrice, had sent a chill coursing through her body. It wasn't her lack of confidence in him as a fighter; far from it. If anyone could beat Beatrice and that creature she'd been able to conjure earlier, it would be Dante. But as long as she was around, he wouldn't have to do it alone.

Beatrice pounded her fist into Isis's head, her strength surprising for a mortal. But the blows only served to anger Isis. With a low growl, she chomped down even harder and managed to sever the lower part of the witch's arm. Isis landed on the ground and spat out the offensive limb.

The witch screamed in agony as blood shot from her amputated stump in a rush of crimson death. "Noooooo! This shouldn't be possible!"

Good. Suffer, bitch. Isis didn't get a chance to relish her minor victory because something strange happened. The rest of Beatrice's arm fell off at the shoulder, to be replaced with a long, slimy, log-like protrusion with spindly fingers and sharp, thick nails. It oozed a green sulfur-scented substance that sickened her. Holy shit. The arm belonged to that thing she'd seen earlier.

Out of the corner of her eye, she saw Dante attempting to stand though he seemed shaky on his feet. That last hit he'd taken had probably been more powerful than anything he'd ever come up against, and Isis figured it would only get worse once Beatrice transformed completely. She had to get them the hell out of here before that happened, and fast. Isis ran to his side and nudged him with her snout. *"Let's go or else something really bad is about to happen."*

Dante shook his head as though to clear his mind. "I told you to stay away from me."

There was no point arguing with him about whose side she was on. What was important was getting them away from that monster. *"And I told you to let's go. Whatever your feelings toward me, you need to get over them, because this situation is about to get really ugly very fast."*

Dante opened his mouth as if to argue, but when he looked over Isis's shoulder, he closed it. Balling his hands into fists at his sides, he bared his fangs. "I'm not scared of this bitch." His eyes narrowed to a fierce glare at the subject of their discussion, who swayed back and forth on her feet as though she were about to go out for the count.

"I don't give a goddamn if you're not scared of her, Dante Grimaldi! We're going to need help to defeat her. Look at her, she changing into some kind of monster. I've seen it and it's frightening. Now isn't the time to play the tough guy."

Ignoring Isis, Dante ran in the direction of the half demon, half human, but the seemingly disoriented Beatrice was ready for him. Throwing out her arms, one normal and the other grotesque, she sent out a visible wave of energy like an electrical current. The force of her magic hit them like a nuclear bomb. Isis howled in agony as her fur was singed and fell off in clumps. She and Dante were knocked to the other end of the hallway, their fall broken by the stone wall.

Isis landed on her side, letting out a whimper instead of the howl she'd intended. Using her residual strength, she put herself in between Beatrice and Dante, shielding him from further harm. Shutting her eyes tightly, she braced herself for the next attack. After several seconds when it didn't come, she opened one eye and then the other to see Beatrice wobbling from side to side, moving in a circle as if she'd been the one who'd been hit with that tsunami-powered assault. Stranger still, the witch appeared to be having a conversation with herself.

"You promised I'd have my revenge. This is my time!" she raged, her arms flailing wildly in the air. "You can't do this to me!"

"Oh, but I can," an inhuman-sounding voice answered from out of nowhere, vibrating throughout the entire castle.

Isis didn't know what the hell was going on, but she didn't want to stick around to find out. She'd experienced the power of the monster that dwelled within the witch, and this scene only confirmed they'd need reinforcements. Dante might still be angry with her, but she'd make him listen to her, if it killed her. Ignoring the ache, which had set in once again, she rose to her feet before nudging him in the side.

Breathing raggedly, he made it to his knees with his head bowed. "Go away."

"We need help. Stop being so stubborn and run. We'll get her when we can regroup."

Dante placed one hand against the wall to lever himself to a standing position and held his side with his free arm. "I never asked for your help. And there's no we as in you and me. It's me and my team."

"Get over yourself, Dante. I said I was going to help and that's exactly what I intend to do. I know you don't trust me, but you're going to have to put aside your hatred long enough to see what you're facing. You're only harming your family if you think to stay here and spite me."

"If you think you mean that much to me, then you're the one who needs to get over *yourself*."

Isis ignored the pain his comment inflicted. It hurt far more than any blast from Beatrice's demon. *"Say whatever you want to me but think about your family. You're no use to them if you're dead. Now, let's get help before she stops talking to herself."*

Dante looked down at her, his expression unreadable save the slight tightening of his lips. Finally, he nodded and flashed down the hallway with Isis on his heels.

"Give up, Gio. You know you can't defeat me. I'm not completely heartless. It's not too late for me to grant you that quick death. All you have to do is surrender." Using his magic, Adonis sent a chair flying in Giovanni's direction.

Giovanni ducked, but was knocked off his feet when another chair slammed into his back. *Dio*, it seemed as if his brother had an unlimited amount of magic at his disposal, but the glowing, reddish tint to Adonis's eyes, which hadn't gone away, was telling. Giovanni's plan was working, though this fight was taking more out of him than he imagined it would.

Every ounce of magic he'd stored for himself had been used up and he could now only rely on his natural vampiric skills. The loss of power was like a hunger within, clouding his mind, but he couldn't quit, refusing to give in to the insanity beckoning him into its embrace. "It's not me who needs to give up, but you. Look around you, Adonis. You're holding onto the past. Why would you come back to it when it only brought you misery?"

Adonis raised the utensils on the dining room table and directed them at Giovanni. "Miserable for you because you were unwanted. This was my birthright!"

Though Giovanni ducked, he couldn't avoid all the eating instruments; a fork penetrated his neck and another in his arm. He cried out, not from the pain, but from sadness. Despite his resolve to harden his heart against the one who'd caused so much despair, he couldn't bring himself to hate his brother. Adonis had clearly lost his grip on reality. How could one feel anything but pity for him? Even still, he planned to take Adonis down.

Hoping to dredge up one last bit of magic, he whispered a chant under his breath and shot an energy ball at Adonis, hitting him directly in the chest.

The other vampire's eyes widened in apparent surprise that Giovanni still had such power in his arsenal. Adonis soared through the air and crashed onto the dining room table. Giovanni was over him in a flash, grabbing him by the collar and rained several blows into his face.

Adonis clawed the side of Giovanni's face to free himself, furrowing his nails into the skin as if it were butter. Still holding onto his brother by a handful of shirt, he rammed his fist into Adonis's torso. Adonis placed his hands on Giovanni's chest and gave him a mighty shove.

Giovanni's grip loosened but he lost his balance in the process. Taking a few steps backward before righting himself, he was met by the hard force of Adonis's fist to the chin, but this time he stayed on his feet. Returning the favor, Giovanni threw a quick uppercut.

It went back and forth, each vampire evenly matched in strength going blow for blow. Their fight was a brutal dance, a battle of good versus evil that neither intended to lose.

As they fought on, Adonis's eyes turned to the deep shade of his minions'. His magic was waning. This had become a battle of endurance, neither vampire giving an inch. To Giovanni's surprise, Adonis was plucked backward by a pair of muscled hands.

Clasping his hands together to create one big fist, Romeo swung at Adonis, knocking him to the ground.

Niccolo appeared in an instant and dealt Adonis a kick to the ribs before he could stand. Giovanni took that moment to catch his breath, but he knew Adonis wouldn't be down for much longer.

Proving his supposition correct, Adonis dissipated in a puff of smoke and reappeared behind them, dealing Romeo and Niccolo vicious blows to the backs of their heads.

Adonis looked as though he was ready to deal out another assault when he was swept off his feet, lifted into the air until he hit the ceiling, and then slammed into the floor as if he'd been picked up by a large, invisible hand.

Giovanni looked over his shoulder. Liliana had gotten back to her feet and had shot out everything she had. Her face had lost all color, as if her life force was draining away.

Adonis, however, vanished yet again and appeared directly behind her. Wrapping a thick lock of hair around his fist, he yanked back so hard the sickening sound of cracking bones could be heard. "No!" He raced forward to save his friend, silently praying that she wouldn't die on his behalf.

Adonis chuckled. "Didn't I tell you, there was no use?"

Giovanni hit what felt like an invisible wall standing between him and Adonis. Romeo and Niccolo flashed forward and they, too, were stopped by the invisible barrier.

"Let her go, Adonis. Your fight is with me, not Liliana."

"Oh, but you're wrong, little brother. She has been a thorn in my side as much as you have over the years. I think it's only fitting you watch her die as well."

Liliana didn't struggle, scream, or cry out. Instead, a single tear slid down her ashen cheek. "I'm sorry I let you down, Giovanni."

Giovanni pounded against the invisible shield, desperate to save Liliana, whose friendship had been a comfort to him over the past several decades. He couldn't let her die like this.

Adonis cackled again, his voice filled with a maniacal glee that chilled Giovanni to the core. "As touching as this tender scene is, I'm unfortunately going to have to end it."

To Giovanni's horror, a fist exploded through the witch's chest. Her eyes briefly widened in surprise before a serene look of peace entered them and she slumped in Adonis's arms.

"*Figlio di puttana! Bastardo!*" Giovanni beat against the obstruction until his fists bled. Never before had he been this filled with rage.

Adonis taunted him with a warped laugh. "You share the same bloodline as me, so what does that make you?"

Giovanni kicked and hit at the invisible force. He was so focused on getting his hands on Adonis, he didn't notice Romeo, Niccolo, and a few others attempted to break the wall as well. Adonis's powers would eventually fail him, and when they did, he'd be here waiting.

Dante flashed through the castle, hoping that thing wouldn't catch up anytime soon. Isis raced alongside him, keeping up. As much as he hated to admit it, Isis had been right. There was no way he could take that thing alone. Anything that could knock him out like that had to be powerful.

If Isis had not intervened, he probably would have stubbornly stayed behind to face the monster. He'd also be dead. He didn't know why she had even bothered. She had to realize no matter what she did, there was no going back for the two of them. She'd broken a trust he didn't freely give to anyone beyond his family and a small group of allies. Dante had to accept her fighting with him for now, but there would be nothing else beyond that.

They made it downstairs to the great hall where the big rumble still took place. To Dante's relief, he saw Marco, Romeo, and Nico standing alongside Giovanni. They looked to be beating against some kind of force field that Adonis had taken cover behind.

He surveyed the room to see that all but a handful of the rogues had been dispatched. There were a few missing members of his team, and his heart lurched because he immediately knew what that meant. His gaze fell on Sasha and her brothers, who worked together to fend off a few of the remaining villains.

"We're going to need Sasha to help us with that demon Beatrice is transforming into."

Isis cocked her head to the side. *"Demon? Is that what that thing was? And what can Sasha do? She's a young witch. Would she be any match against it?"*

Dante nodded. "She's much more powerful than you think. There are rare occasions when age does not determine the strength of an immortal, and she bears an extremely rare mark. Besides, she wouldn't have to face it alone. I'm sure Nico, her brothers, and her son wouldn't allow that to happen either."

Just then, the castle shook again as something released a loud, bellowing roar that sounded like a noise from the depths of the darkest hell. The creature was near. Everyone in the hall paused for a brief moment apparently startled by the sound. Their time was short before it caught up with them, he ran toward his brother's mate.

"It was the demon, wasn't it?" Sasha asked the moment Dante approached.

"Yes. The thing is stronger than I imagined it would be, and I suspect we still haven't seen the full extent of its power."

Taking a deep breath, Sasha inclined her head. "Then, I'll do all I can. Take me to it."

Jagger grasped her shoulder. "I'm going with you, Mama."

She shook her head. "*Nyet!* I'm not going to lose you again."

Steel placed his arm around his sister's shoulder. "Sasha, your little boy is a man. He won't go down easily. He has Romanov blood in his veins."

"And Grimaldi blood most importantly," Nico growled as he joined them.

"Fine," Dante agreed with both factions. "There's no time to argue about it now, because here it comes."

Beatrice, or what sort of looked like her, toddled into the hall. Her good arm had fallen off so now both of her arms were monstrous. Her face had contorted beyond recognition, and those sharp, off-colored teeth were larger than ever. Clumps of skin had fallen off her face and only thin strands of stringy red hair remained on her head. She'd grown at least a foot since Dante and Isis had left her behind. It was by far one of the most gruesome sights he'd ever seen. He instinctively knew the thing would not be easily beaten.

Giovanni continued in his endeavor to break through Adonis's barrier with the assistance of his brothers. Even the roar that had shaken the castle hadn't distracted him from his goal. He was determined to tear the target of his ire limb from limb. Although Niccolo had abandoned him to aid his mate, it didn't matter because the force field trembled beneath one of Giovanni's blows. Adonis had weakened. He wouldn't be able to hold this thing up much longer.

Adonis's eyes were now completely crimson as he continued to taunt them. "You can never hope to beat me, Gio. You were always jealous of me, weren't you? That's why you stood in my way all these years. You wanted me to be as big a failure as you are." He redirected his spiteful gaze to Romeo. "And you are supposed to be the bad boy of the family, aren't you? I'm not so sure about 'bad,' but 'boy' certainly suits you."

"Shut the fuck up!" Romeo pounded against the force field, battering it so fast and hard that his movement would have been invisible to human eyes.

Adonis turned his attention to GianMarco. "How does it feel to know you weren't strong enough to protect Bianca and your son? Ah, her screams were delicious. Do you know I tasted her before I ripped out her heart? So sweet. I can understand why you fell for such a tender morsel. And the baby, you should be very proud. He barely cried as I tore off his limbs one at a time. Do you think your little girl will be so brave?"

Adonis continued to work Giovanni, Romeo, and GianMarco into a frenzy of passionate anger, alternating between taunts and laughter until he paused to gaze over their shoulders. Whatever was behind them had captured his attention enough for him to end his verbal tirade. "*Dio!*"

Giovanni looked back and stilled. His mouth fell open and he could do nothing but stare. A horrific caricature of his mother, half demon, half human, stood in the middle of the room. Gone was the beauty she once coveted and in its place was a misshapen caricature. It not only confirmed his suspicions that a demon had attached itself to her, but that it had also been *within* her. In his studies, he knew a demon could detach itself from its human host without causing damage. But this one chose to exit through Beatrice's body in a gruesome manner, meaning one thing: She'd run out of usefulness to it.

And from the looks of things, she knew it. What was left of her face held an expression of rage, agony, and dismay. Giovanni had known this moment would come for her, but he never believed he'd actually witness it. The creature roared, and a woman's scream echoed in the midst of the unholy sound. Beatrice's. "You promised me eternity!"

"In hell," the thing answered.

As the internal struggle continued, bursts of power shot from her body as hair and skin fell to the ground in piles. Her body stretched, bursting her clothing to shreds, and she grew another foot taller. Spikes popped out of her back in a mockery of a spine. Narrow shoulders broadened to hulk-like proportions as the demon inside Beatrice continued to grow taller.

And all Giovanni could do was stand and stare, frozen in horror at the thing his mother had become. It was a fitting end to someone who'd only ever been pure evil, but she was still his mother. A wave of sorrow that he hadn't expected to feel touched him. He didn't have a chance to dwell on those feelings before rays of light shot from the demon's body, attacking everything and everyone within its wake.

"Mother!" Adonis yelled out, racing toward the beast, the barrier gone.

"No, Adonis!" Giovanni screamed involuntarily. He reached out to grab Adonis's hand only to be shoved backward with a force that sent him tumbling to the ground.

"Mother!" Adonis attempted to touch the beast and was lifted and thrown the length of the room.

Exactly as Giovanni had feared, the creature could no longer be controlled and it was seeking souls to consume. Which side they came from didn't matter to it; it was hungry.

Desperately scanning all the occupants in the room, Giovanni's gaze fell on Sasha, and he made his way over to the witch whose magic could be powerful enough to combat this minion of darkness. He grasped her by the arm. "I'm going to need you to give all you've got to the demon. Black magic will have no effect on it."

She moistened her lips with the tip of her tongue and nodded. "What spell should I use?"

"Do you have a light spell?"

Uncertainty puckered her forehead. "I do. I haven't practiced it much, though."

"We will back you up, *sistra*," Steel assured Sasha.

"Everyone will need to help. I'll need you all to use everything you have while the rest of us attack. Like I said before, it won't be easy taking this thing down."

The creature lurched forward with a low growl, waving its hands in apparent fury. They needed to act quickly before the monster got any closer. "Surround it now!" Giovanni commanded.

Dante moved next to him. "What do the rest of us need to do?"

"Attack it as best as you can, but be careful to avoid any of the magic bursts it may shoot out."

Dante nodded. "When?"

"Now, Sasha, do it!" Giovanni shouted.

Sasha, her brothers, and Jagger circled the demon, standing far enough away from it so it couldn't touch them. Rubbing her hands together, Sasha murmured a chant before shooting out a beam of light so bright Giovanni found himself squinting against it. Steel, the twins, and Jagger followed suit.

The monster howled louder than ever. Giovanni turned to the rest of the group. "Now! Give it everything you've got!"

Chapter Twenty-One

Isis had never been more frightened in her life. The creature seemed to be absorbing the energy Sasha and the warlocks shot at it, seeming unaffected by the hits. But no matter how long it took to take the thing down, she wouldn't back down.

Springing forward, she pounced on the demon's chest and sank her teeth into slippery flesh. The foul taste of rotten meat assaulted her taste buds and the need to throw up threatened to take hold of her, but she wouldn't let go of it. The monster, however, had other ideas.

Ripping her off its chest, it squeezed her body until she felt as if her bones would crush. Each breath she took fought to leave her lungs and it felt like her insides were hemorrhaging.

"Isis!" Dante shouted her name. If she didn't know better, he sounded as if he actually cared. It gave her hope and the strength to claw and fight to free herself from the demon's grasp. Out of the corner of her eye, she saw Dante pound into the demon's stomach. His attack was followed by several others from various team members.

Without warning, the monster flung her over its shoulder as if it were discarding an insignificant piece of trash. Using every bit of agility she possessed, she landed on her feet. She turned, ready to deal out her next assault. This time she settled for a ground attack, catching it on the ankle. Clamping her jaws down as hard as she could, Isis found its skin harder to cut through than anything she'd ever bitten into.

Biting and clawing, she ripped at its flesh, frustrated she was barely making a dent. The other shifters appeared to face a similar dilemma. Paris seemed to have more success, managing to slice off a hunk of the creature's leg with his claws. Being an older immortal made his attacks more lethal, though the demon was still stood with little injury.

The warlocks pounded the beast with light and it still only seemed to be a minor deterrent to it. Isis didn't know how long she clawed and chewed at the monster while fending off its kicks. With an abruptness that took her by surprise, it stilled. But she wasn't fooled into thinking they'd beaten the thing. Without warning, it bent over and pounded its fists into the floor, making the ground shake. Something akin to the attacks she'd experienced earlier shot from its body, sending every single team member surrounding it flying. A tidal wave of agony shot through her body.

She fell to the floor, her body convulsing. The demon raised its foot as if it intended to stomp her. With a whimper, she attempted to move her paralyzed limbs, but it felt like the creature had some kind of hold on her. Helplessness wrapped its fingers around her like a taunting caress and gripped her entire being. Her breath caught in her throat and her fur stood on end.

Isis had been prepared to die fighting, but she hadn't expected it to end this way. Closing her eyes against what she knew was to come, she opened them again when strong arms slid beneath her and she was pressed against a warm body. Dante gripped her tightly and rolled away just before the demon brought his elephant-sized foot down.

Instead of releasing her right away like she believed he would, Dante held her close. As the seconds passed, her muscles relaxed and she could finally move freely again, though her breathing was still ragged and hard to get out due to his nearness. Even in battle, Dante had this effect on her. They had to help the others but she selfishly gave herself another moment in his arms before raising her head to meet his gaze. *"You can let me go now, Dante."*

What she wanted to tell him was the opposite, but this was neither the time nor the place. Besides, that cold, hard mask had settled over his face again, shutting her out. He'd saved her life, but just as quickly, he withdrew from her, locking his emotions away and throwing away the key.

"Are you all right?" He asked it so matter-of-factly he could have been talking to a stranger.

Isis nodded, hoping her expression didn't give away the pain embedded deep in her heart. *"I'm fine. That blast took me by surprise."*

His lips tightened grimly. "It took us all by surprise. You should be more careful. Just don't think my saving you means anything. I pay my debts and the one I owe you has been paid in full." Releasing her, he hopped to his feet and turned his attention toward the demon that now shot its dark magic at anyone in its path. Reaching out, it caught Giovanni in its grip and squeezed.

Dante sprang at the beast, wrapping his arms around its neck and holding on in a death grip. He sank his fangs into the back of the demon's head. It was Isis's cue to join in. The creature finally let go of Giovanni but he released another ball of demonic power in the process. This time she was ready for it. Racing away, she managed to dodge it and darted forward.

A pattern ensued. The team ganged up on the demon and it would swat and kick them away and release a power wave of strong energy, knocking most of them off their feet. Exhaustion soon set in after several rounds. However, as they continued, the demon's attacks grew weaker. She only hoped it was the case and not just her imagination or they were all doomed.

As the creature knocked Dante back yet again Giovanni was at his side, offering a hand to help him up.

"It's weakening." From the way he felt, Giovanni was certain his eyes were now completely red. The pinkish tint of his normally olive skin spoke of the powerful blood rush coursing through his body. "I know what you're thinking and I'm fine. I have the craving under control for the most part. We almost have the demon where we want it. Look, it's getting smaller."

Since they'd started their attack, the demon had lost a foot in height. It didn't seem as broad, either. Sasha, her brothers, and Jagger held hands as a bright beam of light emitted from the circle they'd created, firing into the demon. The end was near. Giovanni could feel it.

The demon's movements became more erratic, and it flung a couple shifters out of the way as it tried to get to the team of warlocks and witch. Giovanni made his way toward the monster and began to pummel it.

The demon dealt a blow to the side of Giovanni's head, but he barely lost his footing.

Dante gripped Giovanni from behind and yanked him away. "My turn." Dante nudged him aside and continued to rip into the demon.

It now shot out weak bursts of power. It's energy was nearly drained. The remaining team surrounded the demon, ready to finish it off, but something caught Giovanni's attention. In the far corner of the room, he noticed Adonis and Nya in their own battle. His brother's hands were wrapped around her throat and though she clawed at him to break free, she didn't really seem to be fighting back. It was almost as if...

Fuck.

The demon forgotten, Giovanni joined the pair and yanked Adonis away from Nya. Giovanni backhanded Adonis with all the force he could muster. "You will not kill another tonight."

Giovanni stumbled when Adonis sprang to his feet and returned the hit and then followed with an uppercut. "You're wrong, little brother. If I go down tonight, it won't be alone."

Giovanni charged toward Adonis, but he was stopped in his tracks when the redhead grasped him by the neck with one hand and punched him in the face with a hard fist. "Did you think I didn't figure out what your little plan was? To weaken me? Even without my magic, you're no match for me, but I thought I'd save a little something for you."

Jolts of power shot through Giovanni like a million sharp razors, cutting him from the inside out. It was a struggle not to crumble to the floor, but stubborn pride kept him erect.

"Fall!" Adonis screamed.

"Never!" He gritted his teeth against this twisted bout of torture. The cool, wet kiss of blood trickled out of his nostrils and ears. It rose from his throat to spill from the corner of his mouth.

"Then you are a fool, Gio. You always were."

Just as it seemed like every single organ in his body would explode, he was shoved aside and knocked to the ground. Nya wrapped her arms around him and held on tight.

"Let...me...go...Nya. This is between Adonis and me."

Her grip tightened. "No. I won't let him do this."

"So this is your final choice?" The soft tone of Adonis's voice didn't fool Giovanni for a second. He'd heard it too many times before and knew this was the quiet before the storm.

Nya raised her head, her dark eyes narrowed to slits. "You knew the answer to that long before now."

"I should have killed you instead of allowing you to lurk in the castle. I had thought...Well, it doesn't matter. You will die with him."

Seeing the fierce glow in his brother's eyes, Giovanni realized he'd only had a taste of what Adonis had left within his arsenal. He should have been able to easily push Nya off him. She was less than half his age, but she held on with a tenacity that surprised him. As he struggled to break free of her grip, Adonis delivered another burst of power, but this time, Nya took the brunt of it.

Her eyes were now tightly closed as she braced herself against the attack. If not for the gasp that escaped her lips, Giovanni would never have known it hurt her.

Nya's eyes popped open and she gave him a brief look, which he immediately understood. She *did* want to die.

He'd already lost Liliana, and he'd be damned if he let her go without a fight. He tossed her off with great effort but before he could get to his feet, Dante appeared, catching Adonis off guard with a fist to the midsection.

Dante followed up his assault with a kick right between Adonis's legs. "That's for my parents, motherfucker."

Adonis dropped to his knees. Dante didn't give him a chance to retaliate, dealing out a left hook. "That's for Bianca and baby Giovanni." He followed up with a right cross. "That's for Flora." And he finished with roundhouse kick to the head. "That one was for me."

Adonis wasn't down for the count, however. As Dante pulled his fist back to hit him again, Adonis dissipated and reappeared behind Dante and sank his fangs into the side of the younger vampire's neck.

Giovanni jumped to his feet and dashed forward. Muttering a prayer for forgiveness under his breath, he clawed through Adonis's back with every ounce of strength he possessed. Giovanni didn't stop until his hand was inside his brother's chest. He circled his brother's pulsing heart with his fingers.

Adonis cried out in his apparent surprise and stiffened.

Using Adonis's distracted state, Dante freed himself and when he looked as though he would mete out another blow, Giovanni shook his head. "No, Dante. If anyone does this, it has to be me."

Dante flared his nostrils and for a brief moment Giovanni thought he wouldn't relent, but he slowly lowered his fist. He met Dante's gaze. *"Thank you."*

"You owe me."

"I know. But, I need this moment."

"I'll go back and help the others. The demon is wasting away." Dante flashed away before Giovanni could reply.

Adonis slumped against his body, gasping for breath as Giovanni held onto his heart. Once it was destroyed, his brother would be as well. With his life force in the Giovanni's palm, Adonis could no longer wield his black magic.

"Go ahead and finish it, Gio, I—" Adonis broke off abruptly to cough up blood.

The life force that had once been so strong within Adonis slowly drained away. It was just one simple squeeze, but Giovanni didn't want to do it. It would probably have been easier to let Adonis kill him than to suffer through this scourging of his soul. This final task was almost like destroying a part of himself. He couldn't stop thinking of the man Adonis had once been, and a great sorrow gripped him. That it had to come to this was what he'd dreaded from the day he'd finally chosen sides.

Collapsing to his knees with an arm locked around Adonis's waist and the other hand still gripping his heart, Giovanni rested his forehead against his brother's shoulder.

A weak chuckle escaped Adonis's lips. "Even now, you hesitate to kill me? You've won. Relish it."

Though he held Adonis's heart, it was his own that was breaking. "You know I could never do that."

A genuine smile crossed Adonis's pained face. Giovanni could see a glimpse of the boy who had once been his best friend. "No. You couldn't. That was always your problem, Gio."

The hot scald of bitter tears raced down Giovanni's face. He opened his mouth to speak, but no words were forthcoming. One of his favorite memories of the past was when they were children and they'd race around these very castle walls, causing holy terror to everyone in their wake. He thought of those warm summer days when they would swim in the pond. And the times when they'd spin around with their arms straight out, until they were so dizzy they could barely walk. He remembered the nights when there was a thunderstorm and Giovanni would run to Adonis's room for protection. His older brother would tell him stories until he fell asleep. He remembered the boy with ready laugh, who had a kind word for everyone. That was the Adonis who would remain with him.

Adonis must have felt the dampness against his neck because he stiffened. "Tears, Gio? Be a fucking man and get this over with. Or do you wish to gloat? Do you want to rub your victory in my face?"

Ignoring Adonis's last statement, he tightened his arm around him. "There was a time you used to care. Is it wishful thinking on my part to think you never stopped?"

"I don't know what you're talking about." The protest was weak enough to give Giovanni hope.

"There were several times you could have killed me, and Nya for that matter, but you didn't. You cared. And you lied, too."

"What are you talking about, Gio? I think you're reading more into things than you should." Adonis moved as if to straighten himself but winced from his obvious discomfort. His sharp intake of breath told Giovanni he was in pain, but still something kept Giovanni from granting Adonis the sweet release of death's embrace.

Giovanni raised his head and bit back a cry that rose past his throat. Adonis had lost all color. He was ash white and his eyes were no longer red. They were not even their usual dark blue, but a pale, near white shade. In that moment Giovanni would have gladly traded places, but knew he must continue on his course.

"You said I was never wanted. But that was a lie, wasn't it? Someone wanted me around."

"And who do you think that was?"

"You."

Adonis looked over his shoulder at Giovanni with narrowed eyes. "Not...true."

"Admit it. At least, give me that. *Please.*"

Giovanni closed his eyes, squeezing them tight against the pain coursing within him. Every physical and verbal assault he'd ever received couldn't compare to this hurt Adonis meted out. "No matter what you feel toward me, Adonis, I never stopped loving you and I'm sorry it had to end like this. Whether you accept my love or not, you have it."

Just when Giovanni thought he'd be greeted by silence once again, Adonis released a long sigh. "You're right," he said so softly Giovanni thought he'd imagined it. "I never stopped caring about you, either. And...thank you."

"What for?"

"Not letting them finish me off."

Giovanni figured by "them" Adonis meant Dante and his younger brothers. "I wouldn't have allowed it to be any other way."

"Most of my existence, I craved power, but you had the greatest weapon at your disposal all along: your love."

"You're my big brother. Of course, I love you. I just wish Beatrice had never gotten her hooks into you. If only, I could have saved you from her clutches…

Adonis shook his head. "It's true our mother had nothing but malice in her heart, the choices I made were my own and now, I must repent for them. " He looked around him and his gaze fell on Nya, who stood close by, her expression blank. "Come." He motioned her to him.

She slowly made her way over and knelt beside him. Adonis reached up and grazed the side of her face with the back of his hand. "*Bella*, I should have been honest with you, but I thought it made me seem weak if I admitted my feelings. I love you. I've loved you since the moment I laid eyes on you. I'm sorry I changed you before you were fully aware of what that meant but I couldn't bear living without you. I apologize for binding you to me when I had no right. But…I thought perhaps you might love me a little, too. Did you?"

Nya hesitated for a second before nodding. "I did. I do. I just didn't like the things you did and because of them, I didn't want you to know how I felt. But maybe if I had, you—"

Adonis pressed his finger against her lips. "Shh. Not even you could have deterred me from my course, my lovely. Don't blame yourself for the choices I made. When I released you, I knew you hadn't left the castle and were a danger to my plan. But, I was just happy to have you close in any capacity. But now, my time has come to an end. I release you. And, I want you to find happiness and love with someone who can give you the life you always deserved. You're far too beautiful and full of spirit to carry on as you have. Your joy will eventually come." He caressed her cheek.

Her eyes suspiciously damp, Nya took Adonis's hand in hers.

"No tears, *Bella*. May I have a final kiss goodbye, my love?"

Nya sniffed as she leaned forward and pressed her lips against Adonis's. When she straightened, she hastily wiped a tear that had trailed down her cheek.

"Do it now," Adonis whispered. "And, no more tears for me. This was the destiny I chose." He closed his eyes.

Giovanni pressed his forehead against Adonis's. "Goodbye, brother." While he still had the courage, Giovanni squashed Adonis's heart in his palm, finishing him off. When his brother drew his final breath, Giovanni wrapped his arms around the corpse and held it close, letting his tears fall at will.

Nya released Adonis's hand and placed her arm around Giovanni's shoulders as he rocked his brother back and forth. It was over, and they'd won. So why did it feel like he'd lost the fight?

True, Adonis had masterminded several acts of evil and had perpetrated even more, but it wasn't him. When one had been manipulated by a self-centered parent who emotionally, physically, and even sexually abused her child to maintain control for her own twisted reasons, it was bound to warp one's mind.

Giovanni didn't place all the blame on his mother's shoulders. Adonis was just as responsible. He'd had the opportunity to break away but didn't. Giovanni also held himself responsible for not trying to help his brother more. Maybe, he shouldn't have given up his attempts to convince Adonis to come away with him when they were younger. He should have stayed around in those lean years, and things wouldn't have ended this way. Over and over, he replayed how he could have done things differently.

"It's not your fault, Giovanni," Nya said softly.

He didn't answer, not trusting himself to speak.

In the end, Giovanni did get his brother back, but at the cost of his life.

Dante leapt away from the demon as it waved its arms in the air erratically and emitted green ooze from every pore of its body. The thing's skin began to ripple as if there were creepy crawlies living beneath the surface. It let out an earthshaking roar before falling to the ground facedown. Slowly, it began to dissolve. Sulfur-scented smoke blanketed its disappearing form until it was a thick, gooey puddle on the floor.

They'd done it. It was finally over. But there was one piece of business he needed to take care of. Glancing across the room, he saw Giovanni kneeling on the floor, his head in his palms and his shoulders heaving. Nya sat beside him, her arms around him. There was no sign of Adonis, which meant it truly was the end.

Unlike his older brother, Dante couldn't conjure up much remorse for Adonis. After all, he'd set out to do everything within his means to destroy the Grimaldi clan, shaking their foundation and leaving a trail of destruction behind him. The torment and anguish he and his family had suffered was something Dante would never forgive or forget.

A small part of him felt regret, however, because he'd never known this brother. Maybe if there had been no Beatrice, things could have been different. But he knew there was no point dwelling on the what-ifs. Adonis had signed his death warrant when he killed Dante's parents and screwed with his family.

And then, there was Giovanni. It was clear from the trembling of his body and the raw agony stamped on his face that Adonis had meant something to him. In the short time he'd known his older brother, Dante found Giovanni to be honorable, and if he said there was another side to Adonis, Dante had to take his word. It was disappointing that Adonis had let the dark side take over. But, all Dante's sympathy lay with Giovanni. He could imagine what the older vampire was going through.

Awkwardness kept him rooted to the spot. He wasn't sure if he should go to his brother and offer comfort or leave him to his grieving. He didn't have long to ponder his question when a hand fell on his shoulder. Dante turned to see Marco, and he immediately knew something was wrong. "What's the matter?"

"The children. We've searched the castle and can't find them anywhere, but I feel Gia near. Do you think someone is still holding them?"

Nya stood abruptly and joined them. "I can take you to the children."

The words were barely out of her mouth when she was surrounded by the others. "Where's my baby?" Maggie demanded.

"Are they safe?" Christine asked, her eyebrows knitted in worry.

"Yes, follow me." Turning around without waiting to see who followed her, she lead his family out of the room.

Dante decided to let them enjoy their reunion. He would see his nieces and nephew later. Taking a deep breath, he walked over to Giovanni and hunched down. Not sure whether he should hug him, Dante kept his hands in front of him. "I'm sorry, Giovanni. I know Adonis meant a lot to you."

Not bothering to look in Dante's direction, he nodded. "Thank you. But you and I both knew this was a long time coming. I can't excuse all he's done, but Adonis wasn't all bad. The funny thing is, neither was Beatrice. Granted, she was a self-centered, malicious woman, but she was an ambitious woman who lived in a time when a woman's only commodities were her connections and her looks. She had plenty of the latter and used it to get what she wanted. I think in a another era she might have been a different person. But after the demon had taken hold of her soul, there was no hope for her. She and I were never close, but she was my mother."

"You're right, she wasn't completely bad. She had you." Dante reached out to take his brother's hand in a comforting gesture, not caring any longer whether Giovanni would welcome his touch or not.

Giovanni didn't pull his hand away as a smile spread across his face. "Thank you. It means a lot to hear you say that." He squeezed Dante's hand.

"You may have lost a brother today, but you have four more and we'd very much like you to be a part of our family, the proper way."

Giovanni's smile widened. "I'd like that a lot. These years have been tough, wanting a relationship with the four of you when I knew I had to stay away."

Dante grinned. "You're going to wish you hadn't said that because there's no getting rid of us now."

Giovanni's expression turned serious as his smile faltered. "This is what Papa wanted: for all his sons to be together. He never gave up on Adonis, you know. He always hoped to bridge that gap between father and son one day."

Dante pondered this. It sounded so like his kindhearted papa. "Let's just hope that wherever he and Adonis are right now, they'll finally get that chance."

"Yes."

Silence fell between them for a moment until Dante released his brother's hand. "Should we go catch up with the others?"

Giovanni shook his head. "You go back to the villa and I'll join you later to participate in the celebration you and the family are due."

"Are you sure you'll be all right on your own?"

Giovanni raised a brow. "Dante, I've been alone for longer than I can remember. It's what I've grown accustomed to."

There was a wealth of meaning in that statement, and it tweaked Dante's heart to hear the sadness within

Giovanni's voice. "You're no longer alone." When Giovanni didn't answer, Dante sighed. "We'll head back. Take as much time as you need."

He stood up, then, and headed out of the hall when something brushed up against him. Isis, still in wolf form, glanced up at him. With Adonis and Beatrice taken care of, he had all the time in the world to deal with the issue of her, but he didn't want to. Dante didn't have the energy or the desire to talk to her.

"What do you want?"

"Is that all you can say to me, Dante?"

"What exactly would you like me to say to you, Isis? That I forgive you? That I understand you're a lying whore?"

She reeled back as if he'd kicked her, and for a brief second, he felt ashamed at the harshness of his words. Then, he pushed his shame away. She'd done this to herself with her lies. Turning away from the wounded look in her eyes, he left hurriedly, not bothering to look back.

Chapter Twenty-Two

Isis could not have predicted the level of Dante's cruelty, but he'd cut her to the quick with those last words. Instinctively, she wanted to run away with her tail between her legs and forget Dante even existed but she couldn't. How could she truly love him if she didn't fight to be with him? She would confront him and make him listen to her. And then if he turned her away, she'd try again.

Isis understood why he'd believed she'd betrayed him but he'd gone a bit overboard in his condemnation. In her heart, Isis believed beyond a shadow of doubt that they belonged together and he knew it, too. It was why she'd gone back to Giovanni's villa, uninvited. She didn't know how she'd be received, but Isis didn't care about what the others thought, only Dante.

So why couldn't she bring herself to knock on the door? For the third time, she raised her fist and then dropped it. Just as she was building enough courage to go for it, the door swung open and she met the questioning gaze of Paris Kyriakis. His nephew was behind him and they looked to be heading out.

"I was wondering when you'd show up." His tone surprised her; it lacked the edge she had come to expect from all their exchanges. It almost sounded like he was pleased to see her. It had to be her imagination. There had never been any love lost on his end where she was concerned.

"Well, um, I, uh, had to freshen up. I needed to shower and get some clothes so I kind of let myself inside of an unoccupied villa." She owed him no explanation but she found herself babbling nonetheless "Is Dante inside?"

"Yes, he is, but may I have a word with you before you go in?" He turned to his nephew. "Aries, go ahead and wait for me in the car; I'll be with you shortly."

Aries Kyriakis inclined his head toward her in acknowledgment, closing the door behind him before he left.

Once she and Paris were alone, Isis tensed. She hoped he didn't intend to tell her to stay away from Dante because that was one request she couldn't comply with. Or he could tell her that he no longer wanted her to contact Persephone anymore which would have been almost as bad. She tensed as she waited for him to speak.

"Relax, Isis, I won't bite your head off, although sometimes I do give that impression." He was actually smiling.

Isis took a step back. Who was he and what had he done to Paris Kyriakis? "No? Then what did you want to talk to me about?"

"Not about what you think."

She crossed her arms across her chest defensively. "And what am I thinking, Paris?"

"That, I'll warn you off. Before we began our adventure, it might have been something I would have done, but no more. Truce?" He held out his hand to her.

She looked at his outstretched palm, debating whether she should take it. Finally, releasing a deep breath, she placed her hand in his engulfing grasp.

Paris offered her a smile, the first genuine one he'd ever given her. "Now that wasn't so bad, was it?"

Slowly, she relaxed and let her guard down. "No. It wasn't. But, I wonder what's brought on this about-face."

Paris released her hand and raked his fingers through his dark hair. "I know I've made no secret about my thoughts on lone wolves. In my experience, a lot of them were bad seeds, kicked out of their packs for whatever reasons. I've put up with you because Persephone believes in you and I should have listened to my daughter."

She raised a brow. "Oh?"

"Yes. I've misjudged you."

"You no longer believe I was working both sides?" Isis couldn't help challenging him. She'd been on the receiving end of his disapproval for so long that it wasn't easy to accept this turnaround.

"I admit when Dante had told me what had happened between you and Black Adder, it made me think about how you fought against those rogues. If you were really on their side, would you have gone at them as hard as you had? Besides, you were clearly smitten with Dante. It was clear your feelings for him are genuine, I was simply too blinded my own prejudices to admit it. And then, there was tonight when you went after that demon. You had our backs and no traitor would have done all the things you did."

"I still had an association with the Serpent Gang."

"This is true, but I would be a hypocrite to say my past is pristine. My biggest concern about you was the influence you have on my daughter. My judgment about you was so clouded I couldn't see that Persephone is quite strong-willed when she wants to be, so there's nothing you can make her do that she doesn't want to. And then, there was Dante. He's a good friend of mine, and he's been through so much I didn't want to see him hurt again. Do you understand what I'm saying?"

"Yes. I think I do."

"I'm glad because I was wrong about you. While I can't say I'm happy with the friends you kept in the past, what you did then should have no bearing on the present, and for that I apologize. Put it down to me being an overprotective father and friend."

Isis realized it couldn't be easy for Paris to express regret to someone of inferior rank, a wolf without a pack's protection. "Thank you. I only hope Dante will be as forgiving as you."

Paris rubbed his chin. "He's been distant since he returned."

She frowned. "How so?"

"Oh, he's all smiles for everyone, but I can tell something's the matter. I think he's probably more hurt he didn't learn the truth from you. You knew how he felt about rogues. That he learned of your association with an entire gang of them and that you and the leader were lovers hurt him the most. I'm not saying it's right, but that's probably more in line with his reasoning. When you go in there and confront him, it won't be easy, but you have my support. And if things don't work out, you have a place in Pack Kyriakis."

Isis was so touched by his generous offer tears sprang to her eyes. "Thank you. Your offer means a lot to me."

Paris smiled, showing off even white teeth. Bending over, he brushed her cheek with his lips. "Good luck, Isis."

Nervous laughter trickled from her lips. "I'm definitely going to need it. "

"Aries is waiting for me. We have to get back to the island and check up on Constantine and Sarah."

"Send them my love and tell Persephone, I'll be in touch."

"Will do."

When he was gone, she was left facing the same dilemma she had earlier. Should she go in? Gathering every ounce of courage in her reserve, she tried the doorknob instead of knocking. Isis decided to brazen it out. She had nothing to lose and everything to gain. It was unlocked. Making her way inside, she closed the door behind her with a gentle click, but before she could turn around the hairs on the back of her neck stood on end. He was near. Not just near, but he was next to her.

Isis slowly pivoted to see Dante so close the breath from his flared nostrils caressed her face. "Dante!"

"You don't fucking listen, do you?"

Catching her bottom lip between her teeth to hold back her gasp, Isis squared her shoulders to show him she wouldn't be intimidated, despite the quivering of her insides. She raised her chin in defiance, meeting his cobalt gaze. "I was hoping we could talk and I don't plan on leaving until we do."

Raising one dark, sinisterly arched brow, Dante crossed his arms over his broad chest. "Is that so?"

She moistened her lips with the tip of her tongue, holding onto the last thread of her courage. "Yes, it is. Are we just going to stand here or am I not allowed any farther?"

"Everyone else has either left or retired for the night. I was about to do the same, so say whatever you need to say to me and leave."

She took a step closer until their bodies touched. "Won't you offer me someplace to sit?"

Dante took a step back, his arms falling to his sides. "What kind of game are you playing, Isis?"

"This isn't a game, Dante. It never was with me."

His gaze raked her face, his expression unreadable. Finally, turning on his heel, he gestured her to follow. He led her to the living room.

As he'd said, everyone had dispersed for the night, but she didn't want to take the chance of being interrupted. "Can't we go to your bedroom? It would be more private, wouldn't it? You're staying the night here, aren't you?"

"I am. You aren't."

"I never said I was. Please, Dante. All I need is five minutes of your time. In private."

Releasing an exasperated breath, he rolled his eyes. "Even though I owe you nothing, I'll give you those five minutes, but not a second more. And if you try anything, I just might strangle you."

"What exactly do you think I could do to you with a house full of your family and allies? I wouldn't make it out of here alive."

He grunted in response, but turned and led her down a hallway until he reached the guest room he occupied. Unable to help it, she allowed her gaze to stray toward the large four-poster bed. It was the same bed they'd shared not so very long ago. A shiver raced up her spine as she remembered how passionately he'd fucked her and the way he'd held and kissed her afterward. God, she wanted that back, but from the look of him, this wouldn't be an easy task.

His arms were folded across his chest and his face was a tight, unreadable slate. Isis shivered from the iciness of his stare. "You've wasted two of your minutes already. I hope you can sum up what you need to say in the next three."

She closed her eyes against the harshness of his tone. "Please don't." Isis wished her voice didn't sound so wobbly and unsure.

"Don't what, Isis?"

"Don't be so cold. I can't bear to see you like this."

He raised a dark brow. "How should I act toward you, Isis? Do you think I should take you in my arms and say all is forgiven despite how you lied to my face and continued to do so even after I practically begged you to tell me what was bothering you?"

She took a step toward him, but he backed away. Isis flinched, but squared her shoulders and met his gaze. "I swear I wasn't in on the plot with Black Adder and his gang. I'd distanced myself from them long before I met you. If you don't believe me—"

"I believe you, Isis, about that part at least. That's the one thing I'm willing to concede to you. When I look back on events more closely, you couldn't have been aligned with them. I remember the look in your eyes when Black Adder revealed himself. I'd almost forgotten it."

"I thought you still believed I betrayed you."

"I did up until a few hours ago."

"What changed your mind?"

"I didn't have Adonis and his evil mother to contend with. I had time to think things through properly."

"So why do you continue to treat me like a pariah? If you know I wasn't working for the other side, why do you continue to push me away?"

"You can ask me that when you know I've been fighting people like you for most of my life? You may have disassociated yourself from them, but do you think you could possibly mean anything to me when every time I look at you, I'll be thinking of what you did? I don't want to know all the gruesome details, Isis, but if you were in league with that crew, it stands to reason you've killed innocent people."

Isis winced as he reminded her of her past. She was ashamed of many of the things she'd done which she desperately wished she could take back. It was on the tip of her tongue to tell him exactly that, but didn't know if he would care about her regret so she went another route. "We've all done things in our past we're ashamed of. I explained to you what it means to be a lone wolf, alone and without the protection of a pack. I did what I had to do to survive and along the way, I made some bad decisions. But that's in my past. It's not who I am, now."

Dante twisted his lips into what looked like a cross between a sneer and a smirk. "That's where you're wrong. You still have the heart of a rogue."

"You told me yourself, we've all done things we weren't proud of. Were you lying to me when you told me that, Dante?"

"You don't get to fucking turn this back around on me. I wasn't a fucking rogue and I never killed innocent people. Can you say the same?"

"I can. I robbed, stole, conned, and did whatever I thought I could do to fit in, but I never killed an innocent."

"Bullshit."

"It's true. Being a lone wolf, I had run-ins with those who wanted to kill me and I did what I had to. So yes, in those cases I did kill, but never while I was with the Serpent Gang. When they'd gotten involved with Beatrice and Adonis, I left them but even before then I'd began to distance myself from them. They killed this innocent family while I just watched and I did nothing to stop them. I know it sounds horrible and it was. I should have stood up to them. I tried to save the child but they found her and there was nothing I could do because if I stopped them, they would have turned on me. I admit I'm a coward for that and it haunts me daily. I'll never forgive myself for that."

Shaking his head, he snorted. "You don't get it, do you?"

Isis balled her hands into fists at her sides. She wasn't sure what he wanted her to say. "Obviously not, but I hope you'll tell me."

"I asked you repeatedly if there was something you needed to tell me, but you kept the secret of your past to yourself. You're a liar, and who's to say your past won't come back to haunt you? It usually does, you know. There may be someone you crossed that you didn't quite finish off. They could be lying in wait to take their revenge on you. Do you think I would allow my family to be put in that kind of danger after what they've already been through? I don't need that shit, so I suggest you get the hell out of here, while I can still think rationally."

His words hurt far more than any of the wounds she'd suffered in battle. However, his small display of emotion gave her enough hope to remain in the room. If he didn't care for her, he wouldn't be so passionate in his conviction. Torn between anger and sadness, Isis strode over to Dante and grabbed him by the collar, hot tears scalding her cheeks. "I was scared, Dante! From the moment we met, I fell head over heels for you. And when I learned what Black Adder was up to, I volunteered to help, not only for the sake of your family, but to be with you. I wanted you to get to know me before I revealed my past to you. I never lied to you."

His dark blue gaze narrowed. "A lie by omission is just as much a lie as one spoken."

He attempted to shrug her off, but she held on, refusing to let go of this man, her heart's true mate, without a fight. "Well if you believe nothing else, know that I love you. That wasn't a lie. We belong together and I know you feel it, too."

Dante stiffened. "Isis, your five minutes are up. Let go and get out."

"No!" With her pride already in tatters, where he was concerned, she had nothing to lose. She couldn't let things end this way. "Dante I didn't imagine you telling me you cared about me. You're not the kind of man who would lie about something like that. Love isn't something that can be turned on and off at the snap of your fingers."

"You don't know shit about me!"

"I do! I know you're passionate about the things you believe in. I know you love your family. I know I've hurt you by hiding the truth from you and if I could change it, I would. I know you still have feelings for me. You couldn't have made love to me the way you did or kissed me so tenderly, if you felt nothing."

"We didn't make love, Isis. We fucked. I've fucked a lot of women in my lifetime, and I can't say there was anything particularly memorable about my experience with you."

He could have punched her in the stomach and it wouldn't have knocked the breath out of her the way his cutting statement had. There was no need for Dante to push her away because she released her tight grip on him as if her fingers had been scorched. "You don't mean that," she croaked in a hoarse, shaky whisper.

With a vindictive tilt of his lips, he reached out and pulled her roughly against him. "I don't? How about I prove it to you?"

Even now when she should have pulled away in the face of his cruelty, Isis found herself trembling within the circle of his arms. She was hypnotized by his stare as he lowered his head and the warmth of his breath touched her lips. Isis tilted her head back, ready to feel the press of his mouth against hers.

Instead of kissing her as she'd expected, he chuckled. His cobalt gaze turned to a dark glowing gold and his fangs descended. "So eager for it, aren't you, Isis?"

His taunt was a bucket of ice water to the face. Splaying her palms against his chest, she gave him a shove, but he was unmovable. She gasped when Dante gripped her ass in his large hands, forcing her pelvis against his. The thickness of his cock seared her through their clothing. "Let me go." She wanted him, but not like this.

"What's the matter, Isis? Don't you like this? I thought this was what you came for; my cock in your hungry little cunt. You really should make up your mind about what you want. First you need me and you love me; now you want me to let you go? Which is it?"

Isis realized he was still angry with her but she didn't expect him to be so vicious toward her. "I came to talk to you. I was hoping you would allow me to explain to you why I had lied but now, I see you're in no mood to listen. Please let me go."

Again that cruel smirk curved his lips. "I told you I didn't want to talk to you when you arrived, but you insisted so now here we are. You don't get to play the victim now. Besides, the last thing you want is for me to release you. The heat from your body gives you away every time, Isis. You want me, don't you?" Dante lowered his head again, but instead of kissing her, he grazed her neck with his fangs.

Isis trembled involuntarily. He was right. She was hot. The heat within her core spread through her body as Dante ground his dick against the juncture of her thighs. She opened her mouth to deny him, but closed it immediately. She would be fooling no one. She couldn't deny him this even if she wasn't happy with the circumstances.

Dante kept one hand pressed against her lower back as he gyrated his hips against hers. He worked her body into a frenzy while he used his other hand to thread his fingers in her hair. He gave it a hard tug, forcing her head back to expose the column of her neck. Then he raked his incisors against the tender flesh, pricking her skin but not burrowing those fangs into her neck as she secretly desired him to.

Chuckling, he raised his head to meet her gaze. "You don't have to answer. Your body says it all, but I wonder if it's me or would any vampire do?" His grin widened as he gauged her expression. "Oh, you didn't think I knew about your vampire fetish? I have a way of finding these things out. Would it give you a thrill for me to sink my teeth into your delectable skin? Would you like that as I finger that tight little pussy? Or do you want it rough? Do you want to be fucked like the bitch you are?"

She whimpered as his words flayed her like daggers. Even he continued his verbal assault, she felt helpless against his touch. Her body was his to do what he whatever he wanted to it. Isis pressed herself against him tighter still. She couldn't help herself. Besides her love for him, Dante Grimaldi had a powerful sexual hold on her she couldn't deny.

"There's no point in lying about it, Isis. You want it bad, don't you? And guess what? I'm going to give it to you." Dante gripped her shoulders and twisted her around until his erection pushed against her backside.

Hooking one arm around her waist, he wrapped his hand around her throat, his fingers pressing against her windpipe until she could barely breathe. "What? No words, Isis?" he softly taunted.

She closed her eyes, ashamed of easily she had surrendered to him no matter how cruel his touch. This was a mockery of their earlier lovemaking but she couldn't help herself where this man was concerned. Moistening her lips, she leaned her head against his shoulder, craving the feel of his lips against her skin while silently cursing her weakness.

Dante shoved his hands inside the elastic waistband of her pants and brushed his fingertips against her mons. Isis shuddered violently. "Oh!" she cried out in a mixture of surprise and delight. Arching her back, she wiggled her bottom against him, silently encouraging his erotic exploration.

"No panties? It seems you've come prepared."

She shook her head as much as she was able to. "It wasn't like that."

"Of course it wasn't, Isis." His tone clearly underlined his disbelief. "Spread 'em. Show me how much you want me, my deceitful little shifter."

When he had made love to her before, Dante had been tender, whispering words of endearment. But not now. He seemed hell-bent on shaming her, and he was doing a pretty damn good job of it. But she couldn't bring herself to leave. The insatiable need to be near him was too strong to fight. Isis wished she weren't so damn needy where he was concerned. She'd vowed to never be one of those women who let a man use her. But here she was, giving in to a dark carnality she knew couldn't be healthy.

He continued on, shoving his hands farther between her thighs and pinching her outer labia together until she cried out from pleasure and pain. Something this wrong, shouldn't have felt so right. "Dante," she sighed, fearful her knees would give out from under her.

Dante slipped his fingers into her damp folds and caught her clit between his thumb and forefinger, rolling the tiny bud of nerves until it grew thick and sensitive to the near pain. "I shouldn't want you so much, but I can't help myself," he muttered, rubbing and twisting her nubbin until she writhed against him uncontrollably.

His admission should have made her happy, but it didn't. He still fought their attraction and it frustrated her. "You want me because we're bonded forever."

"The only bonding between us will be my dick in your pussy. Don't read more into this than there is." As if to prove his point, Dante released her clit and roughly shoved two fingers inside her. There was no gentleness or finesse in his touch, but it still drove her insane with passion.

She bit her bottom lip, drawing blood, to stop herself from crying out again. Even before this battle of sexual domination had begun, Dante had been the victor and they both knew it. This depraved desire she derived from his careless caresses only showed what little shame she had where he was concerned. Isis however, tried to break through his anger toward her. "I'm not the one who's mistaken, you are. You're my mate and I'm yours."

He continued to finger her, shoving his digits faster and deeper into her. The hand resting on her throat tightened as his incisors nicked her skin again. She rode his fingers, moving closer to her peak. Dante pushed another finger into her soaking wet channel, stretching her vaginal walls to their limit. But it seemed he wasn't finished with her yet. He was on a quest for sexual torture. He slipped yet another finger into her, and Isis stiffened as she realized what he meant to do. "No! Don't. Please don't!" For the first time since he pulled her against him she tried to break away, but his grip tightened around her.

Dante moved his hand away from her throat and circled her body with his arm until it rested under her breasts. His menacing chuckle caressed her ears. "Why not, Isis? You love me, don't you? We belong together, right? Those were your words, were they not? Why shouldn't I be able to express how I feel to the woman I supposedly love beyond reason?"

"Because, this isn't you! I don't want this!"

"No? Then why am I able to slide my fingers so easily into your cunt? Why are you so fucking wet, juices are running down your thighs? You want all of it, don't you? Don't pretend you don't like this now because this doesn't fit into your perception of how lovers should act."

She squeezed her eyes shut, wishing she could wake from this nightmare, but despite this cruel side to Dante, Isis realized there was some truth to his words. Her body did respond to his extreme brand of sensual domination. It was her mind that fought against it, wanting things to return to the way they were before. "No," she offered a token protest, although it sounded false even to her.

"You're so adept at lying you're even lying to yourself, aren't you? Shall I prove you wrong? You're so fucking wet, I bet I can get my entire hand inside you."

She shook her head frantically. "Please," she whispered, unsure of what she was asking for.

Dante, however, would afford no quarter. "Please what, Isis? Please let you go or please fuck this delicious, wet pussy with my fist?"

The words remained lodged in her throat. If there was ever a time to pull away from him, this was it. But something kept her within the circle of his corded arms.

When she didn't answer, Dante laughed with menacing glee. "That's what I thought. Let's see how far this cunt stretches, shall we?" Easing his fingers out of her pussy, he guided her toward the bed and pushed her forward.

Isis threw her arms out to brace her fall. "Keep your hands on the bed and don't move, unless I tell you to." Slowly, he peeled her pants down her thighs and legs. Then he lifted her feet one at a time to discard them. He settled himself between her legs and rubbed her slit slowly, driving her to the edge of insanity.

Unable to keep still, she wiggled her hips, shivering with need. For her disobedience, the flat of his palm fell heavily on her ass. "I told you to be still," he growled. He flipped her onto her back, and without waiting for a reply, Dante pushed all four fingers back inside her cunt. Isis let out a squeal. He was on a take-no-prisoners mission and wouldn't be satisfied until he had her complete submission.

He worked his fingers in and out of her, and to Isis's horror and secret delight, her body accommodated him, taking him deeper into her wet cavern. She grew more slippery for him by the minute. Just as she had accustomed to those long digits fucking her to distraction, Dante eased his thumb inside and curled his fingers into a fist.

"Ahh!" It fucking hurt! But it was an erotic hurt that hovered on the fine line of pleasure and pain. Tears burned the backs of her eyes because she wanted to hate this, but she couldn't. She had to be insane to allow him to do this to her. As she stretched for him, all Isis could think of was the dark desire pulsing through her entire being and that Dante had given it to her.

"Relax, Isis. We're immortal. Your body can withstand this. Besides, it's what you wanted, right?" He slowly moved his fist inside her to the wrist, making Isis squirm.

Dante gripped the side of her hip, digging his nails into her skin. "Look at what I'm doing to you. See how wet you are. You just can't help yourself, can you, baby?"

Isis kept her eyes tightly shut as she shook her head. "Don't make me."

Leaning forward, he nipped her earlobe with the sharp point of one of his sharpened teeth. "Look, goddamn it!"

She willed the tears not to come when she slowly opened her eyes and did as he commanded. Moving to her elbows so she could get a good view of what he had done, she released a sharp cry at the sight that greeted her. Isis abruptly brought her head back up, unable to look anymore.

"What? Aren't you enjoying the show?" Dante chuckled, moving his fist within her with tight little pulses. He took her slowly, deeply, and skillfully. When she came, it took her by surprise.

"You're a dirty little bitch, aren't you? But you're still hungry for me, aren't you? Even now your pussy is clinging to my hand as if it doesn't want to let go. Well, I've got something even better for it."

When he slowly eased his soaked hand out of her pussy, she murmured in protest at the empty feeling within her, but the barren sensation didn't last. Within seconds of hearing the sound of pants being unzipped, Dante thrust his hard, thick cock balls deep inside her. He filled her pussy so wonderfully and completely she could just melt into a puddle right then and there. She squeezed his cock, clenching her muscles around him, not wanting to let go.

"*Dio!*" His sharp intake of breath indicated Dante might not be as in control as he wanted to be. Isis decided to turn the tables. She gyrated her hips forward and slammed her pelvis against his as she tightened her vaginal muscles around him at will.

He felt good. Isis doubted she would ever get enough of him. She was addicted and her drug of choice was his cock. "Mmm, Dante, I love you so much," she sighed with contentment.

Obviously, it was the wrong thing to say, because the next thing she knew, he pulled out and flipped her over to her hands and knees. As he shoved his cock into her wet pussy, Dante smacked her ass with his palm.

"Oh!" She turned her head to meet his gaze, but he cracked her on the rear again.

"I told you not to move, and now, you'll have to suffer the consequences."

"Dante, what—"

"No words," he growled. "Not until you're spoken to, understand?"

Her declaration of love had made him go berserk. But she didn't regret telling him. She would continue to tell him until he believed her.

He brought his hand down on her butt again, this time even harder. She let out a yelp.

"Dante, what are you doing?"

He smacked her rear in a succession of rapid spanks. "Teaching you. Now, answer my fucking question. Do you understand?" Grasping her hips in one hand and winding a handful of hair around his other hand, he slammed his cock deeper into her hungry pussy. "Do you under-fucking-stand?" He yanked on her hair.

"Yes!" she screamed with a mixture of arousal, pain, and humiliation.

"Good. Because I don't want you to pretend this is anything other than what it is. And don't play the injured innocent. You want this just as badly as I do. Even now, your pussy is gripping my cock like you can't get enough of me."

She couldn't argue because that's exactly what was happening. Isis gripped the coverlet, her nails tearing into the fabric while Dante rammed in and out of her, thrusting with unrestrained power. His cock was so deep inside her, he nearly hit her womb. And she loved it. Needed it. Craved it even though she realized this was a form of revenge for him. This conflict between body and mind was a torment that would drive any sane person mad.

It didn't take long for her next orgasm to hit, sending waves of passion through her. But, Dante still wasn't finished with her. Pulling his cock out of her pussy, he grabbed her ass and parted her cheeks. She stiffened.

"Don't play coy, now. The night is still young and we've only just started." He rubbed his fingers along her dripping pussy, dampening them. Dante slowly moved those wet digits to her tight anal ring, lubricating it with her juices.

She shouldn't have been excited by this, but she was. Still, she couldn't help but ask, "Why, Dante? Why are you trying to destroy every shred of feeling I have for you?"

He replaced his fingers with the velvet-smooth tip of his cock. "What feelings, Isis? Your need for a good fuck? That's exactly what I'm giving to you." Gripping her hip in one hand and his cock in the other, he pushed past the puckered bud and slid his length into her rectum, inch by deliciously torturous inch.

Unable to help herself, she pushed her ass against him, eager to be filled.

Dante chuckled. "Easy, baby. I'll give it to you soon enough." He fucked her with slow, steady precision, taking her on a carnal ride of wild passion. "Finger your pussy for me," he commanded.

She'd hate herself after this was over but she couldn't help herself. Without hesitating, she slid her fingers along her wet slit before slipping two fingers into her channel. Isis could hardly think straight from the pleasure overload she experienced at the hands of this lusty vampire.

As he pumped harder and faster into her ass, she worked her fingers in and out of her pussy in a frenzy, moving closer to yet another climax. Dante had to have a magic cock because no one had ever made her feel desire the way he did, taking her to the very heights of passion until she didn't want to come down. He felt so good and she didn't want it to end.

Dante's grip in her hair tightened as he slammed into her. "I'm going to come."

"Don't hold back!" she yelled, caught up in the whirlwind of emotions flowing through her.

Hot spurts of his essence filled her bottom as he climaxed. He shuddered against her with a groan, sending her spiraling into another wave of bliss.

Unable to hold herself up any longer, Isis fell forward on the bed, breathing heavily. Dante pulled his cock out of her. His seed slid down her crack and coated her pussy.

Dante remained standing. "Mmm, as much as I hate to admit it, you have a gift. You're a great fuck."

The second he said that, something inside her died. Her mind shut down completely and it felt like he'd robbed her of air because she couldn't breathe. Her tender lover from before was gone. He was a stranger to her now. Though she would never stop loving him, she refused to let him treat her so callously. She'd just let him use her as if she was no more than a piece of meat, and for what? For him to make her feel lower than dirt? Less than nothing?

Isis had tried to reach him, to explain herself to him but he had humiliated and used her, and what was worse, had made her like it. She might not have much pride where he was concerned, but she did have some left and she wouldn't allow him to strip that away from her, too.

Rolling off the bed, she reached for her pants. Dante grabbed her arm. "Where are you going? The night is still young. Don't tell me you've had enough."

She wrenched her arm out of his grip violently. "Take your fucking hands off me." Isis refused to look at him because she knew if she did, she'd burst into tears.

"What's the matter? You love me so much, right? Why are you running away because you couldn't have your way?"

Refusing to answer him, she shimmied into her pants and headed for the door. Dante grabbed her arm again and turned her around to face him. Isis wouldn't be manhandled by him any longer; she gave him a hard shove with all her strength and sent him sent him flying across the room. "Don't touch me ever again, Dante Grimaldi!" she screamed at the top of her lungs, not caring if she woke the other occupants in the house. "You know you what your problem is?"

As he made his way back to his feet, Dante glared at her. "No, but for shits and giggles, enlighten me."

"You are an emotional cripple. You don't know what love is, so when you're presented with it, you act like a spoiled brat. You accuse me of being upset because I can't have things the way I want them, but that's only because it's something you see in yourself, not in me. You think I should be some perfect little flower you can wrap in cotton wool and cosset so you can feel like a fucking hero. You don't want a real woman who's strong enough to stand by your side, Dante. You want a mindless puppet you can control and put away in an ivory tower so you can feel superior. Yes, I've done some things in my past that I'm not proud of and that I deeply regret, but if you're so fucking perfect, then good luck finding someone else who is. Congratulations, you've won. I'll stay out of your life, and you stay the hell out of mine."

Turning on her heel, she headed for the door but paused and turned to see Dante standing as still as a stone, his expression unreadable save for the muscle jumping in his clenched jaw.

When she slammed the door behind her, her heart shattered to a million little pieces.

Chapter Twenty-Three

"She's so beautiful, isn't she?" Maggie sighed as she watched her daughter sleeping soundly in her bassinet.

GianMarco smiled indulgently at his wife, sharing in her happiness, his heart more full of love than he thought possible. It had been nearly a month since they'd found Gianna and her cousins in that abandoned shack in the woods. For the first several nights after Gianna's return, Maggie wouldn't let the baby out of her sight. Gianna slept in her basinet beside their bed. Only in the past few days had GianMarco convinced his mate to let the baby sleep in her own room.

It wasn't that he didn't adore his daughter to distraction—he did—but he felt the sooner they fell into a normal routine, the faster they could put the ordeal they'd suffered behind him. What Maggie didn't know, however, was each night when she was asleep, he'd tiptoe into their daughter's room and stare at her for hours. Sometimes, she'd wake up as if she knew her papa was there and a smile would flit across her little face before she fell back into a restful doze. He vowed to never let any harm come to his *bambina* again as long as he drew breath.

He'd also wanted his daughter to sleep in her own room for purely selfish reasons. He needed some privacy with his woman. Making love with the baby so close wasn't quite as satisfying because Maggie held back from fear of waking their child. GianMarco wanted the wild, abandoned, passionate mate he knew his wife was capable of being.

And that's exactly what he got when they finally had their bedroom to themselves again. Sometimes, he had to pinch himself to make sure he wasn't dreaming. The nightmare of the past few centuries was over and his family was safe. Their daughter was back where she belonged.

GianMarco put his arm around Maggie's shoulders and kissed her temple. "Of course, she is. She's your daughter."

"I do make beautiful babies, don't I?"

He chuckled, giving her another kiss. "Yes, you do."

"I'm so proud of all my babies. I love Camryn and Darren, but I'm glad *we* made this baby together. Our family feels complete."

"I know. I've come to love Camryn and Darren as my own and I'm happy to be a part of their lives. Speaking of Camryn, she barely lets Jagger out of her sight since his return, not that I think Jagger minds. He likes all the attention." GianMarco chuckled, remembering how hard his stepdaughter had fought against her love for Jagger and now, the two were inseparable.

Maggie giggled. "That's Camryn. She never does anything in half measures."

"And poor Oliver, I think he's quite smitten with Montana. Heaven help him." He rolled his eyes.

She slapped him playfully on the chest. "Hey! What's so wrong with that? Montana is a wonderful person."

"The poor guy has suffered from a rather messy divorce, and you, yourself, have admitted Montana plays a little fast and loose with men's hearts. I don't want to see my friend hurt."

"She's really not so bad. Maybe Montana is just the kind of woman Oliver needs in his life. Anyway, he's a big boy, capable of taking care of himself. I'm sure if something happens between the two of them, he'll go in with both eyes open."

"You're probably right." GianMarco sighed. "I suppose we should get back to our guests, or do you think we can sneak away to our room for a quickie?" He wiggled his eyebrows at her.

Maggie threw her head back and laughed. "You have a one-track mind. We have a houseful of guests and all you can think about is sex?"

He pulled her against his chest and wrapped his arms around her waist before dropping a hungry kiss on her mouth. *Dio*, she was sweet. He lifted his head just enough to trace the seam of her lips with his tongue before allowing his gaze to roam the contours of her beautiful face. She made his heart flutter with joy whenever she was near and it was a sensation he would never tire of. "When it comes to you, *ciccina mia*, it is. I love you so much, and I can't tell you how very proud I am of you for your bravery. Though, I don't think I'll ever allow you to participate in another one of our missions should there be more rogues that need to be taken care of."

"And why not? Granted, there were a few close calls, but you have to admit I kicked ass. How about when I shoved my fists down that one rogue's throat and pulled his heart out of his mouth?"

He winced at the memory. GianMarco didn't realize his wife had such a brutal streak. He made a mental note to himself to never piss her off. "Yes, I've been meaning to bring to that up. Never take an unnecessary risk like that again. You could have been killed."

"That asshole shouldn't have taunted me about Gianna. It pissed me off. There was nothing stopping me from taking every single one of those creatures out because my child was in danger."

He took her hand in his and brought it to his lips. "I know. And like I said, I'm very proud of you, but you have no idea how frightened I was at your being in harm's way. I don't think my heart can take another scare like that."

Maggie stared at him with warm brown eyes as she brushed a stray strand of hair off his forehead. "But, I'm fine now. You're stuck with me because I don't intend to go anywhere."

"You'd better not, because I'll be damned if I'm letting you go. Before you came into my life, I was only half-alive. You and Gianna, Camryn and Darren have made me whole again."

She pressed her face against his chest. "You have no idea how much it means for me to hear you say that. Everything is so perfect right now. I almost feel guilty at being this happy when…"

GianMarco caught her chin between his fingers, tilting her head back to meet her gaze. "When what?"

She shrugged. "Maybe I'm imagining things, but I get the impression something is troubling Dante. He seems distracted and he's been staying away again. Remember the last time he did that? He smiles and responds to conversation at the appropriate intervals, but his mind is elsewhere."

He sighed with regret. "No. You're not imagining things. I've known something has been wrong these past weeks, but I was hoping he would work things out for himself."

"What do you mean? Why haven't you said anything?"

"You're a worrier, Maggie. I didn't want to alarm you unnecessarily, but if you've noticed it, Nico and Romeo have as well."

"What's wrong with him?"

"If I'm reading the signs correctly, I'd say he's entering the first stages of la morte dolci."

She gasped. "Isis?"

"Who else? I had hoped he would swallow his stubborn pride and go to her, but something is stopping him. I don't know what it is, but I can't believe he's foolish enough to deny his heart's desire."

"I don't think she betrayed Dante, not after the way she helped us."

"Neither do I, nor does Dante, for that matter. It's much more complicated than that. I think it has more to do with her past and him not being able to trust his feelings on that front. Keep in mind, he'd been lured into a false belief that one woman was his bloodmate when she wasn't. And then, there was the confusion of his feelings for you. I think he's afraid of this not being real, which is why he's fighting so hard."

"That makes sense. I hope he snaps out of whatever funk he's in over her. I really like Isis. I think she's just the kind of woman he needs."

"I do, too. The problem is he doesn't realize it himself. I think part of the issue is that he's so used to taking care of others, and Isis is the kind of woman who can take care of herself."

Maggie frowned. "Do you think he's intimidated by her?"

"No. I wouldn't say that. I just don't think Dante knows how to relinquish his role as protector and finds it hard to give himself over to someone so completely. He has a bit of a hero complex and Isis is definitely no damsel in distress. It challenges his ideal of how things should be between a man and his mate."

"Doesn't he realize they can be strong for each other? Is it that he feels she doesn't need him?"

"I think that's part of it."

Maggie rolled her eyes heavenward. "Sometimes, I'll never understand men. So, what will you do about *la morte dolci*?"

"It's early stages yet, but I'll monitor him to see how this thing progresses. He may be fighting his feelings for Isis, but eventually biology will take over and when it does, I may need to intervene so that Isis is not harmed. She's a shifter and is able to take a battering, but not against one in the throes of this madness."

"Then, I'll help you. Dante is my family, too. We need to help each other out and Isis will need all the support she can get."

"Are you sure? You do understand what it will entail by *helping*, don't you?"

"I don't know a lot about *la morte dolci*, but it was frightening when you were in the midst of it. I thought you were going to kill me." She shuddered as if reliving the memory.

GianMarco kissed the side of her neck. "I'm so sorry for that, *ciccina mia*. I live in constant regret of that night."

"It's okay. I know you couldn't help yourself. Besides, it didn't turn out too bad." She grinned and winked at him.

"You're just asking for it, aren't you?"

"If I am, will you give it to me?"

"You know it," he growled, swatting her on the backside. His cock was rock hard and he wanted nothing more than to take her to their bedroom and fuck her senseless, but he needed to clarify a few things with her first. Reluctantly, he pulled away from her. "Maggie, I don't think you fully understand what helping Dante get through this difficult period will mean."

"Then, make me understand."

"Remember how Dante was there for me and helped calm me down? He was allowed certain liberties with you as well to ease the passage of the night. Dante could seriously harm Isis and it would be up to us to see that doesn't happen. Do you understand now?"

Her brows flew together and suddenly her eyes widened as comprehension dawned. "You mean…?"

"Yes. Are you prepared to go to those lengths? I won't be upset, if you're not. You're aware there is a special bond between Dante and I. I can't ignore him in his time of need."

"I won't allow you to, and I want to help any way I can. I knew my life would never be the same when you made me a vampire. I fully accept I'm different and I'm more open to our culture."

In that moment, GianMarco couldn't love her more. He pulled her into his arms and brushed his lips against hers. This time he couldn't ignore the calling of his body. His cock was stiff to the point of pain and he needed pussy. Maggie's. "Now, about that quickie…"

Dante sat on the patio table in his brother's backyard watching the merry partygoers around him, yet he had never been in less of a mood to party. He threw back another shot of tequila, his eighth, wishing for once he had the ability to get drunk. The alcohol gave him a nice buzz but it didn't allow him to pass out and forget his pain like he wished it did.

It had been four weeks, three days, seven hours, and—he glanced at his watch—forty-two minutes without her. And, it had yet to get any easier. He played that scene of from when they were last together in his head over and over again and cringed each time. For as long as he lived, he'd never forget the pain lurking in the depths of Isis's beautiful eyes. He'd put that pain there and for that, Dante cursed himself a thousand times over.

In all his years, he'd never been as sadistically cruel to anyone as he'd been to her that night. He'd used, degraded, and humiliated her, and for what? Because he couldn't handle his feelings for her? She more than likely hated him now, but she couldn't possibly hate him as much as he did himself. The very thought of what he had done to her made him sick to his stomach.

Dante had had a lot of time to put things into perspective since their parting, and he realized he'd made things between them more complicated than they should have been. Instead of listening to his heart, he'd gotten some crazy notion in his mind that she'd betrayed his developing feelings for her, when in truth he was the one who'd betrayed her. He'd turned his back on Isis, leaving her with Black Adder, not caring if she was injured or killed. He hadn't fought hard enough to investigate the truth, even when it was staring him in the face. But she'd still come to him to try to inject some reason into his insane line of logic.

When she'd walked out on him, he was finally able to admit to himself what he'd probably known from the beginning. He was in love with Isis and she was his bloodmate. He'd let fear rule him and ended up pushing her away. But the worst part of this ordeal was dealing with the shame. He couldn't face her after how badly he'd hurt her. He had no right to go to her and plead his case after what he'd done.

Right now, he wished to hole himself away in his penthouse and be alone, but the week's festivities wouldn't allow him. Gianna had been christened earlier this week, and the entire family had gathered for the weeklong celebration. There was no graceful way to back out of this. Besides, this was a happy time for everyone. The threat of Adonis and his mother was gone, and for the first time in centuries, he had a lot of time on his hands. While he was happy for his brothers, he was miserable.

He poured himself another drink and tossed it back in one gulp, relishing the sting of the strong fluid running down his throat. Dante was so caught up in his own misery, he didn't notice the little figure approaching him.

"Can you hand me my ball?"

Dante snapped to attention to see his young nephew standing in front of him. "Your ball?"

The little boy sighed with exaggerated patience. "My ball rolled between your feet. I was playing catch with Jagger and he threw the ball too hard. Look." He pointed in the direction of the baseball.

Dante bent over and, sure enough, there it was. He picked it up and held it out to Jaxson. "Here you go, kiddo."

As Jaxson stepped forward to take it from Dante's hand, his little face crinkled. "Peeeew! Your breath stinks!" He narrowed his eyes. "Why are you drinking? Are you sad about something?"

Dante reeled back. Romeo had said his son was blunt to a fault, but finding himself on the receiving end of the child's frank observation put him on the defensive. He grabbed the near empty bottle of tequila and capped it. "What makes you think I'm sad?"

"My first mommy used to drink when she was sad and her breath smelled like yours. Are you sad, Uncle Dante?"

Leave it to a child to not beat around the bush. He wasn't sure why, but something compelled him to say, "Yes. I am. I'm very sad."

"Oh." Jaxson took the empty seat next to Dante. "Why are you sad?"

"I was very mean to someone I care about."

"Then, you should say you're sorry."

"It's not that simple, Jaxson."

"Yes, it is."

Dante snorted. He wasn't going to argue with a six-year-old. "Jaxson, trust me when I tell you it isn't. I've lived a lot longer than you."

"I'll be seven next month, so I've lived a really long time, too. If you want to show someone you care, you say you're sorry. And if you're so smart, you would know that."

"Jaxson!" Romeo, appeared with his daughter in one arm, gave his son a stern, narrowed glance. "Apologize to your Uncle Dante." Romeo turned to Dante. "I'm sorry. We encourage the kids to speak up, but never to be disrespectful."

Dante waved his hand dismissively. "It's okay. He wasn't bothering me."

"No matter, he *will* apologize." He focused his attention on his son. "Apologize."

Jaxson sighed, sliding out of his seat. "I'm sorry, Uncle Dante." Then the child grinned, the corners of his lips tilting mischievously. "You see? Saying sorry isn't so hard." The little boy ran off before his father could scold him.

Romeo plopped down in the chair his son had vacated and adjusted his daughter on his lap. "I'm sorry. Jaxson can be a handful but you have to admit, the kid is entertaining."

Dante chuckled for the first time in weeks, unable to help himself. "No harm done. And I understand what a handful children can be. I seem to remember you and

Nico giving me a run for my money when you were children. You have no idea how many sleepless nights you gave me. You should be very proud of your son. He's wise beyond his years."

Romeo grinned. "I am very proud of both of my children. I have the smartest boy and most precious little girl in the world. Isn't that right, *piccola*?" He kissed the top of his daughter's head.

She smiled around the thumb in her mouth in response.

"Did I hear my name?" Niccolo joined them with a smile plastered on his face. Dante had to admit his brothers had never looked as relaxed as they did now.

"Yes, I was telling Ro what brats you two were when you were younger."

Nico's hand flew to his chest in mock surprise. "Me? Never. Romeo was the mastermind behind most of our schemes. I merely went along with him."

Romeo chuckled. "Aww, I was the one who suggested the activities, and you actually planned them out, so I suppose that would make you as guilty as me."

"Slander," Nico retorted.

Dante laughed. "I think Romeo and I would both agree, you're full of it."

"Sure, go ahead and gang up on the younger brother. Hey, there's Marco. He'll side with me."

Marco stepped out onto the patio, followed by Maggie, who had that just freshly fucked afterglow. "I'll side with you in what?"

"Romeo and Dante are saying I was a troublemaker when I was a child. I was the picture of innocence."

Maggie rolled her eyes. "Oh, brother. I'm staying out of this one. I think I'll join the ladies. You boys are welcome to your little debate." She sauntered off, shaking her head.

Marco laughed. "I think, I'd have to agree. What brought on this conversation anyway?"

Romeo sighed. "My kid was popping off at the mouth."

Dante shook his head. "It wasn't such a big deal. We had a difference of opinion about something, plus he took exception to my drinking, I believe. I should have been more cognizant of my surroundings."

Romeo frowned. "He's very sensitive about that. You never touch the stuff unless… are you okay, Dante?"

"I'm fine." He hoped his brothers would leave it at that.

"No, you're not," Marco interjected. "Tell them the truth, Dante." The atmosphere suddenly grew tense.

"I'm fine," Dante repeated tightly.

Adrienne must have sensed the unease between the brothers because she whimpered and squirmed in her father's lap.

Romeo carefully set his daughter on her feet. "Go find your mama, *piccola*, and tell her to give you a cookie." He gave her a gentle swat on the rear, shooing her off. Once the child was out of earshot, he turned to Marco. "What are you talking about, Marco?"

"Shut up, Marco." Dante spoke through gritted teeth.

"Look at him." Marco pointed at him. "Don't you see the elevation of color in his face, the moodiness, the need for seclusion? It's starting."

377

Dante hopped out of his seat. "For the last time, I'm fine. And I would thank you to mind your own damn business, Marco."

Marco raised a brow. "You are my business, Dante. We're brothers and though you may think you don't need anyone, you do. Stop acting like a jackass and go to her, for goodness' sake. If you let this go on any longer, you know what will end up happening."

"Listen to him, Dante," Nico agreed.

"Nothing good can come out of denying your feelings," Romeo added.

"What the fuck is this all about? Is it gang up on Dante day? I don't need this shit. Giovanni tried to have this conversation with me earlier. I didn't want to hear it then, and I certainly don't want to now, so get off my back." He leaped from his chair and pushed past his brothers, shrugging off a hand that fell on his shoulder.

He knew what he needed and it was to be alone. He'd go back to his place and try to forget. Only then, could he heal. It was too bad the image of injured blue-gray eyes wouldn't leave his mind.

Chapter Twenty-Four

"You are so damn stubborn, Isis. Why don't you just go to him and tell him how you feel? Don't you think two months is enough time for him to have calmed down? And, Uncle Dante is a reasonable man." Persephone Kyriakis flipped a long strand of blue-black hair over her shoulder with an exasperated sigh.

Isis slumped deeper into her sofa, watching the television but not really seeing a single thing on it. She only half listened to what her friend was saying. Persephone had been going on and on about contacting Dante, and frankly it was getting old.

Isis wanted to forget him, not have a constant reminder every time her friend opened her mouth. Wasn't it enough that the pain of being away from him ate away at her heart, keeping her awake at night? Didn't she deserve a break from the steady barrage of images that randomly popped in her head? What about the sensation of total and utter devastation, as if she was missing a part of herself? Why was it necessary to talk about it?

"You're starting to sound like a broken record, Seph. This isn't something I want to discuss."

"Well, you're going to have to talk about it sooner or later because all you seem to do is mope around your apartment. You never visit anymore, even though you're welcome in our home anytime. My father has even offered you refuge on our island. It can't be healthy to stay cooped up in here all day."

Isis shrugged. "Sorry, I don't live in a huge mansion like you."

"That isn't what I meant and you know it. Have you even gone on runs the last two full moons?"

Isis flipped the channel, not bothering to answer. Persephone ripped the remote out of her grasp and flung it across the room where it hit the wall and shattered into several pieces. "Will you at least acknowledge me when I'm talking to you?

Isis turned her attention to her friend, more than a little annoyed at the attempts to engage her in a conversation she didn't care to participate in. "Fine. I'm acknowledging you. Now what?"

"You know what I mean. You're a fighter, Isis! My best friend wouldn't sit around and sulk; she'd go and fight for her man."

Maybe part of the reason Persephone was pushing so hard was because Isis hadn't told her what had happened that night. She was only aware of a falling out. "I did go to him and was humiliated for my efforts."

Persephone's eyes widened and her mouth flew open. "What?"

Isis twisted her lips into a humorless smile. "You heard me. My body may have wanted him, and it still does. But, he made me feel so dirty. He looked at me like I was less than something on the bottom of his shoe."

"No." Her friend whispered her disbelief.

"It's true. I don't think he could have made it more clear how he felt about me. So you tell me, what should I do now? Go to him again and have my already battered self-esteem torn to shreds?"

"Oh, Isis, I didn't know." Persephone threw her arms around her.

"Of course, you didn't. I never told you."

"I'm so sorry. And, here you were taking my shit. I haven't been very supportive of you. All I could see was you were hurting and I thought I knew what was going on, but I really didn't."

Isis rested her head against her friend's. "It's okay."

"You're taking it surprisingly well. I mean, you don't look like you want to cry. I'd be bawling my eyes out."

"I'm all out of tears. Besides, crying would change nothing. Whatever Dante's issues are, they're his problems to iron out. They're no longer mine, nor do I care to have this discussion."

"But how can you ignore it when the two of you belong with each other? When I saw the two of you laughing together, I just knew—"

"I thought we agreed to drop the subject. I don't want to talk about this anymore."

"But, you're going to have to deal with it, eventually."

Isis raised a brow, torn between strangling her friend and telling her to leave. "Do I? Since we're on the subject of who belongs with whom, let's talk about your love life, shall we? How do you know the man your father has picked out as your mate isn't the one for you, when you haven't met him yet? From what I understand, the men of Pack Magnuson are quite handsome and I hear Eric Magnuson is no exception."

Blood rushed to Persephone's face, turning it bright red. "You know nothing about it. My father is being his usual overbearing self. He knows of my preference and I won't accept this Alpha just because he says I should."

"Of course not but I bet you haven't told your father about that mortal you've been spending a lot of time with lately. I'm sure if he knew, he'd put a halt to your romance before it properly begins."

Persephone jumped to her feet. "You know nothing about it."

"I know what you told me about it."

"But we weren't talking about me."

"We are now and might I add, in my opinion, the only reason why you date human men is because you can walk all over them. This Hugh guy you're seeing is probably wrapped so tightly around your little finger, you keep his balls in your pocket."

The younger shifter's nostrils flared and she bared lengthened canine teeth. "If that's the way you feel, I guess I don't need to stick around, do I?"

Isis shrugged. "Doesn't feel good to have your life psychoanalyzed, does it? If you want to leave, Persephone, you know where the door is."

Olive-colored eyes grew stormy as Persephone clenched her hands at her sides. "Fine, I will." She turned on her heel and stalked to the door and paused. "Well, I'm leaving now."

Isis stared at her television. "Okay."

"And when I leave, I may not be back for a very long time."

Isis shrugged. "Suit yourself."

"And, you can sulk all you like on your own."

"That's the plan."

"Okay. Good-bye, I'm leaving."

Isis examined her nails. "Yeah, you said that already."

There was no reply, but Persephone stayed rooted to the spot as if she was expecting Isis to stop her. Finally, she opened the door. "I'm going now."

"Later."

The door slammed shut and Persephone came storming back to the living room. "I can't believe you were willing to let me walk away just like that. I thought we were friends!"

Isis glanced up to see the hurt brimming in her friend's eyes. She released a long sigh and stood up. "We are friends, Seph, and I apologize for being so obstinate. This is just a sore subject for me. And you're right; I have been holed up in my apartment for days. I don't think I've seen sun or moonlight for at least a week."

"Let's make a deal. I won't mention Dante to you, if you come out with me. We can catch a movie and have a bite to eat or just go for a walk. How's that sound?"

For the first time in days, Isis smiled. "I'd like that."

Getting over Dante wasn't going to be easy. Honestly, she wasn't sure if she ever would, but life would go on whether she did or not. And Isis intended on living it, no matter how much it hurt.

"I hope we make it there before he does. Are you sure we're going in the right direction? I think we may have taken a wrong turn." Maggie looked out the window with a frown.

GianMarco groaned in frustration. "Have a little faith in me. Paris said this is where Isis lives and we're going in the right direction."

"But maybe you should pull over and ask for directions. We've been driving a lot longer than I think we should have."

GianMarco silently counted to ten and took a deep breath. "Maggie, I know where I'm going. I know this area a little better than you. Trust me." After Dante had left their party nearly four weeks ago, no one had heard a word from him despite constant phone calls and attempts at communication.

But because of the bond they shared, GianMarco knew his brother wasn't doing well, could in fact feel him getting sicker by the hour. It wouldn't be much longer before he was too far gone and he knew he and Maggie had to get to Isis before Dante did. Dante would seek Isis out and when he found her, there was no telling what would happen.

When GianMarco had been in the throes of the illness, it had only been a matter of a few weeks when he'd succumbed to it but Dante had been holding on longer, and because he'd fought so hard against it, the grip of the madness would be hard to break.

These past few nights, GianMarco would wake in a cold sweat, yet his skin was hot to the touch. Pain would tighten around him like a fist, squeezing him from the inside out until he could barely breathe. He couldn't control his body's functions at times. He'd be in the middle of a mundane task and all of a sudden he'd be so horny he couldn't think coherently. Thank God for Maggie, because in those moments, he'd take his mate aside and fuck her until she nearly fainted. Not that he or she minded that last part, but it was getting worse.

Earlier today, he'd been in the middle of feeding his daughter, when an agonizing, searing ache had seized him. He'd clutched the baby tightly against his chest and didn't even realize that he was still holding her until she let out a cry of protest. It was then he knew with absolute certainty his brother needed him.

When he'd tried to reach Dante, he got a headache for his efforts. It further confirmed what he already knew. He and Maggie had contacted Paris and found out where Isis lived, hoping if they could get to her first and explain the situation, she'd be fully prepared when Dante finally put in an appearance. When one didn't understand something, it was only natural to fight. And Isis had proven that she wouldn't take anything sitting down.

They had taken Gianna to Romeo and Christine's and then, headed north to Isis's Long Island residence.

Even now an incendiary heat pulsed through his veins, threatening to erupt in an explosion of massive fury. He was irritable as well, but GianMarco knew his symptoms were nothing compared to what Dante was probably suffering through at this moment. Romeo and Nico were feeling it to a lesser degree, but neither had ever been in the full throes of *la morte dolci*, rendering them incapable of completely understanding the illness. For that reason, he had volunteered to take care of this issue, although his brothers would step in, if needed.

It didn't seem like they could get there fast enough. He breathed a sigh of relief once he noted the street they needed to turn down. "See? Here we are."

"Hmph. I think we could have gotten here sooner if you'd made that right on Main Street."

"Maybe, but it doesn't matter now." He parallel parked his vehicle on the side of the street.

GianMarco took Maggie's hand as they walked toward the large brownstone. At the front door, he pressed the button next to Isis's apartment number. "Let's hope she's home."

There was no immediate answer, and he pushed the button again with growing impatience. The heat in his body was starting to take over, and the veins in his head began to throb. Dante was near.

Very near.

He rang the bell again. "Shit. Where the hell is she?"

"Well, it's not like she was expecting our arrival. Maybe, we can let ourselves in. I think Isis wouldn't mind under the circumstances."

"What wouldn't I mind under what circumstances?"

GianMarco jumped. He hadn't heard her approach, yet another sign that he was losing control of functions he normally had an easy handle on.

He whirled around to see Isis standing there with her hands on her hips and an eyebrow raised. Her body was encased in a pair of worn jeans and a simple white T, yet the clothing skimmed every single curve. Dante's feelings for her manifested themselves through him, and GianMarco's body tightened in awareness of her. He panted, unable to control his reaction.

He'd expected something like this might happen because of his own period in the madness. Maggie rubbed his arm. "It's okay. I'm here with you, baby." She stood on tiptoe and kissed the side of his mouth.

"Will someone please tell me what's going on here?" Isis demanded.

Maggie released GianMarco's arm. She walked toward the shifter and took her hands. "We're here because we have something to tell you and it's of grave importance."

Isis snatched her hands out of Maggie's grasp. "If it's about Dante, I'm not interested in hearing it. As far as I'm concerned, he's made his feelings quite clear."

GianMarco couldn't tear his gaze away from her. *Dio*, she was beautiful. Not as lovely as his Maggie, but in that moment he wanted her. Needed her. "Isis, whatever Dante may have told you, please believe, he loves you. He's just a stubborn fool and—ah!" A sharp pain seared through his chest. He gritted his teeth and took several deep breaths to slow the erratic beating of his heart. Was this how Dante had felt when GianMarco was going through this?

Isis frowned and jerked her thumb in his direction. "What's wrong with him?"

"He's in pain," Maggie explained.

Isis's brows flew together as concern worked its way across her face. The wary stance she'd taken before was now gone. "What's the matter? Is there anything I can do to help ease his suffering?"

"Yes, actually, there is."

"What?"

"When the time comes, you'll have to give yourself to him."

Isis shook her head. "What! Did I hear you correctly?"

Maggie took her by the arm. "I think we should take this conversation inside."

Isis nodded and looked as if the wind had been knocked out of her.

"Maybe you should explain this to me again because none of it is making sense." Isis shook her head. This had to be part of some weird dream. *La morte dolci*? Although it was clear something was wrong from looking at GianMarco, who now paced the floor in agitated motions, Isis couldn't fully process what she'd been told.

He suddenly turned to her, his amber eyes glowing and his fangs bared. "I've already explained three times. He's near and he will have you whether you want it to happen or not, but if you don't want to get hurt, I suggest—"

"GianMarco!" Maggie stood up and walked over to her husband. "You're frightening her. Let me try to explain, okay?"

"But Maggie…"

She cut him off by placing her lips over his. "Shh. I know it hurts, baby, and I promise you'll have relief." She kissed him again. "I promise." Maggie turned to Isis with a reassuring smile, but it did nothing to ease her concerns.

Standing up, Isis placed her hands on her hips. "If the two of you are finished, might I remind you that no one is 'having me' without my say-so. Dante, GianMarco, or anyone. Do you understand?"

Maggie approached her, the smile still pasted on her face. "It's okay, Isis. I was scared once, too. When GianMarco and I met, he was a terrible person to be around. I constantly wanted to strangle him."

Isis backed away, suddenly uncomfortable at the other woman's proximity. What the hell? It was bad enough her body had reacted to GianMarco, but she found it particularly disconcerting to be so aware of Maggie, as well. Her nipples had tightened to painful peaks, and all she could think about was getting rid of these two before she made a fool of herself. She crossed her arms over her chest to hide the evidence of her arousal.

Isis didn't want to hear that Dante loved her or how he was suffering from some kind of sickness that drove him insane, all brought on because he'd denied what was in his heart. She most certainly didn't want to feel this pull toward his family members. Shaking her head more vehemently this time, Isis took a step back. "I'm not interested in hearing this."

Maggie moved closer until their bodies touched. "Of course, you do." She reached out and pushed a lock of Isis's hair from her face and placed her hand against her cheek. "There's no use in denying what you feel. It's only natural. Dante is your bloodmate and your body is crying out for his. The pull you feel with us is the connection we all share. Dante and GianMarco are very close, so it's only natural you should want him when he's in this state. And since GianMarco made me, there's a pull between us as well."

"No," Isis whispered, even as her hands fell to her sides.

Maggie smiled, catching Isis's face between her hands. She pressed her lips against the shifter's in a gentle kiss before tracing Isis's lips with her tongue. Isis didn't want to respond, but under Maggie's gentle touch she found herself trembling. Trying to maintain some sense of sanity, she pushed the other woman away. "No! This isn't right. I want you two to leave."

"We can't do that. Don't you understand? When Dante gets here, there will be no reasoning with him." GianMarco practically growled the words.

Isis narrowed her eyes. "What the hell is this? Good cop, bad cop? I'm perfectly capable of taking care of myself."

The words were barely out of her mouth, when her door buckled under the pressure of something that had pounded against it. Unable to help herself, she let out a scream. Dante stood in her doorway, his eyes glowing and his face twisted in what she likened to rage and passion. He'd come for her just as they said he would.

Isis suddenly wished she'd listened to Maggie and GianMarco.

Chapter Twenty-Five

"I need you, Isis." The deep, gravelly voice was a parody of his normal dulcet tone.

Isis froze. He sounded almost as monstrous as Beatrice's demon had. What was happening to him? Despite how they'd parted, with one look at him, any ill will she'd felt toward him was gone. It was clear he had suffered just as much as she had, but his pain had manifested into something that had changed his entire physiology.

Maggie took her by the hand and led her down the hallway. "Which one is your bedroom?"

Isis pointed to the second door on the right, still not fully grasping what had happened.

"Come back here, now!" Dante yelled, taking a step forward, only to be blocked by his brother.

GianMarco shook his head. "No, Dante. Not this way."

"Get the fuck out of my way, Marco. This is between me and Isis."

The younger vampire placed his hand on his brother's shoulder in what looked to be a reassuring gesture. "As it should be…later on, but, right now, you're in no condition to be alone with her."

Dante, however, would not be calmed down. He grabbed GianMarco by the arms and tossed him across the room.

"Come on." Maggie pulled Isis into the bedroom and closed the door, as if that would help. If Dante really wanted to get to her, no door would hold him back.

"We have to go out there and help your husband! Did you see Dante? Something's wrong with him!" Isis demanded.

"Yes. And, I have all the confidence in the world GianMarco will be able to handle Dante. He understands what's going on." A loud crash of breaking glass sounded from outside the bedroom door. Maggie didn't so much as flinch.

"Are you nuts?" Isis attempted to shove Maggie away from the door so she could go out there and stop the commotion. But, the other woman remained immobile. "How can you just stand there? Dante is in some kind of crazed state."

"*La morte dolci*," Maggie stated too calmly for Isis's taste.

"I don't care what the fuck it's called. I'm not going to stand here and let them tear each other apart on my behalf."

"Do you love Dante?"

The question had come so far out of left field, Isis paused. "Huh?"

Maggie nodded patiently. "Of course, you do. I've seen the way you look at him and I saw it on your face when he burst into the apartment." Another loud crash followed her statement, jolting Isis into motion. She grabbed Maggie and managed to pull her away from the door.

"If you go out there, you'll only exacerbate the situation. Let the men handle it. GianMarco knows what he's doing." This time Maggie didn't try to stop her.

Isis yanked the bedroom door open and raced to the living room to see Dante's fingers wrapped around his brother's throat so tightly, GianMarco's eyes bulged.

She jumped on Dante's back and was knocked back with a sharp elbow for her efforts. Hopping to her feet, she grabbed Dante's arm, trying to get him off GianMarco. Again, he slapped her away, but this time with such force she sailed through the air and crashed into the wall.

Maggie was by her side in a flash, helping her to her feet. "Now, will you listen to me?"

"He's going to kill him! Don't you care about your mate?"

"Very much so, but I also have faith in his ability to handle this. Look." She pointed in the brothers' direction. GianMarco had twisted out of Dante's grasp and had his brother pinned to the floor. This time when Maggie led Isis to the bedroom and closed the door behind them, Isis flopped on the bed, dumbfounded.

This had to be some kind of crazy nightmare and she sure as hell wished she'd wake up from it. "Okay, I'm ready to listen." Isis flinched at the loud thud against her bedroom door. She forced herself not to run back outside.

Maggie smiled, sitting down next to her. Their thighs touched and Isis's knee-jerk reaction was to scoot away, but something within her compelled her to stay near this beautiful vampire femme. She'd never been particularly attracted to women in a sexual way, but there was no denying how her body had suddenly responded to Maggie Grimaldi's voluptuously full frame. She couldn't tear her gaze away from the soft-looking curls framing her face and those lips. She couldn't figure out what was happening to her.

Maggie placed her hand on Isis's thigh. "It's okay. This is new for me, as well."

Isis narrowed her eyes with suspicion. "I thought you said you'd experienced this before."

"What I said was the experience of *la morte dolci* wasn't new to me because of GianMarco. I've never actually been with a woman, either. Does this bother you?"

Isis couldn't answer, never having given it thought.

"Ever since GianMarco brought me over, I realize there are so many experiences mortals limit themselves to because they're so afraid to let go and explore who they are. I haven't been a vampire long, and maybe things are a little different for shifters, but our mates are determined by this"—she placed her hand over her heart—"not this." She pointed to her head.

Isis nodded. "I understand." She'd always known vampires were sensual creatures, taking their pleasures anywhere and however, they pleased. It explained Maggie's attraction to her, at least partially. She moistened her suddenly dry lips. "You've explained this madness Dante is suffering through, but do you simply expect me to spread my legs for him and pretend all is forgiven?"

"Like I said, I know how you feel. I had a similar experience with GianMarco. Before we finally admitted our love for each other, he was such a pain in the ass. He was temperamental and difficult to be around. His partner at the detective agency had even threatened to disembowel him. At the point, I just thought it was because his personality sucked. What I didn't realize was that he was fighting his feelings for me because he'd already suffered the loss of his first mate and son. He didn't want to be hurt again so did his best to scare me off. Basically, that strategy backfired on him. By denying his feelings for me, it drove him to madness. *La morte dolci* is a sickness a vampire suffers through when he's denied or denies himself his heart's desire. That's exactly what Dante's done to himself. He loves you, Isis, but he's been hurt, too, so please don't turn him away."

Isis sighed. "I do love him. I don't want to after all the horrible things he said to me, but I do. But that thing out there…it's not Dante. He's become some kind of monster. He shoved me away as if I was nothing to him."

"It's not you, it's the sickness. When GianMarco had come to me, and I discovered he was a vampire, imagine what was running through *my* mind. At least you're already an immortal and have knowledge of others like you. I didn't have that advantage. He attacked me and I fought him and I was nearly strangled because of it."

"By GianMarco?"

Maggie nodded.

Isis's mouth fell open. "He could have killed you."

"He could have, but he didn't because Dante was there to help ease the way. He convinced me to help his brother out and give myself to him. You see, at the time, I wasn't one hundred percent convinced of my feelings for GianMarco, so I was really conflicted. But you, on the other hand, know without a shadow of a doubt what you feel for Dante. You love him. Give him this one night and then from there the two of you can iron your problems out. GianMarco and I will stay throughout the night until we're sure the darkness has left his mind, and then you two are on your own."

"You should have seen him. He was so vicious to me the last time I faced him."

"Isis, I don't know you very well and hopefully, that will be remedied soon. But from what I've observed of you, you're very brave, strong, and kind. I think you're perfect for Dante. Don't give up on him."

Isis lowered her lashes. "I…I don't know how to go about this." Her hands trembled in her lap as she thought of what was expected of her. Dante's hands all over her, his cock pulsing deep within her pussy was enough to send a fiery burst of desire to her core.

"Let me help you." Maggie leaned over and kissed Isis on the neck. "Don't be ashamed of the sensations you feel from my touch. They're an extension of your desire for Dante," she whispered, capturing Isis by the chin.

Isis felt as if she had fallen into some deep trance as she stared into Maggie's dark brown eyes. When their lips met, she reveled at the softness of Maggie's mouth against hers. The kiss was gentle, but insistent. And, she liked it. When Maggie pressed her tongue against the crease of her lips, Isis opened her mouth with a sigh, allowing the femme entrance.

Maggie tasted of raw honey and spice, and Isis pushed her tongue forward to savor Maggie's sweetness. The hands that had been resting on her lap slowly moved up and down her arms and finally cupped her breasts.

Isis found herself pushing into that caress, enjoying the tender touch.

Isis gripped the sides of Maggie's face, deepening the kiss. In the back of her mind, she couldn't believe how turned on she was and how much her body responded to this femme's skillful touch.

It was Maggie who pulled back first, looking slightly winded, her lips slightly parted and her eyes wide. "Whoa. That was pretty intense."

"I'll say," Isis said breathlessly, wanting to continue but not finding the words to admit it. The commotion outside had either died down or no longer registered because all Isis could hear was the pounding of blood in her ears. Her pussy pulsed as her desire increased. She squirmed on the bed.

"What now?" she asked.

Maggie held her shoulders as she guided Isis to lie down on her back and slowly pushed her T-shirt up, exposing her abdomen. The vampire placed light kisses on her bare stomach, sending trails of molten fire through Isis's body.

"Mmm, you're so sweet. It's so different with a woman, isn't it?"

Isis could only nod as Maggie pushed her shirt up and over her breasts before kissing the flesh overflowing her bra. "Lift your arms," Maggie commanded.

Without debate, she raised her arms as she was ordered, helping the femme to remove her T-shirt. Maggie didn't immediately remove Isis's bra. Instead, she began to work on Isis's jeans, in no particular hurry. The anticipation made Isis shiver. There was something titillating about the slow ease with which Maggie undressed her.

By the time she lay naked except for her underwear, Isis could barely keep still beneath that steady dark gaze. She reached out to pull Maggie to her but the vampire jerked back with a chuckle. "Easy, sweetie, there's no rush." She ran her hand down the center of Isis's torso to rest on her stomach. "You're very beautiful. It's no wonder Dante is so taken with you." She looped her finger beneath the waistband of Isis's panties. "Shall I get rid of these?"

Isis caught her bottom lip between her teeth, not trusting herself to speak. Maggie eased her panties down Isis's thighs and discarded them before letting her dark gaze roam her body.

The femme dropped more kisses against Isis's belly and thighs, moving her lips against her heated flesh. Her mouth touched Isis everywhere except the one place where Isis wanted it the most. Unable to help herself, she raised her hips, eager for more. Maggie raised her head with a knowing smile on her face.

Rubbing two fingers between Isis's parted thighs, Maggie raised a brow. "Is this what you want?"

Isis nodded again, still unable to find her voice.

"Tell me."

"I want you inside me."

The warm smile returned. "Ask and you shall receive. Mmm, you're already very wet. You're going to need to be for what's to come later." She slipped those two digits past Isis's labia and slid them deep into her channel.

A groan escaped Isis's lips. There was something to be said about a woman's touch. It was gentle but no less satisfying than any man she'd ever been with, except Dante, who her heart longed for the most. But in this moment, she wanted nothing more than to give herself over to the blissful sensations coursing through her body. Isis had suffered through too much pain and loneliness these past several weeks. She wanted to surrender to the hypnotic effect of Maggie's touch.

Maggie fingered Isis's pussy slowly, pushing those digits in as far as they'd go then pulling them out to the fingernail. Each thrust grew progressively harder and faster until Maggie's fingers were sliding in and out of her at a rapid pace. Isis couldn't keep still, bucking her hips to meet each sensual plunge.

Leaning over, Maggie placed a light kiss on her quivering stomach. "Do you like this?"

"Yes," Isis moaned in return. Never in her wildest imaginings had she thought she would enjoy something like this as much as she did. But she was no longer willing to lie back and let the femme have all the fun. She wanted to do a little caressing and exploring of her own.

Maggie eased juice-coated fingers out of her cunt and slid them in an upward motion along Isis's body, stopping at her lips. Parting her lips, Isis sucked those fingers into her mouth with fervent tugs.

Grabbing Maggie by the shoulders, she pulled the young vampire on top of her, eager to feel the press of those soft lips on hers again. Her hands roamed the femme's back, stopping only when she reached Maggie's rounded bottom. Isis cupped the luscious backside, giving it a squeeze as she ground her pelvis against Maggie's.

Isis wanted to feel the warmth of that silky brown skin against hers. Without breaking the tight seal of their lips, she frantically worked at the buttons of Maggie's blouse and pushed it off her shoulders. With that article of clothing discarded, Isis unfastened Maggie's bra, freeing a pair of sinfully voluptuous breasts.

Gripping Maggie by the forearms, Isis rolled her over and straddled her. "Now, it's my turn." Dipping her head, she caught one chocolate-tipped breast in her mouth, sucking hard.

Maggie threaded her fingers through Isis's hair. "Mmm, yes."

Isis turned her attention to the other nipple, taking her time licking and laving it to tautness. Grasping the waistband of Maggie's skirt, she pushed it down the vampire's hips. The panties followed next as Maggie finally pulled off Isis's bra.

They lay naked in each other's arms, their limbs entwined as they lingered over heated kisses. Their hands roamed soft expanses of skin, drawing moans of carnal delight. Isis hadn't felt this alive in weeks, and a part of her was honored to share this experience with this gorgeous femme.

Maggie suddenly stiffened.

Isis frowned. "Are you okay?"

"He's calling to me. I'm needed out there."

"Then, I'm coming with you."

Maggie shook her head. "No. He isn't ready for you, yet."

Isis bit her bottom lip to hold back from saying what was really on her mind. She was still very hot from what had just happened between them. As if reading her thoughts, Maggie leaned forward and placed a light kiss at the corner of her mouth. "Don't worry. GianMarco will take good care of you."

Isis's mouth fell open. "And, you… you don't mind?"

Maggie smiled warmly. "I know GianMarco and I are truly one — bloodmates; our souls are bonded. That's all that really matters. Anyway, everything I've just done with you, so has he. Just like when Dante helped him through his sickness." She grazed Isis's cheek with the back of her hand.

Leaning into the caress, Isis sighed, feeling slightly envious of the tight bond Maggie shared with her mate. Did she dare hope for the same thing with Dante, especially after all that had passed between them? "I guess that makes sense," she finally replied.

"There are times when we have to do what's necessary to help each other out. Like now, for instance, I've never contemplated being with another woman, or thought I'd enjoy it as much as I just did, but this is no ordinary situation. You seem to have grasped the basic concept of what's happening with Dante, but you won't completely understand until this is all over. When Dante finally comes to you, he won't be gentle, and he might even hurt you, a lot. He'll be wild and untamed but GianMarco and I will ease the passage to ensure you have the optimal amount of pleasure. Your heightened state of arousal will ease your fears and help you relax when Dante takes you." Maggie stroked Isis's hair. "I'm going out there now, but GianMarco will be with you shortly."

Isis grasped her hand, not wanting her to go. "Wait. Won't you be hurt if you go out there?"

"I'll be fine. It isn't me Dante is after, but just like you need relief, so does he." Maggie leaned forward and kissed Isis's cheek then rolled off the bed before heading out the door with a seductive sway of her hips. The chocolate-skinned femme was a full-figured goddess and Isis was certain she knew it.

Another wave of arousal rippled over her body, and Isis rubbed her pussy to temper the burgeoning heat. If Maggie could elicit this type of response from her, Isis knew she would go supernova with tall, blond, and devastatingly gorgeous GianMarco Grimaldi.

"Get off me, Marco. I need her!" Dante growled. The fever blazing within him threatened to incinerate him from the inside out. This unbearable ache was torture and the most excruciating sensation he'd ever experienced.

He'd fought his feelings for Isis for so long, it had become a habit. He knew he was in the throes of *la morte dolci*. In his arrogance, he'd believed he was strong enough to overcome it, despite the onslaught of symptoms he'd battled for the last several weeks. The throngs of nameless women and tight pussies he'd gone through hadn't been enough to satisfy the burning hunger he had for one sexy, shifter.

His thoughts were a jumble and his body raged with unfulfilled desire. Marco was keeping him from her, and though he loved his brother with every last breath in his body, all he could think of was blue murder. He could tell Marco was using every ounce of his strength to hold him down, and if Dante really wanted to, he could throw him off. He had the strength of ten vampires while he was in the midst of this illness, but some semblance of sanity had entered his mind, allowing him to see that Marco was trying to stop him from harming Isis.

"I know you do, Dante, but until you've calmed down a little more, I can't allow you to go in there."

"You can't stop me, you know."

"How about me?" Maggie's soothing voice reached his ears. He glanced over Marco's shoulder to see her striding toward them in all her naked glory. *Dio*, she was beautiful, every voluptuous curve of her, from those generous breasts to her ample hips. His cock stiffened in reaction, and when she kneeled next to him, it took every single bit of self-control he had left not to toss his brother off and grab her.

His heart cried out for Isis, but he needed relief and Maggie could give it to him. "Maggie, you shouldn't be around me when I'm like this," he finished on a growl, his heat rising once again.

Instead of answering, she focused on her mate. "I can handle it from here, GianMarco."

Marco raised a brow. "Are you sure?"

She nodded.

"If you need me, call."

"I will."

They exchanged a brief kiss before Marco released his hold on Dante and headed down the hall.

Dante sprang to his feet. "Where the hell is he going? He's going to her, isn't he?" Isis was his woman! She belonged to him! When he would have charged after his brother, Maggie blocked him.

"Maggie, I don't want to hurt you. Don't get in the middle of this."

She grabbed a fistful of his shirt, her dark brown eyes turning several shades lighter as they began to glow. Her lips were slightly parted to reveal descended incisors. "So, you'd rather hurt Isis? The woman you love? You're not ready to go in there. You need to calm the hell down."

"And you can stop me?"

"Oh, I think I can." She moved toward him with a smile that invited endless hours of wicked delight. When their bodies touched, she wrapped one arm around his neck. Sliding the other hand down the length of his torso, she placed a light kiss against his jawline.

"Oh, Maggie," he groaned, torn between wanting to bury himself so deep inside her, he could barely think of anything else, and pushing her away. Dante had the wherewithal to realize he wouldn't be gentle with her. The last thing he wanted was to hurt her when she meant so much to him.

She slid her tongue along his neck. "It's okay, Dante. I can take it."

Balling his hands into fists at his sides, he shook his head. "You don't know what you're asking."

"I do." Nimble fingers undid the buttons of his shirt before moving to his belt buckle with a determination that took his breath away.

Dante grasped her hands in one last attempt to keep her from stepping over the threshold of no return. "Don't."

Deftly pulling herself out of his hold, she continued her task, wasting no time in unfastening his belt and pants before sliding them down his hips. Dante's painfully hard erection sprang forward, and when she dropped to her knees and wrapped those seeking fingers around the base of his cock, he was utterly lost. The warmth of her breath against his member was enough to send him over the edge of sanity once again. "I fucking warned you!" Clasping his hands on either side of her head, Dante guided her mouth to his dick and thrust forward, practically sending his rod down her throat.

Maggie groaned in response, but not in protest. Tightening those sexy lips of hers around his cock, she sucked him with an enthusiasm that pushed him deeper into the abyss of madness. Even as his fingers dug into her hair and he thrust hard and deep into her mouth, she moved with him. He needed this sweet release more than he needed air.

He fucked her mouth with frantic movements, racing toward the peak his body so desperately craved. Dante burned for this. "Yes, Maggie. Yes." And she took every inch of his cock, swallowing it, driving him closer still to that goal. He shot his load hard and fast down her throat when he came, emptying his balls and savoring the temporary relief.

Sighing, he looked down to witness Maggie feasting on his juices like a woman starved. The sight of her working his cock even after he'd finished sent another pulse of heat raging through him. Dante released the tight grip he had on her hair and grabbed her by the forearms.

Maggie whimpered in protest, as if she didn't want to let go.

"You're a greedy little femme, aren't you?"

"Of course, I am. I haven't fed in hours, and how could anyone resist when presented with this impressive cock?

Dante chuckled, hauling Maggie into his arms. "If I remember correctly, I presented nothing to you. You simply took."

She grinned. "And you're complaining?"

"You're going to make me lose control, again."

"I don't mind."

Growling, he smashed his lips against hers. He shoved his tongue past her full, parted lips to explore the honeyed recesses of her mouth.

Maggie didn't seem content to allow him complete control. Wrapping her arms around his neck and legs around his waist, she pushed her tongue forward to meet his and they fought for supremacy in a battle of sensual delight.

Dante grasped her ample bottom in his palms, molding and squeezing her soft flesh as he ground his dick against her pussy. He wanted inside. Badly. And he intended to take it. How could he not when the heady scent of her arousal drifted to his nostrils and teased him? She was already wet and ready for his possession and he knew from prior experience her pussy would be tight and hot.

Breaking the tight suction of their lips, he reached between their bodies to circle his cock and guide it to her slick entrance.

"Hurry," she moaned, arching her back in invitation.

Dante needed no further encouragement before easily sliding into her cunt, driving into her so deeply she screamed and dug her nails into his back, breaking skin. "Oh, my God!" Maggie buried her face against his neck.

Even if he had wanted to, he couldn't stop himself from thrusting into her harder still. His fingers burrowed into her bottom as he fucked her, thrusting with a possessed fervor. Again, the need for orgasm overrode his ability to think clearly. The only thing that mattered at the moment was how tight and juicy her pussy felt around his cock and how much he wanted it.

He had to taste more of her. Fixing his gaze on the tender skin where her neck and shoulder met, he opened his mouth wide before sinking his extended incisors into that tempting flesh. Her sweet, coppery ambrosia gushed into his mouth, heightening the sensations coursing through him.

Pushing and straining against her, Dante came again, shooting his seed into her cunt as he continued to feed from her.

Maggie was the first to break their embrace, unwinding her legs from around him and letting the tips of her toes touch the floor. "Mmm, Dante, that's enough, you're going to suck me dry."

Her words barely registered at first, but when she yanked at his hair, Dante remembered where he was. Raising his head, he licked his fangs, savoring every last drop of Maggie's life-giving essence. "Ah, shit, Maggie. I got carried away." He cupped her face in his hands. "I lost control and I couldn't help myself. Please forgive me?"

A smile tilted the corners of her lips. "Of course, although I admit, I did enjoy it." She winked at him.

Dante chuckled, hugging her against him as he kissed the top of her head. "Thank you. I needed that more than you know."

She raised her head to meet his gaze. "Oh, I have a pretty good idea. Maybe now that I've taken some of the edge off, you can go to Isis without scaring her half to death?"

Dante groaned at the reminder. "Damn it. It's bad enough I acted like the asshole of all assholes when I last saw her, but there's no telling what she thinks of me now."

"She understands. GianMarco and I have explained your condition and I'd say she's more concerned for you than anything else."

"I hurt her." Shame crept through every pore of his being as the memory of his harsh treatment of her filtered into his mind. Why had he been so stubborn as to push her away when she'd humbled herself before him? He didn't deserve Isis. She was probably better off if he turned around and walked out the door and stayed out of her life forever.

Maggie smacked him against his chest with the flat of her hand. "Stop thinking like that. Staying away from her is what got you into this state in the first place. Don't you dare leave!" Within seconds, she'd turned from seductive sex siren to drill sergeant.

Dante raised a brow, slightly amused at her change in demeanor. "So you're reading my mind, now? It's rare for one as young as you to penetrate the mind of someone my age."

"While you're in this state, you're very easy to read, and stop changing the subject. You will not, I repeat *not*, leave. You will march your ass in there and tell her how you feel…well, after this madness has run its course."

"You make it seem so simple." He sighed, releasing her.

She crossed her arms over her breasts. "It is that easy. You're making it more complicated than it has to be. You love her and she loves you."

"I know, but —"

"There are no buts. You know what, Dante? I never would have taken you for a coward."

He narrowed his eyes. "What's that supposed to mean?"

"You are one of the bravest men I know. You've faced rogues, demons, and all kinds of things that not so long ago I never knew existed, but you're willing to walk away from your bloodmate. Why?"

He wasn't quite ready to admit the truth because it shamed him. Yes, he loved Isis. She was everything to him and more, but could he really trust that love when he'd been wrong before.

Maggie cocked her head to the side as understanding entered her dark eyes. "Oh, Dante. I think you know this time it's right. Love is a lot like bungee jumping. It's a big leap of faith, and if you're not ready to take the plunge, you won't get to experience the rewards. Take the dive."

Dante laughed. "Have you been watching Oprah again?"

She giggled in return. "No, actually, Lifetime movies. But that's beside the point. It's time, and I can't think of a more perfect mate for you than Isis. She's drop-dead gorgeous, strong, brave, and she's got a caring spirit. I know about her past, but I understand. Sometimes, one has to do what one has to in order to survive. Obviously, she's changed and you can't continue to hold that against her."

"I don't. I realize now that it was only an excuse I used to keep her at arm's length." He ran his fingers through his hair. "I guess, I should go in now."

She nodded. "I think so."

Dante pulled Maggie against him again and squeezed her tight. "Too bad Marco found you first. I think I would have given him a run for his money otherwise."

Maggie smiled. "We both know it wouldn't have mattered. My heart belongs only to GianMarco and yours to Isis, you big flirt." She tapped his arm lightly.

She was right. Isis was the only one for him, and when this night was over and the sickness had passed, he intended to spend the rest of eternity showing her just how much she meant to him. Lowering his head, he brushed his lips against Maggie's. "I do love you, you know."

"I do. And I love you, too." She wrapped her arms around his waist and hugged him back.

Theirs was a love born from the night they'd first connected. It was a bond almost as strong as the ones he shared with his brothers. Though he loved Sasha and Christine as well, Maggie would always have a special place in his heart. He no longer fooled himself into believing it was a romantic love, yet it was special nonetheless. No more, no less.

A sharp pain spiraled within him, making Dante double over. The excruciating ache was returning.

"Dante!" She grasped his arms and quickly pulled her hands back. "You're burning up."

"I. Need. Her. Now!" He managed to bite the words out. He could be put off no longer.

"Then, let's go to her."

Chapter Twenty-Six

Isis bounced up and down on GianMarco's cock, clenching her vaginal muscles around the thick member. His dick was nearly as addictive as Dante's. The Grimaldi brothers definitely lived up to their legend in and out of bed.

He lay on his back, raising his hips to thrust into her. GianMarco tweaked her nipples between fingers and thumbs. She was close to yet another climax with him. He'd taken her against the wall earlier with such masterful strokes; he'd left her panting for more.

Now as she rode him, Isis was aroused with an uncontrollable savagery that she couldn't satisfy. Placing her hands against his chest, she raked her nails down his torso, making tracks of passion in his skin.

He inhaled sharply and grabbed her hips before thrusting deeper and harder into her. "So you like it rough, huh?"

"Oh yeah." She moaned, relishing the feel of his thickness sliding in and out of her. It would be perfect if it was Dante. As soon as the thought crossed her mind, she shook her head. Their time would come soon enough, if what she'd been told was true. She couldn't help being a little apprehensive about what would happen, though. Once Dante sated himself of her, would he then turn his back on her again? After their last meeting, she wasn't sure how he'd be, but she wouldn't dwell on it right now.

As GianMarco continued to fuck her senseless, Isis fully understood why Maggie walked around with a permanent grin on her lips. GianMarco's skill could not be faulted. As she gyrated against him with more urgency, he increased the tempo of his thrusts until they moved frantically against each other.

Shudders racked her body when she reached her peak, but GianMarco continued to pump in and out of her channel several more times before gritting his teeth and grunting his release.

Isis slumped against him, breathless. "Oh God, I don't know if I can take much more of this."

GianMarco stroked the back of her head. "You must. Dante needs release, and though my mate can give him a temporary break from the madness, only you can completely heal him."

A shiver slid along her spine. "You said you and Maggie wouldn't leave me. At least not until he's more himself."

"We won't, but there's no need to be frightened any longer, although I don't think what's bothering you is the physical side, is it?"

"Am I that easy to read?"

"Right now, you are. My brother is new at this love thing, so he's going to make a few jackass-proportion mistakes. I know I made my share when I fell for Maggie, as did Nico and Romeo with their mates. Because, we've lived as long as we have and we're so used to having constant control of our lives and emotions, we sometimes do foolish things when we lose it. Don't be afraid to give your heart to him. Dante is extremely loyal to those he loves and you, he'll treat like a queen."

She snorted. "I guess we're going to have to wait and see."

"Actually, you don't."

She raised her head to look at him. "What do you mean?"

"Because, he's coming as we speak."

The door flung open.

Isis rolled off GianMarco to sit up. Dante stood in the doorway with Maggie in tow. He was completely nude, and his cock was rock hard. His skin was still pink-tinged and his eyes were just as red, but there was a calm about him that hadn't been there before.

His heated gaze raked her body from head to toe as he bared his fangs. His gaze never left her face as he strode toward the bed, his cock bouncing with each step he took. Without ceremony, he took her by the arm and yanked her against him, his mouth covering hers in a demanding kiss.

He smashed his lips so hard against hers Isis could barely breathe, yet she was willing to endure any amount of roughness to get him through his suffering. Throwing her arms around him, she opened her mouth underneath the pressure of his probing tongue. Dante grabbed her hair and twisted it around his fist, holding her head steady, making her take the onslaught of his persistent passion, not that she wanted to fight him anyway. His touch was an awakening of her soul.

She'd missed him. Missed his touch, his kisses and caresses. More than anything, she wanted to feel him inside her again, to move together as one until she didn't know where he ended and she began. That was the way it was meant to be between them.

Emitting a low growl from the back of his throat, Dante broke the kiss to toss Isis on the bed, wasting no time in falling on top of her. His menacing red eyes bored into her as he shoved her thighs apart none too gently. Maggie slid on the bed beside him and grasped his shoulders, holding him back. "Easy. I know how badly you want this, but we have all night." Stroking his hair, she placed light kisses along the back of Dante's neck.

GianMarco eased himself beside Isis and pushed her onto her side so he lay behind her. Dipping his head until his lips nearly touched the shell of her ear, he whispered, "It's okay. I said we wouldn't go anywhere tonight. Trust us." He raised his head to look at his brother. "Slow down, Dante."

"That's easy for you to say. You don't ache like I do." Dante molded his body against Isis's, his cock pressing against her entrance.

"I can handle this, GianMarco," Isis reassured him.

GianMarco shook his blond head in protest. "He's relatively calm now, but—"

"No, let me handle this. You, too, Maggie."

"If you're sure," the femme responded.

"I am." It was the least she could do. If this wasn't the ultimate way to prove her love, then she didn't know what was. Eager to be taken, she gripped Dante's shoulders and met his gaze. "I'm not afraid."

"I need you so much," Dante groaned.

"Then take me. I'm yours."

Dante hooked one hand under her knee to lift her leg before pushing forward with one powerful slam. He drove so deep inside of her, she could feel him all over her body.

Isis gasped at the brutal sensuality of his entry. "Dante," she sighed, tightening her hold on him. His possession was rougher than it had ever been, even more so than their last meeting, but she didn't care. She was shameless where this gorgeous man was concerned. He began to ram into her, his pelvis slapping against hers.

There was no gentleness as he fucked her, yet Dante still managed to reach a part of her that only he could. Isis knew her body responded to his because they were meant to be together. Gritting her teeth, she took every single hard inch of him over and over again. The brand of pleasure-pain Dante dealt out had her craving more. "Oh, Dante! Yes!"

She moved her body with his but no sooner did she find his rhythm, than Dante increased the pace, driving with harder, more furious thrusts. The more she gave, the more Dante took. Her gaze locked with his glazed, lust-filled one, and it seemed as if he'd been pushed over the brink of insanity and she was the cause.

The hairs on her body stood on end as though she was ready to transform. In high-stress situations, her body would automatically shift in order to handle any physical or emotional turmoil as a defense mechanism. The pleasure she'd been feeling only a few minutes before was slowly becoming more pain than anything else. No one had ever taken her with so much force or intensity before, and a niggling fear began to creep into the recesses of her mind.

Dante showed no signs of slowing down. In fact, he seemed as if he could continue for hours. Would she be able to handle him? A howl traveled from her throat as her body began to shift, her fur popping out of her pores. It only seemed to make Dante pick up the speed yet again.

"Isis, it's okay to ask for help. It's not a sign of weakness." GianMarco's voice reached into the inner sanctum of her mind.

"We're here to help you," Maggie added. *"We know you love Dante and he loves you, too. There's no need to suffer pointlessly when we can share this burden."*

Isis caught her bottom lip between her teeth, feeling a bit like a failure.

"You're not a failure. You're actually one of the bravest people I know and more than worthy to stand by Dante's side as his mate." GianMarco ran his tongue along the curve of her ear and nipped it gently. He ground his cock against her ass. Isis began to shake in response, knowing what was to come. With Dante in the front and GianMarco behind her, she would soon have two very large vampire cocks inside her, and the anticipation was driving her crazy.

"You're so wet, your juices are dripping all over." He rubbed his thumb over the tight ring of her anus. "I'm going to have no problem sliding in, right here. Would you like that?" GianMarco whispered against her heated skin.

Isis nodded, unable to bring herself to utter the words.

"Good, because I'll enjoy fucking your tight little ass." Parting her cheeks, he guided the satiny-tipped head of his cock against her anus. Pushing forward just enough to get the tip past her tight anal ring, he paused before thrusting into her to the hilt.

"Oh!" she cried out.

GianMarco's intrusion into her body was enough to throw Dante off his cadence and slow him down slightly.

Maggie, pressing her length against Dante's back, bared her lengthened incisors, and sank them into his shoulder, causing him to pause altogether.

"We'll do this together, Dante. Nice and easy," GianMarco instructed.

"Need her," Dante murmured. Sweat glistened on his forehead and his skin was hot to the touch.

"I know," GianMarco replied.

Isis remained still, her body calming down. The metamorphosis that had begun to take place reversed as her heart rate slowed.

GianMarco stroked the side of her face "Are you ready?"

"Yes," Isis croaked in a hoarse whisper. Now that her body had been given the chance to adjust to being impaled by the thick hardness of each vampire, she didn't want to be immobile any longer. Wiggling her hips to signal her needs, she burrowed her nails into Dante's torso.

Dante started to move, not gently, but at a considerably slower pace. GianMarco gradually pulled back until his cock was nearly out of her ass before pushing into her again.

Maggie continued to feed on Dante as she stroked the side of Isis's body, which seemed to have a calming effect on him.

It took several tries before Dante and GianMarco were finally in sync with one another. As Dante pulled back, GianMarco pushed forward and Isis would move her body in time with theirs. A tingling sensation built within the pit of her stomach before it caught fire and exploded into a raging inferno, tearing through her. The light touch of Maggie's hands caressing her body served to make the experience even more pleasurable than it already was.

When Dante increased the intensity of his possession again, Isis was ready for him, as was GianMarco. They moved, ground, and strained against one another, and she realized it wouldn't be long before she reached her peak. And when she did, it would be huge.

Dante and GianMarco's cocks stretched her pussy and anal walls until she began to shake uncontrollably. Being sandwiched between these three powerful, sexy vampires was nearly more pleasure than she could stand. "I'm coming!" she screamed, tearing her nails down Dante's chest.

Bright spots of light danced before her eyes and the sudden sensation of spiraling out of control took over, sweeping her into a huge, tsunami-sized orgasm. Releasing a scream, she nearly passed out from pleasure overload, yet Dante and GianMarco continued to move in and out of her, not finished with her.

Maggie used her mouth and hands to give pleasure, alternating her attention between Dante and Isis, caressing them each in turn, and planting kisses on their bodies.

The brothers fucked her until she reached yet another powerful peak, and Isis knew then that this night would be one she would not soon forget.

As the night progressed, the ache that had been burning inside Dante slowly waned. He couldn't remember all the positions the four of them had tried together, but he remembered being in each of Isis's and Maggie's holes, and Isis's more than a few times. He'd never come so much as he had this night. And though he still felt some of the effect of *la morte dolci*, the worst of it was over. It would probably take a couple more days for him to get back to normal, but at least his mind was finally clear.

He owed so much to Marco and Maggie. Had it not been for the two of them, he wouldn't have made it through the most serious stage of his illness without causing harm. Everything had come full circle. Dante remembered when he'd helped Marco through his illness. It seemed appropriate that it would be Marco and his mate to be there for him in his time of need. That they'd been willing to put themselves in the line of danger as he suffered through the madness humbled him.

But now, the moment had come for them to leave.

A sliver of rose-tinted dawn crept through the venetian blinds of Isis's bedroom window, bathing her sleeping figure. She lay curled into a ball at the edge of the bed, having drifted off only minutes ago.

Marco was in the process of helping Maggie into her clothes as she tried to fight sleep. Dante paced the floor, still full of nervous energy. Once his brother and sister-in-law were gone, he would have Isis again. There would be plenty of time for her to sleep later…much later.

"I can't thank you enough for helping me."

Marco smiled. "There's no need to thank me. I'd do this again in a heartbeat. After all you've done for us, it's the least we could do to repay you."

Dante sighed. "Sometimes, it's hard for me to ask for help, since I've always had to be the one who others depended on."

"You're not alone, Dante. You have a family and we love you. Isis loves you, too. Never forget that and take good care of her. She's a part of our family now."

Dante didn't need to be told that. Isis was everything he never knew he wanted and definitely needed in a mate. He counted himself lucky to have found her. "After I've completely gotten over this sickness, I'm going to do everything in my power to make up for what I've done to her."

"Don't beat yourself up over it. I'm sure she already forgives you."

"She might, but I still think she needs to hear it from me."

"If you believe that'll help, go for it, but I know you'll have no problems on that end." Standing up, Marco pulled Maggie to her feet. She leaned against him, barely managing to keep her eyes open. He chuckled before scooping her into his arms. "I need to get you home, sleepyhead. We can get the baby later, after you've had some rest."

"No. We have to pick her up right away," Maggie murmured drowsily.

Marco placed a kiss on her forehead. "Of course, *ciccina mia.*" He winked at Dante with a grin. "*She'll be too tired to notice the difference.*"

A smile touched Dante's lips. That twinge of jealousy he'd felt when he looked at them was no longer there because he'd found his heart's true desire. Everything had finally fallen into place. "It's hard to believe it's all over. Not just with Adonis and Beatrice, I mean. I'm talking about the inner struggles."

"I know the feeling. We've all had to face our demons in the past several months, haven't we? I only hope…"

Dante didn't need to read his brother's mind to know what he was thinking in that moment. "Giovanni."

Marco nodded. "He showed up at the christening for a few minutes with gifts for Gianna and Romeo's children. But he didn't stick around for long and left with the promise of returning soon. He hasn't been seen or heard from since. Wherever he is, I hope he's okay."

"I think he's still facing his own struggles right now. Liliana's death was rough, but Adonis's death was especially hard on him. I can't say I'm not glad he's gone, but I know how much he'd meant to Giovanni. It must be tearing him up inside."

"I'm sure it is. But let's hope wherever he is right now, he's healing." Marco adjusted his hold on Maggie. "Well, we'd better get going. If you should need us for anything —"

"I know I can depend on you. Thank you, again."

"Anytime. We're brothers and we help each other out."

Dante was truly lucky to have brothers like GianMarco, Romeo, and Nico through thick and thin. He slapped his brother on the back and kissed Maggie on the cheek before bidding them a safe journey.

Only once they'd left the apartment did he return his attention to the sleeping beauty on the bed. A smile curved the corners of his lips as he strode toward her.

Would he ever get enough of her? Never.

Sliding onto the bed, he rolled Isis onto her back and gently nudged her legs apart. He had the need to taste every bit of her. Settling himself between her thighs, Dante slid his tongue along her slick outer labia and parted the soft folds. Her pussy dripped with juices and he relished lapping every single drop up, feeding off her essence, getting high with pleasure from doing it.

He closed his lips over her clit and sucked gently at first, wishing she would wake up. When she stirred, he slid his middle finger into her cum-soaked channel. Dante was far from finished with her.

Chapter Twenty-Seven

Isis was in the middle of the most delicious dream. Dante kissed and caressed her all over, leaving no part of her unexplored, making her feel as if she would combust from an overflow of lust. Licks of flames raced along each part of her body as a warm tongue lapped her pussy. She squirmed, attempting to get closer to that seeking mouth, wanting it so badly she could hardly stand it.

The sharp nip of teeth brought a gasp to her lips. She opened her eyes. It took a few seconds of shaking off the sleepy haze clouding her mind to realize this was no dream. Dante had positioned himself between her legs and was sucking her clit while fingering her hot channel.

Bliss.

"Dante." She sighed and grabbed his head, running her fingers through his dark locks.

She'd never been roused quite like this before, but she could definitely see herself getting used to it. Dante licked her pussy with urgent strokes of his tongue, sucking, tasting, and laving it, ignoring no part of the highly sensitized area.

Dante played with her clitoris, alternating between nibbling and kissing it. He filled her with a savage need for more of his sensual ministrations. After last night, Isis didn't think her body was capable of handling any more

424

pleasure without a long respite, but she should have known better. Where Dante Grimaldi was concerned, the sky was the limit. Despite the playful nips, she noticed as he ate her pussy with such tenderness and care that he'd calmed considerably from the manic beast he'd been earlier.

Isis found herself once again spiraling to yet another climax as his fingers went deeper and his tongue became more persistent. "Dante!" she screamed, mashing her cunt against his face.

Dante continued to lick her until she thrashed from side to side. Only when she stilled, her body weakened from the sexual roller coaster ride he'd taken her on, did he stop.

Finally, with a grin tilting his lips, Dante raised his head. His eyes were now the same deep shade of blue they normally were and his skin had cooled. He slid alongside Isis and wrapped his arms around her waist.

"*Bellissima,*" he sighed as he buried his face against her neck. His hold tightened around her as if he didn't want to let go.

Her heart sang with joy at the sound of the endearment. She'd believed she'd never hear it from him again. "Dante." Without any warning, the overwhelming emotions she'd been holding in for so long burst forth, and she broke into a torrent of tears.

"Isis. *Bellissima,* please don't cry." He stroked the back of her head as he whispered words of love to soothe her.

Isis's tears were an emotional release she desperately needed. Sobs racked her body and the harder she tried to stop, the more she cried until finally she just let it happen. It was an outpouring of everything that had tormented her from past to present—the loss of her parents, the loneliness, the fear and despair. She'd held everything inside for so long this outburst was like a cleansing of her soul.

Several moments passed before her wails subsided to sniffles and finally tapered off to nothing. She appreciated the silence afterward because it allowed her to reflect on what had just happened. "I'm sorry," she whispered at last, wiping a stray tear from the corner of her eye. "I don't know what came over me."

Dante kissed the top of her head. "It's okay, *bellissima*. You needed that. Sometimes, we all need a good cry. I just wish I wasn't the cause. I never want to make you unhappy again. Please forgive me, Isis. My behavior in Florence was deplorable and I've never been more ashamed of anything I've done in my life."

Remembering how nasty he'd been, she pulled back slightly to look him in the eyes. "You hurt me but I know you hurt, too. It's true I was angry but I understand why you fought so hard against our love. But, I trust it will never happen again?"

He brushed her lips with his. "Of course not. I would rather cut out my own tongue than to speak to you that way ever again. I can offer no excuse for my behavior because there is none. I was very stupid for not listening to my heart when it told me that you would never betray me. I'll never forgive myself for it."

Isis cupped his face in her hands. "Love is all about forgiveness and I do forgive you, but you have to learn to do the same with yourself."

His eyes briefly clouded with an emotion that could have been anguish or regret and Isis's heart melted with devotion for him. "It's always hardest when the person you have to forgive is yourself."

"I know what you mean. I've done things in the past that make me cringe when I think about it and those actions will probably haunt me forever. But I can't go back and change them, so I have to learn to deal with it." She paused, knowing it was time to tell him what she should have a long time ago. "About my past —"

He placed a finger over her lips, halting her in midsentence. "No explanation needed. I was a fool not to trust you. I should have given you the time you needed to tell me instead of demanding it. I trust you and I love you."

She caught his hand in hers and kissed his palm. "Thank you. You have no idea how much it means to me to hear you say that, but I want to get some things off my chest. I need to tell you for *me*, okay?"

Dante stroked the side of her face. "Of course, *bellissima*. Please continue."

Isis closed her eyes briefly, savoring his touch against her skin before opening them again with a sigh. "I told you a bit about my part with the Serpent Gang but I need to start from the very beginning so you can get a clearer picture."

"Okay."

"As you know, we shifters are extremely pack-oriented and family means everything to us. Pack Vasquez was a small but tight group. My mother in particular instilled within me the value of family because she'd been kicked out of her pack for falling for a Beta in a pack considered beneath them rather than the mate my grandfather had chosen for her. Not once did I doubt their love for me, although my father was extremely strict at times. But my happy family was all taken away from me within the blink of an eye when Hunters and rogue shifters wiped out my entire pack. I would have died too, had it not been for my mother. She sacrificed her life for me so I could live." She paused as pain washed through her. No matter how much time passed she would always miss her parents.

"It's okay, Isis. I miss mine, too. The heartache never goes away but it does eventually become bearable."

"I hope so. Anyway, I was now what others had warned me about: a lone wolf. I didn't have the protection of a pack and it was a kill or be killed world. I chose to survive. No other pack would have me and that unfortunately led to me making some bad choices. I aligned myself with a member of the Serpent Gang, partly because I was rebelling against my strict upbringing and because I was still hurt from being rejected by my grandfather's pack. I was finally free to do the things I hadn't been allowed to do before. But with that freedom came a lot of trouble."

I was also attracted to the Serpent Gang because that particular band of rogues traveled in a group, which appealed to my instinct for pack life that I'd grown accustomed to. I wanted to put myself in a position where I could never be rejected again, which is why I set my sights on Black Adder, the leader. I admit the relationship was a little scary but it was exciting, too. We were lovers but he never touched my heart, and I know he didn't see me as more than a trophy. He saw that other men wanted me so he decided he must be the one to have me."

"I catered to his overinflated ego and that suited him. I stayed with the gang for years, often doing things I knew were wrong, but I had tuned out that part of my conscience. There was one particular incident, where we went after an innocent human family, children and all. I was only meant to go there to take their valuables but it became a gruesome scene by the time they were done with those poor people. It was then, I realized I no longer had the stomach for that life. It wasn't who I wanted to be and I didn't like what I'd become. Besides, it was around that time the Serpent Gang had gotten involved with Adonis and Beatrice.

"Persephone Kyriakis saved my life. Were it not for a chance meeting with her and her offer of friendship, I can only imagine where I'd be right now. Knowing there was someone out there who still cared for me gave me the courage to turn my life around. And then, I met you. I fell in love with you in an instant, but I knew of your battle against rogues. I thought if you learned of my past, you would want nothing to do with me, so I withheld that information, hoping you would get to know me and fall in love before you did. When Black Adder confronted us, he'd lied to you about the two of us meeting up. Apparently, he had established a powerful mind link to me I was not aware of. Had I known, I would have stayed away instead of jeopardizing everyone. I never betrayed you. You have to believe me." She clutched his shoulders with the desperate need to get her point across.

Dante captured her mouth with a hungry kiss. "I do believe you. I suspected something like that with Black Adder might have happened after all the things I'd witnessed these past several weeks. I think I'd fallen for you from the start, too. You certainly took my breath away on first sight. But now, it's time for a little explaining of my own. In no way am I excusing my actions that night, but I think it's only fair that you should know a little of my background."

"You don't have to."

"I want to, *bellissima*. Anyway, you pretty much know how my parents were murdered and I was responsible for the care of my brothers for years. My need to battle rogues has, in essence, stemmed from revenge and to protect my family. My battle with Adonis has consumed the majority of my years. I allowed no love in my life except that for my brothers. Of course, I've had lovers along the way but I've always been focused on my work with the Underground. Falling in love was a liability, especially considering what had happened with Marco's first family. I kept my relationships light, and when my lovers expected more, that's when I moved on. That was until I met a young woman by the name of Flora. I was instantly drawn to her and she filtered into my thoughts more than anyone ever had. I began to believe nature had other ideas for me and she was my true mate. But something went terribly wrong." He stopped, frowning as though the memory was particularly painful.

Isis stroked his arm. "Take your time." She loved him so much.

"I grew obsessive over her to the point where I needed to be with her every single second of the day. I was consumed with thoughts only of her, and I nearly went insane if she so much as looked at anyone other than me."

"That doesn't sound like you."

"Because, it wasn't me. I later learned Adonis had gotten inside my head. Flora was charmed and sent to lead me astray. I was drawn into a crazed state a lot like *la morte dolci*, but it was more like rage than passion."

"So what happened?"

"I killed her."

Isis gasped. "How? Why?"

"A lot of that night was fuzzy for a very long time, but I came home to find her naked except for the sheets wrapped around her body. She smelled as if she'd just been made love to, and I remember her laughing and taunting me. The next thing I recall was my brothers trying to reason with me. She was dead, and all I knew was that I'd killed her because of my jealous rage. Years later, I learned her lover was a rogue who worked for Adonis. It was his intent to make me so crazed, I'd let my guard down. What he didn't count on was my finding out about her treachery so soon. Since then, I've always been careful to hold my feelings in check."

Her heart went out to him. To believe he had found love only to have it ripped away was probably harrowing. "I'm sorry you suffered through that."

"That isn't all. Not very long before the two of us met, Marco had gone through his own crisis with Maggie. I was there to help but my emotions ended up in a jumble. Marco and I share a deep connection, so some of his feelings for Maggie transferred to me. And how could I not love her a little? She's beautiful, sweet, and loving, everything I could have hoped for in a mate. From that night, I struggled with the idea that I may have fallen for my brother's woman. And then when Nico and Romeo joined with their bloodmates, it only made me long for her more."

"But you didn't really love her, did you?" Isis understood how he felt. Through her bond with Dante, she'd felt a strong attraction for GianMarco and Maggie last night. She could see where he'd get his wires crossed.

"Not in that way, no. I was ashamed of myself and I was scared what I was going through would cause a rift between me and my brother. So, I stayed away. I was jealous of my brothers, Marco in particular, because they all had something I was not a part of. When one has been depended upon for so long, it's hard to let go of that role. Then I met you and I knew what I felt for Maggie wasn't real. I didn't trust myself after being wrong twice, so I made every excuse I could to keep you at arm's length. Even when Black Adder said those things about you, I think in the back of my mind I knew he was lying. I shouldn't have left you with him. But, you came to me anyway and I still pushed you away, because I was scared…"

Isis stopped stroking his arm when he trailed off. "What, Dante? Please tell me," she prodded.

He took a deep breath and closed his eyes. "I was afraid to love you because I didn't want it to turn out to be another false alarm. I've dealt with the Flora and Maggie situations and survived, but if for some reason it turned out that you weren't truly my mate as my heart told me you were, I don't think I could have handled it. I would have died on the inside. But, I'm laying everything on the line right now. I love you, Isis. I'm not even sure if love is the most appropriate word because there isn't a word adequate enough to describe what I feel for you. You're my every waking thought and every breath I take. You are everything to me. And I don't want to spend another day without you in my life."

Tears flowed down her cheeks unheeded, her heart overflowing with her feelings for this beautiful vampire.

"I love you, too. I can assure you this is very real and I pledge my heart to you always. I want to spend my life laughing and crying with you and I want to bear your children. I love only you, Dante Grimaldi, from now until eternity."

His eyes glistened with moisture. "Ah, *bellissima*, those words are music to my ears." Dante covered her mouth with his as he rolled on top of her and nudged her thighs apart. He slid into her tight, wet sheath.

Isis welcomed him inside, wrapping her arms and legs around him. With their mouths sealed together, tongues dueling, her breasts crushed beneath a rock-hard torso, they moved in a syncopated rhythm.

For so long Isis had been on her own, a wolf without a pack, a lost child without a home, and a heart without its mate, but now she had it all: friends, family, and redemption. But most of all, she'd found the other half of her soul in Dante Grimaldi, and from this day forward she'd never be alone again.

Epilogue

Had it only been a week since he had finally declared his love for Isis? Dante had never been happier in his life. Their first few days together, they'd spent their entire time in bed, making love until both of them were weak with sated passion. He couldn't get enough of his beautiful shifter and it excited him to know they had the rest of forever to love.

Now he, too, understood what it was to truly give his heart so completely until his soul merged with another's. He loved Isis to distraction and hoped they would soon have a family of their own. There was no one else he would rather have carry his children. For the first time in centuries, he was truly and utterly delirious with joy and it was all because of Isis.

He'd probably still be back home making love to his woman if his brothers' mates hadn't insisted on a women's outing so they could get to know Isis better, giving Dante the opportunity to hang out with his brothers.

There was only one dark cloud on his horizon, however. Giovanni. He remained elusive. He'd shown up at Dante's penthouse a few days earlier and Dante's mind drifted back to that meeting.

"Giovanni, what are you doing here? Are you all right?" Dante eyed his brother with concern.

Immortals didn't age after they reached their mid-thirties, so it had taken him by surprise to see his brother looking considerably older. There were bags under his eyes and his face was lined.

"The black magic has finally worked its way out of my system and it may take some time for me to heal completely, if I ever do. This is also the result of not having slept a wink for the past several decades."

Dante gaped at his older brother. Vampires could go days without sleep if they so chose, but sleep was important for rejuvenating and healing. "How did you manage?"

Giovanni smiled faintly. "It's not so hard when you have to constantly be on your guard, and dabbling in the dark arts helped. I'm glad I'm finally able to let go of that part of my life."

"Where have you been? We've all tried to reach out to you for a while now."

"I've been roaming here and there — nowhere of importance. It's a difficult adjustment I've had to make these past several weeks."

"I can only imagine what you must be feeling. I'm sorry for your loss," he offered, even though Dante still couldn't bring himself to grieve for a brother who'd caused him nothing but anguish.

"I appreciate it. Actually, I've only come to say good-bye."

"Good-bye? You just got here. Don't tell me you're going to up and leave and that's it. Will we at least see you again?"

Giovanni shrugged. "Maybe. I don't know. I have to get my head straight right now, but I'm touched to know you and the rest of my brothers are willing to accept me into your lives. When I came to the christening last month, I realized I'm not ready for this yet. Don't get me wrong, I do want a relationship with all of you eventually, but I can't right now. I'm not myself, and to be quite honest, I've been so many different things for so long, I don't know who I am anymore."

It saddened Dante to see the pain stamped all over Giovanni's face. He was hurting and Dante ached for him, but he realized Giovanni would need this time of reflection on his own. "Where are you going from here?"

"I have a promise to fulfill to an old friend. And from there, I don't know. I might travel, or maybe not."

"I see. But don't forget us. And if you ever need anything, we'll be there for you."

"Thank you. It means a lot to hear you say it."

There was an awkward moment of silence before Dante reached out and hugged Giovanni to him. "I mean it."

"I know," the older vampire whispered.

When he'd left, Dante wondered if he would ever see him again.

"Earth to Dante." Romeo waved his hand in Dante's face, bringing him back to the present.

Pasting a smile on his face, he focused his attention on Romeo. "What were you saying?"

Romeo shrugged. "It's not important, really. The three of us were just saying the women are probably having a field day on their shopping excursion. Wonder how much it's going to set us back?"

Dante chuckled. "None of you have to worry about your finances. I'm sure your bank balances are safe."

Marco shook his head. "I'm not sure about that. Maggie has a black belt in shopping. We'll have to purchase a larger house soon; otherwise, we'll have nowhere to put the stuff she buys."

"If Maggie is a black belt, Sasha must be the grand master," Nico added with a fond smile.

Romeo sighed. "And they've corrupted Christine. She used to be a conservative spender. You mark my words, if Isis hangs out with those three shopaholics, you'll be complaining along with us."

Dante grinned. "It's possible, but you know as well as I that you'd deny them nothing."

Marco's smile widened. "I'd give Maggie the sun and moon if it were possible."

"As long as Sasha's happy, I am as well," Nico agreed.

Romeo nodded. "Yep. If the women are happy, they'll keep us happy…if you catch my drift." He winked.

Dante rolled his eyes with a laugh. "I believe I do but let's keep that little tidbit between us guys."

A comfortable silence followed until Marco asked, "You were thinking about Giovanni, weren't you?"

He nodded. "Yes. I can't stop thinking of the last conversation we had. I should have insisted he stay."

"He'll come around in time, I'm sure, and when he does, we'll be here for him. That's what brothers are for," Marco reassured him.

"Let's just hope he realizes that," Dante murmured.

"So this is it?" Nya asked, looking every bit as tired as he felt. Her eyes were dull and lifeless. Though her face remained smooth and unlined, she seemed older to him somehow. Giovanni knew she'd suffered, too and wished he could take that pain away.

"Yes. I'm heading down tonight. I've called her and she's expecting me."

"Please, whatever you do, don't hurt her. She's special."

Giovanni frowned, furrowing his brow, annoyed that she needed to remind him. "I know. I would never hurt her. I doubt I could, if I tried. I barely exist to her."

"How do you know?"

"She seems to be involved already."

Nya shrugged. "What does that have to do with anything? You're going there to watch over her, not to marry her. Unless, you're not telling me everything about your last encounter with her."

"I told you everything you needed to know. I befriended her and have checked on her when I was able."

Nya raised a brow. "Everything I need to know? What aren't you telling me?"

"That's private." Giovanni wasn't sure himself. "But like I said, she's already involved with someone."

"So you say. But, it's not like you're an expert on reading women."

Giovanni flinched. "That's not fair Nya. Had it been possible for me to return Liliana's feelings, I would have. I owed her so much and she gave her life for mine. I'll carry that guilt with me always."

She sighed. "You're right. That was uncalled for. I'm sorry. I've been extremely irritable lately. Her death hit me pretty hard and I wish I could have saved her."

"I wish I could have as well."

"It hurts because I only had a few people I was close to. You, Liliana and Christine. Liliana is gone and Christine has a family to take care of. And then Adonis…" She hung her head.

"It's okay that you loved him. Don't beat yourself up over that. It's true the evil in his heart spread and made him a parody of the brother I once knew but I think you kept him as anchored as it was possible for him to be."

"I could have done more. If I would have told him—"

"Don't. You'll drive yourself crazy if you keep going over what you should have done. You have to live your life now, just like he said. That's what Adonis would have wanted. And yes, Liliana is gone, but Christine is not. You two share a special friendship. Don't use her family as an excuse to keep your distance. I'm sure she'd welcome a visit from you."

"We'll see."

"About visiting Christine or following Adonis's advice?"

"Both."

"Glad to hear it. I need to get going soon." He held out his arms to her.

She went into his embrace. "I'll miss you."

"And I you. Will you be okay?"

"Yes, that is if I can shake the Romanov twins. They've become nuisances recently."

He chuckled. "Maybe you should stop running so hard and let them catch you."

She shook her head vehemently. "I'd much rather be alone. I've had enough of men to last a dozen lifetimes."

Giovanni decided not to debate the point with her. Nya had her own inner demons to battle. One of them was resolving her guilt where Adonis was concerned. Even in all the years he'd known her, he still didn't know everything about her. Now that she was free from his brother, he worried about what would happen to her and where she would end up.

Nya pulled away as though her display of affection embarrassed her. "Okay, I wish you well. And please take good care of her. She's my only real connection to who I once was."

"I will take good care of her. I promise."

And it was a promise he intended to keep even when he knew that nothing but trouble could come from it.

About the Author

NYT and USA Today Bestselling Author Eve has always enjoyed creating characters and stories from an early age. As a child she was always getting into mischief, so when she lost her television privileges (which was often), writing was her outlet. Her stories have gotten quite a bit spicier since then! When she's not writing or spending time with her family, Eve is reading, baking, traveling or kicking butt in 80's trivia. She loves hearing from her readers. She can be contacted through her website at: www.evevaughn.com.

More Books From Eve Vaughn:

Finding Divine

The Kyriakis Curse:
Book One of the Kyriakis Series

GianMarco:
Book One of the Blood Brothers Series

Niccolo:
Book Two of the Blood Brothers Series

Romeo:
Book Three of the Blood Brothers Series

Jagger:
Book Four of the Blood Brothers Series